CW01024118

LIBRARY OF CONGRESS CONTROL NUMBER: 2024914044

DEDICATION

To the preservers of what is good.

AFTER ME

BY J. SHEP

The old man stared a full minute at the parcel, a curiosity to him, a mystery awaiting reveal. Why he was hesitating to open it was more so the mystery even to himself. It had come all this way from America, and he could not decipher the smeared name above the return address. His great-nephew had brought it in and alerted him to its arrival, and there it sat before him on the table.

Finally, he lifted it and brought it to his chair in the parlor. He sat, pulled the ottoman close, and set the package on it. Although he had been used to mystery, the old man knew better than to let the unknown fester. He unwrapped it with smooth hands in slow tears of brown paper to reveal a blue box. He lifted the lid on the blue box and found a bound manuscript. As he gently pulled the booklet from the box and brought it toward himself, a letter plopped onto his lap from between the cover and the first page. The old man placed the manuscript back in the blue box and turned his attention to the letter. His name was handwritten on the envelope.

He slid the letter from the envelope and saw his name at the top, but he immediately searched to the end, seeking the name of the sender. When he saw it, he lowered the letter to his lap and stared in the direction of his entryway hall, in the direction of a window lined with fresh mint, in the direction of the shutters that, many years ago, had burst opened to this person.

And then he read avidly, pulling the letter close to his eyes, not taking a moment to reach for the magnifying glass on the nearby side table. When he had finished, the tears he had fought through each paragraph descended from overflowing eyes down smooth, leather cheeks. After a rush of sadness and joy too overwhelming to contain, he held the letter to his heart and wept again.

Over a half hour passed before, worn with release, he returned the letter to the envelope and swapped it with the manuscript. With the text on his lap, he reached for the magnifying glass and leaned over the typed words of the first page. Then he began reading—voraciously reading every word and every scene, impervious to his nephew's check-in, unconcerned by his niece's call to the dinner table, intolerant of his sister's reprimands for having missed the meal, oblivious to his great-nephew's sneaking out of the house to see his girlfriend. He read and read, absorbing every moment, and in some cases, reliving them.

CHAPITRE 1

My sister's rubbing my cheek rifted me from a dream—a glimpse of my mother and father sitting on either side of us on the couch in the living room. My mother held my face in her hands and started caressing my cheek with the smooth heel of her palm to wake me the same way my sister was now.

My sister held back tears as she asked, "Where are we, Ellande?"

Groggy myself, I felt her leg against mine under the coarse sheets and the textured matelassé covers I knew from previous summers, and I rubbed my eyes to take in more clearly the bedroom belonging to my parents—the oak dresser, the Limoges vase, the hanging framed print of Cignac's *Le Pont des Arts*. The sunlight beamed through thin, pale blue curtains hanging in front of the window orifice and the dark brown shutters pressed against the wall on both sides of it.

"We're in France. Remember?" I said. "We arrived last night—I think."

I couldn't be sure when we arrived, but I recalled darkness on a drive from the port to the house. Aunt Adèle had greeted us at the port and escorted us with Uncle Gilbert driving. A few of our cousins greeted us at the house, and then Uncle Gilbert placed my sister over his shoulder to carry her up the stairs while Aunt Adèle took me by the hand and led me up behind them. They put Madeleine-Grace to bed, and I climbed into the same bed with her. Aunt Adèle tucked us in, smiled, and shut the door behind her. A few minutes later, she opened it, said something to Uncle Gilbert in the hall, and left.

"We're at the summer house?" Madeleine-Grace said to me. "I want to go home."

"Me, too," I said, and I turned to the sunlit window. The light made my newly opened eyes water. "We can't go back."

Madeleine-Grace and I propped ourselves up and leaned our backs against the headboard to take in our environs for a moment. The emptiness of the vase on the dresser snagged my attention and reeled my thoughts into a memory of my father as he told my mother that she should never see that vase empty as long as he lived. They were lying in this very bed one morning when he had said it, Madeleine-Grace and myself lying between them. The vase was filled with yellow jonquils, although the green stems, the green leaves, and the green herbs all around the yellow more so stood out to me. Papa abided by his mandate: for as long as he lived, he made sure that she always awoke to flowers in that vase. His favorite were jonquils, what we called *pourions* in Cauchois.

"I don't want to go downstairs," Madeleine-Grace said. She was looking from the bedroom door to the window, and I could tell she wanted to walk to the window to see where we were, to see our summer residence in daylight. She was too nervous to leave my side, opting to lean with her protruding head over my chest for a view through the window.

"We can wait until Aunt Adèle gets us," I said, but then I protruded my head, too. I wanted to check if I heard silence, and I did. "I think everyone is still asleep. If we get up now, we can look around and not have to talk to anyone else."

"I don't want to go down," my sister reiterated.

"We'll go together," I said, sitting upright by swinging my legs to dangle over the side of the bed. "Come on." I gently pulled her by her hand to join me on the side of the bed, both of us facing the window. We rose in unison and walked to the window, pulling aside the curtains. Our room was on the American second story toward the front of the house. Our room did not have a terrace, offering instead a window view of the gray stone side of the family summer house, the green lawn, the empty clotheslines, and an automobile in the pebble driveway. I could not tell from the sunlight how early the morning was. I wanted to reach for Grand-père Guarin's pocket watch, but I didn't have it on me.

Madeleine-Grace and I, hand in hand as we gazed out the window, released our hold to turn toward the bedroom door. I saw at the foot of the bed our trunks with our travel clothes folded neatly on top. I knew the pocket watch my grandfather had given me was left in the pocket of my pants, and I stopped to check it before leaving the bedroom. It was 8:15am France time; I had changed it on the *paquebot* when the lights of Le Havre came into sight.

I pushed the door open and peered down the hall. All the doors were shut. At the top of the stairs, I could see morning light below, and we crept down the narrow, wooden stairs until we arrived in the main hall, from which we walked to the kitchen. The room smelled clean, no dishes and bowls and glasses and silverware cluttered the countertops, and no piles of mail and magazines and homework untidied the table and the chairs. Papa used to leave things out sometimes, and mother reprimanded him; he winked at us and shrugged while she was yelling, and we always laughed.

We walked through the house room by room, and somehow, for as many summers as we had visited, I remembered only the rooms and not a single event that had taken place in them. I saw vague apparitions of my mother and father in them, but they were not quite memories. We stepped through an archway that led from the kitchen to the dining room, we slunk to the foyer and main staircase, and we tiptoed through the *salon*, the living room. I heard a flapping sound, long but fast threshes of movement, coming from nearby, possibly outside. Our curiosity piqued, Madeleine-Grace and I inched toward a window, opening the curtains to see outside. We saw no one and moved to another, repeating until we came to the door to the back veranda. It was not shut all the way.

Slowly pushing the door open, I peered out to see the veranda littered with cigarette butts and boxes of Gauloises and Gitans, loose tobacco, and white paper; brown and green and clear glass bottles, some empty and some almost empty; porcelain plates and crystal glasses, tiny silver forks, and coffee spoons; half an apple tart on a tipped platter on the table, the sweet apple filling having spread but coagulated, the tart distorted in its fatal dive into the tabletop; crumbs and pistachio shells and from-the-tin sardine bits on the table and chairs and benches; and *salon* loveseat pillows and chair cushions on the stone floor. At the end of the veranda stood Aunt Adèle, snapping a tablecloth over the railing, shaking her head from side to side between every snap. When I pushed the door wider, she heard the squeak it made, turned, and rushed to us, whispering to stay inside. We withdrew immediately into the house as she followed us, the tablecloth now crumpled in her arms.

"Come!" she said with straight lips and led us to the kitchen again. "Do you want a *café*? I did not put it on yet. I just stepped outside to see what was done last night."

"No, thank-you," I said to her question. Madeleine-Grace said the same.

"What do you have for breakfast in America? Toast with butter and jam, right? I can give that to you if you would like. Or would you prefer a *croissant*? I asked you last night in the car, but you were too tired. You shrugged at my every question. And no *café*? You have always liked it, but I can make a *chocolat chaud*."

Madeleine-Grace slipped behind me bashfully while saying, "I don't want to eat here." From behind me, she wrapped her arms around my waist as if she were three years old.

"We aren't hungry yet," I said to Aunt Adèle, not wanting to make her feel bad as she offered so much to us. While I wanted to unwrap Madeleine-Grace's arms from my waist, I put my hands on hers where they clasped. I hung my head, not to look at our hands, but in sadness, perhaps absorbing Madeleine-Grace's.

I lifted my head when I heard Aunt Adèle pull a chair from the kitchen table. She was looking at us with the same forlorn expression I imagined Madeleine-Grace to have as she smooshed her face in my back. Once she had sat, Aunt Adèle realized she was still holding the tablecloth. She lifted the clump of *nappage*, sighed, and lowered it to her lap.

"I found it in the corner of the veranda with a piece of *tarte aux pommes* right on it—no plate. There is a big, sticky spot on it I will have to scrub out. That's why I use this one. You see—" and she held up a portion of the tablecloth for us to see a light red stain— "they have already spilled on this one many times. I am tired of scrubbing out their recklessness only to have to find a new one for them to ruin. Now, this one stays out there all the time, and I don't put as much effort into cleaning it. Only this—" and now she held up a different spot, this time the congealed apple tart filling— "I have to get rid of quickly before it attracts insects or birds."

Madeleine-Grace peeked from around my back to see the spot, and once exposed, she remained by my side. I put my arm around her.

"Then I will clean all the rest," Aunt Adèle said, and she sighed again. "But first, I am going to put on the coffee. If you would like, you may join me. The others won't be up for hours."

She set the tablecloth on the chair on which she had been sitting and prepared the coffee at the stove, but not before forbidding us to step foot on the veranda until she had cleaned it. We stayed in the kitchen, watching her in silence. She reached for a door of the *vaisselier*, a large kitchen cabinet, and upon opening it, she pulled first one and then two more cups from an orderly arrangement of cups and saucers, plates and bowls. The way she lined the cups and saucers on the countertop, each in a single-file wait for fulfillment, reminded me of my mother's way of doing the same. Aunt Adèle walked across the kitchen to a door, unlocked it at the top corner, opened it, and leaned in to retrieve a tin box she had left on the floating shelf affixed to the wall lining a narrow staircase to the cellar. The floating shelf, a ledge atop cyma recta molding, jutted dangerously into the doorway so that stepping through required a parry of the head to the right as if slipping an oncoming punch. Aunt Adèle and my mother had asked Uncle Romain to remove the ledge, convenient though it was for temporary storage with easy access, and until he did so, the ladies painted the ledge white to stand out the moment the door opened. Maman said the white ledge was like the cliffs of La Côte d'Albâtre.

Aunt Adèle closed the door and stopped before us with what was once a Berlingots de Nantes tin. She lifted the lid and a layer of cloth to show us a display of homemade cookies.

"Miniature *sablés*," she said. "I made them for you yesterday. I know you love them. They are good with the coffee."

She set two on each saucer and shortly thereafter poured three *cafés*. She brought them to the kitchen table and sat. Madeleine-Grace felt comfortable enough to sit at the table but did not take the coffee and cookie until she saw me pull one set to myself. Then she did the same, blowing on hers to dissipate the smoke. I dipped my cookie without taking a sip, enjoying the two flavors together. Aunt Adèle was right— these were one of our favorites, and the second I enjoyed the familiar flavor, the image of Aunt Adèle and my mother making them three summers ago in this kitchen appeared in my mind.

"You have had a long trip," began Aunt Adèle, sipping the coffee she held in front of her chin. "And you've had many difficulties prior to that. I know you are tired and exhausted and—hurt. Your Grand-mère Armance stayed in Le Havre to talk to Aunt Melisende and will go on to Paris to talk to Grandma'Maud. Your Grand-père Guarin will return to America to get many things in order for you while your Grand-mère Armance continues to London, Calais, and Paris before meeting you for the voyage back to America. She told us to make no fuss for your arrival so that everything would be calm and as routine as your past stays here, yet I did do a few special things, like making the *sablés*." When she smiled, Madeleine-Grace smiled, too, for what may have been the first time since before we left America. "So this summer, like all the others, you will stay with us. Take today for yourself. And later, I will help you with your clothes and washing and meals and everything else.

You will take your parents' bedroom and now—it will be all to yourselves." She lowered the *café* in order to allow herself to cry, and then, as if to dispel the tears, took three quick sips and kept the cup at her chin. "We will talk all summer. I want to hear about this past year in America—your school, your friends, and even your mother and father if you are able. I have missed them very much."

She lowered the cup once more as her eyes welled with tears. To avoid looking at her, I looked at my coffee, which was no longer smoking. I took a sip and glanced at Madeleine-Grace to see that she was silently crying. When Aunt Adèle noticed, she jumped from her chair and crouched next to my sister.

"I know you miss them very much, too. No one misses them more," she said to Madeleine-Grace.

"I want to go home," Madeleine-Grace responded, leaning into my side. Aunt Adèle rested her chin on Madeleine-Grace's shoulder, and for several minutes we remained in this position. Then Aunt Adèle lifted her head, stood, and composed herself. She crouched again to address us.

"I folded your travel clothes, but you are not to wear them. I will include them in the wash. You two can rest more if you'd like or sit on the veranda, but I must clean first. I will clean the veranda and then I have to scrub the floors down here. Everyone else will be up later, and I'll prepare meals. You may join us whenever you wish. I will tell your cousins not to disturb you today. I stopped at the market when I learned you would be coming after all, and I bought Pont l'Evêque for after dinner—your favorite, right? If you would like that tonight, we will have it. This has been your summer place for all your years, so do as you like while I clean."

She stood as if to start her chores and stopped abruptly. She crouched once more and, placing her arms around us, kissed us each on the cheek. Then she rose and carried our cups and saucers to the sink. I heard her reprimand herself for not bringing us sugar.

Madeleine-Grace and I decided to go back to our room, and as we headed toward the main staircase, we passed a window. Outside the window was a bench I used to sit on and read on lengthy days of summers past. From the house to the cliffs, all around were little islands of greenery—islands of flowers and shrubs, of herbs, of vegetables, each enclosed with a tiny rampart of neatly placed rocks. The reading bench was in the middle of one of these, a flower island of light purple phlox, pink peonies, and yellow lilies much nearer the house than the cliffs. I knew I wanted to go outside today, to stand on the cliffs and stare at the ocean. My mother and father had talked about doing that this summer—standing on the cliffs at dusk, holding hands, and listening to the ocean sing.

"The ocean does not sing," Madeleine-Grace told Maman. "It rumbles," and we laughed.

"Sometimes a rumble can make a beautiful song, too," Maman said.

"It's still music to me," Papa agreed.

They would not be able to hear that song, I knew, and to me, it would not sound as beautiful without them.

Upstairs, I placed our travel clothes on the dresser next to the empty vase. We opened our trunks and rummaged through them without a particular agenda. Strapped to the inside lid hung my American magazines. I unfastened them and set them on the dresser. Madeleine-Grace and I washed, changed out of our pajamas, and put on summer clothes. As we made the bed together, with our door open, we could hear occasional snoring, beds creaking, and covers rustling from our relatives occupying the other bedrooms. Then I took my pocket watch out of my travel pants pocket and put it in my current pants pocket, swiped my magazines off the dresser, and headed with my sister for outside. When we arrived at the reading bench, I glanced at the veranda, and Aunt Adèle, who had just finished cleaning it, waved, smiled, and headed in, lifting a tray piled high with dirty dishware.

I walked around to the front of the bench and set down the magazines while Madeleine-Grace smelled flowers in the island. For some reason, that summer in France after my parents' death, I initially had a hard time remembering anything about our French summers prior, yet I did recall a memory from five years before when I was seven and Madeleine-Grace was four. Back then, they called me Jacques:

"Jacques!" Madeleine-Grace had shouted, but I did not respond. My concentration was near impenetrable as I sat on this same bench, imagining I was reading from the copy of *True Detective* opened on my lap, imagining through the words I did not entirely recognize an elaborate tale of down-trodden investigators in pursuit of heartless criminals. At seven, I knew only so much, despite a precocity outweighed only by my imagination.

A second shout, "Jacques!" again from my little sister, finally stirred me, and I looked up. I realized that I had heard the name called before but hadn't noted it was I who was being addressed, for "Jacques" is what they called me in Etretat-au-Delà; I had been there only two days so far. I would more likely respond to "Jack," the American version of my name.

Madeleine-Grace, at that age demure like her brother, but at that moment more sprightly, called me over with a wave. "Let's help Aunt Adèle in the garden!"

I had set down the magazine and ran after my sister as she led the way to Aunt Adèle culling sprigs of thyme in one of the herb gardens. As I approached them, I noticed my other aunts and uncles on the back veranda. They each affected a leisurely mien and acted as if they had colluded to evoke a stagnant atmosphere of oppressive heat, but it was not so hot. Uncle Roul leaned against a post, partially seated on the balustrade, as he brought a cigarette to his lips. The turn of his head as I jogged by barely made a quarter circle before he gave up following my path. Sturdy Uncle Romain, lost within the porch's shade, leaned against the house wall with cigarette in hand, as well. Aunt Pé, his wife, sat at the foot of a *chaise longue* and obliviously caught Uncle Romain's ashes in a *cendrier* whenever he extended his arm toward her; Uncle Roul dropped his over the railing into the lavender bushes. After every few puffs, Aunt Pé took the cigarette from her husband to take a puff, herself. Aunt Mirabelle and Aunt Laure lay in the *chaises longues* as if exhausted and fanned themselves with silk brises. Uncle Gilbert, at table with his elbows propped and his chin resting on one hand, sipped *calva* from a cordial glass in the other hand. Seated in various spots about the porch idled their children—our cousins—all of them pursuing pastimes. Young Roul, Alphonse, and Chardine played *dominos*, little Laure and Wischard colored without much attention to lines in a coloring book, and Astride stared blankly at the floor. I had attributed my own parents' absence to their likely unpacking upstairs.

The herb garden to which I had run was, in fact, one of several small garden islands between the house and the cliffs. All kept by Aunt Adèle, the flower gardens, which comprised more than half the islands, lured honeybees with their treasure troves of pollen and attracted onlookers with their multicolored beauty and fragrances. Lilies in shades of orange, yellow, and pink bloomed, buffered by lush patches of purple phlox. The herb gardens might go unnoticed unless even a faint breeze passed, for then they, too, enticed passersby with their fragrances.

Aunt Adèle held a miniature osier basket already filled with tied bunches of thyme, chives, and mint. She had just finished tying twine around the mint when Madeleine-Grace and I arrived. The sky escaped from her sparkling eyes, nourishing the fresh herbs with something celestial. She smiled when she saw us at her side and broke off two leaves of mint.

"For you and you," she had said, handing one to each of us. We immediately held them to our noses and sniffed, smiles forming on our faces. "This is your favorite one, isn't it?"

"Yes," we said in unison.

"Mine, too," she said, and winked. "Do you remember when you were so little and I taught you what it was called?"

"And every time I saw anything growing, I pointed and said 'mint'! I remember," said Madeleine-Grace.

"Very good, Madeleine-Grace. Now let me pick one more bunch."

"I want to pick it!" shouted Madeleine-Grace playfully. "Which one?"

"Parsley. Over there," she said, pointing to the patch. "You pull a few carefully, and I will tie them for tonight." She pulled from her apron pocket a piece of twine already cut from the spool. "We will have *rôti de lard* tonight."

"I like it when you or Maman makes it," Madeleine-Grace had said as she pulled one last sprig of parsley.

Madeleine-Grace brought her bunch of parsley to our aunt who noticed the thin stems were already discolored by the child's tight grip. She tied the bunch in one deft movement and placed it with the others in the basket.

That was it, my most vivid memory of summers at mother's family's house on the coast. Here again five years later for the next summer stay, I didn't deliberately try to remember things and find myself unable; nothing besides this memory came to mind except strange wisps of personages from the past, specters still and visions dynamic, evanescing before I was sure they were even there.

Sitting on the bench, my magazines on my lap, I did not lift one to begin paging through it. A heaviness came over me, and I could not lift my arms off my lap; they lay clasped on top of the magazines as I stared at the sky and then at the earth. While I knew Madeleine-Grace and I had been moving more slowly than usual this morning, I did not realize until now that several hours had passed since we had first awoken, and the sun's beating lulled me into a drowse. Madeleine-Grace must have experienced the same effect of the warmth, for she ambled to the bench, a lily in hand, sat beside me, and yawned. Within seconds, she leaned her head against my arm and closed her eyes. In my lethargy, I lifted an arm around her and tilted my head toward her, realizing we had not fully recharged from nearly two weeks of travel. I must have fallen asleep within minutes.

When I awoke again, I knew hours had passed on account of the different sort of sunlight and the wisps of lavender in the hues of the sky. Madeleine-Grace woke as I stretched. I was now smooshed into one side of the bench, and she was curled up on the rest of it. The warmth comforted us and did not feel much different from the temperature that had induced our sleep; we must have been especially tired.

Despite the intention of sitting on the bench to read my magazines, a stronger pull compelled me to explore. We had arrived after dark last night, but now in the sunlight of late afternoon, I felt the lure of the sea beyond the cliffs. The property was one among several along the aquatic border of Etretat-au-Delà, high on the short stretch of alabaster white cliffs overlooking the cuff of "the Sleeve." A short walk from the house, through and beyond the flower and herb islands and past an expanse of green lawn, brings one to the chalky cliffs and to a magnificent panorama of sea immortalized in the dashes and strokes of André, Courbet, and Monet. While I wasn't ready for an excursion to the beach, I did desire a closer view of the sea, so I abandoned the magazines, stepped out of the flower island, and walked towards the cliffs. When Madeleine-Grace saw me heading there, she followed.

We stopped several feet from the edge, far enough away to be unable to see the beach below. Made miniscule in the enormity of the endless alabaster and the ongoing azure and lavender of the sky, I held Madeleine-Grace's hand, and high on the cliffs overlooking La Côte, we watched the ocean meet the sky in a soft, held kiss, not unlike our mother's when her lips pressed into our cheeks but never fully released. The water and the sky and where they met seemed so undisturbed despite the movements of waves and wisps of cloud, and I imagined the *paquebot* wading along in its arrival from America. I imagined Madeleine-Grace and myself on board, holding onto the rail of the foredeck as it approached. In this vision, I wasn't so small; I was part of the ocean and the sky and the horizon; I was the touch of Heaven and Earth and the sacred place they melded; I was *within* the moment that is held in a parent's loving kiss.

Hearing quick-paced footsteps nearing from behind us, we turned to see our cousins Wischard and little Laure. They stopped when we turned, not calling to us but preferring to recognize us, to take us in, this first time since last summer. Behind them, Uncle Roul halted in front of the bench, holding a glass. As the kids waved for us to come back to the house, Uncle Roul waved, too, and then returned toward the house. Wischard and little Laure ran to us, more taken by our presence than by the vastness of sky and ocean.

"It's almost time for dinner!" Wischard said, arriving straight to the point before greeting us. "You missed *apéro*."

"Aunt Adèle says you must wash up before dinner," little Laure added.

Our cousins took a step toward the house, assuming we would follow. When we didn't budge, they stopped, unsure. Madeleine-Grace unexpectedly hugged Laure, clasping Laure's arms in her embrace. Laure lifted a forearm, and in a feigned affection, touched Madeleine-Grace's back. Wischard reciprocated more warmly when Madeleine-Grace hugged him, too. I wanted to stay and stare at the horizon until darkness settled, all the while imagining myself on the *paquebot* cutting the waves as it must have last night, but Madeleine-Grace took my hand to walk toward the house. I placed my other arm around Wischard's neck, and Laure gave him a look when I did, suggesting my action odd.

The four of us made the short trek unnoticeably uphill to the house, passing the still-life of aunts, uncles, and cousins on the veranda, not one of whom waved or smiled or nodded in greeting. Our cousins Alphonse and Chardine inched beyond the adults for a better view of us while their brother Roul, whom I had never seen smoke, lit a cigarette. Aunt Adèle, not among them, was tending to dinner.

The moment the house door opened, we could smell the delicious food. Aunt Adèle must have heard our entrance, for half her body lunged into the hall, her torso in the hall and everything below her waist in the other room.

"You found the soap I left in the washroom for you?" she asked.

"Yes, we used it this morning to wash," I said. She had placed a fresh bar of peony soap in the soap dish and had hung clean washcloths and hand towels.

"Wash up for dinner then, and hurry down," she said, smiling afterwards. I think she was smiling at the idea of our having a good dinner, one prepared by her.

Astride stepped into the room and stared from the bottom of the stairs as we made our way up. Once again, she never greeted us, never so much as waved or smiled. When we arrived at the top, I smiled at her, and she turned as if she had seen nothing and departed.

Madeleine-Grace and I washed up using the fragrant peony soap and the washcloths before heading down. We arrived as a caravan of family was heading into the dining area past the kitchen, merging with them as they offered no acknowledgement of our presence after so many months' absence. Passing the window overlooking my reading bench, I realized I had never brought in with me the American magazines I had been reading. I halted and pivoted, ready to dart through the lazy current of family heading for dinner, but Uncle Roul's hand grabbed my arm and stopped me.

"Where are you going? You don't need to be afraid of anything," Uncle Roul said, my arm still in his hold.

"I'm not afraid. I forgot my magazines on the bench outside." I designed the delivery with urgency in my voice so that my uncle could see the importance of this responsibility to me.

But Uncle Roul shrugged and pursed his lips in such a way that indicated he did not care and neither should I. He released his hand from my arm and positioned it on my back, nudging me in the direction of dinner. "Leave it," he said, as he walked me to the table. "Adèle will get it later."

With his hand on my back, he guided me to my chair and stood behind it until I sat. When I sat, I could not refrain from holding several looks out the window. I felt unsettled as if the magazines were domesticated pets now vulnerable to wild attacks, exposed to the elements, neglected.

Aunt Adèle called our attention to dinner when she pulled her chair from the table and sat. She had been standing behind it, waiting for us to take our seats. The food already covered every inch of the runner and its aromas made my mouth water, yet a strange repulsion accompanied the sensation on account of connecting the scent to dinners at this table with my parents last summer and those before it. It's hard to feel excited about a meal when a sadness settles, anchoring my appetite and the happiness I could never again experience. I couldn't remember a specific dinner, yet I knew we had enjoyed this meal often together as a family at this house many times.

Aunt Pé lifted the slotted spoon from the *haricots verts* and served first her husband and then her daughter, and Aunt Mirabelle began to do the same with the boiled potatoes and parsley in butter and cream. Uncle Roul poured himself more wine while Uncle Romain sipped from his already full glass.

"*Le bénédicité,*" Aunt Adèle said, the word for before-meal grace.

Aunt Mirabelle sighed and stopped serving potatoes. Aunt Pé scoffed but had just finished serving her own and easily slumped into her chair.

"Why should we say grace now?" asked young Roul sticking an unlit cigarette in his mouth. His mother pulled it from his lips, and his father chuckled.

"We always say grace," said Madeleine-Grace, unsure why doing so would be an issue suddenly.

"Juliette and Adèle say grace," Aunt Pé said. "So, say grace, Adèle."

Aunt Pé swept one *haricot vert* with her fingers off the rim of the platter and tossed it in her mouth. Our uncles continued sipping wine except for Uncle Gilbert; Aunt Laure gazed out the window with a look of panic in her eyes; and except for young Roul who rolled his cigarette back and forth on the tablecloth, our other cousins stared at their plates—all while Aunt Adèle crossed herself and said grace. Madeleine-Grace and I prayed with her, the other children crossed themselves sloppily, and then Aunt Adèle rose to serve from the platter of *rôti*, known as *porc à la normande* in America. Her serving opportuned an announcement.

"I have prepared *rôti de lard* to celebrate the arrival of Ellande and Madeleine-Grace," and the spoon stopped serving and settled in the platter. Aunt Adèle's head drooped and tears formed in her eyes. "I'm sorry," she continued. "I find myself unable to adjust to your presence here without—." She did not finish her sentence, I could tell from the look she gave me, because she did not want to be another reminder to Madeleine-Grace and me that our parents were no longer with us. Madeleine-Grace looked down and started crying nonetheless, sliding off her chair and onto half of mine. I put my arm around her, and Aunt Adèle could not speak through a wave of sobs. Then she walked around and held us both from behind the chair. I looked up to see Aunt Pé sneaking another green bean, the uncles sighing before taking a sip, including Uncle Gilbert this time, and our cousins staring intently at us. Even young Roul had stopped rolling his cigarette.

The moment of embrace, held for about a minute, ended. Aunt Adèle resumed her position at the platter of pork, Madeleine-Grace slid onto her own chair, and young Roul continued rolling a cigarette. Aunt Adèle spoke again. "We know this is a favorite, so we welcome you with it. May dinners here always feel like home to you." She then began placing a slice onto our plates as we extended them to her while the other aunts piled on the sides.

Once everyone was served, the first moments of dinner held tenuously to quietude except for the clinks of silverware on china, chewing and sips, and soft thunder rolling outside. Then Aunt Adèle finally began conversation.

"You were very tired today after your travels," she said. "I saw you sleeping on the bench this afternoon."

"We didn't mean to fall asleep," I said, unsure how others might react to what must have been a strange sight—my sister and me huddled in sleep on one of the outside benches.

"Good sun for sleep," Uncle Roul said, providing an affirmation for our nap.

"How long were you on the boat?" asked little Laure. She used the Cauchois word "*bat*" as if it were a little dinghy instead of "*paquebot*," a liner, for which the French were known.

"'How long were you on the boat?'" mocked her mother. "Do you forget they had much more travel than just on the boat? Chicago to New York by train. Several days in New York with their American grandparents. Then the liner to Le Havre."

Little Laure looked down as if her question were stupid.

Aunt Laure continued, "You must have been lost, you two. Lost." She directed her gaze out the window for another long, blank stare. As if trying to reclaim her, Uncle Gilbert poured her a glass of wine. She did not move.

"At least they did not have to spend time in Le Havre with Aunt Melisende," added Uncle Romain. After his comment, he smirked, prompting a chuckle from his wife as if this cue and response had been rehearsed.

"She will come here, then," said Uncle Roul. "Is that any better?"

"See what you did?" Aunt Pé said, looking at Madeleine-Grace and me. "You will make us all pay when Aunt Melisende comes here to see you instead."

"What is so bad about Aunt Melisende?" asked Aunt Adèle.

Aunt Pé, who had just lifted her napkin to dab her mouth, threw it on the table next to her plate. "She is no different from my mother-in-law. Cut from the same cloth."

"I should say they are," said Aunt Adèle. "And what's so bad about that?"

"They're both crazy," declared Uncle Romain, knowing full well he was speaking of his own mother.

Young Roul suddenly interrupted by pushing his chair back and rising, slipping a cigarette into his shirt pocket.

"Sit down!" Aunt Mirabelle snapped. "You are not smoking now."
"I have to," he snapped back. "It feels like rain. I saw the clouds before we sat for dinner. I need to have a smoke before the rain starts."
"Sit down!" his mother insisted.
"You can smoke from the veranda after dinner if it's raining," said Uncle Roul. "Sit down."
Roul sat at his father's command, pulled the cigarette from his pocket, and started rolling it back and forth on the tablecloth again. Then he said, "Can I teach Jacques how to smoke?"
"It's 'Ellande,'" said Aunt Adèle.
"Ellande! Ellande!" shouted Uncle Romain. "Why this 'Ellande' nonsense?"
"His name is Jacques," Aunt Pé reiterated.
"His name is Jacques, yes," said Aunt Adèle calmly. "It always will be. But for now, he goes by Ellande. This is a beautiful name, is it not?"
"It is not Normand," declared Uncle Romain. "It's that Basque garbage!"
"It's a disgrace," added Aunt Pé.
"How is it a disgrace?" inquired Uncle Gilbert. "The boy is Basque himself."
"Barely," said Aunt Pé. "And on his American father's side."
Perhaps as someone who married into the Semperrin family, himself, and aware of what his wife's family might want to say about his own children, Uncle Gilbert felt a need to defend me by asserting, "His blood is no more a choice for the boy than who his father is. Did he have any say over his mother's marrying a Basque man?" Of course, Uncle Gilbert was fully Normand, so he must have known he would escape insulting retorts.
I did understand the novelty of my name change to them, but I did not anticipate the anger. In my father's family, there was no naming convention, at least not that he and his parents followed. Of course, my father's parents had immigrated to America but made a conscientious effort to continue the traditions of their upbringing in Normandie. Had there been a naming convention, I image they would have adopted it even in the States. In my mother's family, the males were expected to name their firstborn male after the baby's paternal grandfather and their firstborn female after the baby's paternal grandmother; other than that, there were no traditional requirements. The Semperrin females, not mandated to follow any convention of naming, usually named their children after the babies' grandparents as a courtesy; it was understood

that the females would likely have to follow the naming conventions of their husband's family, anyway.

My mother's siblings did not honor this practice. Uncle Romain never had a male and named his daughter whatever he and Aunt Pé wished. Uncle Roul named his firstborn after himself, and I don't know the story behind Alphonse and Chardine's name. Aunt Laure named Wischard after Uncle Gilbert' father and named Laure after herself. Aunt Adèle did not marry.

As for my parents, Julien and Juliette Avery, since my father's side had no specific naming convention, they felt content to name me after my mother's father, my grandfather, Jacques Semperrin. And Madeleine-Grace was named after our mother's mother, Madeleine-Maud, who had been named after her grandmother, Madeleine-Anne.

For my first few years on this earth, I was Jacques. When I started school in the suburbs of Chicago, the teachers called me Jack. To this day, I don't understand why they did this when our classes were riddled with Jacks. I would have stood out as the only Jacques. So at home, I was Jacques, but at school, I was Jack. By third grade, I was one of seven Jacks in my class. When I tried to switch back to Jacques, the other kids made fun of me, calling me "Frère Jacques" and telling me to wake them up in the morning, or reciting the old nursery rhyme of not "Jack and Jill" but "Jacques and Jill" running up the hill to catch a pail of not water but frogs. So as a wounded eight-year-old, Jacques was off the table. One day while my American grandparents were watching me, my grandfather told me stories about his life in France, about his upbringing, about his parents. He told me a story about his father salting cod he had just caught in the Bay of Biscayne. I asked what his father's name was, and he told me "Ellande." I'm not sure why, but I decided to take up this name. "Jack" never sat right with me, and if I couldn't be "Jacques," after my own grandfather, I would be "Ellande" after my great-grandfather. Somehow, no one objected to Ellande at school when I began sixth grade with new nomenclature. It was news to my parents when my teachers referred to me as "Ellande," but they took it well—and took to calling me by that name, themselves. It has stuck since then.

"His father is not Basque," insisted Uncle Romain. "He is Normand! Julien's father's father was part Basque. That hardly makes the boy Basque, although he is not a thoroughbred."

"Why get so upset over the name? Besides, he is honoring a great-grandfather," said Uncle Gilbert.

"Honoring his Basque great-grandfather. Why is he not honoring his Normand grandfather?"

"The way your children are honoring theirs?" asked Aunt Adèle.

Aunt Pé, who had just lifted her napkin, threw it again on the table. My two uncles puffed air from their mouths in disdain while Uncle Gilbert chuckled.

"One of mine is," he said.

"Ellande, Ellande, Ellande," Uncle Romain muttered, and then heaved a fork full of pork into his mouth, refocusing on his meal.

Then young Roul started again. "I'm going to teach Ellande how to smoke tonight after dinner."

"You'll do no such thing," admonished Aunt Adèle.

"It will help him get girls," added young Roul, rolling away at his cigarette.

"He doesn't need girls right now," said Aunt Adèle.

"What good is learning that when he's spending a summer with family?" asked Aunt Laure. The raised voices over my name had reeled her back to the table, but every time thunder rolled, she stared off.

"He can make use of it back in Chicago," said young Roul. "Girls like a guy who smokes."

"And you get the girls?" asked Uncle Romain.

Young Roul blushed and unbuttoned his shirt at the top. The collar button was already opened.

"Well?" the boy's father asked.

"I talk with some girls," young Roul responded.

"Like his father," said Aunt Laure, prompting a quick glance from Aunt Mirabelle. "When Roul was younger, he smoked and—and attracted many girls." Aunt Laure seemed to tack this statement on to her first few words. Then, as she placed her napkin beside her plate and rose, she said to young Roul, "You look very much like him when he was your age." This, of course, complimented young Roul as rarely did talk of Uncle Roul not include comments about his handsome looks.

After Aunt Laure rose, she stared at me, tilted her head, and smiled. Then she ambled out of the dining room to listen alone, I imagined, to the thunder. Uncle Romain chuckled, tossing his napkin in the middle of the table, rising, and exiting with his glass.

I looked at Madeleine-Grace's plate and saw that she must have been as hungry as I, not having eaten much since our disembarkment from the *paquebot*. Perhaps because it was our first day in the summer house, we were both too embarrassed to request more or to add some ourselves. Luckily, when I glanced at the serving platters to see if enough remained for Madeleine-Grace and me, Aunt Adèle noticed and understood my searching intent. She rose and brought the platters to us, scooping some of every dish onto our plates as our parents would have. Madeleine-Grace smiled at me, and I shrugged, pretending that another helping didn't matter to me. Before she returned to her seat, Aunt Adèle kissed us each on the cheek, her eyes lined with tears again.

While we finished our seconds, the others rose from the table, leaving behind their plates and napkins, until only Aunt Adèle and the two of us remained. Aunt Adèle had been finished for a while and was simply keeping us company. Noting our plates, she asked, "Are you full? Would you like more?"

We both responded that we were full, and she finally rose. As she approached us, she said, "Go in the other room with the children and play awhile. I will clear the table."

I knew my mother always to clear the table with her. I think Madeleine-Grace associated the same practice with past summers' dinners, for she took her plate and silverware before I reached for mine. Holding our plates, we began to follow Aunt Adèle, who had already loaded her arms with the platters of food, but she stopped us.

"Set those down, my doves. I will do this. Go play in the other room."

"It's okay," I said. "We can help."

Young Roul stepped into the dining room.

"Ellande, put those down. Come in here. I want to teach you how to smoke."

"You heard your mother," said Aunt Adèle to him. "You will do no such thing."

"Then I will teach him how to roll them. Girls will like that, too. Come on, Ellande."

I looked to Aunt Adèle who was more interested in my not helping her. She signaled for me to leave the dishes on the table, which I did, and for Madeleine-Grace to do the same. We looked at each other and returned them to the table, hers on top of mine, somewhat content that at least we had piled them neatly for her. As Aunt Adèle carried on to the kitchen, she issued one last warning to young Roul.

Soft thunder rolled and lightning illuminated the sky beyond the cliffs as we gathered in the *salle-en-arrière* off the veranda. At the end of the main hall, between the conservatory and the veranda, this room for all occasions came to be known to us as the backroom, or the *salle-en-arrière*. With couches, *méridionnes*, armchairs, a card table, side tables, floor lamps and table lamps, a radio, a *tourne-disque*, a shelf of books, toys, and games, and a wall of picture windows opening to the flower and herb islands in the fore and the cliffs beyond, we used this as an all-purpose room, smaller than a great room, more expansive in function than a rumpus or games room; in America, it would have been called a family room, which had not developed in France yet. The children played in spots on the floor, Laure and Wischard playing marbles, or what we called *billes*, and Alphonse and Chardine playing *dominos* nearby. Between every placement, Chardine flattened the ribbons that formed the hair on an heirloom *drouène*, a worn doll from her Cauchoise maternal grandmother. Aunt Pé and Aunt Mirabelle sat on the couch passing the time tenaciously loafing, avidly sitting out games of *dominos*, committedly avoiding exertion physical or mental, while Astride sat at their feet staring blankly. Aunt Laure stood with Uncle Romain and Uncle Roul at the entrance to the veranda, stepping out every minute for a puff from a cigarette, a few sips of *calvados*, and a quick look at the sprinkling of rain, a short-lasting kind we called *eune ondèye*. Madeleine-Grace joined the kids playing marbles, permitted only to watch them play, and young Roul sat with me against the wall, his box of Gauloises out. He took one and started rolling it back and forth over the cover of a Douay-Rheims Bible he had grabbed from a nearby end table. He took out another and gave it to me. These were not the hand-rolled cigarettes he had been rolling at the dinner table.

"Do the same," he commanded, reaching for another book and handing it to me.

I started rolling my cigarette back and forth the way he did. As the cigarette passed under my fingers and palms, something occurred to me: every mention of my parents over dinner had been in the present tense. Not wishing to reflect on the implications of this, preferring thoughts of my parents to belong to Madeleine-Grace and me alone for some reason and not to the others, I shifted my attention back to the cigarette. I double-checked to make sure my rolling movement mimicked young Roul's; it did, only my roll was quicker.

"Why am I doing this?" I asked.

"Because girls like it," young Roul responded.

"I mean, what is the good in rolling cigarettes?"

"You're supposed to roll them to pack the tobacco. It's what they do. I've seen it."

Roul's father was within earshot, having stepped in from the veranda, and he interrupted us. "That's when you pack the tobacco into the papers yourself. You are a fool, Roul."

"You don't roll the cigarettes with the filter, Roul," confirmed Uncle Romain. "You are a fool like your father." He knocked Uncle Roul in the back of the head with his open hand. Uncle Roul's lurch forward cost him a few precious sips of his *calva*, and his face turned red immediately. He slammed the drink on the end table as if the ancestral family crystal set were irrelevant and reciprocated with a smack to the back of Uncle Romain's head. Uncle Romain knew it was coming and had set his glass on the table to avoid a spill. When the blow landed, he was already flinging a fist into Uncle Roul's ribs. Uncle Roul grunted, and young Roul stood up, panic masking his machismo.

Uncle Romain added between jabs, "Are you so preoccupied that you don't teach your son how not to be a fool? His stupidity makes us all look bad." After this, Uncle Romain's reddened face slammed into Uncle Roul's chest, in spite of the twisting grip Uncle Roul kept around his brother's torso. Uncle Romain possessed a stocky physique unlike his brother's tall and fit one, unlike the slim ones of his sisters.

The women didn't rise. Aunt Pé scoffed, and Aunt Mirabelle looked over her shoulder at the brawl behind her. "Stop. The children don't like this," she said, and then returned to her loafing. Aunt Laure, with the same look of panic over the state of the skies, stepped onto the veranda. My two uncles stopped fighting and panted.

Oblivious to the men, Aunt Mirabelle said, "Why does she go out on the veranda? It's raining. She's crazy like her mother."

"The veranda is covered," Uncle Roul said between pants, reclaiming his glass of *calva*. "What difference is it to you?"

Aunt Mirabelle rolled her eyes.

"She's still crazy," added Aunt Pé for no particular reason. But her words called her husband's attention, and he noticed a stream of smoke from the cigarette lying in her *cendrier*.

"Why are you smoking inside? Smoke on the veranda," Uncle Romain snapped at her.

"Why?" said Aunt Pé. "Because Adèle doesn't like the smell of smoke inside?"

"I don't care what Adèle likes or doesn't like. I don't want the house to burn down, you fool."

"Yes, then what would we do with our summers?" responded Aunt Pé.

Forgetting his spat with Uncle Roul, Uncle Romain took two loud stomps toward his wife and stopped. She rose abruptly, nearly kicking her daughter out of the way inadvertently, and then ambled around the couch to the veranda entrance, holding the cigarette out the door.

"You almost knocked the radio off the table, Uncle Romain," said young Roul, touching it to ensure its security on the tabletop.

"Roll your filtered cigarettes like a fool," barked Roul's father. "The only girls attracted to that are the ones as stupid as you are." What was designed as a biting remark became an insight to Uncle Roul. "Maybe you aren't such a fool after all," he added.

Young Roul might not have understood what he meant, but to hear the remotest semblance of affirmation from his father brought a smile to his face. Aunt Mirabelle looked over her shoulder at Uncle Roul and then away from him when he never glanced at her. Instead, he patted his son on the back. Young Roul, the panic cleared from his visage, slid back down the wall beside me.

"Give me back my marble!" shouted little Laure.

"The blue one's mine," returned Wischard, clenching his fist around it and contorting his body away from little Laure as she climbed him.

"Give it back!"

The aunts shook their heads at the quarrel, and Uncle Romain snapped at no one in particular. "Will someone shut them up?"

The kids continued to argue over the marbles. No one moved. I could hear the rain striking the windows and the clinking of plates in the kitchen.

"You will upset *Père La Pouque*! He will come out of the cellar to find you! Do you want that? *Marchand de Sable* will be angered and pour buckets of sand on your eyes, sealing them shut!" Uncle Romain's threatening tactic referred to Normandie's Boogeyman and Mr. Sandman, as we called them in America. "Where's Gilbert?" asked Uncle Romain.

"He went upstairs to lie down," responded Aunt Pé.

"Then you shut them up," demanded Uncle Romain.

Now Wischard had rolled the blue marble away from little Laure toward Alphonse and Chardine, who, as if they could not be bothered, rolled it away even farther. Little Laure crawled on hands and knees to catch it but was not fast enough, screaming at Wischard for the duration of her hot pursuit.

"Adèle!" shouted Uncle Romain. "Adèle!"

With an apron over her dress and dishtowel draped over her arm, her sudsy hands dripping, she stepped into the room.

"Adèle," continued Uncle Romain, "Send the kids to bed."

She used the dishtowel to dry her hands as she said, "Children, gather in the foyer for prayers. I'll be there in a minute." She exited.

Little Laure was sitting across the room, the blue marble in her hand, crying, while the rest of us rose and headed to the foyer. None of us grumbled except young Roul, as the oldest seeing this step in the bedtime ritual as unnecessary. I wondered if he had protested participating before and had been reprimanded for it by Uncle Roul, for he never muttered a contrary word but only sighed in disgust.

I made my way into the foyer but not before taking a peek at the dining room. The table had been entirely cleared with only the crumb-topped tablecloth remaining. Aunt Adèle, just entering the foyer, caught me checking. She waved for me to join the others who were taking their seats cross-legged on the area rug along the staircase.

Aunt Adèle pulled toward us an upright chair, one of a pair positioned on either side of the alcove built into the staircase, and sat, her legs crossing at the ankle. My parents used to accompany her. My father pulled the other chair a few inches from the wall for my mother, and when she sat, he leaned on the chair back. Sometimes, his arm dangled over her shoulder, and she reached with her hand to hold his. That chair remained tonight tucked upright against the wall, empty.

We faced not only Aunt Adèle but an all-white statue of an adult Jesus holding the *norma*, the square, at His side in one hand and the *globus cruciger*, a globe—the world with a cross on it—extended before Him in the other, an image of the humility of earthly labor balanced with the majesty of heavenly rule. We were told this foot-high statue had been made along with one other from the same slab of limestone that had been used to make the Alabaster Virgin overlooking Etretat-au-Delà from the dome of the church. The other one-foot statue, also of Christ, belonged to the Galimards.

Our statue of Christ the Worker and Christ the King stood within a niche in the staircase wall. The semi-dome and walls of the exedra were adorned with a hand-painted fresco of the Blessed Mother holding the Christ Child. She appeared to be radiating in a light-blue-and-green sky, her delicate veil and mantle and gown in pinks and blues and whites. Her protective gaze overlooked the statue of Jesus.

While I did participate in evening prayers as Aunt Adèle led us, my attention alighted more so on the vacant chair. I chimed in for only the *Gloire*, having missed the *Notre Père* and *Je Vous Salue, Marie*, not to mention whatever prayerful words Aunt Adèle had uttered before them.

The consolation I found for having missed the prayers came in seeing that the empty chair fell within Our Lady's view, too.

As we rose after prayers and rounded the staircase, Aunt Adèle requested we wait. After returning her chair to the wall, she hurried into the kitchen and then returned, holding a platter of Grand Pont l'Evêque surrounded by cherries and grapes.

"Your favorite," she said, bringing the platter to the foot of the stairs where we awaited her.

Still contemplating the empty chair and that I had frittered away prayer in the keen presence of absence, I identified with the simple Man holding the carpenter's square, and this stunning platter of fruits and my favorite cheese seemed too splendid for me to enjoy. Guilt in combination with mourning compelled me to decline my aunt's gracious offer. The platter and deference behind its making were fit for a king, not for me, so I thanked her and ascended the stairs with my sister, knowing only a good sleep might cast off the forlornness that had overcome me.

Despite the late start this morning and the unexpected nap lasting the whole of the day, I underestimated how tired I still was and fell instantly asleep to the rain gently pattering on the window until it ceased, to the crisp and clean sheets caressing my skin and the floral of some fragrance mollifying my senses, to the recurring flashes of my mother and father lying on either side of Madeleine-Grace and me in this very bed during summers past.

Madeleine-Grace and I again awoke before the others the next morning, except for Aunt Adèle. When we slipped downstairs, I peered into the dining room and saw the tablecloth without crumb and crinkle and the chairs pushed in. We hoped to find Aunt Adèle in the kitchen, but a movement outside the back window caught my attention. We bypassed the kitchen and went straight to the picture window, a vast porcelain-blue sky beyond the cliffs in the background, and in the foreground, Aunt Adèle lifting the water-logged pages of my destroyed magazines off the bench. As she scraped a page off the wooden seat, Madeleine-Grace looked at me with deep concern in her eyes, and I—I looked toward my feet and closed my eyes in shame.

CHAPITRE 2

Two *cafés au lait* and four *sablés* floated to us in Aunt Adèle's light hands as we waited at the kitchen table. After setting them down before us, she returned to the counter. I sank into my chair, freeing a relieving sigh, when she poured herself a cup and joined us. She didn't sip right away. She looked at us, tilted her head with a teary-eyed squint and close-lipped smile, and sighed, herself. As if difficult to release her gaze from us, she finally turned to her coffee for a sip. Only then we, too, dipped our *sablés* and sipped. These quiet moments with Aunt Adèle early mornings at the kitchen table, with sunlight glowing around the opened window and through the thin, yellow curtains, and with my senses inhaling the aroma of fresh coffee and fresh air, I count among my favorite, not just of that summer but of my life. That smile and what it meant, the reason she had made the *sablés*, the unidentifiable but safe moods the coffee aroma released in me—these made me feel good, cheered me, refreshed me.

Aunt Adèle never once mentioned the magazines I had left outside. I know I should have, but I never thanked her for cleaning them up after my negligence and forgetfulness. I wished I hadn't brought out all three yesterday; I lost them all and, later, had to deny the frequent impulse to retrieve them from my trunk for moments of leisurely reading. I don't know why I continued to be drawn to them after I had read them cover to cover throughout the journey to France; I simply enjoyed turning those pages, reading the stories, scrutinizing the advertisements, wondering about the authors, and imagining detective tales of my own printed on the pages. Unless I came across a new one at some point, I would have to learn to do without them.

Aunt Adèle sent us upstairs to wash and to dress, and when we returned, we found her still in the kitchen, now rolling out long flats of dough while the scent of simmering broth perfumed the room. The dough she had placed in four rounds on the end of the flour-dusted kitchen table. A metal contraption with a crank rested on the same side of the table. Our aunt pressed the rounds with the heel of her palms and began rolling them with a wooden pin.

"You have arrived in time, my doves. You can help me make the pasta. Do you remember when your mother and I made the pasta like this?"

I did remember and nodded my head so. I remembered fondly, but for some reason, I was tempted to say that I didn't. Maybe I wanted Aunt Adèle to talk about her; maybe I didn't, and that's why I decided to nod. Not only did I recall my mother and Aunt Adèle making the pasta here in the kitchen various summer mornings, I recalled my mother talking about it the week before she died.

"'How I long for your Aunt Adèle's *piccagge aggétto in to brodo*,'" my mother had said. *Piccagge*, a name for *tagliatelle* in a Ligurian dialect, were long, flat strands of pasta. "Your aunt learned how to make it when we were in Italy with our father." My mother had brought it up because she couldn't wait until summer to enjoy her sister's cooking—that meal in particular. She had shared with me her anticipation of it one day after school. I was sitting at the kitchen table floating my model *paquebot* over the azure and white tablecloth as if I were a kindergartener, and she was pouring ingredients for a *vieux carré* into a *passoire* so that when my father returned, she'd have only to shake it with ice and strain it into glasses. She had set the shaker in the refrigerator, and when she saw me with the model liner, her shoulders dropped and her eyes closed a few seconds and she shared her longing for Aunt Adèle's garlic *piccagge* in broth.

"You remember?" Aunt Adèle said in response to my affirmation, pulling me from the memory. "Then you must assume her role and carry the pasta to the end of the table while I role it out—the way she did."

The image of my mother flashed before me, a light blue apron over her white and pink dress, holding the off-white pasta and casually walking it to the end of the table as Aunt Adèle turned the crank and teased it out. When she stepped far enough from the crank, my mother slid her other arm under the dip in the pasta length, easing the end of it to the edge of the table and gently setting it down. My mother always wore the light blue apron, and Aunt Adèle, the sun-faded, mint green one.

"Come stand here," Aunt Adèle said to me, and I stood beside her near the contraption with the crank. "I will flatten it with the rolling pin, and then we will pass it through the press."

Madeleine-Grace, however, stepped toward the stove where a stockpot released pleasant aromas. "What are you making over here?" she asked.

"That's broth—a delicious tomato and chicken-bone broth that I will simmer until it is much reduced and full of flavor."

"Will the bones disappear?" my sister asked. "Do they melt because the water gets so hot?"

Aunt Adèle laughed. "No, I take the bones out, but that's how the broth gets good flavor. Bones and plenty of time simmering with the lid off. Certainly you've seen your mother make a broth."

"She makes it while we're at school," I said.

Madeleine-Grace stepped closer to the stockpot and, on her tiptoes, peered in. "It looks like weeds in there."

"Those are many good vegetables and herbs that I will strain out. The thick ones—very dark green—are leeks and give it a strong savory flavor. I will add fresh lovage and parsley for the last hour. Do you remember helping me pick parsley, Madeleine-Grace?"

"Yes, I like that one," Madeleine-Grace said, walking to the table to inspect the dough. "But it's not your favorite, Aunt Adèle. Your favorite is mint."

Aunt Adèle stopped rolling the dough, surprised that Madeleine-Grace remembered something so insignificant. "Yes, mint is my favorite. You have a good memory."

"I remember because it is my favorite, and Ellande's, too."

"Oh, I see," responded Aunt Adèle. "That's why you remember it. The others don't like it so much. Can you imagine? After we finish preparing the pasta, we must pick some for you to wear on your nose."

Madeleine-Grace laughed, and I could tell she was excited at the prospect. Since the funeral, she adopted tendencies not unlike a child younger than her age, and cheerfulness over the prospect of a mint leaf stuck to her nose did not surprise me. I, however, was more excited about walking the sheets of pasta in my arms to the end of the table. Within moments, Aunt Adèle had rolled the first portion of a round of dough as flat as she wanted it, and began to pass it through the machine, guiding it out and into my hands so that I could walk it away from the machine. We did the same with the other portions of dough that she first rolled with the pin. We passed every sheet through the press several more times, Aunt Adèle having changed the setting after every two passes.

Once we had several long sheets, our aunt unwound portions of cheesecloth and set them alongside the dough resting on the floured table. Using a knife, she cut lengthwise into a fresh clove of neatly peeled garlic, making a slice that exposed the inner flesh. The smell was strong but nice. She rubbed the cut side of the garlic along the surface of the dough, making new slices periodically to expose more fresh garlic. She sliced thinly a few more cloves and laid them on top of the sheets of dough before wrapping them in cheesecloth.

"This is how the *piccagge* absorbs a light flavor of garlic without being too strong," she explained.

After twenty minutes, she removed the cheesecloth and the garlic and quickly cut the length of the dough into strips. All the strips formed, she lifted them gently with my help back onto the cheesecloth. The cuts of pasta, like the feeling of cool fingertips resting on my skin, did not break as we lowered them onto the cloth. Aunt Adèle murmured affirmations and cautions while my sister looked on, awed by the process. Once she placed the sliced garlic onto the strips, she wrapped cheesecloth once more around the pasta to let it absorb the garlic until cooking.

"Where did you learn how to make Italian food," Madeleine-Grace asked. I knew my mother and aunt had spent time in Italy with Grand-père Semperrin, but I did not know the circumstances.

Although it seemed she had much to clean on account of all the flour on the tabletop and the messy pasta machine, Aunt Adèle sat down, smiling radiantly, as she rested her forearms on the table and clasped her garlicy fingers. I knew this memory to be a pleasant one.

"Your mother and I went to Italy years ago with our father when we were children. As his eyes began to fail, he relied on his children more and more. My father had accounting business in Italy, and we stayed in an inn next to a convent. We shared a room, your mother and I. The balcony of our room overlooked the convent garden. The proximity of the inn, with its walls, windows, and balconies, must have been an intrusion to the nuns. Both were situated on a road near the outskirts of the small town. The inn had been the infirmary of the convent grounds, but before the war, the nuns had sold it to the innkeeper, who added balconies and repurposed the interior. Every morning while our father sat reading the newspaper up close to his eyes in the doorway to the balcony, we sat at a table near the balcony's balustrade, enjoying our *espresso* and *bescheutti do Lagasso*—that's a delicious cookie from that area, Liguria—or a *navette*, for we were close to the French border. From that balcony, we could see the nuns in the garden. We could see as they tended to every detail of their lives—the gardening, the laundry washing, the hanging of their linens—always in prayer. And one day, one nun, Suor Immacolata, seemed to see us through the kitchen dishtowels she was hanging, stopped, peeked beyond one, and really saw us. She smiled and waved as we, unabashed despite having been caught staring, smiled and waved back. Suor Immacolata was sometimes left alone in the garden to do the laundry or the hanging and, once alone, came to greet us and talk to us. She spoke in Italian and we in French, but we made do. One day, your mother and I—" she looked at the table and grinned bashfully— "we did the unthinkable. We climbed over the balcony onto the convent garden wall. It was not so hard, and Suor Immacolata, herself dumbstruck as we did so, stopped hanging sheets as we approached, unable to halt us."

"Why did you and Maman go into the garden?" asked Madeleine-Grace, engrossed in the story.

"Your mother and I always sprayed our sheets after they dried on the lines with lavender water, and we had brought some with us, so we decided, for some reason, to spray the nuns' sheets. So we did just that. We gave each of the hanging sheets—and even the dishtowels—a few sprays while Suor Immacolata watched, and we knew she did not object because her reaction to the scent brought a glowing smile to her face. And when we were finished, we carefully climbed the garden wall and balustrade of the terrace back to our table on the balcony. The intrusion was a welcome one for not only Suor Immacolata but a few of the other nuns, as well. They sometimes wrapped morsels of food from their kitchen in napkins and tossed them to us, and we, in turn, tossed the can of lavender water to them on the days they hung the sheets."

"Did they make you very good food? Maman says Italian food is delicious," Madeleine-Grace said. She, like me, could not shake the present tense.

"Delicious food. The last week we were there, they allowed your mother and me into the kitchen to cook with them. We learned many things, often in silence: *fûgassa all'êuio, torta di bietole, friscêu, pansotti, cundiggiùn.* And on the day before we left Italy for good, the Mother Superior, who spoke French, invited us—our father, too—to their kitchen to watch them cook and to join them for dinner. And they made *piccagge aggétto in to brodo,* and your mother and I had watched them make it from the beginning. To me, it was the best meal I had ever tasted. It was made by the kindest hands as a gift from the warmest hearts I had ever encountered outside my own mother's. I think this is why it tasted so good."

"That must be the reason everyone here likes it so much," Madeleine-Grace noted.

"How can that be? It is not their hands and hearts that make it. It is their recipe, but it is only my hands that make it—not theirs."

"That's what I mean," said Madeleine-Grace, and Aunt Adèle inadvertently lowered her garlic-scented fingers to the table top where the flour stuck to them. She sprung to her feet, kissed us both on the cheek, and washed her hands in the kitchen sink.

Sent away by Aunt Adèle who refused to let us help her clean, we ambled to the window to stare at the cliffs and the sky without much debate about walking there. Halfway to the cliffs, Wischard and little Laure called to us, and we ran back to them. They had awakened but hadn't washed or dressed, strolling about in their pajamas. We huddled about how to pass the time, and Madeleine-Grace convinced them to wash and dress so that we could walk to the cliffs without worry about anyone seeing us.

We passed the kitchen and caught the sound of dishes being washed, walked through the foyer, and hurried up the stairs. Once at the top, Wischard invited us to partake in an activity at which, I came to realize, he was an expert—spying.

"What do you mean?" I asked him. "Everyone is sleeping?"

"We can still spy on them," he insisted and started leading us to do the rounds.

From the top of the stairs, we had two ways to go: to our left and back or to the right and back. The bedrooms to our left included ours, young Roul, Alphonse, and Chardine's, and closest to the top of the stairs, Astride, Wischard, and little Laure's. Along the hallway to the right were Uncle Romain and Aunt Pé's, Uncle Roul and Aunt Mirabelle's, and closest to us, Aunt Laure and Uncle Gilbert's.

Years ago, my bedroom had been my mother's as a child, and when she married my father, they shared it, even with us when we came along. Young Roul's room used to be Aunt Laure's, and Wischard and little Laure's room used to be Aunt Adèle's. Uncle Romain and Uncle Roul inherited their childhood bedrooms. Uncle Roul had shared his with a now deceased older brother, Uncle Léon. And Aunt Laure's room now, the one with the entrance to the terrace over the back veranda overlooking the cliffs, had belonged to Grand-père and Grandma'Maud.

I always felt special to claim the same bedroom that Maman had as a child.

Wischard pulled my wrist down the hall to our left for a peek at our cousins' room. He crouched at the keyhole of the second bedroom and then stepped aside for us to look; it had never occurred to me to peer through a keyhole despite the times I had come across the practice in my detective stories. Through it, I saw young Roul rolled over, facing us, wrapped in the sheets, while Alphonse and Chardine lay beside him facing the window. Poor Alphonse—Roul had all the sheets and Chardine had the matelassé covers, and Alphonse slept in a ball, using his own body to warm itself.

"He's not measuring his muscle with Aunt Adèle's tape measure this time," Wischard said.

"What?" I asked.

"Sometimes Roul makes the bulge in his arm big and measures it, but only when he's alone," Wischard said, pulling me to the next room. Madeleine-Grace had not peeked yet, and shot a glance through the hole before joining us at the next room for a boring look at Astride sleeping and the only one snoring.

"She woke me up with her snoring," little Laure complained.

From there we swept around the top of the staircase to Aunt Laure's room. Wischard again led with the first peek, waving us to follow suit. I saw Uncle Gilbert sleeping alone on one side of the bed.

"Where is Aunt Laure?" I asked.

"Sometimes Maman doesn't sleep in the bed. She's on the faint," Wischard informed us. As I surveyed the room through the keyhole, I saw near the French windows Aunt Laure sprawled on the faint, a lavender blanket over her and the lamp overlooking the faint still on. Madeleine-Grace looked in, too, but Wischard and Laure were already on to Uncle Roul's room, waving us over.

In both rooms that followed, the husbands slept on their backs while the wives slept on their sides, their backs to the husbands.

Little Laure looked at her brother once we had finished with all the bedroom peeking and said, "*Nianterie!*" a word Grandma'Maud used to express "nonsense," implying that "that was stupid."

The only bedroom left to visit belonged to Aunt Adèle; hers was among the storage rooms on the floor above. Although we stood at the foot of the staircase leading to her room in the attic, no one thought to head there.

I whispered, "Hurry up and get dressed so that we can go to the cliffs!"

Wischard and little Laure traipsed to their room, careful not to wake the snoring Astride as they changed, and met us in the kitchen. We told Aunt Adèle that they were joining us for a walk to the cliffs, so she made them a *café au lait*. Wischard downed his quickly. Since little Laure never took more than a sip, I took a sip from hers. We enjoyed our coffees at the kitchen table, which, somehow, Aunt Adèle had already cleared and cleaned; there wasn't a trace of white flour nor the slightest hint of fresh garlic to interfere with the splendid scent of simmering stock. She cautioned us not to descend to the shore as we raced out of the kitchen.

Each footstep in our run for the cliffs made the sky ahead shake, and when the ocean came into view at the horizon, I slowed as the shaking diminished to a tremor. The early morning kiss between sky and sea captivated me to the point that I could not run; I had to slow so that I could concentrate on its vastness, on its beauty. When I slowed, everyone did, and our final steps to the cliffs were a breathless stroll.

I could hear birds this morning, and, in the distance, I saw two sails of small boats. I wished I was on board one. In summers past, while we had made visits to the shorelines and beaches, to the promenades and the seaside *cafés*, we had never taken out a sailboat.

"Papa said that, a hundred years ago," Wischard shared, "fishermen's boats lined the shore below, and they came in with mussels and oysters and sole and cod to sell at the markets. I wish I were a fisherman, too."

I knew Wischard, like me, felt a longing to be at sea when he saw the sailboats in the distance, when he felt the breeze caress his face, when he heard the gannets gliding the line of white *falaises*. I didn't share with Wischard that I felt the same, that I understood.

Shouting the word "*étaillets*," which our grandmother used to refer to seabirds, Little Laure called our attention to two terns. They approached us on foot, and when little Laure opened her arms to welcome the sleek, white and gray birds with fiery bills, they ascended into flight toward the sea. "Flying back to L'Ile d'Aobefein," little Laure said. Grandma'Maud said the terns visited us from this nearby isle.

As the sun bathed us in warmth, as the fresh air encouraged us to take deep inhales, Madeleine-Grace sat on the chalky cliffs cross-legged, and we all did the same. The cliffs, certainly white, contained specks of black and pink, as well, and green gorse climbed their walls. Yet the line of cliffs on either side of us looked so white, so clean. I was glad that Madeleine-Grace sat because I did not want to go back. I wanted to sit on the cliffs and stare and enjoy and think and feel—literally feel, not figuratively—feel the breeze gently skirt my face and race between my fingers, feel the sun warm the back of my neck. I wasn't at all about to feel in the other sense—not joy, not delight, not happiness. This type of feeling may have crept into my being at times, but I was not about to choose to feel them; numbness was better.

The image of the *paquebot* pushing the waters, sending them to our shores, appeared before me again, myself on her deck, La Côte d'Albâtre nearing and nearing. I saw Wischard and little Laure and all my cousins and Aunt Adèle in her mint apron and all my uncles and aunts waving to me on the cliffs, and I waved back. And the *paquebot* cut the waves, and a glance over the railing revealed the sparkling sapphire water with the white alabaster beyond. That the others were imagining themselves at sea, too, crossed my mind, and as my thoughts turned to those beside me, I lost track of my own fantasies. I wondered if little Laure and Wischard saw themselves on small sailboats, scouting the coast to their beloved Dieppe, or imagined their arrival in New York from the deck of a liner. They had never been to America.

Only some family had made the voyage to America for the funeral. Aunt Laure and Uncle Gilbert, Uncle Roul, and Aunt Adèle came, initially without Grandma'Maud, but she arrived at the port in Le Havre, a room, berth, and tickets prearranged, and joined them.

That our aunts and uncles had insisted Grandma'Maud remain behind, too unwell to make the journey to America, we learned from Grand-mère and Grand-père Avery, our father's parents. Our American grandparents admired that she came and were sure to accommodate her, but they mentioned to me that Uncle Romain and Aunt Laure had forbidden her to join. Undeterred by prohibitive mandates, she arranged her own transportation to the port and passage overseas, having taken minimal pains to ensure the Averys knew of her coming. Apparently, my uncles and Aunt Laure refused to speak with her the first few days of the sea voyage, but Aunt Adèle, alone left to attend her, stitched the fraying relationships.

While Aunt Adèle's efforts repaired the rapport between Grandma'Maud and her children well before their arrival in America, those very efforts had, according to Grand-mère Armance, caused a tear in Aunt Adèle's relationship with Aunt Laure. Aunt Laure, who had no intention of waiting on her mother and resented Aunt Adèle for doing so, had snapped at her mother for detracting from their plans. Aunt Adèle had apparently responded, "How is it that you do not understand our mother's need to be here? You are a mother, yourself." Grandmère Armance said that Aunt Laure found this utterance so offensive that she refused to speak to Aunt Adèle until the day of the funeral, and only because Grandma'Maud smoothed things over as she understood the perspective and composition and constitution of all her children. Shortly before they had departed for the return voyage to France, according to Grand-mère Armance, they were all at peace.

I thought, after hearing about this, that it was my mother that had brought them peace. They were there, after all, because of her. And they must have had no choice but to put their anger aside when something so much stronger, their grief over my mother, barged into their worlds. And if anything could stymie their resentment for each other, well, then the hold that that resentment had couldn't be that strong. When my aunts and uncles realized this, and through the guidance of Grandma'Maud, they must have decided to let go of the anger for each other, I assumed. This way, they could mourn my mother better, too.

None of my cousins came. They, too, were not allowed. Aunt Pé and Aunt Mirabelle remained and watched them. Uncle Gilbert insisted he join Aunt Laure and the others as he was close to my mother and father, and they were always more than fond of him. I didn't understand why Aunt Pé and Aunt Mirabelle didn't insist, too; they knew my parents longer than Uncle Gilbert, even, and my cousins had nannies and other relatives to look after them.

Amid the heaviness and sobs of the burial, the gravity and consolation of the funeral Mass, the worry and love contorting the faces during the many paid respects, the upheaval of sudden absence and new presence, the image I saw most clearly over and over, and that had anchored in my recollections of that period, was the arrival of Grandma'Maud at our home in River Forest. The first night without my parents, Madeleine-Grace and I had slept at Grand-mère and Grand-père Avery's brownstone in the city, but after that night, they stayed at our house in River Forest, a suburb of Chicago. And one day, Grand-mère Armance was taking a baking dish of macaroni and cheese out of the refrigerator while Madeleine-Grace and I sat at the kitchen table sipping sparkling water. In that moment, Grand-père Guarin had let in Grandma'Maud. Having slid the baking dish halfway off the refrigerator shelf, Grand-mère Armance stopped, twirled, and met Grandma'Maud in the kitchen. Their embrace was immediate and firm and rife with pain, their sobs resounding and unstoppable. It lasted interminably, and we stared at them the whole time, at two mothers brought together years before through their children's love and now reunited through their mourning of those same children. Beyond their long-lasting lock on each other, I saw the refrigerator door open, resting against the dish of macaroni and cheese that Grand-mère Armance had pulled out only partially. It was letting out the cold, I thought, and I had never seen the refrigerator door not fully shut.

Accepting Grandma'Maud's accompaniment was wise on the part of my aunts and uncles, for she was the only one among the Semperrins who had, on multiple occasions, rendered us visits in America. She knew the ropes of travel in and out of Chicago and the country. Only three days after the funeral, they all departed Chicago for New York, and from New York to Le Havre on the *paquebot*, knowing Madeleine-Grace and I were to spend the summer in Etretat-au-Delà months thereafter.

My reflection on my relatives' visit to America was interrupted by little Laure who had had a question on her mind for some time still. "How long were you on the boat?" she asked, shifting her eyes and looking down as if her mother's voice were reprimanding her for the question. It occurred to me that as Laure and Wischard looked out at the sea, they, too, saw me holding the rails of the *paquebot* heading for La Côte d'Albâtre.

"It took us five days to cross the Atlantic," I said, finally quenching little Laure's curious thirst.

"Is it true there are five hundred tables in the dining room?" asked Wischard.

"More than that," I said. "It is the longest room in the ship, and at one end, the walls open to a grand ballroom."

"And there's a long, long pool, too?" he inquired.

"If you visit us, you will see for yourself," Madeleine-Grace said, inviting him to our country with the sincerity of her smile as much as her gentle words.

"Maman says—" little Laure began but stopped as she and her brother exchanged glances.

"That we wouldn't be allowed," Wischard continued. "Anyway, is there a pool?"

"There are several pools," I said, amusing myself at the memory of the spectacle of scantily clad men and women in swimsuits interspersed among those in suits and dresses. Grand-mère Armance, among the patrons who made a point to rest on the railing overlooking the pool on the deck fully clad in her day clothes, preferred to spectate instead of swim, which I found odd. Why stop at the pool only to observe swimming and not to swim? She said she stopped there to sunbathe, which, too, was odd on account of her long dress and long sleeves and, one late afternoon, evening gloves. She did not permit us to swim in the pool on the deck—only the smaller, indoor one reserved for first-class passengers.

"What's the Eau de Vie Room?" Wischard asked.

"At the bottom of the grand staircase, there's a special lounge called the Eau de Vie Room where they serve, well, *eaux de vie*, brandies, and bourbons. Inside the lounge, there's an elevator that takes us to the Fumée de Vie Room, the *fumoir*. The Eau de Vie Room is lower because it's closer to the water, and the Fumée de Vie Room is higher because it's closer to the steam and smoke emissions."

"When everyone returned from America," Wischard explained, "Aunt Mirabelle got upset at Uncle Roul for talking to a girl in the Eau de Vie Room. Then Uncle Roul got upset at my mother for telling Aunt Mirabelle."

"Maman said that Uncle Roul had made friends with another girl in Chicago before he met the one on the boat," little Laure added.

Through the haziness of the memory of their visit, I recalled something about the woman Uncle Roul had met one night downtown. "*Plaçage*," he kept saying the next day. A historian whom he had met the night before had taught him this word, and Uncle Roul enjoyed touting it like a trophy, some newfound concept he not only found and claimed but prized. I still didn't understand the term.

"Maman said the woman on the boat was different from the woman in Chicago. She said the woman on the boat—."

While little Laure was explaining, Aunt Adèle approached, her steps emitting a crunch on each delicate press into the chalk. We turned but did not rise from our spots. Aunt Adèle seemed to enjoy the warm breeze as much as we did; she smiled as she pressed her light green apron to her body when the breeze lifted it. She had meant to incite us to return to the house after an hour in the sun, but Wischard spoke before she did, his back to her.

"Is that you, Aunt Adèle, or a foolish gannet? I can't tell the difference."

"Maman said that you look like a tiny bird," little Laure explained.

"And do I?"

"No, but sometimes I wish you would fly away," Wischard said.

Hearing the mild insults, I did not recall my cousins overtly teasing our aunt past summers. I did not know they had issues with her.

"Now come, children. You have been in the sun awhile already, especially you, little Wischard."

"Why 'especially' me?" he asked, loath to stand.

"You have the lightest hair and skin of all—your father's blond family," Aunt Adèle said, her smile returning, a genuine joy evident in her voice over the blond that Wischard introduced to the Semperrin line. "Let's go, children."

We arose and followed Aunt Adèle to the house, our pace leisurely behind hers more hurried. As she approached the herb islands before us, she stooped to tend to something and then stood in a sudden. We saw standing at the side of the house a man, brown-haired and about Aunt Adèle's age, holding his cap against his stomach the way Aunt Adèle had held her apron. I recognized him but didn't know from where. They both smiled when their eyes greeted.

The man and we arrived at the herb island at the same time. The man first greeted Aunt Adèle and then turned to us, bowing his head.

"Ellande, Madeleine-Grace, this is our friend Monsieur Vauquelin," Aunt Adèle said. "You have met him before at the market in town and sometimes at Mass other summers. Do you remember Monsieur Vauquelin?"

I did remember him after all. When the market came, sometimes I accompanied my mother and Aunt Adèle into town. Monsieur Vauquelin spoke with them near a stand, and once, we walked with him to a stone house a few blocks from the square. On Sundays, he sometimes awaited Aunt Adèle and my parents after Mass, and they conversed briefly before our return home. When *La Fête du Muguet* had been unseasonably cold and no lilies of the valley, *muguets*, had bloomed, he gave Aunt Adèle a small bouquet of them the first Sunday we had arrived for the summer in June; apparently, it was the first of them in bloom that year.

I nodded that I did remember him, and he crouched in front of us. His eyes had short, thin lines on the far side of each on an otherwise smooth face, lines I somehow knew had formed in laughter. The sun cast a gold sheen on the short stubble covering his face and made his brown eyes look lighter and playful. He had to be around my aunt's age, if not younger. Dropping his cap to the ground, he placed one hand on

Madeleine-Grace's shoulder and one on mine, a gingerly touch but a confident embrace of us both, and said, "Jacques and Madeleine-Grace, we have met only a few times and perhaps you don't remember me. I am Alban Vauquelin. I think the world of your family and have for many years, including your good parents. Please, accept my sincerest condolences."

Madeleine-Grace turned in, nestling her body into my side, and he clasped us more firmly. The sincerity in his eyes never broke. Then he retrieved his cap and rose, keeping a hand on each of our shoulders. As he acknowledged Wischard and little Laure, I thought that this man whom I barely knew had been more expressive to us about our parents than some of my own family, including my cousins who had not made it to the funeral. Maybe it was easier for persons who didn't know my parents so well; maybe my cousins still saw my parents as alive.

"*Merci*, Monsieur Vauquelin," I said, on behalf of my sister, too.

"Please, Jacques," he said, crinkling his smiling eyes. "Call me Alban."

I looked to Aunt Adèle for permission, and she made an expression that captured both disapproval and uncertainty, something of a head-tilted cringe. Instead of deciding one way or another, she said to the man, "You must call Jacques 'Ellande.'"

"Ellande?" he repeated.

Wischard and little Laure exchanged snickers behind me as Aunt Adèle reaffirmed, "Yes, Ellande. Too many Jacques in America."

"Ellande," he said with a smile.

"Children, perhaps your cousins are awake now. Go inside and play with them, and stay out of the kitchen until I return. I must talk to Monsieur Vauquelin."

"Alban," he said, and winked at us.

We walked inside as Aunt Adèle and Monsieur Vauquelin took a seat on the bench in the flower island. From the window, I could see that she maintained a demure composure yet laughed freely and, once, rested her forehead on his shoulder for not more than a second as one laugh trailed off. She looked delicate, dainty, next to his thin but sturdy physique.

Astride, Alphonse, and Chardine had indeed just arrived in the foyer from upstairs, all of them unwashed and in pajamas. Alphonse wore no shirt and was eager to step outside into the warmth. He made for the veranda while the others joined us in the *salle-en-arrière* next to the veranda entrance.

"Where's Roul?" asked Wischard, and oblivious to Chardine's shrug, he flexed his bicep and winked at me.

"Let's play *muche-muche*," little Laure invited, and so we did for about a half hour.

As we organized ourselves for a few rounds of hide-n-seek, Wischard whispered to me a few choice spots he had used effectively to hide from the others and a few he had only considered. Particularly fond of spots that provided the advantage of surveying his immediate environs, he listed nooks in the *salon*, the conservatory, and even the main hall. Wischard had a preference for finding crannies in furniture pieces through which he could peer. He did also mention—to my amusement—tangling himself in philodendron foliage, but only when he's wearing green. His sharing these places with me made me feel trusted by him despite the playful boastfulness behind the array of hiding spots. He would have enjoyed traveling across the Atlantic with me on the *paquebot*, I thought, for he could have hidden between the seats in the cinema, behind the "cabana" walls near the outdoor pool, under the lounge chairs along what we called the Promenade à Tribord, the Starboard Promenade, or within the hazes of smoke spiraling about in the *fumoir*, but only when wearing gray.

We had played *muche-muche*, or *cache-cache*, summers past, and I was happy to take it up again, eager to revisit the nooks and corners of the house I had not thought about since last year, to see their current state, with the inexplicable hope that they remained unchanged. Counting to twenty always took place in the kitchen on account of so few hiding places in there. Rules changed each round, and for these rounds, upstairs was off-limits. While Chardine counted in the kitchen, I made for the dining room, expecting to find an open spot under a china hutch. Wischard followed me in, stopping me with his arm at the dining room window so that he could use my shoulder to hoist himself onto the window sill. Then he pulled the curtains past him so that he was concealed, oblivious to how sheer the curtains were and how easily his shape could be made out.

"I like to hide behind the curtains," he whispered, "because with certain ones, I can see what's happening on the other side of them."

Beginning to detect a trend in Wischard's proclivities—a tendency to peep—I scurried to under the hutch. Once in place, I stuck my head out for one more glimpse of Wischard, his visibility funny to me. Then, pulling my head within my small space, I checked to see if I noticed anything different. There was not even a speck of dust on the wooden legs of the hutch, reminding me of my mother and Aunt Adèle's dusting missions. She must not have let anything slide this summer.

Chardine found Astride first, and the next round, Astride found me—I was hiding in the same place, and so was Wischard. What struck me was that I had foolishly stuck my head out of my spot when I thought Astride might be skulking and by chance caught her with her back to me, staring directly at Wischard's obvious presence behind the thin curtain. Then she turned away, as if never having noticed him, and continued her search within the dining room, calling me out immediately. She shouted my name and pointed, not with a smile but with eyes glazed with satisfaction.

At the point I had crawled out and was entering the main hall on my way to the kitchen, Uncle Roul and Aunt Mirabelle were descending the staircase. Uncle Romain and Aunt Pé, who must have descended moments prior, sat in the *salle-en-arrière*, and Aunt Laure and Uncle Gilbert entered from the kitchen. Uncle Gilbert held a tray with four *cafés*. The children halted in their tracks and ambled to the *salle-en-arrière* to greet them. Aunt Mirabelle saw Uncle Gilbert with the tray.

"Why are you serving us, Gilbert?" she asked, her head turning every which way in search of Aunt Adèle.

"I am not serving *you*. You were not here," he said, handing a cup to each of the three others. "You will have to serve yourself."

"Why?" asked Aunt Mirabelle, a furrow forming across her eyebrows. "Where's Adèle?"

Uncle Roul seemed put off, and I couldn't tell if it was more by Aunt Adèle's absence or by his wife's immobilizing consternation. "I'll make us some," he said, diverting course for the kitchen.

"Is she cleaning the veranda?" asked Aunt Mirabelle, still frozen in the main hall.

"Alphonse is on the veranda," said Uncle Gilbert, "but I didn't see Adèle."

"Aunt Adèle is with Monsieur Vauquelin on the bench outside," said Astride, happy to be the informant. She hurried to the picture window to confirm as we joined her. I saw through the window Aunt Adèle grinning in reaction to something Monsieur Vauquelin was saying, his smiling eyes fixed on her, his head jutted close to hers.

"Monsieur Vauquelin," Uncle Romain said, barely finishing the name as a chortle interrupted its syllables.

"The driver has come for his lady," Uncle Roul said, eliciting smirks from his brothers and sisters.

"Adèle is lady-in-waiting to his real majesty, a lady much more beloved—and valuable," Uncle Romain responded to an onslaught of laughter. Aunt Pé was waiting for her cue and never stopped convulsing in laughter.

"What is so funny?" I asked, smiling and wide-eyed as I looked from laughing visage to laughing visage.

"The man calling on your aunt Adèle is a good-for-nothing. His family are *sauniers*—salt-harvester nobodys—and he cannot hack even that. But he is the chauffeur for a very important lady—"

"Her name is Fleur—" began Uncle Roul, cut off by his own laughter.

Aunt Laure laughed through her words. "He drives the salt to the markets."

"You see, Ellande?" Uncle Romain explained. "Do you understand now? The *fleur de sel* might be worth a little something—his lovely passenger. The lady in his backseat is bags of salt."

"More precious than even your Aunt Adèle because she never gets a ride," Uncle Roul said as they all continued in laughter.

"Not without Fleur's permission, anyway," Aunt Pé added. Now even the children were laughing, but Madeleine-Grace and I, our laughter abated to a stodgy smile.

"Your Aunt Adèle is lady-in-waiting to his more important lady—and duty. Now do you understand?" asked Uncle Roul.

"We should ask Fleur what she thinks of Monsieur Vauquelin," said Uncle Romain.

"She would say, 'he's a lowsy driver,'" Uncle Roul said to fits of laughter.

"You are jealous," Aunt Mirabelle said to her husband, "because he is more handsome than you."

Uncle Roul shrugged off her comment, returning to the kitchen as he laughed.

The bench was difficult to see from the couch, but in that moment, Aunt Adèle and Monsieur Vauquelin stood, and, stepping aside so that Aunt Adèle could lead, Monsieur Vauquelin let Aunt Adèle bring him around the house to his vehicle parked in the front. Our aunts and uncles continued flinging jabs through their interminable cackling while the children followed the couple from window to window around the house, rushing from room to room. Chardine announced her surety of a pending kiss, piquing our curiosity and inciting our pursuit. I knew Wischard, once informed of such a possibility, grew intent on catching a glimpse of the kiss from afar. Instead, Monsieur Vauquelin only bowed his head, took Aunt Adèle's hand in his, and kissed the top of it. We snickered nonetheless.

As his posture returned to its standing stature, Monsieur Vauquelin caught sight of us staring through the dining room window. The smile never leaving his face, his sight zeroed in on me, and he waved me over. My cousins remained in the window, and Madeleine-Grace accompanied me as far as the front veranda. I descended the stairs and approached the pair in front of the car while they exchanged something in murmurs.

Monsieur Vauquelin crouched before me and said, "Ellande, I would like very much to take you to the salt marshes on L'Ile d'Aobefein one day. Would you like that?"

In my impulse to be well-mannered, I said, "Yes," but then a concern came over me. I only vaguely remembered him, and not two minutes prior, my aunts and uncles had been ridiculing him. So I looked to Aunt Adèle the moment after I accepted his invitation and said, "Only if Aunt Adèle comes."

He looked at her and smiled bigger, stirring a blush and a smile from her. Then he turned his head back to me and said, "I would love nothing more than for your Aunt Adèle to join us. We will do this soon." He rose and placed his hand on my head affectionately. "You will enjoy the *marais*. There is peace there. There is peace in what we do."

"Will you teach me?" I asked, unsure what to expect, what even to imagine.

"I will show you how to harvest the salt, yes. Your aunt and I will show you how to use it. You will cook a salt-encrusted chicken for all your friends in America one day, and they will be your friends for life because of it."

I smiled. The thought of me cooking at all, let alone for my friends, amused me. I could tell he saw the humor in it, but I knew he meant business, too, as a pride in his work and the surety of its peace clung to his every word.

Monsieur Vauquelin opened the car door, reached inside, and pulled forth two large bags of salt. He piled the two coarse bags onto my arms. "Please carry these for your aunt, Ellande."

"Thank-you, Ellande," my aunt said, and, holding the bags of salt, I left the couple. Madeleine-Grace held the front door open for me.

I set them down at the entrance, sure Aunt Adèle would find them. I heard my cousins giggling at the dining room window, and through the foyer, bouncing from wall to wall, resounded the derisive laughter of my aunts and uncles.

The sun in its languid ascent stretched every minute of the day, as if a slow dilution into every particle of air weighted the minutes with its warmth, saturating them with a heavy light. The warmth in Etretat-au-Delà was not oppressive, but the lengthening days sometimes felt like a cord, languorously wrapping itself around our necks, until those first indications of dusk when the rope lost its hold, when its girth and tautness dwindled.

My uncles joined Alphonse on the veranda, sipping *cafés* and staring at the sky. Uncle Gilbert brought in the newspaper but kept it folded and unread on the arm of his chair. I was passing through with nothing in particular to do when young Roul entered in pajama bottoms only, like his brother, and, before finding a spot on the stone railing of the veranda, swiped the useless paper from Uncle Gilbert's chair. Leaning against a beam, his knees bent before him on the railing, young Roul opened the newspaper across his legs.

"What are you going to do, Roul?" asked Uncle Romain. "Read it?"

He could not refrain from laughing as he spoke, and young Roul's father, along with all the others, followed suit. Young Roul, his curiosity about the headlines and the velleity of a leisurely read of the paper dashed, folded the paper in half and swept it off his lap to the stone veranda floor. Then he extended and crossed his legs, leaned his head back on the pillar, and closed his eyes to the abating laughter of his father and uncles.

Except for Aunt Adèle, my aunts sat in the *salle-en-arrière*. Aunt Laure from time to time ascended the stairs and returned within fifteen minutes. One time, she stepped onto the veranda and stared with us at the sky, only her stare, unlike any of ours, reprimanded the sky, interrogating it with existential questions and personal ones, too, I imagined, and demanding of it answers about why she felt so anxious all the time.

When Madeleine-Grace stood in the veranda entrance, I walked over to her, intuiting her incertitude about how to pass the time, and we strolled to the kitchen to find Aunt Adèle. We had never encountered such lethargy when we were here with our parents, which isn't to say we didn't enjoy downtime, but it had never stood out so awkwardly before now. She was leaning over the table, on which was sprawled a large sheet of muslin covered with fresh herbs.

"Go upstairs for *mésienne*, my lambs," she said to us with a glance in our direction, quick to return her attention to her work. "I will call you for *apéritifs* and dinner."

"We don't want to nap," Madeleine-Grace said as we approached the table. "We want to help you."

"Can't we pull out the weeds?" I offered, intent on postponing *mésienne*. I could tell what she was doing. She had fresh herbs in a single layer on the muslin and was scrutinizing the bunch for anything that did not belong. A small pile of mostly brown leaves, tiny twigs, and dirt clinging to tiny roots lay in the corner of the fabric closest our aunt.

"Okay," she said, "but do not touch the good herbs. You want to be delicate with something so delicate. I discarded as much as I could when I gathered them, but a few always sneak in. If you see parsley that is too dry or looks too hard or rough, discard it, too."

Leaning our heads over the herbs and scrutinizing them for abnormalities amused us, and we were excited whenever we found something that adulterated the otherwise pristine bunch of parsley our aunt had culled. Madeleine-Grace announced her every find with a big smile, held it up for Aunt Adèle to inspect, and then dropped it in the rubbish pile. How dull was our lives that finding an unwanted, tough sprig of parsley amused us? Our aunt explained while we worked that some she would keep fresh and some she would dry. She let us taste one each. "Alban sometimes chews on the stems," she added fondly.

The herb project did not take long as this had been Aunt Adèle's last batch to come under her scrutiny today. She cleared the table, and we accompanied her to the shed to store the herbs. She hurried because she wanted to close the shutters throughout the house.

The wooden shed rose unobtrusively next to the house in the shade of hawthorn trees and one large beech. At the foot of the beech tree near the wall of the shed, a boulder, sunken in the earth, rose as high as my waist. Obtrusive a presence it may have been, it must have felt welcomed on account of its treatment: mint sprung up around it and the green stems of clinging marjoram decorated it, accented by the delicate petals of many purple flowers. Aunt Adèle lifted the latch of the shed door, and we entered the small edifice, a single room no bigger than half our bedroom with light illuminating it through a window that our grandfather had insisted be built. Shelves lined the two side walls, some stopping at the window and continuing after it. One of these shelves was dangling from its spot as if a single nail in its center were keeping it attached to the wall. Gardening equipment, folded tarps and blankets, wooden baskets and glass jars, and sports equipment like the *viquets*, *crosses*, and *balles* for *la choule* and the *maillets*, *arceaux*, *piquets*, and *boules* for *croquet* leaned against the wall under the shelves. It was difficult to see what lined the shelves on the wall opposite the window because a large mattress lay propped upright against them. On the far wall of the shed opposite the door and perpendicular to the two shelved walls were a wooden table and a stool. This table, lodged into the wall, served as the only wide, flat surface with which Aunt Adèle could work.

Where the table met the wall, jars of fresh herbs, their stems in water, and dried herbs and flowers lined the tabletop, so Aunt Adèle was careful as she set down the muslin with today's herbs. On her way to the table, her foot accidentally kicked the mattress.

"Why is there a mattress in here?" Madeleine-Grace asked.

"I had purchased it weeks ago so that I would have a soft place to sleep in the attic this summer. Monsieur Vauquelin kindly brought it here for me to store since I had not yet made a space for it in the attic. I asked Uncle Romain to bring it up for me, and he still hasn't. I asked Uncle Romain to fix the broken shelf here, and he still hasn't. And there's the hole on Aunt Laure's bedroom wall from the picture that fell and the useless *décrottoir* out front I asked him to remove or at least cover with the flower basket so that no one trips unsuspectingly—all undone. Each one would take minutes to complete, and I can't do them, myself."

"I can help you," I said, perhaps too ambitiously. The mattress was sure to be unwieldy for a single person let alone a boy.

"Thank-you, Ellande," she said, "but these tasks are not as easy as they seem. Your mother and I, we could do the cooking and the housekeeping with our mother all summer long—*all year* long if we had to—but we're not so good with the house upkeep and repairs."

Having unrolled the muslin, she placed the good herbs upright in jars. She shook the cloth outside the door, and then we helped her fold it. As we were finishing, Madeleine-Grace, glancing around, said, "How do you know how to gather the herbs?"

Aunt Adèle set the folded muslin on the table inside and leaned her face into an upside-down nosegay of dried rosemary hanging from the shelf.

"My mother—Grandma'Maud—had taught me plenty, like how to clean and store them, but once again, I learned more on the trip to Liguria. *Prebuggiùn* they called it. One day as we were entering our inn, your mother and I saw a man dropping something off at the entrance to the convent. We stepped over to see as the nun receiving him was Suor Immacolata who, at that point, was already familiar with us. The man was a local farmer, and after scouring the countryside for herbs, he made small bunches of them—seven different kinds of herbs in each bunch. We learned that the process of foraging for these local herbs is called *prebuggiùn* in Ligurian dialect, and they use the same word to refer to that combination of herbs. *Prebuggiùn*—that special, perfect combination of flavors, is used in several Ligurian dishes like the filling in *pansotti*, a type of stuffed pasta. The farmer, Adolfo, he told us that in old wives' tales, a hundred local herbs—not seven—were needed. I remember Suor Immacolata spoke with him in Italian, and I knew they were talking about us. A moment later, Adolfo invited us to join him on his foraging rounds the next morning, and our father consented as long as he could accompany us. So we did. From sunrise to late morning, we walked the rocky, dirt roads of the beautiful countryside, trod the worn paths of his fields, and watched as he bent, picked, and gathered the seven herbs. The budding nettle along the roadside near his farm looked like mint and smelled like spicy lemon if there is such a scent—*ortiga* he called the herb when he picked some and held it to my nose. The red poppies and the fiery pimpernels, and the chicories the color of clouds! These herbs in flower were so delicate, and *he* was so delicate, so caring, in his culling of each one. He was too kind to bring us into his farmhouse kitchen to make us *minestra*, a soup that uses the herbs. It was bitter and aromatic and savory and wonderfully delicious."

Still lost in these remembrances, Aunt Adèle lifted a sprig of borage from a glass jar and smiled. "This is the one he called *boraxa*. Your mother liked it for its bright purple flowers and put one in the same hole as her blouse's button and wore it all day. Borage is one of those herbs necessary for a true *prebuggiùn*." She smelled the herb. "So you see why I can think of this trip with only the utmost affection? We learned so much. We enjoyed learning so much."

"I think you liked the farmer," Madeleine-Grace said, making me snicker.

"He was older than my father! He had to have been at least eighty years old!" said Aunt Adèle to our continued laughter, setting down the herb. "Come now. Let's close the shutters."

We were lucky, she mentioned, not to have in Etretat-au-Delà the heat of Paris summers, but she insisted on keeping the place cool. We helped her close some of the interior shutters, and then she made our cousins and us go to our rooms for *mésienne*. Our aunts and uncles, themselves, strolled to their rooms for afternoon rests.

We washed for dinner when Aunt Adèle visited each room to announce *apéritif* hour. Our aunts and uncles sipped *cidre* on the veranda while Madeleine-Grace and I sipped some in the kitchen with Aunt Adèle as she prepared dinner—that delicious *piccagge aggétto in to brodo*. Aunt Pé walked in once, circled without a word as if a wardress, her hands clasped behind her back, and after a few sniffs and a sip of the broth from the ladle, returned to the veranda.

We dined after grace at the table in the dining room, everyone claiming the same seat as last night, as summer's past, without spaces left for Maman and Papa. The uncles and the children commented that the dinner was delicious, Aunt Adèle smiling and tilting her head each time.

Uncle Roul slurped a spoonful of the broth, clearly delighting in it, and announced, "Mirabelle's *piccagge aggétto*—not so good."

Aunt Mirabelle lowered her spoonful of *brodo* in disgust. Then she turned to Aunt Adèle and said, "You must never make this meal again, Adèle. Every time you do, my husband must bring it up."

"Bring what up?" asked little Laure, perhaps too young to remember even as recently as last summer when Uncle Roul had mentioned the same story.

Aunt Laure hushed her daughter, her shoulders dropping despondently when she saw the slightest dribble of broth on little Laure's chin. She grabbed her own napkin to wipe it.

"The time my wife tried to make *piccagge aggétto*," Uncle Roul said, finishing his announcement with a chuckle and washing it down with a last gulp of *cidre*.

"What was it you did again?" asked Uncle Romain.

Aunt Pé thought her husband was going to laugh and started to laugh, but when he only smiled, she quickly stifled herself.

"'What was it again?' 'What was it again?'" repeated Aunt Mirabelle, feeding herself a spoonful so that she did not have to address him.

"What was it you did, Mira?" asked Uncle Roul. "You had Madame Fioretti, our neighbor in Rouen, give you a recipe for the dough, and you ground up the heads of three or four raw garlics with the mortar and pestle and mixed it with the dough. Is that right, Mira?"

Aunt Mirabelle ignored him, sipping away at the delicious broth. I noticed she had finished all her *piccagge*.

"The pasta was so strong with garlic," Uncle Roul continued, "my mouth felt like fire." He started to laugh, as did his children.

Young Roul added, "Alphonse had to spit it out. Do you remember?"

We were all laughing now, including Uncle Romain, loosening Aunt Pé into interjecting, "And didn't you make the broth with too much garlic, too?"

"Too much garlic? She used five bags of garlic!"

We knew Uncle Roul was exaggerating, but none of us could hold back the laughter now, especially since Aunt Mirabelle was so upset at the recounting of it. Only Aunt Adèle refrained, but even she could not resist maintaining a smile throughout the story.

"She did not know where the garlic taste came from is all," rationalized Aunt Adèle. "She did not know if it was mostly in the pasta or in the broth."

"She did not have to poison us to figure it out!" shouted Alphonse.

"Why did you not just ask Adèle?" asked Uncle Roul.

At that, Aunt Mirabelle glanced quickly at Aunt Adèle, yanking her gaze away before a contempt for her sister-in-law could manifest. I am sure Aunt Adèle sensed it nonetheless. Yet, demure as ever, she continued to defend Aunt Mirabelle.

"The nuns told us that the Ligurian garlic there is subtler than other varieties. Even the one I use here is stronger than what we experienced in Italy. I can't find the Ligurian variety at the markets here."

"Ah, Liguria!" interposed Aunt Laure, thrown from her laughter into irritation at the mention of Ligurian garlic.

"Yes, Liguria," returned Aunt Adèle. "Papa, Juliette, and I never had a better trip together. And look how much we brought back. A recipe we have enjoyed for years."

"And while you were never having a better trip, I was having the worst time of life," replied Aunt Laure. This was the first I was hearing of this.

"So you've decided on that?" asked Romain. "There are so many to choose from—all your own making. I'm so glad you could finally narrow it down to one."

The glare with which Aunt Laure struck him struck us all with its shrapnel. "What do you know?" she snapped. "For a month, I was left alone to stay with Maman, doing the chores, helping with the cooking, accompanying her to the market." Then she shot a glare at Aunt Adèle. "All so that you and Juliette could get your vacation with Papa."

"Papa first asked you to join him, but you refused," reminded Aunt Adèle.

Justifying it, Aunt Laure shouted, "I was seventeen! What seventeen-year-old would leave with her father for a month in Italy?"

"I don't think it was the age that mattered," said Uncle Gilbert. "Wasn't it a boy?"

"What difference does it make?" responded Aunt Laure, on the verge of tears. "I was the one to stay home, to do all the work!"

I knew that my mother and Aunt Adèle had helped their mother with the lady-of-the-house affairs all the time, never with Aunt Laure's help. Her reaction surprised me, considering she had to sacrifice only one month of her life to helping her mother. And the reason my mother and Aunt Adèle, only fourteen and thirteen themselves, accompanied my grandfather was to assist him—hardly a vacation. I did not speak though.

As if to reaffirm her trauma, Aunt Laure said, "It was a month-long nightmare," and then to her chuckling brothers, she exclaimed, "What do you know?"

The smile on Uncle Roul's face cleared in an instant. "What do I know of nightmares?" He lifted his empty glass and slammed it back on the table, arresting everyone with the shock. "You had to help Maman with chores for a month, and I spent a year avoiding explosives and bullets—the very next year after your traumatic spring. Why don't you tell Léon what a nightmare your one month of chores was!"

Aunt Laure finally burst into tears and bolted from her seat and the room. Uncle Gilbert sighed and excused himself to follow her.

Madeleine-Grace and I looked at each other, both aware, as was everyone at the table, that our mother's brother Léon had lost his life in the Second World War. Uncle Roul had fought in it, sustaining a shoulder injury. While young Roul simply pulled out a cigarette to roll on the table, Alphonse motioned with his head to Chardine; she reluctantly rose, walked to her father, hugged him from the side with her head on his shoulder, and returned to her seat, content an obligatory solace had been fulfilled. I noticed her smile as she enjoyed another spoonful of broth.

As we all finished our dinner in silence, Aunt Adèle rose, prompting Madeleine-Grace and me to rise quickly. She motioned for us to remain seated as she cleared the bowls and spoons and returned with trays of fruit and cheese. "No salad tonight. A light meal," she said softly, disturbing no one in his or her solicitude.

The evening continued on the veranda for everyone except Aunt Adèle, who cleared the dining room table and washed the dishes. My uncles brought the trays of fruit and cheese to the veranda, young Roul brought the cigarettes, and Aunt Mirabelle brought the *calva*. And as the setting sun disappeared, we lounged in near silence on the veranda for several hours. That night, I thought about thinking and how much thinking I was doing. If my parents had been here, Madeleine-Grace and I would have been in their company, working through the evening with Aunt Adèle, enjoying conversation with Grandma'Maud about Grand-père Jacques, about the war, about school and work and neighbors and friends in America, about growing up in France, about past summers in Etretat-au-Delà.

Aunt Adèle called us to the foyer for prayers eventually, and after evening prayers, we made the trek to our rooms. As I changed into my pajamas, I glanced at the vase on the dresser, knowing my father would have had it filled with flowers for my mother by now, only two days into our summer stay. But now, it remained empty.

We slept well that night, my sleep interrupted only once before dawn when I awoke to a dream of my parents. My father was pouring a cocktail into the rocks glass from our *passoire* at home—a clear, icy cold drink that Maman had prepared and stored in the refrigerator—and his hand touched my fingers as he handed the *passoire* to me to drain the remaining drips over my head and into my mouth; I knew it to be gin and fresh lemon. I hated that it was only a dream of them. I could taste the icy gin and dry lemon from the few droplets, yet I could not feel my father's hands. And I fell back asleep.

The visit from Monsieur Vauquelin yesterday was not the only significant visit this first week at the summer house. The second arrived with two invitations, the effects of which I could never have realized at the time.

Aunt Adèle had spent the morning handwashing the bed linens and bathroom towels from every bedroom, a necessity that stirred the rancor of all my aunts and uncles for years on account of another necessity— that they rise from bed earlier than usual so that Aunt Adèle could launder them. Only grumbles slipped out as expressions of their frustration because they knew that unless they abided by Aunt Adèle's schedule, the *literie*, our linens, would go unwashed otherwise.

Madeleine-Grace and I helped her hang the sheets and pillow cases to the clotheslines linking the side of the house to the shed. There were so many sheets and towels, though, that Aunt Adèle had planted four more poles into the ground with two ropes linking each pair. These clotheslines were on the other side of the house, past the flower and herb islands, and as we passed the veranda to reach them, Madeleine-

Grace and I each holding a basket of sheets for Aunt Adèle, we could see the grumpy stares of our aunts, uncles, and cousins. Her hands free, Aunt Adèle waved and smiled.

She started hanging the damp linens, requesting that I hold the bottom of each one so that it didn't touch the grass, when Madeleine-Grace asked, "Aunt Adèle, why do you gather the bed linens so early when you can gather them at night and change each one before we go to bed?"

Aunt Adèle stopped pulling a sheet taut, stopped adjusting the placement of a clothespin, and smiled furtively at Madeleine-Grace. She parted her lips to answer when we heard the knock. I heard a voice call "*boujou*," or "good-day" in Cauchois, and we knew we weren't imagining when everyone on the veranda found someone to look at curiously. The call, firm yet distant, propelled over the house from the front door into the lawn in the back. Our next pair of visitors had arrived.

We followed Aunt Adèle in so that she could greet the unannounced guests at the front door, and while my uncles seemed unaffected, our aunts huddled on the veranda, gossiping at the possibility, horrified by the prospect of being seen in their nightgowns. We stood behind her as Aunt Adèle opened the front door. Before us stood Lady Victorine Galimard and Lady Léontine d'Evreux, two ladies my grandmother's age and close friends of hers.

Aunt Adèle greeted them with decorum and piety, her smile wide at their presence, and then led them into the foyer. We remained behind Aunt Adèle, but Lady Victorine never took her eyes off us. For a warm June day, they dressed with unseasonable modesty, in a manner more in keeping with matrons of Bourbon Restoration fashion yet with contemporary touches. Their collars were high with ruffles oozing out of a buttoned redingote, clasped with a brooch, Lady Victorine's a pink and white cameo and Lady Léontine's a faceted amethyst. The same frilly ruffles stretched from the sleeves of their waistcoats, covering most of their hand but not their many-ringed fingers. And their skirts almost touched the floor—all of their skirts, for there seemed to be several layers if not a panier, accounting for how expansive they looked. Lady Victorine's entire ensemble was puce with the iridescence of a martini olive, except for the white of her ruffles and the pink of her *camée*, and Lady Léontine donned a variety of browns, except for the white of her ruffles and the purple of her collar facet. Both wore hats with elaborate flourishes of ribbons, feathers, and pins, and both boasted hair of short, white curls.

Seeing their unwavering intention to acknowledge us, Aunt Adèle stepped aside, and their eyes, once fixed on us unobstructed, welled with tears. Lady Victorine could not crouch but bent at the torso and opened her arms to me while Lady Léontine, a bit nimbler, did the same to Madeleine-Grace. We stepped forward, allowing them to embrace us. Then they switched. Neither Madeleine-Grace nor I felt close enough to them to offer more than resting our hands on their arms. Each embrace lasted at least half a minute, and I felt their bodies lifting and falling with their sobs.

When they stepped back, they pulled out hankies and wiped their eyes. I glanced at Aunt Adèle to see a tear on her cheek.

"We cannot express our condolences," said Lady Léontine. "Words will not be enough."

"Your parents—such beautiful children," said Lady Victorine. Then she looked at Madeleine-Grace and added, "I remember when your mother was no bigger than you are now, and how inquisitive she was at that age!"

"So intelligent," said Lady Léontine. "She went to school and to university!"

Lady Victorine placed a hand on my shoulder as she shared, "Your Grandma'Maud has not recovered. We were in Paris when we received the news, and we went right to her. She was devastated."

"She took the roses from the parlor vase and broke them. She broke them in front of us."

"She was devastated. And she threw the vase and collapsed to the floor crying."

"We were there," said Lady Léontine.

"I'm glad we were there."

"We were there, and I threw myself onto the floor beside her—"

"—and I threw myself on top of her to console her—"

"—but she could not be consoled." Then Lady Léontine looked at Aunt Adèle. "She still cannot be consoled. We were there this past week. We only arrived in Etretat-au-Delà yesterday, or we would have come here sooner."

"The Countess," continued Lady Victorine, "she has remained in Paris and will check on your mother. But Léontine and I had to return to our family staying at the house here, and to see Jacques and Madeleine-Grace, of course."

"You will visit your Grandma'Maud soon," declared Lady Léontine. "She is hoping to see you soon, and your visit will be the only consolation."

"Even news of your Uncle Léon's death she took better—"

"Differently—she took it differently—" corrected Lady Léontine.

"—as if she had expected the news. Her reaction was more—quiet."

"The war. We learned to expect the unexpected."

"We were there, too, when your Grandma'Maud got word of Léon's death."

"She named him after me, I believe," said Lady Léontine incidentally.

"Léon was not named after you," said Lady Victorine before moving to more serious subjects. "I lost a son to the war one month later. My Aubery. We both grieved together."

"But your Grandma'Maud, she took Léon's death differently. She was so still."

"Not this time," reiterated Lady Victorine. "So you must visit her. You are planning to visit her, are you not?"

Although I had expected to see Grandma'Maud, I looked to Aunt Adèle.

"Yes, they will spend time together. They have the whole summer, and they've only just arrived Sunday."

Lady Victorine lunged for me, not permitting me to escape from a tenacious hug that lasted a full minute. She sobbed again through the duration of the embrace before finally releasing and dabbing her eyes with the kerchief.

"Lady Victorine, Lady Léontine, may I escort you to the *salon*? May I offer you a coffee or a tea?"

"We so enjoy a *séjour* in your *salon*, but wouldn't you prefer we enjoy this visit outside?" asked Lady Victorine.

"We so enjoy the late morning before it turns too hot, and your veranda is so lovely," Lady Léontine said to secure the destination.

"Of course," replied Aunt Adèle. "Allow me to escort you to the veranda, and then I will make coffee."

"No need, dear," said Lady Léontine with a brush of the hand as she made for the veranda through the main hall. "We know our way and do not need escorts."

"However, Adèle," said Lady Victorine before budging from her spot, "wouldn't you prefer something cold to drink? I'm sure you would prefer an iced tea or an iced coffee."

"Of course, Lady Victorine." As Lady Victorine followed Lady Léontine, Adèle nudged me to follow them and took Madeleine-Grace with her to the kitchen.

When I opened the veranda door from the *salle-en-arrière*, I saw the last in the phalanx of the Semperrin family marching down the veranda steps and around the side of the house. I surmised they planned to enter the house through a different door so that they could hurry upstairs to change. Luckily, they had not yet made a mess on the veranda. A newspaper lay on the floor against the low veranda wall, and a tray with used cups and saucers, a plate of cookies, and a *cendrier* remained on the balustrade. When I pulled out chairs for the ladies to sit, I surveyed the tabletop and chairs and found no crumbs. Once they were seated, I quickly lifted the tray and the newspaper, ran them into the kitchen, and returned to the ladies, standing at the table with my hands behind my back. They were preoccupied with their discomfort as I heard them discuss Lady Victorine's stiffness of joints and Lady Léontine's puffiness of skin. Then they turned their attention to me.

"We are so glad you continue to spend your summers in Etretat-au-Delà," said Lady Victorine. "That would mean so much to your dear mother—"

"—and to your Grand-père Jacques. He invested much time here, himself, and it was his father who built it," added Lady Léontine.

"Just as our fathers built our home here—ours farther up the *falaises*—"

"—and ours farther still—"

"—but all of us neighbors are good friends. Aren't you so grateful for the friendship of the Semperrins?" asked Lady Victorine.

"I am most grateful." Lady Léontine looked at me intently and then finally sunk in her chair, at last realizing this a place to be comfortable. "We are so grateful to know such good people, little Jacques, and your parents are among the best. We watched your mother grow up, and we, too, fell in love with Julien while your mother fell in love with him, herself."

"Such a good boy, your father." Lady Victorine sighed. "You must tell us, Jacques, if your Grand-mère Armance plans to stay in France now that she has brought you here."

"She must return to America," Lady Léontine answered for me, "to make arrangements for the children."

"Is this so, Jacques? Has your Grand-mère Armance left already for America? We so wished to meet with her."

Finally, I spoke. "Grand-mère Armance and Grand-père Guarin must visit relatives here in Normandie first as well as in London and Calais, and they plan to spend several days in Paris with Grandma'Maud before they return to America and wait for us."

"I did not know this," uttered Lady Léontine incredulously. "Madeleine-Maud did not mention this to us."

A breeze bore a gentle path to the veranda so that all their ruffles and feathers and ribbons fluttered. Both ladies smiled in the breeze and caught notice of the sheets on the distant clothesline billowing in the fresh gusts.

"Here is much better than Paris," said Lady Victorine. "You will see when you visit your Grandma'Maud."

Lady Léontine, her gaze still fixed on me, smiled and said, "I remember when you were little—five years old maybe—"

"—the most adorable children, you and your sister—"

"—and we took you in the car with us to Fécamp—"

"—you, not your cousins—they are not so adorable. You and your sister are the most adorable—"

"—your Grandma'Maud, Lady Victorine and her husband, my husband and I—we drove to Fécamp for the afternoon, and we took you with us, and you saw the Bénédictine advertisements here and there!"

As Lady Léontine laughed at the memory, Lady Victorine continued fondly, "And you pointed and said you wanted that for Christmas—because the bottle and the color of the liqueur are so beautiful. And you were only five!"

"And my husband said, 'We must try it first to see if you like it,' and you said with wide eyes, 'Really?' so with l'Abbaye closed, we went to Café Maôve and ordered the liqueur."

"Do you remember Madeleine-Maud?" Lady Victorine asked of her friend. "She was laughing so hard. She couldn't speak."

I had been told the story several times and knew the outcome. It wasn't much of a story, but to them, it was a climactic ending to a one-page bildungsroman.

"—and you took one sip while we all watched, and—. Do you remember?"

"Yes," I said, somehow still bashful about this.

"And you smiled so big after the first sip. Then you poured the rest of the glass into your mouth all at once before we could stop you!" Lady Léontine laughed again.

"Your smile was so big, and we couldn't believe you enjoyed it so much for someone so young, and then you said—"

At the same time, they quoted me, "'May I have another?'" And at that they bent at the side laughing.

"My husband," said Lady Victorine, bringing the tale to a close, "he sent you a bottle of Bénédictine for Christmas. Do you remember?"

"Yes," I said.

From thick, ice-creamy *crème de menthe* grasshoppers in winter to Galliano over vanilla frozen cream in spring, I had developed a taste for sweet liqueurs early, and my enjoyment of the herbal depth of digestives weren't far off. Sips of Irish whiskey with Jack McCleland's parents and shots of bourbon with Clark Garel and his dad, a spoonful of cherries soaked in vodka with the Krakowskis at my friend Stan's, a glass of homemade red wine at the Pennacchios', and, of course, a stein of ale with dinner at the Pabsts' were not foreign occurrences to us. When these same friends joined me for dinner at my house, we treated them to *calvados* or Bénédictine. Furthermore, both my parents delighted in the making of a good cocktail. Tending bar, I have been told, is a prestigious career in France, Switzerland, Germany—and not treated like a menial job—so we found making a good cocktail honorable. It's no wonder Lord Galimard's Christmas gift brought me so much joy that holiday.

Aunt Adèle entered holding a tray of iced teas, each garnished with a sprig of mint in filled highball glasses. Next to her, Madeleine-Grace held a plate with *sablés*. When Aunt Adèle placed the tray on the table, Madeleine-Grace placed the plate in the tray and then stepped behind Aunt Adèle. Lady Léontine, however, pulled Madeleine-Grace to her side and wrapped her arm around her waist. The ladies' affection for us was genuine, and this encounter with them was the first time I saw them as human, not background vases and flowers and doilies belonging to my grandmother's world; they had been until now, I imagined, taken for granted by me on account of their constancy in my life and their presence in so many of Grandma'Maud's stories. Why did I notice this now?

Madeleine-Grace still in Lady Léontine's embrace, the ladies discussed many topics, from their visit to my grandmother in Paris to their plans to remain a full month in Etretat-au-Delà, from Thiessé Galimard's busy schedule disallowing extended stays at their summer house this year to Monsieur Cuvelier's expressing to Countess Honorine his boredom over uninspired contemporary pieces of music. Every time Madeleine-Grace and I locked eyes, one of the ladies asked me a question to include me politely, only to resume conversation intently with Aunt Adèle. When they seemed to have discussed enough and their iced teas had but a sip or two left, Lady Victorine pulled from within her redingote an envelope. The envelope was quite big, and I don't know how she had kept it concealed. On the outside were written in elaborate penmanship of dark-blue ink the words "Jacques et Madeleine-Grace Avery."

"Well, my little ones, this is an important reason we have visited today, and we do not want to forget," said Lady Victorine.

As she handed me the envelope, I saw Aunt Adèle smile knowingly. I, too, had a hunch, but I couldn't be certain until Lady Léontine added, "It is from the Countess." Then I knew.

I pulled the invitation from the envelope and hadn't a chance to read before Lady Victorine pulled it from my hands and offered it to Aunt Adèle.

"Countess Honorine wishes she could present it to you, herself," Lady Victorine said, "but she had to stay behind in Paris. The invitations went out a month ago, and she did not know if, after—well, if you would be spending this summer in Etretat-au-Delà."

"She wishes very much that you attend," said Lady Léontine to Madeleine-Grace and me, and then to my aunt, "Is this possible, Adèle?"

"Of course," said Aunt Adèle, smiling delicately as she returned the invitation to the envelope without so much as a glance at it. "They are as honored as their cousins to attend and are grateful to share the opportunity."

With the merest nod, Aunt Adèle indicated to respond, so first I and then my sister said, "Thank-you for the kind invitation."

"On behalf of Countess Honorine," said Lady Léontine.

"She will be so pleased when she hears the news. Be sure to stop by Madame Dalmont's to register for the ball," said Lady Victorine. "Now, we must walk back, only this time, it is slightly uphill. The exercise will be good for my stiffness."

"But the sun will irritate my puffy skin. We must walk quickly."

"I cannot walk quickly anymore," said Lady Victorine with an apologetic shrug.

As we walked with the ladies into the foyer, the Semperrin family, now washed and dressed, descended the stairs. Our cousins remained on the staircase, resting chins and hands on the railing, while the adults greeted the ladies in their most proper manners.

"We woke you, did we?" said Lady Victorine to our aunts and uncles. To the children on the staircase, Lady Léontine asked, "And did we wake you, too? Do you help your Aunt Adèle—and your Aunt Laure and your Aunt Pé and your Aunt Mirabelle—with all the chores, or do you sleep all day?"

When my cousins nodded in affirmation while looking at their shoes or at the marble of the foyer floor, Lady Léontine placed her hands on her hips and exchanged a glance with Aunt Adèle.

"My son Thiessé likes to sleep late, too," said Lady Victorine.

"Is Thiessé staying in Etretat-au-Delà this week?" asked Uncle Roul.

"Yes, he is at the house now with his wife. And Hardouin and Marie Loiselier are visiting with their children."

This piqued Uncle Roul's interest. "We must enjoy a *calva* with Thiessé and Célèstène soon—"

Uncle Romain cut him off. "To what do we owe the pleasure of this visit, ladies? Do you bring word from our mother in Paris?"

The smile on the faces of Aunt Pé and Aunt Mirabelle vanished. I sensed that they did not care to hear about news from Grandma'Maud. I assumed it was because they thought to visit her with us soon enough, and maybe they were displeased with the prospect of a few days in the Parisian heat when they could be here.

"Yes," said Lady Léontine, "we spoke to Adèle of your mother. Her spirits are low. Adèle will tell you all."

"Her spirits would remain low if she had heard you have not yet fixed the broken chair rail in the hall," inserted Lady Victorine, chuckling afterwards as Lady Léontine pierced Uncle Romain with her stare. He only grumbled, glancing askance.

"A visit from her grandchildren is sure to lift her spirits," said Lady Léontine.

"But we also visit bearing an invitation for Juliette's children, on behalf of Countess Honorine, to the children's ball this summer," added Lady Victorine, lifting her chin with delight in delivering the news as she looked directly at Aunt Pé and Aunt Mirabelle. My two aunts did not notice her gaze as they looked at each other, for some reason grimacing.

Aunt Mirabelle forced a smile and said, "The Countess is so gracious to include my nephew and niece."

Aunt Pé, also contorting her face into a smile, inserted, "But surely she has forgotten that the date to register with song and dance selection has recently passed."

Lady Victorine chuckled. "It is the Countess's event. Surely, she can grant an extension to whomever she pleases. Besides, the Avery children have been welcomed participants for several years and would be expected at the ball."

"And anyone with even a crumb of sympathy would forgive their late registration," added Lady Léontine. "Surely, you do not suggest that it might be an issue."

"I only meant it might not allow Ellande and Madeleine-Grace time to make selections," Aunt Pé said, her face blanching. She shot a glance at her husband and looked to the floor immediately upon being met with his eyes bulging in disbelief. I assumed he could not believe she would think to question the graciousness of the Countess, also a dear friend of my grandmother's.

"Ellande?" asked Lady Léontine.

"Little Jacques's new name," said little Laure from her step.

"I will explain another time," said Aunt Adèle.

"The things of children," responded Lady Léontine as if to explain away an insignificant, new pet name.

"I recall," continued Lady Victorine once again lifting her chin to my two aunts, "these two doing very well at last year's ball." Then she sighed and turned her attention to Aunt Adèle. "Come now. My joints grow stiffer by the moment, and we must walk home."

"Please give Thiessé and Célèstène our best," said Uncle Roul. "They should expect us to call on them soon, some time before *la choule* on Sunday."

"Why don't you join us at the house this evening? The children, too," asked Lady Victorine. "My husband is having over Arnault and Anne Anquetil, and Léontine, of course, and I'm sure Thiessé and Célèstène would be delighted if the Semperrins join us for the evening. I have already asked Hardouin and Marie Loiselier to stay one more evening, as well. Would you consider joining us for *apéritifs* or cordials?"

"We certainly do not wish to impose, especially at such short notice," said Aunt Adèle, speaking for us all.

Aunt Mirabelle stepped forward as she said, "But I would so like to see Célèstène. And my husband enjoys the company of Thiessé who is so rarely in."

"What would you prefer, my dear?" asked Lady Victorine to Aunt Mirabelle. "To spend *apéritif* hour with us or cordials after dinner?" Before anyone answered, she added, "Wouldn't you rather spend *apéritif* hour with us? It's not far off, and then you can return for a sumptuous dinner that Adèle will prepare in your comfortable home."

"I have every intention of making sure Adèle is not left at home to make the dinner while the rest of you enjoy *apéritifs*," said Léontine. "Did that not happen in the past?"

"Only at Adèle's insistence," interjected Aunt Pé.

"I strictly forbid it this time," said Lady Victorine.

"You must join us," said Léontine.

"And bring young Alban Vauquelin," said Lady Victorine with a wink.

"He is very handsome," said Lady Léontine.

"Alban is on the island tonight. He will not be able to join us," Aunt Adèle said, her cheeks reddening.

"That must not deter you from joining us," said Lady Léontine firmly while still enjoying my aunt's blushing.

"Of course she will come," said Uncle Romain. "She must look after the children. However, cordials sound more appealing to us, do they not?" He did not check for accord from anyone. "Adèle, you will have to forgo the dishes tonight. We will walk over right after dinner. Is this agreeable, Lady Victorine?"

It was not, I could tell. Stiffness crept now to her face, too, and without a smile, she said, "Very well. I will inform Thiessé and Célèstène of these plans, and they will be delighted."

The moment pleasant farewells were completed and the door was shut, the family was astir. The little time to prepare was made littler for Aunt Adèle whose housework had been curtailed by the pleasant interruption of two life-long neighbors. Although they normally may have preferred—what the Cauchois call—*caleuser* on a warm afternoon, my aunts and uncles diverted their attention from *caleuser*, doing nothing or loafing; Aunt Adèle, meanwhile, thought ahead to a return home to beds without bedlinens and turned her attention to avoiding this. We followed her to the linen closet at the top of the stairs, two floor-to-ceiling, white doors with white, double-panel molding and thick, brass handles as knobs. All my summers past, I passed these doors daily and never once considered what lay behind them, never once saw them anything but closed. Then Aunt Adèle opened them in unison.

The small area at the top of the stairs no longer felt like a hall or intersection to the two lanes leading to the bedrooms; it felt like a separate room with a décor unknown to me. On one half were the bathroom towels, neatly piled in perfect squares by color. I could tell each pile included the towel set for a different washroom. The bath towels undergirded the hand and face towels. Between every two piles, a lacey sachet of lavender and herbs protruded, like a closet fairy sticking its head out of a frilly, ruffled collar to breathe a soothing scent on any folded fabric nearby. On the other half were the sheet sets, neatly piled by bed, each encased in a lace reticule. Each smooth, percale flat sheet and fitted sheet, along with the pillow cases, was stacked high, meticulously folded, and enwrapped in lace pulled closed with a drawstring of yellow ribbon, its strands lilting over the side of the pile. Between each of these piles, too, protruded the playful and fragrant, lacey fairies.

"Put out your arms," Aunt Adèle said, and when we did, she placed a lace-wrapped set of sheets in each of our arms, took one more set for herself, and escorted us from bedroom to bedroom, allowing us to help her dress the beds of every room. We repeated the procedure in every bedroom with every bed and then restocked the bathroom with towels, as well. Amidst our intrusions, my aunts, uncles, and cousins huddled in their respective rooms, pulling outfits from armoires, sizing dresses to their physiques before mirrors, sampling shades of blushes and eyeshadows and lipsticks, tearing off pants and shirts, buttoning and unbuttoning dress shirts, and twirling around us with glares and grimaces about our making the beds and replenishing the bathroom towels. Aunt Pé had her hair pulled back as she rewashed her face in the sink, Aunt Laure sifted through a box of foulards as Uncle Gilbert folded a pocket square, and Uncle Roul, with his shirt unbuttoned one too many buttons, puffed his shirt off his chest with pinched fingers while Aunt Mirabelle sprayed her skirt with Vent Vert.

"Adèle!" shouted Aunt Mirabelle when we stepped out of their bedroom. "You must take up my hemline. I haven't worn this skirt once this summer, and it doesn't hang right."

"Leave it on the railing," said Aunt Adèle, running the fingers of her finally emptied hands through her hair as Chardine whizzed by with a beige blouse into her parents' room. Aunt Adèle must not have counted on having one more task to complete in the little time between now and the gathering. We watched as she closed the closet doors with her back to it, as if she had known it her whole life.

"Why is everyone so anxious about tonight?" asked Madeleine-Grace. "We always hang out with them over summer."

"Your aunts and uncles like to associate with people they see as influential and affluent. Your aunts like to learn of what's fashionable and who is——." She stopped and sighed, looking over our heads down the hall of bedroom doors. "They like the company. That's all."

Within several hours, after delicious platters of snacks made by Aunt Adèle instead of a dinner, my aunts and uncles put the finishing touches on their evening attire while we children decided to spend the final moments before departure playing a game. The girls played *muche-muche* around the house while the boys played Candyland on the veranda; I had brought it to France just for the summer house several years ago, and the crease of the board was ripped after so much use. I knew Aunt Adèle had altered Aunt Mirabelle's skirt in the conservatory and was seeing her into it upstairs.

When the adults called for us to leave, we were already what Uncle Romain considered late; his concern wasn't punctuality but not losing out on time interacting with Thiessé Galimard and Hardouin Loiselier. As they rushed out the front door, I noticed that Madeleine-Grace did not stand among the lot of us and darted into the conservatory to find her. Uncle Romain angrily shouted my name from outside, so I stuck my head out the front door to say that I couldn't find my sister.

"Where is your cousin?" demanded Uncle Romain of the girls.

Astride shrugged.

Chardine said, "Madeleine-Grace was the last to count while we hid. She shouldn't be hiding anywhere."

"Go on ahead," said Aunt Adèle. "I'll find her."

Uncle Roul and Aunt Mirabelle, waiting at the end of the front walkway, began their stroll when they heard Aunt Adèle's announcement. Uncle Romain grabbed my arm and pulled me toward the Semperrins heading for the Galimards'. With a glance into the house, I resisted in an attempt to assist Aunt Adèle only for Uncle Romain to yank me toward the others already en route.

We strolled the white gravel road connecting all the houses along the *falaises* of Etretat-au-Delà, the length between the Semperrin house and Lady Victorine Galimard's stretching about a mile. The road rose at a barely noticeable incline, and, passing the homes, we studied the space between properties for a glimpse of the glowing, dusk sky and copper-streaked ocean. Each glimpse blinded me before the next house's blockading relief. All the houses, similar in size and style to ours, showcased a walkway to the main entrance and a variety of flowers and greenery lining the front façade. Ours, to my knowledge, was the only property with flower and herb islands in the back. My father had told me that after the war, the houses along the *falaises* were kept up, renovated, and modernized to varying degrees, evident more so within the houses than in their exteriors.

Astride, who walked beside her mother ahead of me, kept glancing behind her, beyond me. About a half mile from our house, I glanced back, hoping to see Aunt Adèle and Madeleine-Grace. I felt relief as they trailed us in the distance but said nothing to the others. The silence of our stroll broke, however, when Aunt Laure acknowledged a woman on the front steps of the house we were passing.

"Jeuffine!" Aunt Laure called out.

As she leaned over the stone railing, the woman was using scissors to cut a spray rose growing along the front steps. She snipped the stem just when Aunt Laure called her name, and as she stood, her carriage stately and proud, the breeze pushed her long emerald green dress against the shape of her body for a moment and blew her long, dark brown hair. Her face was beautiful—a defined jaw line, high, pink cheekbones, thin lips and a thin nose, and large eyes with softly curved brows—but those eyes never once saw the owner of the voice that called her. They saw only the owner of the head that swung to its left at the word "Jeuffine," his attention to her more eager than Aunt Laure's or anyone else's. Their eyes fixed, and both smiled in a way that, to me, seemed to hold back a more complete smile. Without breaking eye contact with Uncle Roul, Jeuffine flipped her hair to one side and slid the rose stem over her ear. Since I trailed the group, I saw, too, that Aunt Mirabelle in this moment increased her pace so that she no longer walked beside her husband but a few steps in front of him; Uncle Roul did not notice. His smile grew bigger as Jeuffine slowly turned like a top on its last revolution before it tilts to a rest, glanced over her shoulder at Uncle Roul, and walked up the few steps into her house.

By the time we had reached the front veranda of Lady Victorine's, Aunt Adèle and Madeleine-Grace had gained on us. I felt secure in waiting for them at the door as Thiessé ushered the rest of the family in. When he realized I was waiting for others in our party, he told me simply to enter and find them in the drawing room to my left. As they neared, I could tell something was wrong. Madeleine-Grace leaned into Aunt Adèle on almost every step and her visage looked serious. When she arrived at the front walk, she left Aunt Adèle's side and ran to me, hugging me for comfort. Her eyes were swollen from tears, and she buried her faced in my side to cry again. When Aunt Adèle reached us, she led us away from the front door where I had been standing, halfway down the front walk.

"What happened?" I asked. "What's wrong?"

"Your cousin did something unkind," Aunt Adèle said, petting my sister's hair.

"Which cousin?" I asked. Somehow, I knew the answer.

Madeleine-Grace lifted her face from my side and shared, "The girls asked me to play *muche-muche*, and Laure found me the first round, so I had to count. And when I went into the kitchen to count, Astride told me that I had to count behind the cellar door. I stood behind the door at the top of the stairs to count and told her to leave it open a crack so that I had light, but she shut it. Then I heard a sound. It was her locking me in. I told her over and over to open the door, and she said, if I counted quietly to fifty, she would open it for me. So I did, but then no one came. Finally, Aunt Adèle opened the door after everyone had left."

I knew the latch to lock the cellar door was at the top of the door on the kitchen side. And I knew that the light for the cellar stairs was installed only a few years ago, a hanging bulb with a chain that Madeleine-Grace would never have been able to reach. And I realized not only the fear Madeleine-Grace must have felt but the danger she had been put in, unable to see the stairs she was atop.

"You must have been very scared," I said and pulled her back to my side, this time by an impulse of my own to hug her. I was not surprised to hear Astride was the culprit.

"I was scared. It was dark, and I couldn't see if *Père La Pouque* was coming. I was afraid to pound on the door for help," Madeleine-Grace said, crying again. "Why did Astride do that?"

All I could think to say was, "Lady Victorine said that you are more beautiful, so Astride is jealous."

"When I went into the kitchen, I saw the chair beside the door and the latch at the top closed. I knew this was not right and called for Madeleine-Grace," Aunt Adèle said.

"I am never going to play *muche-muche* with them again," Madeleine-Grace said, wiping her eyes.

"Come," Aunt Adèle said. "Let us greet Lady Victorine and her family and enjoy our evening. Stay away from Astride, and I will tell Uncle Romain about this after the soirée. If Thiessé's children are here, you will play with them this evening."

Aunt Adèle smoothed down any wrinkles in our clothes, dabbed at Madeleine-Grace's tears, took us each by the hand, and entered the house. The bustle to our left called us to the drawing room where Thiessé and Célèstène Galimard greeted us cordially, offered condolences respectfully, and ushered us into the small gathering. After acknowledging Lady Victorine and Lady Léontine, seated in upright chairs on either side of a small table and lamp within perfect proximity to the bar to maintain unnoticed vigilance, we were welcomed by little Maclou Galimard. The Galimards took delight in greetings between their children and us, eager to ensure our joy through immediate playtime together. We had, of course, met and played with Thiessé and Célèstène's children, Ansgot, Brigitte, and Maclou, many times before on past stays in Etretat-au-Delà, but on account of months having elapsed between each visit, the parents always deemed necessary a formal albeit quick introduction.

From the window at which Aunt Laure and Uncle Gilbert stood approached Hardouin and Marie Loiselier, friends from Fécamp. They called over their children, Henriette and Collot, and all greeted us cordially. Henriette and Collot had been speaking with young Roul and hurried to him after greetings. Other guests of the Galimards, mostly of my grandmother's generation, acknowledged us in their own way, sometimes with simple tips of the head or waves of the hand.

Clasping us by the wrists with gentle holds, Ansgot, Brigitte, and Maclou led Madeleine-Grace and me to our cousins and several other children in the adjoining drawing room to play *p'tits chouaux*, known outside Pays de Caux as *petits chevaux*, on the floor. Brigitte took Madeleine-Grace by the hand and sat next to her in the circle, and Ansgot made room for himself and me in the circle. When we entered, Astride rose from the circle, grabbed Brigitte by the hand, and pulled her to another room. Luckily, this left Madeleine-Grace next to little Laure. Although Aimée Anquetil had just learned how to play, she explained the rules with cheerful animation, and we novices played eagerly.

The evening carried on as these evenings usually did: conversation and clinks and laughter emanated from the drawing room while joy and shouts and laughter sprung from amongst the children in our drawing room. Uncle Romain and Aunt Pé, Uncle Roul and Aunt Mirabelle, and Thiessé and Célèstène Galimard sat along one wall, the females on the same divan and the men in upright chairs; Aunt Laure and Marie Loiselier remained standing in the recess of the bay window as they chatted; Uncle Gilbert and Lord Galimard spoke together with Arnault and Anne Anquetil, standing at the bar piece. Aunt Adèle sat with Lady Victorine and Lady Léontine for gentle laughter and conversation; the children interacted within the game or jumped up to enjoy brief excursions into the main hall, the powder room, or the other drawing room; and everyone, adult and child alike, had a drink in hand or within reach.

More so than at our summer house thus far, I felt an alleviating freedom this evening. Even though, in the house of someone where I had to mind my ps and qs and take every precaution against abusing the hosts' hospitality, where I had to act within certain strictures, the Galimards' welcome, the playfulness of the children, and the care of Aunt Adèle nearby made me feel more at ease than any time in Etretat-au-Delà since my arrival, with the exception of calm morning coffee. The same could not be said of Madeleine-Grace's experience here. Between rounds of *p'tits chouaux* and amid our joking, she shifted about for quick searches for Astride's whereabouts. On one survey of the room, she found Astride behind her talking to Henriette. When Madeleine-Grace glanced in their direction, Henriette smiled and waved amicably. As she stepped toward my sister, Astride pulled Henriette by the wrist to the adjoining drawing room, saying, "You don't want to play with her. Maman says her mother's no fun, so neither is she." Henriette, too old to buy into such foolishness from youngsters, allowed herself to be pulled away, but only because it brought her closer to young Roul who was entering from the main hall with Collot.

After an hour, Lady Victorine called us into their room, for a servant had rolled in a cart of desserts, placing plates of cookies and pastries, assortments of cheeses, nuts, and fruits, and trays of *mousse au chocolat* on the various tables about the room. No one demurred from reaching for a sweet, and some even used doing so as a means of escaping their circles. As Aunt Mirabelle probed Célèstène for names of tailors at the Paris and Rouen clothing shops, she took no notice of young Roul leading Henriette to the main entrance and onto the front veranda for a cigarette. When Marie stepped from the bay window for a *palmier*, she drifted instead to Aunt Adèle, engaging her in conversation about her sewing and blouse patterns. Aunt Laure, left alone, shifted her attention to her children, and as Wischard and little Laure reached for their own *mousse au chocolat* from a side table, she slapped the top of little Laure's hand, prohibiting her claim on one. Brigitte entered with Astride on her trail, her eyes on a *tarte aux pommes*, but when Brigitte saw Madeleine-Grace and me heading toward Aunt Adèle, she zig-zagged to our nook of the room where we welcomed her; Astride stopped following her, turning her attention instead to Chardine and Alphonse playing with two neighbors.

I could make out snippets of conversation throughout the evening and knew Lord Galimard to be commenting about banking, and Uncle Roul and Thiessé, more casual in their chats, to be anticipating tomorrow evening's World Cup match, Aunt Laure to be reflecting aloud to Marie, again next to her, on her wish to travel, to be at sea, to be standing on the terrace of a mountain chalet, Aunt Pé and Aunt Mirabelle to be teasing out information about fashionable lounges from Célèstène, Lady Victorine to be regaling anyone within earshot with tales of Lady Léontine and my grandmother as young mothers. While past summers had young Roul interacting playfully with Henriette, he intimated to Ansgot that he liked her now. Just as Wischard was characteristically making all of us laugh by getting *mousse* on his nose in forgoing the spoon and using his tongue to ingest the treat, Lord Galimard called my name, using "Ellande."

I turned toward the bar to see him holding a bottle of Bénédictine in one hand and a cordial glass in his other. His smile grand and summoning expressed more than words. I smiled in return and walked to him amid jolly laughter from the ladies.

"We always have a glass of *béné* awaiting you," Lord Galimard said. "You must never forget that." He poured into the cordial glass the Bénédictine and handed it to me, requesting I wait one moment. He poured several more and passed them around the room, some accepting and some declining. Finally, he poured one for himself, he smiled at me with a bow, and we all drank.

After my first sip, I was incited by Lady Victorine and Lady Léontine to follow it up with a gulp, which I did to more laughter from all. I was happy to see Madeleine-Grace smiling too, now nestled in the embrace of Lady Léontine.

"Now, *calva*!" shouted Uncle Romain. Lord Galimard withdrew from the bar a bottle of *calva* to serve. Prior, everyone had been drinking Chambord neat and kirs royales.

Thiessé approached the bar to help his father with the distribution of the *calva*. As the glasses were poured, I heard Lord Galimard whisper crankily, "Damn Semperrin and his fat wife—will clean us out if they could." I knew he was talking about Uncle Romain when Thiessé responded, also *sotto voce*, "His brother is no better—." Uncle Gilbert, who had stepped to the bay window to check on Aunt Laure, returned at that moment to the bar to lend a helping hand, and both Galimard men reinstated conviviality and handed him two drinks.

"And for Ellande?" asked Lord Galimard.

Célèstène said from the divan, "Only a little for the children, Father."

Thiessé retorted, "Little Bertin was drinking *calva* when he was a baby—did him no harm!" Little Bertin, a little older than young Roul, was the son of Thiessé's sister Marie. The mention of little Bertin prompted Aunt Pé and Aunt Mirabelle to turn toward Célèstène to inquire about Thiessé's sister and later his brother Bertin after whom little Bertin was named. The tugs for information for no reason other than gossip fodder pulled distastefully, judging from the dour expression on Célèstène's face and the look she and her husband gave to the pestering of my oblivious aunts.

Aunt Adèle turned to us at the bar and said, "Ellande may have his last glass for the evening, Lord Galimard. Thank-you for your generosity."

Lord Galimard's countenance grew genuine with fondness and appreciation as Aunt Adèle spoke sensibly and graciously. He handed me a glass of *calva* and patted me on the head with that big smile.

So the evening's joviality continued despite the yawns from Lady Victorine and soon thereafter from the children. The plates of sweets ransacked and all variety of glasses empty, the evening came to a close, and we bid our adieux. The Semperrins idled on the front veranda a moment as cigarettes were lit and a short search for young Roul ensued. Alphonse found him with Henriette on the tree swing along the side of the house, announcing, as he pulled him to our clan, that his shirt was unbuttoned more than usual. Young Roul, too, lit a cigarette, and we left the glow of the Galimard house for the dark walk home. A large cloud obscured the moon, but many stars twinkled in the midnight blue above.

No lights illuminated the windows of the houses along the road during our walk back, quiet except for the crunch of the gravel, the friction of fabric moving with our steps, catching the breeze, and the incoherent rumblings of Aunt Pé and Aunt Mirabelle discussing their latest discoveries about socialites. After ten minutes, though, I noticed interior lights glowing from the picture window of one house ahead. In such darkness, making out the houses was difficult for me, but when I saw the stately figure rise in the window, as if having been seated there in anticipation of our passing, I recognized the place as the one with the spray roses growing along the front railing and the figure as Jeuffine. In a moment, the figure disappeared from out of view of the window, the light turning off. Not a minute later, a light on the second floor rendered a window aglow.

Before we had fully passed the property, Uncle Roul placed a hand on Uncle Gilbert's shoulder, then one on mine, chuckled under his *calva* breath, and veered from our group, nonchalantly walking up the side path of Jeuffine's house, disappearing into the darkness, as we continued to our house without pause.

When we reached our house, we entered through the front door and stood in the main hall. I saw Aunt Adèle lead Aunt Pé back out the front door and realized she must be informing her about Astride's actions this afternoon. Only a minute later, the two reentered the house, shutting the door behind them. Uncle Gilbert told the children to go directly to bed. As Madeleine-Grace and I were the first to obey, we began to ascend the staircase. We stopped, Madeleine-Grace two stairs behind me, when Aunt Adèle said, "Astride, do you wish to apologize to Madeleine-Grace?"

Astride, still standing in the main hall, looked up at us. Everyone else, none the wiser about what she had done this afternoon, turned to Astride and then to us with curious stares. Astride said nothing.

"Astride will do no such thing," interjected Aunt Pé suddenly. Uncle Romain, off balance, leaned into the doorframe of the *salon* as he glared back and forth between his wife and daughter.

"What do you mean?" asked Aunt Adèle. "It is the right thing—and the least thing—to do, considering her actions today."

"What actions?" grumbled Uncle Romain.

Aunt Pé stepped toward the railing so that she could look Madeleine-Grace in the eye and said, "Astride will not apologize for the foolishness of an orphan. You went into the cellar, where you did not belong, and if I had my way, you would have stayed there until we returned."

She placed each fist on each hip and stared menacingly at Madeleine-Grace. Madeleine-Grace, however, stared directly back at her. And that's the moment something, if not everything, shifted. In this moment, Madeleine-Grace changed, the horror of such words taking a stick to her sight, to her mind, hurtling her into a reality she did not want but was ready to take on. In this moment, Madeleine-Grace did not nestle her head into my side as she removed Aunt Pé from her sight. Instead, she walked past me, and once two stairs above me, stopped, turned to Astride, then to Aunt Pé, and said, "An apology only means something when it comes from someone I care about. You can save it." The ferule of the acrimony in Aunt Pé's words, the cane of the resentment in Aunt Pé's eyes had been brandished before my sister and swung at her, a stinging disillusionment taken to my sister's understanding of family, clobbering the sense out of it, flogging the security from it. Looking Aunt Pé in the eyes, she said, "At least I have a mother who cares about me, as I always have. Poor Astride. With a mother as useless as hers, she might as well be the orphan."

Insouciant about the commotion that ensued, she continued to our room as I followed, unaware I would not again see the Madeleine-Grace I had always known.

CHAPITRE 3

Only three full days into my summer stay and I felt an obligation to be at Aunt Adèle's side early and often to help with tasks around the house. While Aunt Adèle discouraged our participation, preferring we experience restful hours of play and relaxation, she never pushed us away and always taught us what we did not know. A number of the tasks needing tending to that first week, however, benefited from our presence, including a declutter of our travel trunks and our fittings for the ball.

The morning after the party, Madeleine-Grace had already been awake by the time I awoke. She was lying beside me with her arms clasped over the covers, staring at the ceiling, not budging from her musings even when I rolled, greeted her, and hopped from bed. Aware the sun had risen only a half hour or so prior, we slunk out the bedroom door, down the hall, and down the staircase to the kitchen where Aunt Adèle characteristically greeted us and hurried to the stove to pour us a *café au lait*. Madeleine-Grace's entrance into the kitchen was circumspect as she carefully eschewed proximity to and even eye contact with the cellar door. At table, she twisted herself in her chair to ensure her back was to the cellar. Afterwards, we left to wash and dress, and upon our return, Aunt Adèle invited us to sit with her on the veranda while she ironed the clothesline-dried bedlinens. We insisted on helping.

As we walked from the kitchen to the veranda, passing the *salle-en-arrière*, we could not avoid seeing Uncle Roul asleep on the couch in last evening's pants, one leg up and one off the side, one pillow under his head and the other on his chest. His shoes, his shirt, and one sock were strewn alongside the couch, cluttered with another couch pillow and the throw Grandma'Maud had made. He did not snore but his breaths were long and loud, his sleep deep.

Aunt Adèle stood between Uncle Roul and us, waving us through the *salle-en-arrière* and onto the veranda without a word. Once on the back veranda, she gently pushed the door to an inch from the doorframe and approached the work station she had established while we had been washing. The iron sat atop a portable ironing board, and the cord traveled through the partially open doorway to an outlet on the inside wall. Next to the ironing board, the sheets were piled high in baskets, recently removed from the clotheslines outside.

Although she must have done this ironing many times on her own during the many months my mother was not present to accompany her, she found ways for Madeleine-Grace and me to help. She assigned to Madeleine-Grace the task of lifting the fluffy sheets from the basket and placing them neatly over the ironing board, and to me the task of making sure the edges did not touch the veranda floor. She assigned us both the task of spraying the basil water onto the sheets every so often before she applied the hot iron. Madeleine-Grace and I took turns spraying different sheets. I loved the smell of the basil water. That scent combined with the fresh lavender of the laundry spray had me wanting to bury my face in the sheets for minutes.

After she finished ironing each sheet and before requesting Madeleine-Grace reach for the next, she had me walk with two corners of it away from her and assist in folding. Taller than Madeleine-Grace, I could ensure that the sheets not swipe the floor. Madeleine-Grace, however, knew how to fold better than I as she more often assisted our mother with the sheet folding in America.

If we hadn't been helping Aunt Adèle fold the sheets, my mother would have been.

After the sheet set had been folded into the neatest square imaginable, Madeleine-Grace asked if Aunt Adèle was going to store them in lace. We had, after all, seen them thus adorned in the linen closet yesterday. She told us that she would tend to this task later at her sewing station in the conservatory.

When my mother and Aunt Adèle used to work, sometimes they worked in silence, happy, I imagined, to be accomplishing necessary tasks and to have each other to rely on. Sometimes they talked idly, sometimes they discussed issues, and other times they sang or recited "L'Abbé Trupot," a Normand poem by Charles Lemaître about Julie the *blanchisseuse*, the laundress. As the narrative unfolds, the abbot needs someone to starch and iron his surplices, so he turns to Julie Tancrède. He gets them back from her, but things don't turn out quite as he would have wished: when Sunday rolls around, he finds his vestments so stiff that he can't move. Julie rendered the man's surplices cardboard by over-starching them. Picturing the priest unable to turn his head, my mother and Aunt Adèle laughed through the reciting of it, especially Julie's response to the priest, but they always switched the name from Julie Tancrède to Juliette Semperrin.

They could never make it through the whole poem because they were laughing so hard. Two summers ago, after having finished the folding of Wischard and little Laure's clothes and having stacked them in neat piles, Aunt Adèle knocked the piles off the ottoman as she bent at the side in convulsions of laughter; they had not only changed Julie's name to Juliette but had changed the abbot to Uncle Romain and the surplice to our uncle's shirt. They could not shake the image of stocky Uncle Romain immobilized by starching and ironing. Neither my aunt nor my mother minded as they fumbled through the refolding of the fallen clothes, their laughter far from subsiding. I was laughing, myself, simply because they couldn't stop, and when my father entered and tried to help them, he laughed with them because the spectacle was so absurd. I couldn't imagine laughing that way again, not through housekeeping, not through anything. As Aunt Adèle, Madeleine-Grace, and I ironed and folded the many sheets, we took this time not to laugh through Normand poems but to talk quietly.

"Do you still feel scared after yesterday, Madeleine-Grace?" Aunt Adèle asked.

Madeleine-Grace did not answer. She sat in a veranda chair holding the spray can, bringing it to her nose for a sniff as pressing the lever tempted her.

"I should not have told Astride's mother last night," Aunt Adèle continued.

"Because she was drunk?" I asked.

Aunt Adèle stopped mid-motion with the iron when I said this, and then resumed.

"Maman said a lady shouldn't drink to drunkenness," I continued. "Papa said that, as a gentleman, I must see to this. The other ladies, they did not get drunk."

Refraining from comment on this topic, Aunt Adèle said, "I should not have told your Aunt Pé at all. I should have waited until today and told your Uncle Romain. I had intended to tell him to begin with—"

"—but he was drunk, too," I said.

"I will ask Uncle Romain today to talk to Astride. You should not be afraid of your cousin. She sometimes does foolish things, as we all sometimes do foolish things."

Madeleine-Grace did not look up as our aunt spoke on this matter. With Aunt Adèle's attention on eliminating a wrinkle, Madeleine-Grace aimed the spray nozzle at her hemline and pulled the lever halfway so that a tiny mist spread onto her skirt.

"Later on, my doves," Aunt Adèle said, "we will go through your trunks together. I will wash your travel clothes, and I will tidy your trunks. Once they're dry and folded, I will put the clothes in the dresser and the armoires for the summer. Your grandparents brought us another small trunk with gifts and odds and ends for the house, but they told us a few other gifts and odds and ends remain in your trunks."

Although travel had not caused much disorganization to the contents of our trunks, the inside of each looked far from the way Grand-mère Armance had packed it. I looked forward to the pending order and the forthcoming clean clothes.

"I will wash and hang the clothes this morning. Afterwards, we will walk to town to buy fabric for your suit and gown for the children's ball."

"Have you already begun making the others' suits and gowns?" Madeleine-Grace asked.

"The ones your aunts bought were finished suits and gowns, not the fabric. They preferred them that way this year. We still made alterations and adornments."

"Have they been practicing their dance?" I asked.

"I have not heard any practice, no. And you," she said, lifting the iron and staring at us, closing her lips and then her eyes for a moment, "you certainly could not have chosen a song let alone practiced."

"We have a song." Madeleine-Grace responded like a boxer delivering a decisive jab.

"You have a song?" asked our aunt, her attention remaining on us as she cautiously held the iron in the air, away from the sheets, the board, us, and herself.

"We have a song," Madeleine-Grace reiterated before shooting a glance at me.

In that moment, I realized to what my sister was referring. In the weeks prior to the accident, in mid-February, my mother had secured the sheet music to a *tourdion*, a traditional French dance, and she played it on the piano for us while my father made percussions of tabletops and chairs and pillows, smacking his hand into them with the rhythm while his foot tapped the floor. Madeleine-Grace and I danced, having learned long ago the near extinct steps, and we had a great time one night after dinner dancing with our father. Maman played the piano, swaying and smiling with the rousing, majestic melody in triple time while Papa, thumping on a pillow in his hand, danced with us. Maman looked over her shoulder to see us and one time stopped playing to suggest more elaborate choreography, which Madeleine-Grace, a natural, absorbed easily. We quickly took to her arrangement of traditional steps, and laughed and laughed the whole time learning it. I knew Madeleine-Grace saw that night as an amazingly good time and was determined to bring to France all the associations of that night, from the tradition to the joy, connecting my parents in America to their presence in our immediate future. I was on board.

Maman had been so excited to have found the piece. Her avocation of playing the piano occasioned stops at the music store in Chicago. She knew exactly where the piano music was kept, and she knew always to make a stop at the "new releases" display where Mr. Stueck conspicuously posted all the sheet music and collections that had come in. Sometimes, weeks if not months elapsed between visits, so this was a time-saving stop for Maman. Over the years, she had grown acquainted with Mr. Stueck, and he not only alerted her to new oeuvres from French or francophone composers, he enlisted her help with translations from time to time.

I'll never forget her entrance into our house the day she found it. The elation exuded from her red, frost-chilled cheeks, and her scarf danced in anticipation of her playing as she twirled it off and hung it on the coatrack. "I stopped at the music store today," she announced, "and Mr. Stueck asked me if I had heard of Jacot Galienne—a new piece had come out by him. 'No,' I said, and he handed me the music and replied, 'a *tourdion*.' Can you imagine? Mr. Stueck had not heard of *tourdions*, but I assured him I had—and I bought the piece on the spot!"

We didn't spend much time wondering who this Galienne was nor what this new *tourdion* might sound like. Maman made a cocktail for Papa moments before he arrived home. She hurried through making dinner, we ate disrespectfully hastily, and we sped without clearing the table to the living room for a sample of the new *tourdion*. Within minutes, we had fallen in love with it—haunting and reminiscent—and spent at least an hour enjoying the tune and dancing.

"Maman found a *tourdion*," Madeleine-Grace announced at last, and Aunt Adèle, simultaneously understanding and grief-stricken, smiled, looked a moment at the iron in her hand, and returned it to her sheets at the board.

The memory of our first evening with the Galienne *tourdion* reminded me of evenings of family dancing here in Etretat-au-Dela. French hits on the radio by Jacques Brel and Dalida could lure us to our feet in the *salle-en-arrière*. Without fail, Maman grabbed Papa by the arm and began some energetic sort of light-hearted but modish dancing. Aunt Adèle and the children were never long in following suit. Then Maman might grab Aunt Pé and Aunt Mirabelle and Aunt Laure, and the children might grab their fathers, and we all danced. Usually, Uncle Romain sat it out and scoffed from an armchair, Astride hopped offbeat with her mother, and Aunt Mirabelle danced with a smooth fluidity that made Uncle Roul smile. I always got a kick out of when an American song came on, like recent hits by Paul Anka or The Diamonds. My cousins tried to sing along but didn't know what they were saying. Listening to Wischard sing along with Paul Anka to the first lines of "Diana" had my parents and me in stitches. The *pièce de résistance* of such evenings was Grandma'Maud's inevitable joining us for these trendy, quick-paced songs she knew nothing about; she danced to them waggishly as if they were *courantes* or *rondeaux* or *farandoles*. To recall her dancing and kicking and laughing made me hope our visit to Paris was not far off.

As we carefully carried the perfect, pre-wrapped packages of folded sheets to the conservatory, tiptoeing through the *salle-en-arrière* as Uncle Roul slept, I didn't imagine we would have more of these dance parties in the backroom anytime soon. Besides Elvis Presley having enlisted a few months ago, Grandma'Maud remained in Paris, and the initiators of the frivolity were not among us. We left the sheets in piles on a table for Aunt Adèle to wrap.

Then we went with Aunt Adèle to our bedroom where she helped us empty our trunks, placing clothes, clean or worn, into the same pile to be laundered. In the bottom of Madeleine-Grace's, wrapped in undergarments, rested two bottles of American whiskey for the Etretat-au-Delà house, and in the bottom of mine, boxes of Pall Mall cigarettes and records for the *tourne-disque*. Aunt Adèle told us that the other trunk with which we had traveled here, now in a closet on the main floor, also contained bottles of gin and bourbon, along with Hershey's kisses, pixy stix, and Hostess cupcakes. Our relatives loved our American chocolates and candies, and they were fascinated last summer when Papa said he remembered when Hostess cupcakes had no filling, prompting the request to bring these treats on our next visit. I was looking forward to a tube of the elvish green pixy dust, myself. Also in the trunk were the board games Careers and Wide World. Grand-mère Armance thought my cousins would enjoy them after the avidity with which they played Candyland when we had brought it several summers ago.

Before leaving our bedroom with baskets full of our clothes, Aunt Adèle surveyed our room, as I was sure she did every day at the times we left it unoccupied, as I was sure she did every day with everyone else's rooms when unoccupied. Our bed already made, our pajamas already folded, our shutters not yet shut, we had met her approval, having kept it tidy, but she did find washing the soap dish in the adjoining washroom necessary.

She washed our clothes at a washbasin outside next to the shed, and we talked with her about Grandma'Maud while she washed. She hung our clothes on the clotheslines to dry, and we talked with her about baseball and tennis and other sports in America.

Before noon, we were en route to town to pick up fabric for our suit and gown. We walked in the direction of the Galimard residence, and two houses before arriving at Jeuffine's, we met a main road that took us straight into *centre-ville*. This road served as a main artery, the connection from *centre-ville* Etretat-au-Delà to our stretch of the *falaises*, to the shores and beaches below the *falaises*, and to neighboring towns. Once in town, shops, stands, and cafés lined either side of this road. It intersected with the town square, usually freeing and open except for days the market set up, encompassed by more cafés, the *terrasses* of restaurants, and the church, Notre Dame de Préservation. Constricted alleys, walkways, and streets connected to other side streets where residences abounded in concentric circles beyond the town center.

The market did not clutter the town square this late morning, and before passing through to arrive at the fabric store, we stopped inside the church. Our aunt headed directly for the candles before a statue of St. Joseph the Worker in the vestibule. She lit three candles. As she lowered the flame to the candle and the white, opaque glass glowed, I noted the dimness of the small church. The stained-glass windows were thin but filtered much light. The gray, unburnished stone walls between them were thicker than the windows. Along the side aisle, only several feet from the statue of St. Joseph, high on a pink marble pedestal stood a prodigious statue of The Blessed Mother. She was of the purest white stone from toe to crown, except on the tip of her crown glowed even in the faint light a star-shaped, light blue gemstone. Aunt Adèle turned to invite us to the candles, but, as if mesmerized, we gravitated toward the statue of The Blessed Mother. It wasn't the star but her glowing white, smooth skin that drew me to her. My sister seemed entranced.

"That's La Vierge Albâtre and our Notre Dame de Préservation," Aunt Adèle said, nearing us. She spoke softly but did not whisper as no one else occupied the church. "You are not used to seeing her here. When she's in the church, she usually overlooks from the choir loft, but this year, they brought her here. She is beautiful, is she not?"

"Yes," I said, still mesmerized by her smooth, white skin and gentle smile.

"Are you looking at her crown?" our aunt asked.

"I'm looking at her eyes," Madeleine-Grace said, herself still entranced. "They are sparkling more than the gemstone."

"The gemstone on her crown is a sapphire—a rare light blue, like a star. 'Marie' means 'of the sea.' La Vierge Marie, she is 'Star of the Sea,' and the blue sea is in her name. She is the preservation of us all as she guides us to her Son, but especially of sailors and fishermen. The rest of her is alabaster, fashioned from the stone of the *falaises*, the very cliffs below our house. On special occasions, the men of the parish hoist her to the top of the dome over the altar, and she glows in the moonlight as a beacon of hope and safety for us all."

Breaking her gaze from the eyes of the Alabaster Virgin took longer for Madeleine-Grace than for me, but she eventually followed Aunt Adèle and me to the candles. The three our aunt had lit flickered side by side.

"One I light for my parents and one for my brother Léon. And now I light one for your parents," Aunt Adèle shared. "Would you like to say a prayer?"

Wishing to do so, we both slipped in to a pew, knelt, and prayed. Initially, I began praying for my parents, but my intentions wandered to my sister, and then turned to prayers of gratitude for her, Aunt Adèle, and *la préservation* and protection of the Alabaster Virgin.

Before leaving the church, we crossed ourselves with holy water and sent our hope in one last glance to The Blessed Mother, our appreciation and awe in one last smile to the Alabaster Virgin. Then we stepped into the brightness and warmth of the town square. In two blocks, we had arrived at and entered the fabric store.

Madame Maillart stepped from around a counter to embrace Madeleine-Grace and me moments after entering *la mercerie*, the fabric store. Approximately the same age of Grandma'Maud, she wore a black dress, black shoes, a crocheted, black shawl, and a metal thimble that I could feel pushing into my shoulder blade on each embrace. She offered condolences and burst into tears. Once she had wiped away her tears with a hanky, she told her adult son behind the counter to bring us candy. He walked around and extended a dish of wrapped *pastis* hard candy. We each took one.

As Aunt Adèle conversed with Madame Maillart and her son about us, about Grandma'Maud, and about the fabric, Madeleine-Grace and I took in the small shop, two walls lined with rolls of fabric of many colors and patterns and materials, and another wall with spools of every thread in different hues and thicknesses. Along the bottom of this wall and in tiered, wooden bins throughout the small *mercerie*, skeins of yarn heaped from their bin. On the shelf of the counter with the register hung manifold knitting, crocheting, sewing, and embroidery supplies, tools, and notions, and on the shelf behind the main counter, each in its own pigeonhole rested layers of laces and ribbons and jars of buttons and snaps. I could see that Madame Maillart had been making a blouse as the design pattern had been laid upon the countertop, dressmaker shears and needles next to it. Aunt Adèle leaned close to it when both the proprietor and her son had their backs turned, no doubt inspecting the quality of their cutting or sewing or something minute.

Once she had the fabrics, we left, taking a minor detour to the first street parallel to the main street. Madeleine-Grace had forgotten, but I remembered what we were passing. When Madeleine-Grace asked Aunt Adèle why we were walking out of our way, I responded before she could. "It's Monsieur Vauquelin's house," I said, grinning at my knowing. Aunt Adèle confirmed the pronouncement, blushing but cheerful to be passing. She suspected he was working on L'Ile d'Aobefein today but had wanted to pass nonetheless.

Our walk home was quick, and when we arrived at the fork in the road, the Galimards' to our right and the Semperrins' to our left, Wischard and little Laure shouted to us a short ways down the road as they ran over. Wischard, his blond hair sticking up in the back and matted to his head in the front, had been out of bed for a half hour now and craved his "morning" *café* but lacked the knowhow to prepare it. He urged us home for his coffee, but we could not speed up after having been working or on our feet for almost nine hours already. Realizing we could not run home with him, Wischard adjusted his pace to our stroll, asking us where we had been.

A glance over my shoulder held the hope of catching a glimpse of the woman whom Aunt Laure called "Jeuffine" since hers was the residence a few places down. I did not see her, and, after Aunt Adèle had explained to Wischard that we had stopped at the *mercerie*, I could not help asking her who Jeuffine was.

"Mademoiselle des Gervais," Aunt Adèle said. "She is the great-niece of Monsieur des Gervais. Do you remember him? We visited him several times when you were in for summer."

"Yes," I said, "the monsieur with the *hydromel*, the *bauchet*." The synonyms referred to a honey liqueur popular here.

"Yes," she said as she chuckled. "He made his own *hydromel*. He passed away two years ago and bequeathed this house to his great-niece, Jeuffine. He had no children, and his brother lives with his family in New York. Mademoiselle des Gervais moved in a little over a year ago. I don't know much, but I believe she had been living in England before taking up residence here."

For some reason, I smiled to recall her long brown hair, her green dress blowing in the breeze, the rose in her hair, and Aunt Adèle saw.

"She is very beautiful, is she not?" she asked me.

I smiled, nodding that she was. Wischard patted me on the back and laughed.

"Too bad she's Uncle Roul's *brouillèe*," he said. I know he was messing around in using *brouillèe*, a Cauchois word for girlfriend. "Aunt Adèle, why does Aunt Mirabelle get so upset about Uncle Roul's *brouillèes*?"

The smile on Aunt Adèle's face straightened. The package of fabric under her arm for the moment crumpled as her arm stiffened.

"How would you feel if your father had a *brouillèe* and not just a wife?" she asked.

"Father does not have a *brouillèe*," Wischard declared, a furrow between his eyebrows.

"No, he does not," Aunt Adèle said. Noting Wischard's reaction—a defensiveness in his crackling voice like the white pebbles underfoot—perhaps Aunt Adèle felt she needn't say more on the subject. "Let's not talk of Aunt Mirabelle and of your good Uncle Roul."

"Uncle Roul is a funny man," said little Laure. "He is sleeping on the couch in the *salle-en-arrière* this morning."

"Yes," agreed Aunt Adèle, staring at the horizon between houses. "He is a—funny—man. Now, children, perhaps I must teach you how to make the coffee yourselves. That way, you will not have to wait for me if I am not here."

"I don't want to learn how to make it," declared Wischard. "I want *you* to make it for me."

"You'll always be here," said little Laure.

Aunt Adèle sighed, loosened the grip on the package of fabric, and escorted us to the house for coffees. Shortly before our arrival, she passed the package to me, took Wischard in her arms, and used her fingers to untangle and groom the blond hair she adored so much.

With only Wischard and little Laure awake when we entered the house, Aunt Adèle kept busy with odds and ends, including taking a few measurements of Madeleine-Grace and me and preparing for tonight's *apéro*. France was playing North Ireland in the World Cup tonight at seven o'clock, and the family planned to listen to the game on the radio. There had been talk of this at the Galimards' soirée yesterday, and Wischard had explained to me that his father had been much angered to have had to pick up my sister and me Sunday evening during France's previous match, but the rest of the family had stayed home to enjoy the victory over Scotland. Wischard said that Aunt Adèle had not made dinner that evening—only an extended *apéritif* hour—and she planned to do the same tonight. My memories of the 1954 World Cup vague at best, I was excited about the evening's unfolding with snacking and sipping and smoking and listening to the match on the radio.

While the four of us ascended the stairs for *mésienne* and washing up, most of the others descended, passing us on the stairs groggily without greeting. As Astride passed Madeleine-Grace, she turned toward the wall while Madeleine-Grace, on the other hand, focused an undemonstrative stare at her cousin. While we lay on the bed, we heard the others eventually return, wash up, and dress. From my spot on the bed, I saw that the vase on the dresser was still empty. Next to me, however, a small glass vase with a few short sprigs of purple-flowered borage and leafy mint from the garden fragrance from the nightstand. I was sure Aunt Adèle must have taken note during her inspection this morning that our room lacked flowers and at some point cut these and filled the tiny vase. When she found the time without us to do these things confounded me sometimes.

When Aunt Adèle knocked, we all headed downstairs—to the veranda instead of the dining room. The radio, usually on the table in the *salle-en-arrière*, had been relocated to a side table on the veranda near the door. Aunt Adèle had loaded the main table on the veranda with platters of victuals. Thick, bite-sized cubes of delicately pan-fried mackerel, *maqueré*, each sprinkled with salt, pepper, and a caperberry, formed a single layer on one platter. On two others, small mountains of yellow-green *picholine* olives rose over hillsides of cured, hard sausage slices, crumbled *parmiggiano reggiano* from Italy, and sprigs of fresh chives. On another two platters, wedges of *camembert* and halves of hard-boiled eggs intruded like cliffs into a sea of tangy *aioli* on which floated cornichons and thinly sliced Tyrolean *speck*, all dusted with the faintest trace of powdered thyme. Although most cheeses were usually reserved for after dinner, they were allowed for an *apéro* that blurred the bounds of a pre-and-post-dinner meal. Four bottles of *cidre*, alcoholic apple cider, stood in the middle, still fizzing when I had stepped onto the veranda.

Madeleine-Grace and I waited near the door for everyone to claim a spot at the table, in a chair against the wall, on the steps leading to the cliffs, or on the stone wall of the veranda. Aunt Adèle was folding napkins, piling them in two stacks next to a tower of small plates. Aunt Pé sat in a chair, her right hand rubbing her left upper arm, and Astride approached her mother, hoping to stand at the table beside her. Her mother, however, brushed her aside, so Astride plopped down against the house wall and crossed her legs. When Aunt Pé lifted her hand to swipe at Astride, I noticed a large bruise on the arm she had been holding.

Young Roul asked if he could have a cigarette, and when his mother insisted he wait, he protested. "It's different tonight. It's the match. Besides, we're outside." Young Roul directed these entreaties not to Aunt Mirabelle but to his father, who signaled with one shake of the head a firm "no."

Uncle Gilbert tuned the radio to the soccer match, and soon the sportscaster was summarizing highlights of the World Cup, revealing tidbits about the players, and announcing kick-off. Uncle Roul poured *cidre* while Uncle Romain brought in another bottle, the American whiskey, and everyone reached for plates and bites from Aunt Adèle's buffet. Ten minutes into the game, my uncles began to smoke, upsetting young Roul, who shook his head in dismay from his spot on the stone veranda wall, his back against a pillar. Ten minutes beyond that, my aunts, while holding *cendrier*s for the men, began to smoke, too, except for Aunt Laure and Aunt Adèle. Aunt Laure stood at the top stair of the three steps leading to the cliffs with her back to the rest of us, little Laure sitting at her foot. Aunt Adèle, between egret-like, inspective glances at the food supply on the table and at the whereabouts of the children, sat in a chair away from the table with a small plate of food, enjoying the broadcast herself.

At moments when the announcers' voices crescendoed in bursts of excitement and our attention snapped to the possibility of a break-away or a goal, our energy escalated, too. Aunt Adèle was the only female caught up in the game, but her reactions, silent ones, manifested in stiffening her frame on the chair, freezing in place with an ear to the radio, or bulging her eyes while spinning her hand in the air as if urging a player to go all the way with the ball. The men took a swig or splashed a refill into their glass after every momentous rush in the match, spilling across the table as they yanked the freshly poured glass to their lips. Once, when all seemed calm in the game, Uncle Roul took a sip, and when the momentum of the game shifted and the announcers erupted with enthusiasm, he accidentally spit out the whiskey and coughed on the bit of liquid that must have trickled down his throat. The spray from his mouth landed on the table, and Aunt Adèle sopped it up with a napkin that moment. Before long, young Roul, too, smoked, passing his cigarette to Alphonse, Wischard, and me in a generosity begotten by joy over the game. Every so often, we heard other families hoot and holler from their houses on the stretch along the *falaises*. I heard a delightful female laugh halfway through the game that I was certain belonged to Jeuffine—to Mademoiselle des Gervais. I may have been mistaken, for when I glanced at Uncle Roul, he did not react to it.

Reaches for snacks, spurts of conversation about players, messy pours that cascaded over both sides of the rim, reclines in tilted chairs, abrupt sittings-to-attention, quick inhales of tobacco, deep, gray exhales of smoke, clinking glasses over small battles won, spills on the tabletop and into laps and onto the floor, cigarette boxes strewn as they emptied onto the ravaged table, cheers for France escalating into song, punches into each other's shoulders and open-handed slams across the back, all the frenzy of a World Cup match complemented the cooling air and the yellows turning to pinks and blues as day darkened to twilight.

Although I knew Aunt Adèle would admonish us if she saw us younger ones sneaking puffs of young Roul's cigarettes, I felt content in those moments. Madeleine-Grace stood beside me, smiling as Wischard and I passed the cigarette from and to young Roul. Amid the vociferations and the delicious bites and sips and enthusiasm over France's momentum over North Ireland, seeing Madeleine-Grace smiling pleased me after her ordeal yesterday. The cheerfulness of almost all of us as our neighbors' cheers echoed across the cliffs oddly comforted me, short-lived as the feeling was.

With ten minutes left in the game and France in the lead, a burst of laughter and hoots and claps sounded from another house before our party did the same. Aunt Laure, standing at the same spot at the top of the steps, now holding a glass of *calva* that Uncle Gilbert had walked over to her, looked from the horizon and the cliffs to the direction of the clatter. "They ought to quiet down," she said.

As my uncles and older cousins and Aunt Adèle cheered and clapped, Aunt Laure turned to us for the first time since the match had started and snapped, "You all ought to quiet down! You're animals!"

Paying her no heed, our cheers continued and abated naturally, not at her urging. Uncle Romain slapped Uncle Gilbert on the back and said, "I think we have this one!"

"Shut-up!" Aunt Laure said, her eyes flashing between Uncle Romain and her husband. "You act like animals, all of you!"

"You pick now to have your breakdown?" asked Uncle Romain. "You can't wait five minutes so that we can enjoy the victory?"

Uncle Roul lifted his glass for a sip and then clicked it for some reason with the *cendrier* Aunt Mirabelle was holding. Whether it was the sound of the click or the comment from Uncle Romain, I do not know; something irritated Aunt Laure to the point that she threw her glass of *calvados* against the wall of the house, smashing it just above the seated Astride's head. The shards and liquid doused the child.

Uncle Roul, incensed in a heartbeat, threw his glass at Aunt Laure, smashing it against the low veranda wall next to the steps. "We're breaking glasses now? I can break them, too, Laure!"

Aunt Pé leaned toward Astride for inspection without rising from her place, insufficient for Uncle Romain, who grabbed his wife by her left arm and flung her from her chair in his attempt to be at his daughter's side. Aunt Adèle was already crouching beside Astride, picking glass out of her hair. I would never have known Astride had been affected, judging by the unperturbed expression she maintained since the beginning of the match.

As the announcers plodded on, as Aunt Mirabelle helped Aunt Pé to her seat, as Uncle Gilbert flung a chair out of the way between him and his wife, Aunt Laure turned and screamed and ran toward the cliffs. Wischard and little Laure stood, staring frantically at the flash of their mother zipping away and their father bolting after her. Aunt Adèle rose, and, taking in Uncle Gilbert's pursuit of his wife and the terror in their children's eyes, rushed to Wischard and little Laure and embraced them both from behind, an arm around each, and turned them toward her. Young Roul, Alphonse, Chardine, Madeleine-Grace, and I, however, stared over the veranda railing to see Uncle Gilbert gaining on Aunt Laure, a shrieking, unbroken mare on a mad dash. And as she never slowed, Uncle Gilbert accelerated and overtook her, flinging her to the ground with his arm around her waist. We heard her screams through strange, heaving sobs as the ground crunched under their bodies. Our distant neighbors cheered over the game once more, and the announcers erupted in victory cries on the radio.

In the eerie stillness of that moment, the radio announcers declared France the victor.

The next few days unfolded like variations on a theme: Aunt Adèle worked on odds and ends from early in the morning until late in the evening while Madeleine-Grace and I offered help, paused for coffee and *mésienne*, enjoyed dinner, and idled on the veranda. Wischard became more inquisitive about our life in America, which I appreciated, but any mention of life in America brought to mind my parents and evoked a sullenness that sometimes took hours to shake. The same feeling lingered whenever I dreamt of them.

I awoke the Thursday of the soccer match to a commotion in the middle of the night, which I determined to be wailing from Aunt Laure, whom Uncle Gilbert had carried to her faint in the bedroom. This commotion woke me from a dream about my mother, and I resented the interruption. She was more real to me in my dreams than in my recollections. In the dream, she brought me a muslin dishtowel and opened it over me, allowing freshly picked herbs to fall on and around me as I sat in the lawn. I picked up a sprig of parsley, surprised to see how clean and trim it was, as if Aunt Adèle and my mother had already sifted through them for imperfections. Yet here she appeared, pouring them on me with a big smile instead of saving them for a delicious meal. I looked up at her, ready to ask why, when the noise from the hall woke me. At least in this case, I fell back asleep, escaping the prolonging of the feeling of emptiness, the one that accompanies the reluctant knowledge of possessing a void never again to be filled.

Aunt Laure, confined to her room, never made an appearance in any of our affairs those next few days, and Uncle Gilbert spent most of his time in the room with her. Wischard and little Laure were allowed in only to kiss her good-night. When we went upstairs for our *mésienne*, I could not resist looking through the keyhole to see Aunt Laure sprawled on the faint with her eyes closed, her arm straight and hanging over the side, while Uncle Gilbert sat in a chair near the terrace doors reading. My poor little cousins—they knew something was not right with their mother but did not know how to express concern and knew better than to inquire about it.

"Are you worried about your mother?" Chardine asked Wischard one evening while the cousins sat cross-legged in a circle trying to play *p'tits chouaux* like our friends down the road. Wischard was on my left and Madeleine-Grace on my right.

"I know everything will go back to normal in a few days," he replied without eye contact.

"Maman said she would have run straight off the cliff if Uncle Gilbert hadn't caught her," Chardine added as she gripped a figurine.

Wischard looked up as if to say, "I know," but he could not say the words. He looked at me for some sort of understanding or sympathy, I think, and to my regret, I looked away. I did not know how to respond to the plea in his eyes, to the breath that he lost, to the possibility of him becoming like me. When I looked back, Wischard was staring at his hands, and I could see a tear running down the side of his face. I don't know what compelled me to do so, but I put my arm around him the way my father would when I cried. Wischard sunk into it before rising and leaving the game.

He wasn't the only one to cry that evening. After we had gone to sleep, I had another dream, this time of my father. I was sitting on this very bed facing the window as morning gold illuminated the room. I heard my father's voice say "*pourions.*" Father was placing a small bunch of jonquils in the vase, and turned and smiled at his accomplishment of having gathered flowers first thing and having filled the vase for Maman before she awoke. He was still in his pajamas and with a smile unfading sat beside me on the bed and put his comforting arm around me. I leaned into him, knowing he was appreciating his work with the flower vase; I felt his warmth and in that dream could smell him. And then the dream ended, and I woke with tears in my eyes. I sat on my bed, my legs over the side facing the window, just as I had in the dream, only I was alone. I think I hoped living the dream might bring my father there in real life. Madeleine-Grace awoke and crawled over the bed to me.

"You're crying," she said.

"No." I don't know why I said no.

"I can see your tears in the moonlight. Are you crying about Maman and Papa?" she said in a hush.

"Yes," I replied. I wiped away my tears from my eyes but knew some remained on my face. Madeleine-Grace wiped one away with her finger and then hugged me.

"I know," she said.

We sat like that in the moonlight for I don't know how long.

The vase was still empty.

After a few minutes, we crawled back to our spot on the bed and fell asleep.

I was tired the next day and almost fell off the footstool on which Aunt Adèle had me stand for a fitting. No one noticed. Aunt Adèle, Madeleine-Grace, and I were in the conservatory, which, aside from her bedroom in the attic, was the place she did most of her sewing and knitting, her ironing, and her folding. Large picture windows occupied two full walls of the rectangular conservatory, offering glimpses through the blinds and beyond the myrtle-green drapes of the herb and flower islands, the lawn, and the cliffs. Hanging vines and marble-topped étagères holding potted plants lined the perimeter of the room, and within, wicker couches, armchairs, and ottomans with forest-green cushions and cream or chalcedony pillows furnished the center of the room. Between the furniture and the far wall of windows, Aunt Adèle's work station boasted her wooden tables and chairs, her mother's sewing machine, her *mercerie* baskets, and countless other tools and knickknacks in compartments and drawers of waist-high wicker shelves interspersed among lush, tall ferns and stiff mother-in-law's tongues in floor planters. Recessed into half the wall parallel the lawn and cliffs was a closet with open-weave rattan doors housing more of her notions, piles of fabrics, skeins of yarn, spools of thread, and several more *mercerie* baskets with yarn, knitting needles, and crochets.

When Sunday rolled around, Aunt Adèle woke all the young cousins for church. She had placed our Sunday outfits at the foot of the bed, calling our attention to them when she woke us. Although she woke us earlier than even Madeleine-Grace and I were used to waking, she had also sent us to bed earlier on Saturday. Our other uncles and aunts had gone to a soirée at the Graverand house in Fécamp and left Aunt Adèle at home to watch us. Uncle Gilbert remained home to watch after Aunt Laure but kept confined to their room. Aunt Adèle had full authority to send us to bed when she wanted, and she chose an uncharacteristically early hour, so much so that falling asleep actually took longer than usual. She wished to guarantee the ease of our next morning's waking.

Once we had all washed and dressed, we lined up in the foyer as Aunt Adèle looked over each of us. She pushed our hair down in places, pulled my shirt cuffs from under my sport coat, and brushed all the girls' hair except for Madeleine-Grace.

"Why are you not brushing Madeleine-Grace's hair?" Astride asked.

"Madeleine-Grace knows to brush her hair at night and then again in the morning," Aunt Adèle said.

"My mother taught me to do that, of course," Madeleine-Grace said, looking bluntly at Astride.

All the girls then placed a lacey mantille on their heads.

Having passed Aunt Adèle's inspection, we walked from the house into town. Once in the town square, we joined the many Etretat-au-Delà residents as they, too, donning their Sunday bests, entered the church. Several persons acquainted with my aunt also greeted us, some offering condolences, some sufficing to pat us on the head. The priest standing at the door spoke only to Aunt Adèle, never to us, about our return.

The Semperrin family took up one pew on the left side of the center aisle. Aunt Adèle sat farthest from the nave, but one row behind us across the nave sat Monsieur Vauquelin with his family. I saw Aunt Adèle smile and wave to him, and once he greeted her, he waved to Madeleine-Grace and me, his smile crinkling his eyes. In the light of stained glass, I saw that he was younger than Aunt Adèle, and somehow I knew this youth would stay with him all his life.

After Mass, we remained in the pew for prayer, and although I should have been praying, I looked across the nave for Monsieur Vauquelin. He and his family no longer occupied their pews in the nearly empty church, but a look beyond their pews revealed Monsieur Vauquelin standing alone before the alabaster statue of La Vierge. At the moment I recognized him, he knelt before her, smiled at her, and then bowed his head as he crossed himself and prayed.

"I want to say hi to the Alabaster Virgin," Madeleine-Grace whispered, unaware Monsieur Vauquelin was occupying her. "She told me to visit."

I assumed she meant Aunt Adèle had told her, but I didn't know when she had made this suggestion. Then it occurred to me that perhaps our aunt knew Monsieur Vauquelin to visit La Vierge and thought a visit from Madeleine-Grace would occasion them to unite.

"You'll have to wait until Monsieur Vauquelin is finished praying to her," I said.

"He is now," Madeleine-Grace responded as she took my hand to walk to the statue. Monsieur Vauquelin had just arisen, crossed himself, and stepped from the statue. When he saw us approaching, he stopped and watched us kneel before Our Lady. I prayed for our parents foremost, prayers of gratitude for them and prayers of protection over them. I also prayed for our family, suggesting Our Lady ask God to make Aunt Laure better so that Wischard could feel better. Madeleine-Grace, as she prayed, glowed in white light, as if the alabaster of La Vierge radiated and illumined her.

By the time we had finished praying, Aunt Adèle was lighting a candle with Monsieur Vauquelin by her side and our cousins behind her. Madeleine-Grace dipped a candle's wick into the flame of Aunt Adèle's newly lit candle, and lit one herself. Aunt Adèle dropped a few coins into a slot and ushered us out quietly. Outside the church, many had huddled in small clusters to chat, and Lady Victorine and Lady Léontine called over Aunt Adèle. Before heading to them, she said to Monsieur Vauquelin, "Alban, will you join us for dinner Thursday night." He grinned in the twinkling sunlight warming the town square, and said he would be glad to join us for dinner.

As Aunt Adèle led the way to her friends, I reminded Monsieur Vauquelin about his invitation, asking, "Are you still going to take me to L'Ile d'Aobefein one day?"

He placed a hand on my head and said, "Yes, I would like to arrange that soon."

I smiled and rejoined my aunt and cousins.

After chatter had subsided and gatherers had dispersed, we walked to our house, a leisurely stroll through a day growing hotter. If Aunt Adèle had noticed Wischard and me unbuttoning our cuff and collar buttons, she did not deter us, and she certainly did not reprimand us for taking off our sport coats, nor the girls for taking off their mantilles. Of course, she did have a few words for young Roul when she saw that, by the time we had reached the final stretch of road to our house, he had taken off his sport coat and shirt entirely, walking in public bare-skinned.

I had expected, once we had arrived home, to see our uncles playing *la choule* across the yards with their friends, but Thiessé Galimard and Hardouin Loiselier, along with a few other regulars, had left Etretat-au-Delà for a weekend with their families in Deauville, so the usual Sunday games went unplayed. The expectation of the sight brought to mind my father playing with them last summer, and it dawned on me that today was Fathers' Day. The Semperrin family had not adopted the new custom of celebrating the holiday on the third Sunday of June but preferred to maintain the older tradition of celebrating it on St. Joseph's Day. Their celebration had come and gone, and Madeleine-Grace's and mine would never be. Before long, I felt glad there was no game to watch because seeing the fathers would have made me miss mine all the more, and I hadn't picked out a present for him, hadn't even thought of one.

With most curtains clasped and the inside shutters closed, the house, dim and cool, offered relief from the onslaught of heat. We all changed into everyday clothes, and after a snack of canned sardines on fresh bread, we dispersed to spend our day at our leisure. Madeleine-Grace and I of habit now followed Aunt Adèle to the kitchen to help her prepare dinner. For tonight she was prepping pork chops! By the time we arrived in the kitchen, she had already set up.

Our aunt had set the plate with the chops towering on them next to a giant, wide-brimmed bowl of water. We watched her lift a chop, puncture it several times with the tines of a fork, and set it in the bowl of water. Madeleine-Grace and I scooched our chairs close for a keen look, Madeleine-Grace crouching instead of sitting on the chair bottom. Aunt Adèle lifted another chop, punctured it with the fork, and set it in the bowl of water.

To our surprise, Aunt Pé entered the kitchen. She had evidently already washed and dressed and was up for the day. Before approaching the stove or the cupboards, she stopped to see our activity, leaned a hand on the table, and scoffed. Then she folded both arms and stood straight.

"Makes no difference, putting the pork chops in the water. Why do you waste your time?" she declared. Despite the interrogative, her words had no intonation and required no answer.

"It does make a difference," Aunt Adèle said, repeating the procedure with another chop.

"I watched your mother make it, and I made it myself. It does nothing. It's but a wives' tale," Aunt Pé persisted. Bending toward us, riled by Aunt Adèle's insistence on continuing, she said to us, "This was your father's mother's recipe. They brought it back from America and made it for Grandma'Maud in Paris. She loved it. She made it for us one night, and I watched her. Really it was delicious when she made it, so my husband asked me to make it. I soaked the meat for hours beforehand, and it did nothing."

"Maybe you were doing something wrong," Aunt Adèle said, placing another piece of punctured pork in the bowl, moving on to the next in the shortening tower of chops.

"How hard could this be? The next time I made it, I did not soak the chops. It tasted the same as the time I made it when I had soaked them. Exactly the same. My husband said so."

"But did they taste exactly the same as Maman's or Armance's?" asked Aunt Adèle, not removing an eye from her task.

Pé scoffed, interlocked arms, and turned her back on her sister-in-law. "It's pointless, I tell you. Go ahead and waste your time."

Aunt Pé left the kitchen where Aunt Adèle continued in silence to our avid vigilance, especially now that we knew it was Grand-mère Armance's recipe that had met Grandma'Maud's approval. As she worked, a smile formed. I noticed and smiled, too, unsure why. With three more chops to go, she stopped and looked at us, her smile wide.

"Come here and look," she said, giving us a few seconds to hop from our chairs. "Look at that. Does that look like water to you?"

We looked into the bowl of water, somewhat clear but now murky with particles of pork.

"I don't want you to taste it now, but your mother and father were not so stupid, and neither was your grand-mère. But Aunt Pé—." Whatever she was thinking she did not say. We giggled but did not know why. "This isn't just water, Ellande and Madeleine-Grace. It's water with apple cider vinegar and *sel gris*. I stirred it in so that all the salt dissolved, and then I put the chops in to tenderize and flavor the pork. It's called a brine."

"Is a brine a secret potion that only Grand-mère Armance knows, and she told it to Maman and Papa? And they told it to Grandma'Maud in Paris one day?" Madeleine-Grace asked as if she were learning of a clandestine meeting among fairies sharing spells in a folktale.

"No, it is no secret. Everyone would know you don't soak pork chops in plain water. Everyone would know you need a brine of some sort if you're going to soak them at all. But Pé, not her. She says she watched and learned, but she never has."

We remained next to Aunt Adèle as she finished the process, and as she submerged the last chop, Madeleine-Grace asked, "Aunt Adèle, did Monsieur Vauquelin give you the *sel gris*?"

Madeleine-Grace and I both smiled at the insinuation, and so did our aunt as she rose to wash her hands in the kitchen sink. She dried them with a dishtowel and then rubbed them down her apron, forming deep green spots amid the expanse of light green, like a shadow over an open field of mint. Then she said, "Yes, Monsieur Vauquelin brought the *sel gris*, so these chops will be extra delicious." We giggled again.

The conversations over dinner that night broached many truncated topics, from France's upcoming World Cup match against Brazil to the World Cup stadiums in Sweden, which neighbors Norway, which Uncle Léon had visited in May of 1940; from our walk to church—a pointless one according to Uncle Romain—to Grand-père Semperrin rolling over in his grave to know his children had slept through Mass, according to Aunt Adèle; from Uncle Gilbert's expectation of Aunt Laure's imminent return to Young Roul's inability to advance in his new romance with Henriette Loiselier. Every one of the topics made someone feel uncomfortable or had someone defensively or angrily slamming a fist on the table while bringing someone else to a beaming smile if not a burst of laughter.

To me the deliciousness of the dinner stood out most that evening. The platter of chops before us had, since the brining earlier that day, been seasoned with herbs and other flavorings and broiled to perfection. Aunt Pé could not hide the shock on her expression after her first bite of the moist, salty chop, and her husband rendered her speechless when he announced that they tasted exactly like the ones my parents had made on a visit to the Paris residence. I took a special delight in knowing that my parents and grandparents were responsible for something so good, something so catching that the whole family wanted to be in on.

Grand-mère Armance used to come to our house in River Forest just to make special meals for my father and to teach my mother some of her recipes. I was grateful Aunt Adèle learned these things so keenly. To be enjoying one of her recipes as my father would have—it made me smile and prompted me to lift my glass of cider and, before taking a sip, to wish Papa a Happy Fathers' Day. I thought he would have been happy to see Madeleine-Grace and me enjoying one of his mother's dishes on this day, and I was glad to conceal a toast to him.

CHAPITRE 4

I stood on the stepstool while Aunt Adèle took some kind of measurement—something for the hems of my pants for the ball. With the windows of the conservatory unblocked, not only did the sunlight brighten the room, but it warmed it, and I was growing restless standing so still in the heat. Madeleine-Grace stood before the open closet door enjoying the fabric tiers of many colors. I knew she could not wait for her ball gown to be realized by Aunt Adèle, but our aunt had reminded us that making the outfits would take some time.

While my aunt worked with needles on the hemline of a pant leg, I did not wish to interrupt her concentration with a question I decided was pressing. Prior to our fitting and tailoring, as I was about to round the corner of the upstairs hall for the staircase, I had seen Aunt Adèle at Aunt Laure's bedroom door. Uncle Gilbert was blocking the doorway of her admittance and any view of Aunt Laure, and I heard him say, "You know you will only make things worse for her." Aunt Adèle said that she hadn't seen her sister in days and was concerned, but Uncle Gilbert assured her that his wife had improved and was rejoining the family soon. I decided to pretend that I hadn't heard what Uncle Gilbert had said about making things worse. My impatience overtook me as I stood on the stepstool, immobile, for what felt like an hour.

"Aunt Adèle, have you seen Aunt Laure yet?" I asked at last.

She stopped what she was doing, but not out of some sort of alarm. She had finished in that moment and, releasing my pant leg, reclined onto an ottoman behind her.

"I have not seen her in days, Ellande," she said, looking at the needle and thread in her hand. Madeleine-Grace walked to us and sat on the ottoman beside Aunt Adèle. For some reason, I stayed on the stool. "I tried to visit her this morning, but—."

When she did not finish, I fessed up. "But Uncle Gilbert turned you away," I said, suspecting that Wischard, who would have been proud of my eavesdropping, would have disapproved of my admission.

"So you heard?" Aunt Adèle said. "I was not sure who was standing in the hall, but I was sure someone was."

"What did Uncle Gilbert say to you?" Madeleine-Grace asked.

"He said that I could only make things worse, so I must wait for her return to the family on her own."

"How could your checking on her make things worse?" I asked— the real question I wanted to ask.

Aunt Adèle did not answer, but as her eyes reddened and watered, she sighed and shrugged.

"Is it because Aunt Laure has resented you for many years?" Madeleine-Grace asked, stopping Aunt Adèle, who was about to rise from the ottoman.

"Aunt Laure does not resent me. She is undergoing a serious illness, and any one of us would be a distraction to her recovery. Uncle Gilbert is being cautious. He would have said the same to Uncle Romain or Uncle Roul."

"Uncle Romain or Uncle Roul would not have visited. You or—my mother—would check on her, and you and my mother are the two she most wishes to avoid," Madeleine-Grace said. And I knew she was right. I knew from conversations at dinner since arriving here and from looks Aunt Laure had given Aunt Adèle and from innuendos in conversations with my mother and father at home.

"Aunt Adèle!" shouted Wischard from outside. We could hear him through the glass of the conservatory windows easily. I stayed on the stool as Aunt Adèle and Madeleine-Grace went to the window to see him wave us over.

We hurried through the *salle-en-arrière* and out the door. With a smile on their faces, Wischard and little Laure began running toward the cliffs and waving us along. We followed, and as the sea came into view, we saw a *voilier* nearing, a sailboat, and a woman in a wide-brimmed hat waving from within it. She was accompanied by two men, one of similar venerable age and one younger, doing the sailing. Aunt Adèle waved back, and we did the same, unsure to whom we were waving.

"Aunt Melisende!" shouted Wischard. "We saw her first!" Little Laure held her brother's arm as she jumped up and down, less out of over-excitement at the arrival but more to ensure being noticed, and Wischard stood on his tiptoes as if to make sure his continual wave was seen.

When Wischard said "Aunt Melisende," which is what we all called her, he meant "Great-Aunt Melisende," for she was our Grandma'Maud's sister, the gentleman beside her her husband Ferdinand, and the young sailor their great-nephew on Uncle Ferdinand's side, Jules. Aunt Melisende lived year-round in Le Havre but spent much of the year visiting relatives and friends in Paris, Rouen, and Etretat-au-Delà on her side and Fécamp and Dieppe on her husband's side. Between them, they knew all of Pays de Caux, it seemed.

I looked at Aunt Adèle to see her reaction to Aunt Melisende's nearing the shores below, and the smile on her face was one of both joy and relief.

Within the interminable hour of the late morning, Aunt Melisende arrived by car to the front drive, and by that time, Aunt Adèle had already made iced tea and a platter of finger sandwiches, returned her sewing materials to their places in the conservatory, and tidied the veranda, to which she had tended much earlier that morning. Aunt Melisende's step through the front door was accompanied by a wail of lamentation over us, a howl of joy over Aunt Adèle, a sigh of exhaustion over arrival, and, within moments, a stern admonishment from Uncle Gilbert at the top of the stairs over the commotion that could rile his wife. He did not greet Aunt Melisende expressing the slightest cordiality, and she did not greet him feeling the slightest slight over his brusqueness. His point made, he stormed back to his bedroom, and while Wischard and little Laure shrunk in fear, Aunt Melisende pulled them into her embrace with Madeleine-Grace and me.

A young man—not the sailor—carried a valise to the door, setting it beside Aunt Melisende. He ran to the car and back with a bag that he set on a foyer table. She kissed him and sent him on his way. "Ferdinand's nephews—they are good boys. Jules sailed us here, and Marguerin met us in the car and drove me up. Ferdinand and Jules continued by sea to Fécamp to visit his brother, and Marguerin will meet them there. They are good boys, taking care of their aunt and uncle this way, as are you, helping your Aunt Adèle and now your Aunt Melisende, am I not right?"

She sent little Laure to the kitchen with the bag from the foyer table, and Aunt Adèle, unable to leave little Laure to the easy task alone, followed her. Aunt Melisende corralled the rest of us into another embrace, holding it until Aunt Adèle returned.

We sat on the veranda, and Aunt Melisende, relieved to sip the iced tea, fell back into the cushion of the chair and laughed. She wore a gray dress that hit above the ankle and had black needlework along the bottom hem, matching the work at the bottom of mid-arm-length sleeves and the neckline. She kept on her wide-brimmed hat, the brim and crown straw in color with a band of black and gray ribbon. Where her hat met her forehead, I saw beads of sweat, which she dabbed with a kerchief after her first few gulps of tea. Aunt Adèle refilled her glass.

"Thank-you for the cheese, Aunt Melisende," Aunt Adèle said. "*Pecorino?*"

"I know you like that one, and Ferdinand's friends the Thuilliers brought back many cheeses from their trip to Italy. I set aside the *pecorino* for you. Did you see also the *cigliege di Vignola* and the *coppa Piacentina*? They spent days in Ravenna. They are too good to bring us back so much, so I must share it with those who enjoy it."

"You did not have to do so. Thank-you, Aunt Melisende," Aunt Adèle said, blushing and shaking her head.

"It was no bother," she continued. "They brought so many varieties. You love the Italian cheeses, my Adèle. Do you remember your trip with your father to Italy before the war? You talked about it every day and would not have stopped had war not broken out."

"I could never forget my time in Italy—just my father and Juliette. To Liguria and then to Rome and Napoli and Sorrento." Aunt Adèle glowed as if the sun reached the shaded veranda.

"You and Juliette. You and Juliette," Aunt Melisende said. Then she looked at Madeleine-Grace and me and drooped her head, heaving with sobs. Unable to lean forward to us, she called us to her with her hands, and we rose from our chairs to allow her to embrace us again. Then we returned to our chair and poured ourselves some iced tea.

"Though uncustomary, I will serve the *pecorino* tonight for *apéro*, Aunt Melisende, with *cidre*."

"I look forward to this," responded Aunt Melisende.

Aunt Melisende explained that she had grown bored of drives, having spent Friday and Saturday with Grandma'Maud in Paris, and convinced her husband to sail to Etretat-au-Delà and Fécamp. Their great-nephews Jules and Marguerin, all too happy to spend a day sailing and driving, saw to every convenience for them. As she described the gentle, breeze-heavy passage on the *voilier* from Le Havre to Etretat-au-Delà, I wished I were with them; the *paquebot* journey kept me at a distance from the water whereas a sailboat journey allowed for dips of the hand into the water and even dives and short swims.

When Jules brought them to shore below the cliffs, Marguerin met Aunt Melisende and brought her up in his car. Uncle Ferdinand stayed behind in the sailboat so that Jules could continue with him to Fécamp. Uncle Ferdinand planned to stay with his family in Fécamp for several days while Aunt Melisende stayed here. Then, Marguerin would pick up Aunt Melisende and drive her to Fécamp to join her husband for a few days before they returned to Le Havre.

"I spent two lovely days with my sister in Paris," Aunt Melisende said, "but Paris, it's much too hot. The heat is not a problem for children, however. Your Grandma'Maud wishes very much to see you and is expecting you this weekend. Are you not happy to see her, too?"

We both smiled, excited at the prospect of visiting Grandma'Maud and the city, although I felt a longing for the days when Grandma'Maud joined us in Etretat-au-Delà for much of the summer. Apparently, her health precluded extended stays or even short visits to the summer house.

"She longs with a broken heart to see you," Aunt Melisende continued. Then to Wischard and little Laure, she said, "Where is your mother? Sleeping? She is sleeping so deeply she could not be disturbed by my humble visit?"

"Laure has not been feeling well," Aunt Adèle said before the children had to explain.

"But Papa says she will be returning to us today," Wischard announced, smiling with the love that a son feels for his once absent, soon-returning mother. "I asked Papa last night, and he said that she wishes to come down today."

"It is almost noon, and she has found it decent not to come down?" questioned Aunt Melisende. "Alas, they all have found it so." She scoffed, and after a shake of her head meant for Aunt Adèle to see, took another long gulp of iced tea.

No one spoke for a moment, and then Aunt Melisende signaled for me to come over. She asked for a hand up, and I helped her stand.

"Do you know what your grandmother and I sang together in Paris after dinner?" she asked. "We sang 'Meunier, Tu Dors' over and over, faster and faster! We did not grow up with this one. Your uncle Léon learned it somewhere and taught it to us." She laughed and then began singing to us the nursery-rhyme tune about a miller, a *meunier*, who sleeps so much that the watermill, the *moulin*, spins too quickly. She repeated the refrain, each time more quickly, laughing through the lyrics. "*Meunier, tu dors*," she said to Wischard, and mercurially added with detectable disgust, "*Et tes parents et toute la famille Semperrin dorment, n'est-ce pas?*" She looked at Madeleine-Grace and smiled again to the refrain.

We talked more on the veranda, and between every line of conversation, Aunt Melisende told me that we must visit our grandmother in Paris and chased the demand with a rousing rendition of "Meunier, Tu Dors," inciting us all to join.

In America, we learned nursery rhymes like "Jack and Jill," "Peter, Peter, Pumpkin Eater," and "Little Miss Muffet." "Frère Jacques," another famous French *comptine* involving sleeping, was one all the American children knew, too. But our parents had also recited to us "Il Etait une Fermière" and "Une Poule sur un Mur," which had been sung to them in France. "Meunier, Tu Dors" was not a traditional one for us but one more recently established, one Grandma'Maud got a kick out of and adopted as her own.

Aunt Melisende, after a while, insisted that she not keep Aunt Adèle from her housework, but reiterated amazement that the others had not risen. She shadowed Aunt Adèle as Madeleine-Grace and I were wont to do, only at a much slower pace than we. Wischard and little Laure grew weary of Aunt Melisende and embraced any opportunity to avoid housework, so they walked to the cliffs to sit on the lookout for more sailboats. When Aunt Melisende suggested a nap, she found respite on the couch in the *salle-en-arrière* as no bedrooms were available. At the same time, Aunt Adèle had sent us up for our *mésienne*.

We returned, washed and refreshed with the parade of others for *apéritif* hour, which, as usual was waiting upon our arrival downstairs. Our aunts and uncles exchanged greetings with Aunt Melisende on the veranda as we gathered around the table. Uncle Gilbert, the last to join, apologized to Aunt Melisende for his abrupt greeting, but the conspicuous absence of Aunt Laure stirred worry and consternation for Wischard and little Laure.

"Where is Maman?" Wischard asked.

"She promised to return today," little Laure reminded him.

"She—she remains unwell," Uncle Gilbert said as if choosing his words with care.

The expression of worry on Wischard's face and the expression of anticipation on little Laure's turned to pure sadness. Little Laure did not resist crying, and Wischard swallowed the ache in his throat in order to fight tears of his own.

"In what way is she 'unwell?'" asked Aunt Melisende without the least bit of concern.

Uncle Gilbert, I could tell, did not want to answer and at first turned red but then furrowed his brow, as if her question had put him on the spot deliberately and sought to attack the character of Aunt Laure. But before he could respond in any way, with a lie for an explanation or an indignant disavowal of answering, Aunt Melisende started singing "Meunier, Tu Dors." Except for Uncle Gilbert and his children, everyone chimed in with her through the lyrics.

Then she turned on them all. "The windmill is spinning too quickly because the miller is sleeping. Ha, at least he works at all, is that not right, Romain? At least the miller is a miller at all, right, Roul?"

The accusation had no chance to sink in before Aunt Melisende grew cheerful again and sang the refrain once more. "Your mother and I sang this the other night after dinner, and we laughed. Do you remember when Léon taught it to her? She made him sing it again and again until she knew the words, and then she sang it with you."

I could tell Uncle Romain wanted to respond to Aunt Melisende's question but could not find a way through her barrier of song, and when his brother sang along, he resigned.

"Your mother wishes very much to see her grandchildren. Therefore, you must visit this week," she announced.

Uncle Roul stopped singing as he lifted *cidre* to his lips. Aunt Mirabelle and Aunt Pé, who had not yet smiled nor joined in song beyond a murmur, looked at their husbands with stony faces. Uncle Romain, the only one to betray his sentiment with reddening cheeks and rolling eyes, said, "This week will not work. Maman will have to wait."

"I told her you would arrive by this weekend at the latest. That gives you plenty of time to alter your busy schedules," Aunt Melisende said.

"This weekend? It's already—." Uncle Romain realized how hollow and futile finishing the sentence would be. It was Monday.

"This weekend at the latest," Aunt Melisende repeated. "The Loiselier children often visit their grandmother without her having to request an invitation, as do Ansgot, Brigitte, and Maclou Galimard. What a laughing stock you would become if you didn't afford your own mother the same courtesy when she already has had to make the request."

Uncle Romain refused to hide his ire as he slammed his *cidre* on the table and stormed down the veranda steps toward the cliffs. Once in the lawn beyond the veranda, he shouted, "It is the World Cup!"

He marched for the cliffs as Uncle Roul reiterated Uncle Romain's concerns. "France has recently beaten North Ireland in the World Cup, and there is sure to be a match this weekend," he said to Aunt Melisende, more composed than his brother.

"Surely, we must see how France does tomorrow night, should we not? I predict this Pelé of Brazil will be a wonder," she said, finishing her *cidre*.

"Fontaine is a wonder!" reported Uncle Roul. I think he had not been expecting Aunt Melisende to have any knowledge of the World Cup matches. He turned his back to his aunt and walked to the veranda rail, leaning on it with his *cidre* in hand. Uncle Romain had begun his saunter back to the house.

I reached for a chiseled piece of *pecorino*. Aunt Adèle had placed a rugged hill of *pecorino* the color of white gold in the middle of a plate with a stream of herbed honey around it the color of yellow gold. She had ground the mint, lavender, and thyme so finely that each fleck looked like a speck of forest green powder. I dredged the coarse piece of cheese through the speckled honey and bit the honey-dipped end. The granules crunched in my mouth, their salt mixing pleasantly with the sweetness of the honey, the sweetness tempered by the aromatics of the herbs. I enjoyed a sip of *cidre* to wash it down. Aunt Adèle saw my smile after this taste.

"You like it, Ellande?" she asked. And as I nodded yes, she explained, "When your mother and I were in Italy, a friend of our father served us a dessert of *pecorino*—just a small wedge—a dollop of *millefiori* honey, and half a pear. It was so simple. It was so delicious."

"So the *cidre* takes the place of the pear," said an impressed Aunt Melisende, "and adds a little something else. I see why you could not wait until after dinner to serve this."

"She is a genius," said Aunt Mirabelle, tossing a piece of *pecorino* in her mouth.

"I'm just glad Laure isn't here to throw another tantrum over your trip to Italy," said Uncle Roul. Aunt Melisende turned her head to him slowly, wondering at the comment's meaning, when Uncle Roul released a burst of laughter, as did Uncle Romain as he reentered the veranda, and immediately thereafter, Aunt Pé. Uncle Gilbert scoffed and turned his back on us.

"I think it is delicious this way, too, Adèle," said Aunt Melisende.

"Me, too!" said Alphonse, swiping a few pieces of cheese, dragging them through the honey, and tossing them in his mouth. "Maman is right," he added, unaware that Aunt Mirabelle found her son's words and reaction to the food unsettling; she threw herself into a chair.

"What did you put in the honey?" Uncle Romain asked, squeezing his face as if he had just sucked a lemon.

"I infused it with ground thyme, lavender, and mint," Aunt Adèle responded.

"You ground it so finely that I can't spit the herbs out," Uncle Romain said.

"I like the herbs in it," Alphonse said, passing a piece of dipped cheese to Chardine.

"I like it, too," Chardine said, enjoying her piece.

"I'm afraid I am not getting any younger, my dear ones, and must think of retiring early tonight," Aunt Melisende said, directing her words to Uncle Gilbert, whose back was still turned. "Will my room be ready for an early bedtime, Gilbert?"

Aunt Melisende and Uncle Ferdinand always took the room with the terrace over the veranda, the former room of my Grandma'Maud. It was always understood that when she visited, everyone accommodated so that she could occupy this room at the top of the stairs with the least walking and the most beautiful view of the cliffs. Her stays never lasted beyond a few days, and as my mother had stressed summers past, deferring to the generations before our own was the unquestionable action to take. To my limited knowledge, she had never had to ask for the room, so I assumed she brought it up this time on account of uncertainty over Aunt Laure's unwellness up there and her desire to adjourn early.

Uncle Gilbert turned and said softly, "Laure will not be able to relinquish the room this evening. She remains unwell."

"I have a better word for it than 'unwell,'" Aunt Melisende said.

Oblivious to Aunt Melisende, little Laure, flailing her hands, said as if protesting her father's announcement, "But Maman said she would return to us today."

Uncle Gilbert lifted a hand to his daughter, indicating to her to desist. She stopped talking and flailing in the same moment. At the suddenness of his daughter's halt, he seemed to feel guilty and lowered his hand.

"My wife has asked that you request another room," he said, maintaining composure before turning his back once again, slowly this time, and entering the house.

"She has 'asked,' he says," said Aunt Melisende, staring at his back as he walked away. Then to us, she said, "Our dear Laure has asked that her aunt request another room, conveniently no longer able to return to her family."

After a moment of silence broken only by a sniffle from little Laure trying to hide her crying, Aunt Adèle offered her room. "Please, Aunt Melisende, I know it is not convenient, but you are welcomed to my room. I will prepare it right now."

"Thank-you, my dear Adèle, but I am sure I, regretfully, cannot do two sets of stairs both up and down. You are most kind to offer, but I must decline."

Aunt Adèle knew not to contest her aunt's wishes, but no one else spoke. Every one of my aunts and uncles on the veranda, along with every one of my cousins, looked either at their feet or toward the horizon. The sun, just over the horizon, loomed oppressively in the right spot to make a glance in that direction blinding. The silence felt more blinding than deafening.

Aunt Melisende, waiting for someone to reconnect with her, spoke. "Then perhaps I must—"

"You can have our room," I blurted, looking at Aunt Melisende. I looked to Madeleine-Grace, and she smiled at me. I had her approval and felt at ease then.

"We can sleep in the conservatory," Madeleine-Grace said.

"No," Aunt Adèle said. "It takes much too long to cool off in there."

"We can sleep on the couch in the *salle-en-arrière*, then, like Uncle Roul," I suggested.

Aunt Mirabelle looked at Uncle Roul who preferred another bout with the blinding sun over looking at this wife. Uncle Roul's unwillingness to disturb his wife while she slept, opting instead to stay downstairs on the couch, seemed to me a display of courteousness.

"Why don't you share the bed with Wischard, Laure, and Astride," Aunt Adèle said.

"I don't want to share my bed with Madeleine-Grace—or Ellande," Astride interjected.

"Nor I with her," said Madeleine-Grace. "Sharing a couch will give us a better night of sleep than having to listen to her snoring. We'll be fine on the couch."

"I feel I have caused much inconvenience," said Aunt Melisende. "I never intended to be such a bother."

"You must never feel as if you are a bother," said Aunt Adèle.

"You would never have thought anything should be different about this visit," I said.

Aunt Melisende bent at the waist toward me, took my face in both hands, and looked me in the eye. "Juliette is not only in your eyes. She is in your character." Then she switched to Madeleine-Grace and held her face the same way. She did not smile at either of us, as if pained by the whole ordeal. Then, without provocation, she turned from Madeleine-Grace and reached for the tray on the table. Aunt Adèle had carried the food and bottles on it onto the veranda, and some dishes and napkins remained. She lifted the tray and walked to the steps.

"Grab the *cidre*, Madeleine-Grace," she ordered. "Grab the *pecorino*, Ellande. Tonight, we will do *apéro* on the cliffs. Join me, everyone!"

We obeyed as she marched toward the cliffs. Holding only a bottle of *cidre*, Madeleine-Grace was able to use her other hand to block the sun, but I, using both hands for the plate of cheese and honey, looked before me at the white alabaster past the lawn. Aunt Melisende stopped well before the edge and set the tray down.

Holding only her glass of *cidre* as we all joined her, she looked to the sea and began singing a traditional Normand song, "Ma Normandie." Something about the lilt of the tune and the enthusiasm with which Aunt Melisende sang invited us all to sing the familiar tune with her.

We sang a bit faster than the tempo required. Accompanying her with the lyrics, I experienced an unknown appreciation of the sea glistening before us with a thickening stream of sun spilling onto it.

"Louder!" shouted Aunt Melisende before singing the first verses after the refrain, laughing through the melody, locking arms with Uncle Roul, and swaying. Uncle Roul locked arms with his unmotivated wife, Uncle Romain and Aunt Pé locked arms, and all of us children formed one long interlocked chain as we sang louder.

I wondered why we didn't go so far as the cliff's edge, but I soon realized why she had positioned us close to the house. I caught Aunt Melisende looking toward the house, over the veranda to the terrace. Behind the glass window of the door from the bedroom to the terrace, I saw Aunt Laure. She shielded most of her body behind a long curtain but poked her head well into view, staring at the lot of us. Aunt Melisende, I believe, was hoping for this, and smiled widely when Aunt Laure appeared.

"Louder!" she cried, swaying with the family as we entered the next refrain. While our voices reached the sky, she took a sip of *cidre* with her free hand and lifted her glass to the terrace window.

Aunt Melisende stayed through Thursday evening, the evening Monsieur Vauquelin was to join us for dinner. Aunt Melisende's visit prompted a change within the household as everyone became more attentive to doing anything but sleeping, with the exception of Aunt Laure, who remained in her room, waited on by Uncle Gilbert and taking no visitors, until Aunt Melisende had departed. Monsieur Vauquelin's stay, more extended than he had intended, prompted a different kind of change as the languorous manner of my aunts and uncles became more active, not out of obligation or presenting appearances, but out of ghoulish desire to engage in attack mode, as wardens intent on seeing him not as a guest or even a suiter but a marauder. The major events of the summer—life-changing ones—took place in the weeks ahead while this week held a tenacious grip on the quotidian routines to which we were all becoming accustomed, but a change was taking place within these routines that, as visitors ourselves, became viscerally noticeable to us.

Early Tuesday morning, Aunt Melisende made the walk to Lady Victorine's and spent the morning chatting with her and Lady Léontine, returning with excitement over Madeleine-Grace and my inclusion in the children's ball, which she had forgotten about. She helped Aunt Adèle throughout the day, taking her *mésienne* a little earlier than ours. Wischard and I helped Madeleine-Grace and little Laure play *saut à la corde*, jump rope, near the cliffs, interspersing our rounds of *vinaigre* with lazier ones. Passing, calming sails in the distance distracted us between rounds. Madeleine-Grace, the first to withdraw from *saut à la corde*, didn't take to games much, nor did I, so she left to wander the herb and flower islands near the house, bending and smelling them and occasionally smiling. Wischard and I continued playing with little Laure until we, too, grew bored, preferring instead to sit cross-legged on the cliffs and watch the sea, imagining and wondering and hoping. I saw Wischard and little Laure flash glances to the terrace over the veranda, and I knew the reason. We returned to the house to help Aunt Adèle dust as Aunt Melisende returned from her nap. As the two insisted we go upstairs for our rest before the match, our aunts, uncles, and cousins began to assemble in the *salle-en-arrière*.

Uncle Romain stepped into the warm conservatory where Aunt Adèle was dusting the plants. With a damp cloth, she traced the lengths of the mother-in-law's tongue and the contours of the pothos leaves and the twists of the nephthytis vines and stems. Aunt Melisende was knitting in an armchair. While Madeleine-Grace watched attentively over Aunt Melisende's shoulder her every stitch, I sat on the ottoman watching Aunt Adèle's delicate dusting.

"May I try that?" Madeleine-Grace asked Aunt Melisende.

"It's a tricky stitch," she said, passing the needles to Madeleine-Grace who took to it instantly. After inching toward the clicking needles, Aunt Melisende sunk into her seat and rested her hands in her lap. "You are a fast learner."

"You spend too much time with the women," Uncle Romain said to me. "Why don't you do the things that boys do? Do you wish to become a butler?"

Pulling my attention from Aunt Adèle's dusting, I looked over my shoulder at him and shrugged. I had seen my father joining my mother so many times to fold the laundry or to do the dishes—and she, for that matter, so often helping him while he changed lightbulbs or pulled the weeds outside—that it did not dawn on me that I might be spending too much time doing something only girls did, or something boys did not do.

"You will become the town *blanchisseuse* like Julie in the poem they recite! Where do you keep your *amidon*?" He laughed, and I heard Aunt Pé's echo from the next room. Using the words in the poem, he told me I would be a laundress and asked where my starch is.

Her intense gaze fixed on her needles, my sister said, "Ellande plays sports and drinks with the boys at home. He helps Papa in the yard. He helps with repairs around the house if they're easy."

"You should try that some time," Aunt Melisende said to Uncle Romain. "You might start with the broken chair rail in the front hall that guests can see."

Uncle Romain scoffed. "It will get done," he grunted.

"As long as the house is habitable, you will wait, right? *Après-moi le déluge*," Aunt Melisende said.

Uncle Romain crossed his thick arms over his paunch and glared at his sister who had been all the while listening while working.

"Dusting the plants," Uncle Romain complained.

"They must not be neglected," said Aunt Adèle with her attention focused on the pothos.

Aunt Pé, within earshot, stepped into the conservatory. "If the plants were outside like the rest of nature, would they need dusting? Do you go to the herb garden, too, and dust every sprig of parsley and leaf of lovage?"

Maintaining a gentle smile to complement her gentle touch, Aunt Adèle said, "That's a little different. Dust accumulates differently indoors."

"What difference does it make if the plants have a little dust?" asked Uncle Romain, too grumpy for someone who had slept so much.

"A little dust turns into a lot of dust if not tended to," Aunt Adèle explained. "If there is too much dust on the plants, they cannot absorb the sunlight as easily and won't be as healthy."

It had not occurred to me. My lessons at school on photosynthesis in that moment took on a worth previously unattached to them.

"What does it matter to you if Adèle dusts the plants?" asked Aunt Melisende.

"She shouldn't be wasting her time dusting the plants when she needs to be in the kitchen preparing for tonight's match," Uncle Romain declared.

From the other room, Aunt Mirabelle added, "And she still hasn't sewn the curtains for my sister's dining room in Rouen, nor sewn the button on Laure's handbag."

Aunt Melisende chuckled in a way that sounded like the sinister laugh of a cartoon villain or a mastermind criminal I might read in the detective stories of *Black Mask*. Holding her knitting and rising, she said, "I hear voices but see no one. Where have you all gathered? I will join you."

She followed Uncle Romain and Aunt Pé to the *salle-en-arrière* where everyone except Aunt Laure had gathered, sipping black coffees and snacking on Biscuits Lefèvre-Utile *petits-beurres*. The men occupied the chairs, and Aunt Mirabelle the couch. When Aunt Pé sat beside her, Aunt Melisende, too, sat, forcing them to separate to make room for her.

"Tonight, France must go head to head with Brazil, is this not correct?" Aunt Melisende did not expect an answer as she resumed knitting. "And we will enjoy the match. And tomorrow? What shall we do tomorrow?"

"How long do you intend to stay?" asked Aunt Mirabelle.

"What difference does it make when among family?" asked Aunt Melisende, rhetorically. "Mirabelle, Pé, you must go to the market in Fécamp tomorrow morning."

"To the market? Surely if you need something, Aunt Melisende, Adèle will go to the market," said Aunt Mirabelle.

"*Adèle* goes to the market," Aunt Pé reiterated.

"Surely, Adèle has much to attend to here, what with your curtains and Laure's handbag. What with clearing the tables after the match and—"

"And tomorrow is washing day for the bedlinens!" interposed little Laure.

"What of Laure?" asked Aunt Mirabelle. "Why not ask her?"

"We should know better than to expect Laure to—accompany you," said Uncle Roul.

"With so much to do, surely you can lend a helping hand to your dear sister Adèle," stated Aunt Melisende.

"Adèle is very particular," protested Aunt Pé, "and will insist on going to market herself."

"I see," said Aunt Melisende. "Then perhaps I alone will accompany Adèle to the market, though I had hoped to remain home and help her in the kitchen as she prepared snacks for *la choule*. And, of course, Célèstène Galimard and Marie Loiselier will be most disappointed not to see you."

The two younger aunts looked past Aunt Melisende curiously, and Uncle Romain turned to Aunt Melisende with attention, Uncle Roul placing his cup on the table. Even Aunt Adèle stepped into the *salle-en-arrière*.

"*La choule?*" said Uncle Roul.

"Yes, if you'd like, Roul," said Aunt Melisende. "I thought for sure you would not object when Thiessé and Hardouin suggested a match tomorrow afternoon, having missed it last Sunday."

"You have spoken to Thiessé? He was here?" asked Uncle Roul.

"I visited Lady Victorine this morning. She, Lady Léontine, and I, along with Thiessé and Célèstène, enjoyed a coffee together, and Thiessé had hoped to enjoy an afternoon of *la choule*. I said the Semperrin men would be overjoyed for the recreation, but now I must cancel. It would be so embarrassing not to have proper drinks and snacks, and I'm afraid if Adèle and I are the ones to go, we will have little time to make the food with all the other odds and ends."

"You mustn't cancel," said Uncle Romain. "Our wives would delight in going to the market."

"I certainly have heard from your wives. They insist Adèle go. You heard it, too, Romain. And the ladies will be so disappointed. They were to join us in Fécamp. And they hoped to join Adèle in preparing. I will send one of the children to the Galimards' to inform them of the change. I must apologize for my presumption."

"*Nianterie*, Aunt Melisende," said Uncle Roul, using his mother's favorite word for nonsense. "We will play *la choule* with Thiessé and Hardouin."

"Our wives will go to market first thing," declared Uncle Romain.

"I couldn't impose on your schedules. I feel terribly presumptuous."

"Pé and Mirabelle will be overjoyed to see Célèstène and Marie. Will you not?"

Aunt Pé and Aunt Mirabelle never missed an opportunity to interact with Célèstène and Marie, ladies of society as they saw them. They affirmed with nods of the head.

"Good," said Aunt Melisende. "I'm glad you feel the same, Romain, because I volunteered you as chauffeur. You will pick them up from Lady Victorine's at five in the morning—with Pé and Mirabelle, of course—and drive them to the market in Fécamp."

Uncle Romain sunk into his seat despondently and shifted his gaze of disdain—for the early morning rising, no doubt—from Aunt Melisende to the windows.

"And I will leave it to you, Mirabelle, Pé, to discuss with Adèle what she might need by way of provisions," added Aunt Melisende.

"Of course," said Aunt Mirabelle softly, looking only at the full coffee cup resting in her hand on her lap.

"I will also require you to inquire of Ellande what you must purchase for the cocktail his father and he were working on last summer. Do you recall, Ellande?" Aunt Melisende asked me, an affectionate smile on her face. "I imagine the liqueur is ready now and awaits in the same place you left it in the cellar."

How she remembered I know not, but I certainly had forgotten. Last summer, my mother thinking out loud had tossed out that she would enjoy a liqueur of the cantaloupe we ate one evening after dinner, and my father set out posthaste to try his hand at it. The next day, we went to market with Aunt Melisende, bought twenty cantaloupes, and spent the day chopping the flesh into chunks, pouring a clear grain alcohol over it, and leaving it for days. My father, I'm sure, had taken other steps I did not see over the span of days before bottling it. Not one to be wasteful, Aunt Adèle shaved away the rinds of its corky, beige skin and boiled the remaining green rind with sugar for several hours. She had planned to pickle them, unsure how they'd turn out, but my father insisted on using them for a bottle of the cantaloupe liqueur to learn of their effect on the taste. Days later, my father, Wischard, and I carried all the bottles to the cellar where we planned to leave them until this summer. After we returned to America, several times after school, I talked with my mother about how to use the liqueur in a cocktail, and we brainstormed several ideas. Of course, none of us knew if the liqueur would turn out.

"I know we will need lots of lemons," I said, thinking to one recipe we considered trying.

Aunt Melisende laughed and said, "So you remember now."

I had rushed to these memories unguarded and did not armor myself for the aftereffect of utter loss, loneliness, and sadness. The initial joy was the past. My present without my father was emptiness, and he would not be able to taste with me whatever drink I had concocted, nor would my mother be able to try the liqueur we had made specifically for her. Would it taste how she imagined? The thought of making and trying the liqueur without my parents disturbed me, and the thought of making a cocktail using the bottles of liqueur my father had touched saddened me. The compulsion to leave everything as it was overtook me, and I resolved to pretend that the liqueur had not turned out right and could not be used for a cocktail. I would shout this from the cellar tomorrow and leave everything as it was.

"But first things first," said Aunt Melisende. "We must enjoy tonight's World Cup match."

"And Wischard and little Laure, and Ellande and Madeleine-Grace must take their *mésienne*," said Aunt Adèle.

"Do enjoy your coffee," Aunt Melisende said to the others, "and when you go up to wash, Gilbert, be sure to give your unfortunate wife my best. Please tell her I hope to see her over dinner one night before I leave, though I do not expect to and certainly wish not to pressure someone so—fragile."

The World Cup match came and went, unfolding similarly to the last one minus a sudden mad dash for the cliffs by anyone. Although Aunt Melisende knitted through the entirety of the match with only short breaks for food and drink, observation of the children, and attention on the game, especially when Jonquet injured his leg, Aunt Adèle, on the other hand, sat in her chair listening avidly. These World Cup matches were one of few activities in which I saw Aunt Adèle throw herself entirely into relaxing as if tending to a more important task did not exist.

Brazil beat France that night, and we skulked off to bed dejected after rushed, sad prayers. I think the next morning may have been one of only two days that summer that anyone besides Aunt Adèle woke before Madeleine-Grace and me. Begrudgingly or not, they had gone to the Galimards' and Fécamp before we awoke that morning. The plan for the day included the usual washing and hanging of the bedlinens, putting on the new ones, the *choule* match along the cliffs, and *apéritifs* with everyone.

Aunt Adèle, grateful for Aunt Melisende's help, did much of the washing and tidying before the others returned from the market. Young Roul, Alphonse, Chardine, and Astride went back to bed after their new bedlinens had been applied. Uncle Roul took a walk, and Uncle Gilbert locked himself in his room with Aunt Laure for the better part of the day.

Uncle Romain quickly disappeared after he and the women had returned. Aunt Melisende, who had taken the lead with the bedlinens, was hanging them outside. Aunt Adèle led the recently arrived women into the kitchen where, through laughter and chatter, they managed to accomplish much. Madeleine-Grace and I swept in an out of the kitchen, not wishing to intrude but not finding much to occupy ourselves otherwise, even with helping Aunt Melisende outside. On one pass through, I heard Célèstène and Marie moon over Adèle's announcement of making several asparagus *frittate*; they were something she could make in advance. When she looked at the bunches of asparagus Aunt Pé had brought home, her shoulders drooped. Aunt Pé noticed and inquired about the reaction. The other ladies gathered around the five bound bunches, and they, too, drooped their shoulders and sighed. Aunt Pé was befuddled.

"This bunch," Aunt Adèle said, pointing to one with fat, green-turning-brown stalks, "will be no good for using, even when I blanch them."

"Did I not tell you?" said Aunt Pé to the others. "She is overly particular."

"She is overly correct in this case, Pé," said Célèstène. "We cannot use these to cook."

"How do you know? The plump ones are the juiciest," said Aunt Pé, bending for a closer look at the one bunch.

"Sometimes that is so, but when the tips are not tight, they are likely older and harder," explained Aunt Adèle.

"Can you not see the split at the top?" said Marie.

"And the stalk here is almost brown. It's like a tree trunk," added Célèstène.

"I'm afraid my sister-in-law does not even look at these things. She took the first five she reached for," said Aunt Mirabelle, trying to establish a place with the others but drawing a severe look from Aunt Pé for the betrayal.

"I will make do with just the four," said Aunt Adèle. "I will blanch them now."

"They will cook in the *frittata* with the eggs," stated Aunt Mirabelle. "What need have you to blanch them, too? Always adding unnecessary steps."

"She is always making a fuss over everything," said Aunt Pé. "The asparagus tips. The blanching. None of this makes any difference, I tell you. You should use all five."

I saw Célèstène and Marie look at each other, and Adèle took the five bunches of asparagus and smiled, preferring to work than to respond to her sisters.

"I do wish we had more good asparagus to use," said Célèstène "on account of one more mouth to feed."

"We will make enough for one more mouth," said Aunt Adèle confidently. "Who else will be joining us?"

"Only Alban Vauquelin," said Célèstène, grinning when Aunt Adèle stopped untying the asparagus. "We saw him at the market. He was wheeling bags of salt for his sister to sell."

"When did you talk to Alban Vauquelin?" asked Pé. "I did not see Alban Vauquelin."

"The one time we left you was for you to acquire the asparagus—"

"And we should have stayed with you for that—" interjected Marie.

"—and we went to acquire the eggs. We passed the charming Alban Vauquelin and invited him to join the men for *la choule*."

"He will be coming?" asked Aunt Adèle, squeezing the bunch of asparagus in her hand and lifting it to her head.

"He suspects he cannot arrive in time for the game, but he promised to come for a drink and 'Adèle's cooking.'"

The other ladies seemed more excited than Aunt Adèle for Monsieur Vauquelin's arrival. Aunt Adèle did not respond and, after a blush, returned to the counter to continue with preparations. I was pretty sure her grip on the asparagus had already blanched them.

Moments thereafter, Célèstène's sons, Ansgot and Maclou, arrived, sent by their grandmother Lady Victorine, to offer help with preparations. Maclou said, with a voice like a little bird, "Grand-père and Grand-mère thought it might be too much to leave all the work to poor Roul and Alphonse alone."

Aunt Mirabelle excused herself immediately, and Madeleine-Grace and I followed her upstairs out of pure curiosity, at a distance that maintained our cover. Although we went into our bedroom, we could hear her admonish the boys for sleeping when they could be helping downstairs. Our mouths covered with our hands, Madeleine-Grace and I laughed without emitting a sound as we stood at the partially opened bedroom door and waited for Aunt Mirabelle to pass and rejoin the others in the kitchen.

Once we returned to the kitchen, Uncle Romain entered to inquire about bottles of *calvados* in the cellar. The question called to Aunt Adèle's mind the cantaloupe liqueur, and, neglecting to address her brother, she said, "My dear friends, Ellande plans to grace us with a cocktail made from cantaloupe liqueur that he and his father made last summer."

I could see that the smiles of Célèstène and Marie upon mention of my father and our liqueur making were colored with sadness. Célèstène brought her hand to her heart, and her eyes welled with tears.

I said, "We have never made the liqueur before, so we don't know how it will turn out. Maman thought it would be a nice idea, and at home in America, we came up with ideas for cocktails, that is, if the liqueur turned out."

"I am sure it will be delicious," said Marie. "Your mother had a brilliant idea."

"And I'm sure your father would have not given up on the liqueur until he perfected it had he——." Célèstène had meant to pay my father a glowing compliment of character, I know, but like so many others could not finish certain sentences about him.

"Ellande, why don't you, Ansgot, and Maclou help Uncle Romain bring up the *calvados*, and then you can bring up a few bottles of the cantaloupe liqueur," Célèstène suggested.

The boys lined at the cellar door as Uncle Romain reached for the lock at the top and pulled the pin. Madeleine-Grace turned her back to the door and pretended to inspect the asparagus lying on the counter. When the door opened, he reached for the short chain next to the light over the top of the stairs.

"You must replace that with a longer chain, Romain. I have asked many times," Aunt Adèle said, only to be shrugged off by Uncle Romain.

The bulbs illuminated the top of the narrow stairwell and not much else. There was no railing on our right—only the cold roughness of brick wall; however, a wooden railing began on our left for the last five steps. When Uncle Romain grabbed hold, it shook without a sound, unlike the many creaks of the wooden stairs on our every step. Where the shaky railing began, the stairs felt wobbly, too. Maclou never left the bottom stair, creaking it every time he shifted his weight during his nervous inspection of the dim, scratchy-aired room.

At the bottom of the stairs, Uncle Romain reached up and pulled the short string of another light bulb, revealing the contents of the small, dank cellar. Against the wall at the bottom of the stairs were several tall, wooden shelves lined with canned vegetables, fruits, and jams. I suspected cheese rested in a few of the tied burlap sacks I saw. Shelves had been built into the length of the perpendicular wall, each with square compartments. I knew my grandfather had put these in to store wine on its side, and bottles of wine and spirits still occupied these compartments. Several were specifically for *calvados* and *hydromel*. In the corner, a few crates of *cidre* remained, and I could see webs connecting them to a glob of dried mortar at the top of the brick wall. I surveyed the room cautiously for spiders only to spot more webs. Off to the side in three stacked boxes, my father's cantaloupe liqueur awaited. I did not know which box contained the special bottle with the sugared, boiled rinds.

My mind drifted to the memory of my father carrying the boxes down last summer, his hands likely the last to have touched these boxes and bottles. Before I could ponder the theory, Uncle Romain shouted an expletive when he banged his hand reaching for a bottle of *calva*. I stepped around the railing as he shook his hand, and, despite a web connecting them to the compartments of wine, I ran my open palm over the side of the boxes to ensure my touch was the first to touch something I decided my father had touched last.

We helped Uncle Romain bring up a few bottles of *calva*, and he carried for us a box of six bottles of cantaloupe liqueur. In the natural light of the kitchen, I recognized them immediately and knew that these, unlike one of the boxes we had left in the cellar, did not contain the rinds.

"We have the lemons you requested," Aunt Adèle said. "I will give you two big pitchers to try your cocktail. What else will you need, Ellande?"

"I will also need the gin and the orange bitters from the bar, a few egg whites, and the swizzle sticks." I was excited to try the liqueur, to prepare the cocktail, and to have the help of Ansgot and Maclou. I entertained the prospect of telling Lord Galimard about it and of his asking me to make it at their next gathering. Of course, I did not know the process to make the cantaloupe liqueur from beginning to end since I had not observed my father's every step.

"What will you call it?" asked Célestène.

"I don't know yet," I said. "Maybe a cantaloupe fizz."

I sped off to experiment with the cantaloupe liqueur in the backroom, but really, I sampled the liqueur in a cordial glass, its pour syrupy but not too viscous, and imagined my mother's serious stare as I handed her the glass, her eyes shifting in concentration as the piquant scent tickled her nose, and her slowly forming smile as the cool, sweet-yet-tart flavor coated her tongue. I knew the way I saw her reaction was correct. An observant son knows these things.

When Ansgot approached offering help, I decided to make the cocktail on the spot after the match instead of experimenting now. Trusting the idea my mother and I had discussed, I reasoned, honored her more than fiddling around with ingredients and proportions now, even if our concoction proved disastrous. An initial pang of guilt over not leaving the bottles in the cellar as I had intended yesterday did burrow a nook in my mind.

Uncle Romain and Uncle Roul procured the equipment for *la choule* from the shed while young Roul and Alphonse watched from the veranda. The ladies had finished all they could in the kitchen and had gathered on the veranda, as well, to talk. Aunt Melisende asked the boys to bring chairs down to the lawn, past the flower and herb islands toward where *la choule* match would take place. We all took a chair from the veranda for the ladies while the ladies gathered their *mercerie* bags. Aunt Adèle had given Madeleine-Grace permission to knit with some of her yarn, so Madeleine-Grace ran to the conservatory closet to pick her favorite color.

We made a row of chairs that every adult female occupied. The girls sat at the feet of their mothers, and Madeleine-Grace and little Laure sat between the feet of Aunt Adèle and Aunt Melisende. With Thiessé and Hardouin recently arrived, bringing Brigitte, Henriette, and Collot with them, the daughters found a place at their mothers' feet. Of course, Aunt Adèle had supplied all the girls with blankets suitable for outdoors. Snacks and drinks for *la choule* players topped the main table on the veranda.

I wasn't sure where to be. The boys were gathering around the *choule* equipment on the far end of the lawn closer to the cliffs, but I was not used to playing *la choule* without my father. Something—an invisible barrier around only me—kept me from joining the players. I did not feel at ease among the females and could not turn to Madeleine-Grace for diversion or stalling, for she was avidly crocheting something circular amid conversation, as the others did the same.

Standing to the side of the row of females, I noticed that Aunt Pé and Aunt Mirabelle were struggling to start something from scratch while the other adults had projects already begun. Aunt Pé and Aunt Mirabelle held crochets and yarn, Aunt Melisende and Aunt Adèle held knitting needles and yarn, Célèstène worked with crochet, and Marie worked with embroidery needle and thread. Among the girls, only Madeleine-Grace worked on anything at all—crocheting light blue yarn. Chardine tried to make herself appear helpful or busy by holding the skein of yarn for her mother, although her mother did not incorporate the yarn quickly into anything.

Chardine asked after a few minutes of silence, "Maman, why do neither Astride nor I know how to knit or crochet or sew, but Madeleine-Grace does?"

Aunt Mirabelle shifted in her chair as Aunt Melisende answered in her stead, noting, "Madeleine-Grace's mother taught her, of course." She chuckled as if to herself.

Causing her mother's cheeks and forehead to redden, Astride asked, "Why didn't you teach me how to crochet or knit, Maman?"

Once more, Aunt Melisende answered instead of the intended. "That's a good question, Astride, but let's not dwell on the reasons. It's never too late to start. Why don't you teach her now, Pé?" After she said this, Aunt Melisende leaned over to look at Aunt Pé's crocheting and then shrugged. Tending once more to her own knitting, she said, "Chardine, what about little Laure? Don't forget to include little Laure among the Semperrin girls whose mother has not imparted any skill with hooks or needles."

"Ellande!" I heard Ansgot shout from down the lawn. "Come on!"

For some reason, I looked to Aunt Adèle for permission. Aunt Adèle, already looking at me, said, "Go play, Ellande," and I ran to the *choule* field the men had designed. I wondered had Ansgot not called me, opening a gate in the barrier I could only sense, if anyone else would have.

The field spanned several neighbors' lawns, and none of them minded. Every now and then, some of those neighbors joined the game or watched from their lawns for a leisurely hour. As I stepped near the Galimards, Maclou asked me if we had *la choule à la crosse* in America, and I reported that we did not, but that in parts of the country we had la crosse and rugby. Maclou's father asked what I played in America, and I told him baseball, to his approving nod; in Pays de Caux, *la tèque* is played and is considered an ancestor of baseball. Ansgot said that he wanted to ask me about American football afterwards.

We made teams—the boys versus the men—and we ran and grunted and swooped our *crosses* along the cliffs where the lawns turned to white rock. The simple goal of getting the ball, *la balle*, into the *viquets*, the goal, using our netted sticks, *les crosses*, had us invested in game play quickly. The men moved in a relaxed manner, passing the *balle* high over our heads at times, laughing and hooting at our inability to intercept them. Once, Wischard launched his *crosse* high in the air as the perfect throw could hit the *balle* mid-air, and we all laughed; when Collot Loiselier did the same, his father told him he was not to throw it again. In the late day's heat, the men straggled off the field every now and then, climbed the three veranda steps, and took a sip of something before trotting back. We boys played with more conviction to win, with more speed and urgency, and with no breaks.

After a half hour of playing, my *crosse* clashed with Hardouin Loiselier's, and I slipped backward on the white rock and dropped my stick. I slid a little when I fell and scraped my leg, but it didn't hurt. Monsieur Loiselier said, "Be careful with your *crosse*, Ellande," and extended his hand to help me up.

Uncle Romain shouted, "Leave him! The Basque don't know how to play Normand games."

Monsieur Loiselier helped me up anyway, patted me on the head, and sauntered down the field toward where the *balle* had action. I, however, stayed in place, and started to cry. Some combination of hearing Uncle Romain say, "leave him" and being identified as too Basque to play a Normand game stung. I no longer wanted to play the Normand game because, in an instant, I didn't feel worthy of playing the Normand game. I wanted my father to be there and foolishly surveyed the field and the cliffs and the veranda for him. Instead of rejoining the game, I ran toward the house.

Ansgot saw me and shouted, "Ellande, come back!" When I didn't stop, he followed me as I ran past the hanging sheets toward the side of the house, hoping to avoid the men and women altogether. Once the sheets could shield me from being seen, I stopped.

"Ellande, did you hurt yourself?" Ansgot asked.

"I scraped my leg," I said, wiping away my tears. "I'll be all right. You can go back."

"Okay, but come back," Ansgot said as he ran to the group. I knew he would explain that I had scraped myself so that I would not have to explain the real reason for my tears and departure.

Madeleine-Grace appeared from the other side of a swaying sheet. "Aunt Adèle sent me over to make sure you are okay."

"I'm fine," I said. "I just scraped my leg."

"Are you going back?" she asked, intuiting that I did not want to rejoin the match.

Before I could answer, Ansgot reappeared.

"Let's go make the cocktails instead. They're almost finished playing anyway," he said.

Ansgot, my unexpected savior, needed no verbal response as he slapped me on the back. We walked past the knitters and up the veranda steps. In two hours, the ladies had made so much progress; Aunt Pé and Aunt Mirabelle, at that point, were smoking.

From the veranda, we entered the *salle-en-arrière* and set up for cocktail making. Aunt Adèle had made me a tray with glasses. I poured a shot of gin into a jigger to smell it. "We're going to have to work fast if we're going to make twenty at once. I think I can make two at a time," I said to Ansgot.

"What can I do?" he asked, rubbing his hands together in eagerness. Unsure what to expect of him as a helper, I perceived Ansgot to be an intellectual, fascinated by philosophy and Theology, curious about inventions and history. A reader who tore through books, he played *la choule* for exercise and diversion and not under a compulsion to become a star player unusually dexterous with the *crosse*. I wondered if his lack of athleticism might affect his cocktail mixing. Then again, I was far from the epitome of athleticism, carried by an intellectual fascination with mixing drinks, combining flavors, and applying different techniques. Certainly, the good Ansgot could help.

"I'll show you how to use a swizzle stick to make the foam. It's just like a gin fizz."

"I've never made a gin fizz," he said. "I've never had one! I've never even had gin!"

"Drink," I said, handing him the jigger. "It's straight gin."

He took one quick sip.

"I know," I said. "It's not usually drunk alone, and if it is, not warm. When we mix it with the other ingredients and ice, you'll like it more."

"I hope so," he said.

I taught him how to use the swizzle stick to make a foam once the drink was poured into the glass, and he got the hang of it right away. I poured ice, gin, cantaloupe liqueur, a wooden spoonful of egg white, fine sugar, and two drops of orange bitters into the *passoire* before squeezing a large, half lemon in each. I shook it intensely.

"How long do you have to shake it?" Ansgot asked.

"Without egg whites, I shake it for one 'Notre Père.' With egg whites in there, I shake it for one 'Notre Père,' one 'Je Vous Salue, Marie,' and one 'Gloire.' That's how my mother taught me."

"I like that!" said Ansgot, "But when Maclou gets here, he will like it more."

Once I finished shaking, I poured the drink through the *passoire* lid into the glasses. Some foam had already formed. Ansgot dunked the swizzle stick into one glass at a time, sliding his hands back and forth vigorously with the swizzle stick between them, hoping for more foam to form. It took a while, but we made twenty of them—the first twenty.

I carried the tray onto the veranda. The guys were clearing up and heading in as the boys helped the ladies bring the chairs to the veranda. Aunt Adèle whizzed by us, flashing a smile, to start bringing out platters of food, including three giant, asparagus and red pepper *frittate*, sliced neatly and garnished with parsley, on a bed of lightly dressed *frisée*. A perimeter of thinly sliced Italian *coppa Piacentina*, plump tomato wedges, and crisp endive leaves surrounded each *frittata*. On one large slice of one *frittata* only, a pitted black olive lay; I don't know why I foolishly assumed Aunt Adèle had dropped it without noticing.

As the table and chairs were arranged, Thiessé stepped off the veranda and strolled to the hanging sheets, inhaling through his nose. When he returned, he used the bottom of his shirt to wipe beads of sweat from his forehead. He said to Aunt Adèle, "Your sheets smell fresher than we do."

"Perhaps she can spray you with the lavender water," offered Aunt Melisende to our amusement.

"Attention!" Célèstène said, spreading her arms to each side of the tray of cocktails. "Ellande has made us a cocktail—for which he does not yet have a name. This cocktail features a cantaloupe liqueur that he and Julien made last summer. We must all try."

"Ansgot helped me, Madame Galimard," I said.

As everyone reached for one and took their first sips, I watched their faces. I saw no grimaces, which was pleasing, as everyone studied the flavors on their tongue. Expressions of concentration on the flavors turned to nods of approval. I did not ask for critique, in part because I wished to sample the drink myself, but also because Lady Galimard, Mademoiselle des Gervais, and Monsieur Vauquelin stepped onto the veranda, having showed themselves into the house from the front.

"I am just in time," Lady Victorine said as we all greeted her.

"Where is Papa?" asked her daughter.

"His sciatica compels him to remain at home. He sends his best."

"So you came on your own?" her daughter asked.

"I walked on my own, yes, but I have brought guests. On the walk here, I saw Jeuffine des Gervais on her front steps picking flowers and invited her to our *apéro*, sure the Semperrins would not object to welcoming our newest neighbor. And when we arrived at the house, Alban Vauquelin had just arrived, himself. I am happy to see at least one gentleman who is not panting and sweating." She chuckled at her own attempt at a joke as she eyed Aunt Adèle.

"You do not work up a sweat transporting bags of salt, Monsieur?" asked Uncle Romain, inciting chuckles from Aunt Pé and Uncle Roul.

Monsieur Vauquelin did not acknowledge the comment. He nodded to Uncle Romain while the cap in his hands before him spun through his fingers like a miller's wheel.

"Perhaps Adèle would like to spray you with lavender water anyway," joked Aunt Melisende, causing a burst of laughter from the ladies. Monsieur Vauquelin blushed.

I stepped to the three recent guests. "You must try my new drink. Everyone is enjoying it," I said, proud of the smiles I had seen and eager for all three to taste it, as well.

Aunt Adèle and Célèstène Galimard explained once more the circumstances of the cocktail as all three reached for one, happy to have a cold sip after their short walk and, in the case of Monsieur Vauquelin, a day's work. Their first sip, like the others', was trepidatious, but they, too, smiled with surprise and delight at the taste.

"I will have to have you make one for my husband," Lady Victorine said.

"Very good, Ellande. You must teach me how to make it," Monsieur Vauquelin said.

"Only after you show me the salt marshes," I said.

"You have a deal," he said.

"It is sweet and tart and bitter," the pretty Jeuffine des Gervais said, dipping her finger in and licking off the foam. "I have an idea, if I may be so bold to try—a true Normand touch."

She had everyone's attention, including Uncle Roul's and Aunt Mirabelle's. My uncle leaned forward on the table while his wife crossed her arms and receded to the back of the group of us, standing on her tiptoes to see. Mademoiselle des Gervais had set just inside the door two bottles of her uncle's *hydromel*, and brought them over. She took my drink and hers, setting them next to each other on the table. She pulled a rose from her hair and, to our astonishment, splashed it with *hydromel* in a deft movement of the bottle. Using the wet rose, she sprinkled the froth of our two drinks with the *hydromel*. She reached for the swizzle stick on the tray, stirred each drink once, and lifted her glass. I did the same. She clicked her glass to mine, and we each took a sip.

"Honey and cantaloupe," she said, thinking through the flavors. "A good combination, and not too sweet—just right. Do you like it?"

"I like it," I said, excited about the touch of honey flavor.

"We must all try, then," said Wischard.

Beginning with Lady Victorine, the *hydromel* began its way around the veranda so that everyone could add a splash to their drink. Elated to have teamed up with this prettiest of women, I said, "I will name it *the Jeuffine*!" In that moment, Aunt Mirabelle, who had just been handed the bottle, dropped it. We jumped at the thud, unaware that it had not broken.

"Not to worry," Mademoiselle des Gervais said. "My uncle has many more in his cellar. Perhaps Ellande can accompany Roul over to acquire them. Four hands are better than two when it comes to holding things."

"That won't be necessary," said Aunt Mirabelle, brandishing the bottle to indicate that it remained unbroken. "A little spill but nothing broken. If I wanted to break this bottle, I could find something better to hit it against."

"We would not wish to do harm to anything belonging to your good uncle, however," added Aunt Melisende.

To encourage eating, Aunt Adèle began placing a piece of *frittata* and a sprig of parsley on each plate, handing a plate to someone after each cut. The large slice with the pitted olive went to Aunt Pé. Our guests topped their plates with slices of cheese and *saucisson*, olives, and *vinaigre*-marinated *haricots verts*, plus the garnishes around each *frittata*.

"Adèle made a scrumptious asparagus *frittata*," Marie said to her husband.

"She has been turning to the Italian cuisine much recently," said Uncle Gilbert.

"I have to wait until summer to get good cooking," Uncle Roul said. When he and Uncle Romain laughed afterward, neither Aunt Mirabelle nor Aunt Pé followed suit. Instead, the former crinkled her lip into a voiceless pout and the latter furrowed her brow and glared at Aunt Adèle.

"Are we eating later than usual? When do I get mine?" asked Uncle Romain, standing empty-handed.

"I think you are hungrier than usual after *la choule*," said Lady Victorine, sidling to Aunt Melisende with her plate full.

"It wouldn't take so long to get your food if Adèle didn't insist on taking ten extra steps for every dish—for everything she does. Slice and plate and sprig of parsley. She knows how to waste time, that one."

Aunt Pé, miffed by her husband's comment, did not hide a reproach for Aunt Adèle, and her last statement incited a hush upon the group. Used to such comments, Aunt Adèle continued serving the last of the *frittata*.

"It's not a waste of time," Aunt Adèle said in defense of her actions, "when it makes a difference. Why should I not do things right?"

"It makes no difference," Aunt Pé snapped. "Buy this asparagus, not that. Iron this direction, not that. Soak the pork chops for hours. Spray lavender water before ironing the sheets, but first make the lavender water. And for what? Makes no difference."

Monsieur Vauquelin, who had receded to the doorway, now stepped just behind Aunt Adèle. He said, "It does make a difference." Aunt Adèle touched the top of his hand with her palm, an indication to stop talking.

"How much do others enjoy your laundry and your meals? You skip the steps," Aunt Melisende said, casually taking a bite from her wedge of *frittata*. "Delicious!" she exclaimed and then added, "Everyone loves what Adèle does because she does things correctly."

Aunt Pé rejoined with stiff casualness, "It's all a show. She wastes time because she wants to look busy. Everything is a fuss with her."

"What are you doing with your time that you can't be bothered with an extra fifteen minutes to get something done well?" asked Madeleine-Grace, followed by a reach for a piece of *camembert*. Aunt Melisende placed a loving arm around her, drawing her toward her body.

"From the mouths of babes," Monsieur Vauquelin said, causing Aunt Adèle to redden nervously. "You know it makes a difference when Adèle takes the time to preserve the correct practice for these things, so what takes up so much of your time that you can't keep the same good practices?"

Aunt Pé glanced at Uncle Romain who, along with Uncle Roul, was eating heartily with intermittent sips of the Jeuffine cocktail. With no recourse from him, she reverted to a scoff.

"Adèle, no matter what pains you took to make this, the *frittata* is delicious," Aunt Melisende said.

"Flavorful and tender," Thiessé noted. "You must teach Célèstène how to make this."

"I watched her make it," Madame Galimard said with glee in her voice. "I'm eager to try it at home."

"Tender?" Aunt Pé started again. "Mine is like pulling twine through my teeth."

We could see her pull a string of asparagus through her teeth, and indeed it was fibrous and thick. Although troubled by the unbreakable green strands, she took a satisfaction in this spectacle as she glanced at the ladies.

"I used the fifth bunch of asparagus for your portion—and I didn't blanch it first," Aunt Adèle said.

The reaction of grins and blushing and stopped-in-place chewing deafened us all. Even Aunt Pé stopped pulling the tough asparagus from her mouth and dropped it, letting it hang over her chin as ire flashed across her eyes.

"Certainly, you must approve, Pé," Monsieur Vauquelin said. "She did not bother spending extra time on yours."

Apéro hour continued with conversation, most of it more pleasant than the jabs at Aunt Pé and Aunt Pé's rants about Aunt Adèle. Although Aunt Mirabelle and Aunt Pé withdrew to the *salle-en-arrière* after a short while, uncharacteristic of them when Célèstène and Marie were present, the group remained convivial on the veranda eating and drinking. After my round of cocktails, *hydromel* and *cidre* were passed around, and the ladies took a stroll to the cliffs. At one point, the sheets whipped in a strong, warm breeze, and Lady Victorine boasted her friendship with the Semperrins, saying, "sheets hanging with guests about is a sure sign of a good friendship—one that is rooted in a respect for each other's hard work."

As evening fell and children yawned and chatter subsided, Monsieur Galimard said to his children, "We must head home now for prayers, and then it's right to bed for the lot of us."

"Can we do evening prayers with the Semperrins?" Maclou asked. His chirp of a voice warmed even my heart, especially coupled with his craving for prayers together.

"Is that okay?" Monsieur Galimard asked Uncle Roul.

Uncle Roul shrugged and looked to Aunt Adèle.

"Of course, the children may join us," Aunt Adèle said.

"Children? I'd like to join you," said Lady Victorine, locking arms with Aunt Melisende.

"We say prayers in the foyer in front of Jesus," Aunt Adèle said.

We brought chairs for Lady Victorine, Aunt Melisende, and Aunt Adèle from the dining room, and then all the children sat on the hall floor facing the statue, the ladies seated behind us. Monsieur Vauquelin stood behind Aunt Adèle's chair, resting his hands on the chairback. Mademoiselle des Gervais slipped through the front door onto the front veranda. The Loiseliers and Célèstène Galimard sat on the floor behind the children. My other aunts and uncles, along with Monsieur Galimard, had congregated in the *salle-en-arrière*.

"Romain and Pé, Roul and Mirabelle, Gilbert?" called Aunt Melisende. "Won't you be joining us? We are ready to begin prayers."

Uncle Romain placed an arm around Thiessé Galimard and began walking him toward the back veranda, away from us, while the others schlepped over. Uncle Roul lit the votive before the statue at Aunt Adèle's request.

"Thiessé," called Lady Victorine. "We are beginning prayers now."

Monsieur Galimard stepped from Uncle Romain and headed toward us.

"This is why we leave our mothers in Paris," Uncle Romain said.

Monsieur Galimard did not stop to entertain my uncle's comment before arriving in the foyer and plopping onto the floor with the rest of us. Uncle Romain shrugged and continued onto the back veranda as he pulled a cigarette from his pocket.

Aunt Adèle led prayers, and we all said a "Notre Père," "Je Vous Salue, Marie," and "Gloire." We also took turns expressing to God our gratitude for various people and things. As we began, Uncle Roul opened the front door and stepped onto the front veranda. Ansgot shared his gratitude for his books, Henriette for her grandmother, young Roul for his cigarettes, Alphonse for his brother's cigarettes, Chardine for her dolls, and little Laure for big boats. Wischard expressed his gratitude for witnessing Bette Tranchaud throw up in a planter when young Roul tried to kiss her in the town square the week before Madeleine-Grace and I arrived. Astride shrugged, unable to offer anything for which she was grateful. Maclou announced his gratitude for baby Jesus, and Madeleine-Grace for God's giving the world La Vierge. I found my sister's response, at first, a curiosity until it occurred to me that one of the last gifts Maman had given her was a statue of The Blessed Mother for her bedroom dresser. She had purchased it in Paris last summer, keeping it hidden from my sister until Christmas.

After prayers, Lady Victorine told us something I had never learned in that the fresco on the interior wall of the alcove, an image of La Vierge with L'Enfant Jésus in her arms, had been painted by my Uncle Léon the year before he went to war. She reminded us that the statue of Jesus we housed in the foyer alcove had been a gift to my grandfather's father from her father, an act of reciprocation for the statue that my grandfather's father had given to her father when their place was built a year before ours in Etretat-au-Delà.

"Everywhere I look tonight, I am reminded of such a beautiful friendship. The Galimard-Semperrin friendship is a tradition that must continue, like the traditions of our households and those of our region, through these young ones." Lady Victorine began to weep, and Aunt Melisende and Aunt Adèle placed arms around her. "My heart aches with joy to see the little ones praying together, and my heart breaks with sadness to see Madeleine-Maud not here to enjoy it with us."

Only while talking with Ansgot the next morning in the apple orchard, I realized how quickly I had forgotten my hurt when Uncle Romain used my Basque heritage as an insult. With one more day in Etretat-au-Delà before heading to Deauville with his family and then, with a group of other students in a summer program, to an archaeological dig outside Rome, he walked to our place early in the morning to see if I could hang out. He had brought his French translation of F. Scott Fitzgerald's *The Great Gatsby* and had some questions about it. Since most of the Semperrin household was still sleeping, we decided to walk to his; however, we found a shady spot under a tree in the apple orchard across from Jeuffine des Gervais's, at my suggestion.

Ansgot wanted to know what a mint julep was, and luckily I knew, despite not having read the book myself. My father had read it and mentioned the drink to us one night at dinner, having seen it in the novel, himself. Once we had determined the specifics, my mother and I put one together for him one evening before he returned from work.

Our blue kitchen in River Forest contrasted with the subdued ecrus and creams of the summer house kitchen in France. Standing at our powder-blue counter, my mother with the shaker and I with the muddler, we dropped in the fresh mint leaves and poured in the simple syrup my mother had made. We had the bourbon on hand, the bottle a regular gift from our friends the Garels, but first I had to muddle the mint and sugar.

"The key," Maman explained, "is not to destroy the mint. You want no visible particles of mint in the drink that we might ingest. Press the leaves just enough to release the oils and flavor." She was excited to have learned this from a friend of Creole heritage in her woman's group. "A few rips in the leaves are fine, but don't shred them."

My push into the mint and sugar, perhaps too gingerly at first, warranted more pressure upon my mother's inspection. "Press a little harder, but don't twist too much. This is what Theadora suggests," she instructed. Following her instructions availed, for the mint leaves softened but didn't shred, and, when we added the bourbon and ice, we could taste all the flavors without ingesting the leaves. My father enjoyed his. A man used to the strong brandies, *eaux de vie*, and cognacs of his fatherland, he said after a few sips, "I could get used to bourbon."

I could see the mint julep in his hand as he sat in the armchair after work, the condensation trickling down the glass as mother played the piano. Her own mint julep rested on a square, hand-sewn coaster on top of the piano. Even when Papa sipped his drink, he listened intently to Maman's playing. She was playing Chopin's Berceuse, Opus 57.

While we were talking and the memory of my father and mother was lingering, Ansgot noticed the blotches on my leg, scratches so faint that didn't seep blood, and said he was glad I was feeling better. That's when I realized I had gotten over the insult quite quickly, distracted by the making of the cocktails. It occurred to me then that getting over it so quickly might have disappointed my father who was equally as proud of the predominance of his Normand heritage as he was of the minimal Basque blood in his line. I wondered how I could so soon forget having felt so bad, and I questioned my own allegiance to my heritage.

After an hour of talking about the book, the English language, and what schools were like, we rose under the tree to depart, and Ansgot didn't realize the branch above him was so low and hit his head. It wasn't a hard hit, but the shake caused an apple to loosen and plummet, falling on my head. We laughed for what felt like another half an hour, and I'm glad that's the last moment I ever had with Ansgot, whom I always thought of as a good guy. He never attended the children's ball because he was still away on the dig, and we left Etretat-au-Delà before the end of summer when he and his family returned for a few more weeks. He walked toward the Galimard house, and I walked toward the Semperrin house, each leaving for the rest of his own summer.

When I arrived home, Monsieur Vauquelin had just pulled up, and together, we walked around the side of the house to put away the *choule* equipment. Aunt Melisende had asked Uncle Roul and Uncle Romain several times to bring it from the field to the shed, and they delegated to young Roul and Alphonse at each request. Young Roul nor Alphonse wanted to do it, so some time before evening prayers, Monsieur Vauquelin, Wischard, and I went out in the dark and carried what we could to the shed. This morning, Monsieur Vauquelin wanted to make sure we hadn't missed anything in the dark, and sure enough, upon final inspection, we saw one *crosse* in the distant lawn near the cliffs. Even though retrieving it took no more than one person, we both walked to it and returned it to the shed.

"Can I teach you how to make the Jeuffine cocktail, Monsieur Vauquelin?" I asked on our trek back.

"I was about to ask you to teach me."

"Good," I said. "We will have them for *apéritifs* again. We made lots of liqueur, but I don't know what we will do when it runs out. I don't know how to make the liqueur part."

"We'll figure it out, relying on your memory of it and what we know of liqueurs."

"Aunt Adèle invited you to dinner tonight. You're staying, right?"

"Yes, I'm staying for dinner, and I have arrived early to help her. We're making salt-encrusted chicken. I'd like you to watch, that is, if you'd like."

"I like to watch Aunt Adèle cook. I watch Maman and Papa cook, too. That's how I learn."

"That's smart of you, Ellande. Salt is not the only thing that preserves, you know. So do observation, practice, and patience."

We entered the house to find Madeleine-Grace working on her ball gown with Aunt Adèle in the conservatory and listened momentarily as Aunt Adèle explained her plan to complete strands of lacework and sew them into the hem of the dress and the border of the bodice. Madeleine-Grace shared ideas of her own, likening her vision of the dress to overlapping teacup doilies that she had seen in the dining room. Aunt Adèle had made those one summer, too—medallions of thin lace my mother said were so beautiful that they should never be covered with cups and saucers.

Aunt Adèle turned her attention to accommodating Monsieur Vauquelin and left us kids to ourselves, informing us that she would call when they began the chicken. Since Wischard and little Laure were sleeping longer than usual, Madeleine-Grace and I practiced our dance together. Not wishing to disturb anyone with the noise we might make, we took our practice to the cliffs, and there with the view of the sea and the cloudless sky and the stretch of alabaster cliffs, we danced. Madeleine-Grace took choreographing seriously and incorporated all sorts of moves that she insisted we practice over and over until she thought of the next addition. And we carried on this way until we saw Aunt Melisende waving to us from the house and ran to her.

She sat with us on the bench in the flower island and reminded us that she was leaving today. I had forgotten and wished she could stay longer, but we had only as long as it would take her husband and nephews to arrive with the car from Fécamp.

With her arms crossed in her lap and Madeleine-Grace and me on either side of her, the scent of lilies hovering over us, she spoke to us in confidence, saying, "Now listen to me. You are both the two beautiful children of the beautiful Juliette Semperrin and Julien Avery, and you must never forget what that means the way your parents never forgot what it means to be the children of their parents. But I must share something important with you now that you no longer have the shield of your parents. You have Aunt Adèle, yes, but she can do only so much on account of the many obligations she has been given. The curse of the responsible, yes? They cannot *not* be responsible, and that is the reason your Aunt Adèle has delayed so long in marrying young Alban Vauquelin—too many responsibilities she has placed before her own happiness, which she does not see as a responsibility. We will help with that, won't we?" she chuckled as she lifted her hands and placed them on each of our knees. While her words were poignant, she seemed to ramble, and I wasn't sure where she was going.

"With the possibility of Adèle being pulled to other responsibilities, I must explain that your mother and Adèle spent hour after hour with their parents, taking in the customs of our people and our family. Young Léon was the same. Only Adèle now knows the meals, knows the techniques of the domestic arts—and you must never feel sorry for that wicked Laure!"

What attached itself as an after-thought about our Aunt Laure also had attached to it a vivid anger as Aunt Melisende grabbed our knees and shook them when she uttered our aunt's name. When we both stiffened upright at the shock, she chuckled, realizing an unexpected rancor had gotten the best of her.

"I apologize," she said, rubbing the fear off our knees. "She resents Adèle and Juliette for learning all these things when she knows she had the same opportunities to do so but never took them. She made everything else more important."

She looked to the horizon now, her anger replaced with lamentation. The rubbing of our knees stopped as she said, "My Adèle is certainly outnumbered, but, when you get older, you must not let that happen.

You must hear this from me, my dears, because my sister, your grandmother, will be discredited at every syllable, and while she sees with a more perceptive eye her own children than I do, her understanding is clouded by love. That is inevitable. She forgives what she knows is true, and they, in turn, step on her forgiveness by never changing."

She started sobbing and placed her arms around our necks, pulling us toward her body. "I miss your mother," she repeated through heaves of sobs. As they subsided, she said, "You must have a good visit with your Grandma'Maud. You must have many good visits with her."

Pressed against her, we nodded yes.

Releasing us from her grip, she said, "Everything I'm saying is true. You will question it, but as sure as Laure will emerge from her room the moment she knows I am gone, everything I have told you is the truth. And let me tell you, I told Gilbert I will be leaving on Sunday when you two leave for Paris, so she is unaware of my departure today. You wait and see. She will be down today, and you will know all that I say, then, has been true."

Uncle Ferdinand, Jules, and Marguerin arrived not moments after these words, calling from the veranda. Uncle Ferdinand spent a few moments talking with us and then, with his nephews, brought Aunt Melisende's bags to the car and walked her to the door. With no one up yet, Madeleine-Grace, Aunt Adèle, Monsieur Vauquelin, and I were the only ones to see her off, which we did with kisses and long embraces through Aunt Melisende's tears. We walked with her to the car, and when she was settled and the car began pulling away, we heard her burst into "Ma Normandie," the others in the car joining. Her hand waved to us out of the car, and we waved until the car drove out of our sight.

Monsieur Vauquelin and Aunt Adèle directed us to the kitchen to help with tonight's chicken, and together, we prepped not one but three birds. Monsieur Vauquelin had brought large bags of salt, and he poured their contents into one large bowl our aunt had placed on the table. She brought over dried herbs and pulverized, dried lemon peel, and they set them on the mound of salt in the bowl. With a large pestle, she ground the dried herbs and peel into the salt, emitting pleasant crackles on every push. After several minutes, she and Monsieur Vauquelin buried their hands in the salt and crushed it more with their palms.

"Now you do the same, and give it all a stir so that the herbs and salt are mixed evenly," Monsieur Vauquelin said. With our freshly washed and dried hands, Madeleine-Grace and I dipped them and swirled the salt and herbs around. "This is *sel gris*," he told us.

"And the herbs are thyme, sage, and lavender. The yellow dust is lemon peel I ground into a powder," Aunt Adèle shared.

Next, we brought the bowl of salt to the counter where the tied chickens sat in a giant Dutch oven. Lifting one, Aunt Adèle positioned the first chicken for the salt crust. Monsieur Vauquelin handed me a bottle of *calvados*.

"The secret ingredient," he said. "Pour a little of this on each chicken before we salt it."

"Not only does it help the salt stick better throughout the cooking, it helps flavor the chicken," Aunt Adèle said.

I followed their directions. Aunt Adèle patted the *calvados* all over the chicken, and then they poured a portion of the salt mixture on top and rubbed it all around. They positioned the next chicken, and Madeleine-Grace poured *calva* on that one. They repeated the salt encrusting process. And finally, we did the same procedure for the third chicken. Aunt Adèle grated fresh lemon peel over all the chickens as Monsieur Vauquelin filled some of the space between the snug birds with the remaining salt. They placed a lid on the Dutch oven.

"We'll let it sit like this a while before putting it in the oven," Aunt Adèle said.

Monsieur Vauquelin helped Aunt Adèle with several chores before we put the chickens in the oven. Tablecloths and runners to iron, rooms to dust, shutters to close, floors to sweep and mop occupied our time at a pace quicker on account of all the helping hands after good instruction. Our coffee break included sealing the Dutch oven with a clamp and placing it in the oven to begin cooking. As our *mésienne* neared, Madeleine-Grace asked Aunt Adèle to teach her how to crochet the doilies for the teacups, ones so thin that they appeared to be lace but apparently weren't. While Aunt Adèle and Madeleine-Grace relaxed with their crochets on the divan in the *salle-en-arrière* and Monsieur Vauquelin switched from one bead to the next of his rosary on the armchair, I wished I had my magazines to peruse but did not dare mention them. Instead, I thought about cocktails, from making them at home in Chicago with my mother or father to making them here with Ansgot and soon Monsieur Vauquelin.

We returned from *mésienne* to a smiling Monsieur Vauquelin anxious to learn how to make the Jeuffine cocktail. I taught him as I had taught Ansgot, allowing him to help with the swizzle stick stirring, unnecessary it may have been. We took our first sips as our aunts, uncles, and cousins arrived.

"You have made a true drink—one the world should know some day," Monsieur Vauquelin said.

"A true drink of Normandie now that the sprinkle of *hydromel* has become essential," I said, reaffirming to myself my allegiance to my Normand heritage.

Uncle Roul placed a hand on my shoulder, and without acknowledging Monsieur Vauquelin's presence, said to me after a sip from my glass, "I will go to Jeuffine's now for another bottle of *hydromel*."

"May I come with?" I asked, hoping to see her house and her store of what I imagined to be crates and crates, walls and walls, of her uncle's homemade *hydromel*—and her.

"Next time," he said, already at the front door.

Wischard joined us while most everyone else headed to the veranda for snacks and drinks. "I like your drink for the foam," he said, as I handed him a freshly made cocktail. He took a sip in such a way that allowed his upper lip to emerge full of white froth afterwards. He smiled as he tried to lick it off. His smile was already so wide when the sight of his mother at the bottom of the stairs caught his eye that his eyes bulged with joy. Calling for little Laure, he ran to her without the drink and hugged her. His sister ran in from the veranda and hugged her mother.

"Papa said that you said you would not be well until Sunday," Wischard said, his head pressed against his mother's chest.

"I had told him that, yes, but I felt better tonight and—"

"It's because you couldn't miss us anymore, isn't it?" asked Wischard.

"Yes," Aunt Laure said. "I couldn't bear another evening without you, my little ones."

To give them a few moments of reunion, Monsieur Vauquelin brought me into the kitchen to show me the finished chickens, releasing an herbaceous and succulent odor when he lifted the lid. My mouth watered.

In the dining room, Aunt Adèle led grace and served the chicken and sides of potatoes and hard-boiled eggs—a savory, tangy salad—and leeks and sweet onions braised in olive oil. Wine and beer were passed around this evening as we took our bites of moist, salty chicken that our aunt had sliced so perfectly.

"Why has Papa not returned from his walk?" asked Chardine.

"He probably is talking to Mademoiselle des Gervais still, to be polite," I said.

"Mademoiselle des Gervais?" questioned Aunt Mirabelle, as if she had not known her to be the destination of Uncle Roul's walk.

"He walked to her place for *hydromel*," I shared.

"Roul said he was a little sorer than usual after *la choule* yesterday. He must wish to soothe his muscles," Uncle Romain said.

"With a walk?" asked Alphonse.

"With *hydromel*," Wischard said, to which we all laughed.

"'With *hydromel*,'" said Uncle Gilbert. "That's precisely what I was thinking."

"And you, Romain? Are you sore, too?" Aunt Pé said.

"I did not play so hard," he admitted. "I am not too sore."

"All this talk of *la choule*," said Aunt Laure. "You do not usually play on weekdays. How much has changed after a few days of rest."

"You missed so much!" said little Laure, full of enthusiasm at the chance to regale her mother with stories of the past several days. "You missed *la choule* and Ellande's new cocktail and—"

"Hush, Laure," her mother said. "You must not carry on so loudly."

Little Laure's smile crumbled like dried lemon peel turning to powder, and she turned her attention to cutting a piece of chicken on her plate.

Wischard picked up where his sister left off, careful not to betray too much animation. "Ellande named his cocktail 'the Jeuffine' after Mademoiselle des Gervais. And you missed *la choule*—"

"I said that!" interrupted little Laure.

"Laure!" corrected her mother, and the child set her fork down, dropped her hands in her lap, and fought tears.

"—and a visit from Aunt Melisende, and we sang outside," continued Wischard.

"Aunt Melisende?" said Aunt Laure. "I did not know she had come. How strange for me to have missed her visit. How I wish I had known she was here."

And I saw her on the evening of song in the back lawn looking at Aunt Melisende and the rest of us from her glass terrace door over the veranda.

"We spent a lovely evening with the Graverands in Fécamp," added Aunt Pé.

"An evening with—?" repeated Aunt Laure, turning to her husband. "How is it I did not know about this, Gilbert?"

"You were ill," Uncle Gilbert said.

"What difference does it make?" asked Uncle Romain. "You could not have come."

For some reason, Aunt Laure looked at her husband and shook her head at him, as if he had done her a great wrong.

"Aunt Melisende was not our only visitor," continued Uncle Romain. "We must not forget Alban Vauquelin who graces us again with his presence and the salt of the earth."

"My husband bought a new, modern refrigerator for the house, Monsieur," Aunt Pé said. Her seeming impertinent proclamation was received with dumbfounded looks. "Therefore, you needn't bring as much salt. Perhaps this will reduce your visits."

She smirked as she enjoyed a piece of the chicken he had made, and when Uncle Romain chuckled with his mouth full of leeks and chicken, she chuckled, too. Monsieur Vauquelin stared at them for three seconds and then shifted his gaze to the vexed face of Aunt Adèle, putting her at ease with his grin. I did not understand what Aunt Pé had meant, but suggesting that he reduce his visits did not sit well with me.

"Had you joined the men for *la choule*?" asked Aunt Laure.

"No," Monsieur Vauquelin said. "I came for *apéro* only."

"Salt, she is a cruel mistress," said Uncle Romain. "She does not permit him to stray from her side."

"He arrived with Mademoiselle des Gervais, did he not?" said Aunt Pé, a smirk forming on her face.

"Let us not forget I had Lady Victorine Galimard on my other arm," said Monsieur Vauquelin, bringing a smile to Aunt Adèle's face.

"How many mistresses do you have?" asked Wischard, once again inciting our laughter.

Amidst the flow of earthy wine and the more than occasional bitter conversation, we finished another delicious meal and found plenty at which to laugh. Uncle Roul still had not returned by dinner's end, and, once settled on the veranda with a cigar, Uncle Romain grumbled to Uncle Gilbert about having to drive me to Paris. All the aunts except Aunt Adèle lamented the imposition on Uncle Romain who scoffed, puffed on his cigar, and finished what must have amounted to his fourth glass of wine.

"I wish we could go to evening prayers and right to bed," Madeleine-Grace whispered.

"Me, too," I said, not wanting to hear any more about what an inconvenience my sister and I were to have to drive to Paris, especially as my uncle grew more and more vehement about the hassle. My aunts fueled his anger.

"Do they not need salt in Paris, Vauquelin?" asked Uncle Romain. "Can you not drive the Basques there this weekend along with your mistresses?"

Aunt Pé laughed mechanically but Aunt Adèle admonished him, saying, "Don't refer to them by that."

Alphonse, standing on the top step of the veranda, passed his cigarette to young Roul for a light, but young Roul, extended on the balustrade with his back against the pillar, refused him a light. With an unlit cigarette in his mouth, Alphonse stepped from his brother on the balustrade toward Uncle Romain, sticking the tip of his cigarette to his uncle's cigar for a light. He inhaled deeply until it was lit. Once it was lit, he glanced at his idling brother and then to the rest of us, saying, "Roul has a mistress now, too."

Uncle Romain jumped from his chair and lurched for Alphonse. Lifting him by the shirt with one hand so that the boy's cigarette fell from his mouth, he swung at his face with his other hand. The blow hurled Alphonse across the floor into the balustrade, knocking young Roul over the edge. As the women rushed for the boy and the men for Uncle Romain, I saw Alphonse touching his bleeding lip.

"Mind how you talk!" Uncle Romain shouted as Uncle Gilbert and Monsieur Vauquelin subdued him in his chair.

"Romain! Romain!" screamed Aunt Pé.

Searching beyond his approaching wife, he said to Aunt Mirabelle, "Slap him! You let him talk that way! Slap him!"

"Romain!" shouted Aunt Pé. Then, muffled into his chest, she said, "Alphonse was speaking of his brother."

Uncle Romain, about to shout something again to Aunt Mirabelle, did not continue. Young Roul ascended the veranda steps, scratched across the face from the shrubbery and holding his shoulder. He saw Alphonse in Chardine's arms and his mother at his side. Aunt Mirabelle rose from her son, stepped to Uncle Romain and, ripping Aunt Pé off him, slapped him across the face. As she stepped back to her son, Uncle Romain made for her, only to be held down in his chair by Uncle Gilbert and Monsieur Vauquelin.

Finally resigned not to pursue Aunt Mirabelle, he shouted at Aunt Pé, "Why did you not tell me he meant his brother?"

The men held him in place for another half hour as Aunt Adèle tended to Alphonse and young Roul. Aunt Adèle soon hurried the children through prayers in the foyer and walked us all upstairs. Monsieur Vauquelin remained at the bottom of the stairs as if guarding the domain of the children. I fell asleep to my own prayers, telling God I was sorry for being the cause of Uncle Romain's anger, deciding that if he hadn't been so angry about having to drive us to Paris to begin with, he would not have struck Alphonse.

The next morning, Madeleine-Grace and I found Uncle Roul sleeping on the divan in the *salle-en-arrière* again, but we found someone else lying on a usually unoccupied piece of furniture. On the bench in the flower island, sprawled with one leg over the armrest and the other in the flowers, fully dressed in yesterday's clothes, slept Monsieur Vauquelin. Sleeping lightly, he awoke when we approached, not particularly startled, and sat upright.

"Your aunt was afraid and asked me to stay," he shared. "But you mustn't tell anyone. It would pain her to think her family knew I stayed."

I didn't understand the pain that could come from such an act of honorable protection, but I said, "I promise not to tell."

CHAPITRE 5

It was decided. Uncle Roul agreed to drive us to Paris, especially after Uncle Romain had sustained a black eye from his brother's punch upon learning of the cause of Alphonse's broken lip. Uncle Romain called his black eye a good turn of fortune as it spared him a visit with his mother. This aversion to his mother I had yet to understand. Aunt Mirabelle and Aunt Adèle both insisted on accompanying us, but Uncle Roul forbade them, the former on account of her being a distraction and the latter on account of her being needed in the Etretat-au-Delà house. Wischard had also requested to join us, but Aunt Laure forbade that, too, on account of three grandchildren at once being too much for Grandma'Maud to handle. Uncle Gilbert announced concern over civil unrest in Paris after a bombing in Algeria. All these reasons, understandable as they appeared, I perceived as phony. I just wasn't sure why they struck me that way. Uncle Roul had the final word on all matters of transportation and the visit to Paris, and he decreed that we leave Etretat-au-Delà the three of us when we returned from Mass on Sunday, allowing him time to sleep in and ready the car.

Two other suggestions had been made, the first by Aunt Adèle. She suggested taking us by train, herself. All the adults squashed this suggestion for the same reason Uncle Roul had squashed her accompanying us in the car: only God knew into what disarray and bedlam the household might fall in her absence. The second suggestion came from Astride, teasing the *guenilles* out of the old doll of Chardine's.

"Why doesn't Monsieur Vauquelin drive them? He certainly has a car."

At first, those present in the *salle-en-arrière* chuckled, thinking she was carrying on her father's line of "Alban, the chauffeur of Fleur" remarks. The reaction was lost on Astride who hadn't meant to be funny at all but had, maybe, meant to be conniving; I was not convinced she fully realized she was being so. Madeleine-Grace and I did not realize this at the time but sensed her mischief nonetheless.

"I saw his car here Friday morning," she added through the chuckles.

Of all the mornings she woke early, it was the one of which Monsieur Vauquelin dreaded anyone learning. I saw Aunt Adèle's face blanch, and I remembered Monsieur Vauquelin's words early that morning. Still unsure about why his sleeping over would render Aunt Adèle so troubled, I spoke anyway.

"He was here in the morning to check on young Roul and Uncle Romain, but he left when I told him they were well and sleeping soundly," I said, looking at my hands. I glanced at the side table for something to take casually into my hand and hold but saw only the radio—too awkward to grab.

"So you saw him then? He was here?" asked Aunt Pé.

"Yes, I saw him outside by the bench in the back. Once we talked, he returned to his car and left. I think I assured him everything was fine." So far, I hadn't told a lie, except for the part about checking on young Roul and Uncle Romain, and omitting that he had slept here over night.

"Where was Adèle?" asked Aunt Mirabelle.

"She hadn't come down yet," I said. "Madeleine-Grace and I awoke earlier than usual."

"I am disappointed," said Uncle Roul jovially, a hand on each hip. "I thought he had stolen the convent life out of you. Now I guess there's still hope for the convents!"

Everyone laughed except Aunt Adèle, who, like a rising thermometer in the cartoons, turned bright red in a flash, only what had first manifested as concern now turned to anger.

"Do not talk that way in front of the children!" she snapped, but their laughter did not abate.

"I might like him more if he had stayed," said Aunt Mirabelle.

"I might like *Adèle* more if he had stayed," said Aunt Pé.

"Why?" asked little Laure.

"What does it mean, 'stolen the convent life out of you?'" asked Wischard.

"Stop speaking this way in front of the children!" insisted Aunt Adèle.

The children's questions went unaddressed through the adults' laughter. Uncle Roul declared at last that Monsieur Vauquelin could not be imposed on to drive us to Paris since he was "a laborer" who could not afford to miss a day of work.

Astride was stuffing some of the raggedy strands of fabric back into Chardine's *drouène*, taking no great pains to ensure the Cauchois heirloom looked anything as it had prior to her disemboweling it, and the look of satisfaction on her face reflected more the onslaught of laughter of which she considered herself the source.

For a short while, I couldn't take my eyes off the green—every which tint of it—as we rode the country roads of Normandie's *bocage*. The venerable barns and shanties and carts hiding amid thickets of apple and pear trees, glimmering in the sunlight, and the sparkling waters of ponds pulled our attention beyond the gulches and into the confines of the *closmasure* enclosures as we passed. A sheep among its fold studied our car from its grassy pasture and returned to its grazing unbothered, as if our presence were not an intrusion. Beyond the fold, I saw the alternating dark-gray flint and salmon-pink brick layers of a farmhouse rising to the dun thatch of roof. Thin, worn walkways crept into groves of oaks before disappearing in flickering verdure. The rows of beeches, the fields of flax, the clover climbing to the low summits of chalky limestone rocks, the patches of marguerites, all reached for the cloudless blue of a Cauchois sky. The white of alabaster cliffs, the greens of the foliage, and the blue of the sky—these, to me, are the colors of Normandie and always will be. With Madeleine-Grace at my side in the backseat of Uncle Roul's auto and the countryside all about, I did not feel at peace, especially as the drive and the surroundings and the destination brought a longing for my parents, but I did feel a rare sense of belonging, which I had not felt at the Etretat-au Delà house. I felt that my indescribable appreciation of the beauty meant I must belong to Normandie, or at least that the Normandie of my mother and father accepted me.

Earlier, Aunt Adèle had corralled all the children for Mass as she had in the past and escorted us into town, attended Mass, and walked with us home. Uncle Roul had just awoken, so Aunt Adèle did not feel rushed in supplying us with gifts for Grandma'Maud, including some blouses she had made her, a few bags of salt, two skeins of jonquil-yellow yarn, and the bottle of bourbon Grand-mère Armance had packed as an American gift from us. She requested Uncle Roul pick up several packets of mint seeds for her as the merchant in the market hadn't been bringing them of late; she was planning on growing another mint garden closer to the shed on account of complaints from her brothers and sisters-in-law about the smell of mint from the islands near the back veranda. By early afternoon, Uncle Roul had rolled out of Etretat-au-Delà with us for what he anticipated would be a four-hour drive to Paris.

My sister never took her eyes from all that she saw through her car window while I at times turned my head around for views through every which window. Content after a while to peer through solely my own window, the irony of the stillness of the surrounding trees and shrubs, rocks and ponds, green fields and blue sky struck me, for we were moving at thirty kilometers per hour, and faster had my uncle not gained on a pokey car. The trees and the shrubs barely rustled but maintained such composure; if a wisp of white or pink passed the blue sky, its incremental movement went undetected; even our gaze sitting crossed-legged on the alabaster cliffs had caught flecks of waves' rises and dips but in a way that looked serene like the shimmering of a Seurat seascape. The memory of my father making cantaloupe liqueur with me was not animated in gestures and turns of expression and peeling and cubing and pouring, but comprised of unstirred images of him with a piece of fresh fruit in his mouth, of him pouring the pulp into a bottle through a funnel, of him placing the last of six filled bottles in a box. The dream of my father had placed him on the bed, sitting next to me, immobile. None of these visions thoroughly lacked movement but all were simple and contained and calm. And here we were ripping through the stillness of the Normandie countryside for the Paris bustle at thirty kilometers per hour. Here I was charging through my summers unaware of my pace because everything around me and within me masked itself in stillness here. Maybe this is the way with youth. Maybe I would come to find this is the way with life.

I felt the car come to a slow and then to a stop by the time we had been travelling a little over an hour. I leaned forward for a look through the windshield to see an obstruction in the road. My uncle released an expletive, and our car accelerated just enough to pull to the side of the road behind a few other waiting cars. Uncle Roul stepped out of the car and then popped his head in and said to us, "Step out and stretch your legs. It appears we have a delay."

A rickety flatbed truck transporting live chickens had veered off the road when a boy from a nearby farm stand had kicked his soccer ball into the street. The driver had pulled his truck out of a low gulch and parked it half on the road, as much to the side as he could, while he and the weepy boy picked up the fallen crates of chickens and loose hay. As the two reloaded them, the chickens clucked and cawed, and a few loose ones scurried off the road as the two chased them. The few drivers and passengers that had pulled over occupied themselves with the produce of the farm stand that the father of the boy oversaw. He kept more of an eye on his son, making sure he indeed helped the driver, than on making sales of the beets, onions, and garlic of which he had an abundance. He had positioned his roadside stand next to the crumbling remains of a pink brick wall of a farmhouse. The vague rectangular remnants of the structure made me wonder what had brought about its ruin: a bombing during the war, a fire, a peasant revolt? I did not know my French history well but allowed my imagination to run wild nonetheless.

"Sit here," Uncle Roul said, sitting on the rubble of the low wall while he lit a cigarette.

"No one is helping them," said Madeleine-Grace as she trotted over to lift crates of chickens onto the bed of the truck.

I sat next to Uncle Roul, who passed the cigarette to me after taking several puffs. I took one and passed it back, aware that my parents did not want me smoking but did allow a puff here and there. I did not know if Uncle Roul knew this or not, nor if he cared, as he offered me another in our silence of minutes. I accepted it, puffed, and passed it back. Madeleine-Grace returned, for the driver of the truck shooed her away with a friendly smile; such labor was not fitting for a girl. She leaned against the wall next to me while keeping an intent eye on the work of the man and the boy.

My mind raced to the prospect that the farmhouse whose remaining wall on which I rested had been destroyed during the war, which I knew had devastated Normandie, but I did not know much more. Of course, I knew that while my Uncle Léon had not survived that war, my Uncle Roul had. I think because Uncle Roul had proffered the cigarette, I felt at ease enough to say, "Maman said I should never ask a soldier about the war. Why must I never ask?" I regretted asking as soon as I had uttered it.

Uncle Roul had just inhaled and responded without a pause, the smoke pouring out with his soft-spoken words, "The war, it changes a man because of what he has seen, because of what he has done, and some men don't like how they have changed. So they don't want to talk about it. I suppose it's polite to assume this and not bring it up."

More at ease, I asked, "Would you not want me to ask questions about the war because of what you have seen?"

"I will be honest with you out of respect for my sister," he said, looking above a distant row of beeches at the end of a field across the street. "I was ashamed less of what I have seen and more of what I have done. And now—now, I have learned not to be ashamed, but I cannot change what I have done and what I have become. Soldiers come to this conclusion. They must."

With her sight fixed on the man in the truck bed receiving a crate of chickens the boy lifted to him, Madeleine-Grace asked, "If it was what you had done—your actions—that had made you change, cannot different actions change you now, to become someone new once more, someone of whom you are not ashamed?"

Uncle Roul smiled without looking at either of us. "You are wise, little one. There comes a point after war, once the soldier has returned, when, even though he wants to be grateful to have survived, he feels utterly defeated by the war, by life; some never recover from this feeling. For me, it's like the boulder next to the shed. Your Aunt Adèle grew herbs around it so that now it is overgrown with clinging marjoram and hidden behind tall mint. The greenery is pliant and soft and can bend around it. It is still alive, so it can change, growing taller and fuller. I have become like the boulder. Even though it's hidden behind years of growth, it's too hard to change into something else or to be budged. Willing my own change, except for the worse, is too difficult when I know how terrible such a change makes me feel, when I know I am—."

He brought the cigarette to his lips, inhaled, and blew out white smoke. His smile was gone.

"Still ashamed," Madeleine-Grace offered, to complete his thought. "It is why you walked out during evening prayers after *la choule*."

Tears formed in my uncle's eyes. I saw this when he passed the little bit of remaining cigarette to me. "No more questions about the war, little ones, for now."

I took my last puff and he his. The driver of the truck had run around to the driver's seat and started to pull away while the boy stood on the side of the road wiping away another tear, his foot resting on the soccer ball. The others reclaimed their cars, and, in a swirl of dust from the road, we took off single file behind the truck until it turned off and we could accelerate past Rouen and onto Paris.

The traffic of Paris proper slowed us after having made good time on the road. We still moved easily, though, through the sunny streets that coursed through a city of white and gray buildings—apartments and hotels, monuments and churches, shops and cafés—dotted with streetlamps and hanging flowers. On one corner, an iron railing under an iron archway led to a Métro stop below, and across the street, a group of locals rose en masse to the sidewalk from an exit staircase of the same stop. Lines of cars rolled without horns blaring, without aggressive jolts to the bumper of the preceding car. The middle-aged driver of the black Delage next to us advanced with steady concentration, his grip firm on the wheel, as Citroëns, Renaults, and even a Poinard Tourisme hastened along. Once stopped at a light near Grandma'Maud's place, I saw pedestrians and cyclists enjoying a leisurely Sunday in this tame part of the city, Arrondissement 15. An old man in navy blue plants and white button down, sleeves rolled and a brown *feutre* on his head, came to a stop on his bicycle at the intersection. In the basket of his bicycle, two bottles of wine and a *boule* of bread rested. Two teenage girls, one in white capris and thin, yellow sweater and the other in yellow capris with pink blouse, walked down the sidewalk together laughing. When they stopped at the crosswalk, the one in pink pulled out a tiny mirror and looked at herself.

"This is a different world in some ways," Uncle Roul said, a big smile forming when the girls' laughter caught his attention. Perhaps they reminded him of someone back in Etretat-au-Delà, for he asked me, "I know you like Jeuffine des Gervais. She is—." I don't know what he was thinking but not saying. Then he said again, "I know you like her."

"She is very pretty," I said, although somehow, while she did not fit in entirely with the crowd of Etretat-au-Delà, I could not see the woman in long, silky dresses with flowers in her hair fitting in with the chic crowd of Paris either. "She helped me with my cocktail."

"You like beautiful women, Ellande?" he asked me.

I didn't answer and looked immediately at Madeleine-Grace in my embarrassment over the question. I felt my face heating and wondered if my cheeks were turning red.

"I enjoy beautiful women, and you will, too," Uncle Roul said in my silence. "Do you have a girlfriend?"

It struck me that this was the first time Uncle Roul had asked me about my life in America, about my life at all. This is what he wanted to know about?

"No," I responded with a grin, and left it at that.

"You must have a girlfriend soon. When you do, you will see why I enjoy beautiful women."

"Isn't it because they are beautiful and laugh with you and talk with you?"

Uncle Roul chuckled and then said, "It is because they kiss you and make you feel good. You will see one day. Do you talk about girls with your friends?"

Madeleine-Grace raised her brow and then looked out the window.

"No," I said. Except for planning ways to help my friend Jimmy Mertens avoid Mary Beth Narble, who announced to the whole class that she liked him, and discussing ways to spray Brigid Staples with the hose because she ratted out my friend Jack McCleland for borrowing her pencil during grammar, we didn't talk about girls, at least not in a way that expressed a relationship with them.

"Then what do you do with your friends?"

"They play baseball, tell jokes, and drink," Madeleine-Grace said. Although uncharacteristic of my sister to chime in so casually about me, I chalked it up to Uncle Roul's well-known ability to induce easy conversation, even among strangers. That's how he must have become acquainted with the recently arrived Jeuffine des Gervais, I figured. I had heard he did this on his recent visit to Chicago. He had slipped off for an evening in the city alone, had talked in French at a bar with a professor of Cajun, Creole, and American history, and spoke about *plaçage* among the first French settlers the next day at breakfast. That professor showed Uncle Roul around the city that night after having known him a matter of minutes; that was my uncle's effect on others.

"You drink the whiskey," he said as a matter of fact, the liquor he associated with Americans.

"I have a lot of Irish friends," I said.

"You must share with them our *calva*."

When the light changed, my uncle nodded to the girls as he accelerated, receiving no notice from them, and proceeded to explain that baseball moved much too slowly and that, especially before the World Cup, I should have been playing soccer with my friends, if not tennis before the French Championship that had spanned the last week and a half of May. I shared that only a few of my Italian and Polish friends knew soccer, and even they, like I, played baseball or football in America; a few of my friends played tennis, I not among them. He did not like this but did not have much time to protest as we pulled up to Grandma'Maud's flat on the corner.

After parking, Uncle Roul led the way up the interior staircase of the dim building. Once one flight up and into Grandma'Maud's flat, our laden arms readied themselves to relax on account of the elevator carrying us to the "noble" floor, *l'étage noble*. The building, which formerly had included a *boulangerie* and a *papeterie* on the ground floor, was the only one in Paris designed by architect Maurice Allard and updated years later with elevator, *demeures*, which are residences on the ground and mezzanine levels, electricity, and other advancements.

When first built, shops and businesses occupied the main floors, and domestic units began on the floors above, the finest on the first few floors above the shops. According to design specifications, the buildings could not exceed six stories. Grandma'Maud's place occupied all six floors; however, the main living quarters began on what the French call *l'étage noble*. Her bedroom and sitting rooms occupied the floor above, guest bedrooms and small anterooms the fifth, and servant quarters and attic space on the topmost floor. The installation of the elevator in every apartment facilitated transportation among floors, but Grandma'Maud divided her time between only the two floors, *l'étage noble* and her bedroom.

While I appreciated it for its familiarity, the foyer of her flat boasted no ornamentation nor splendor. A lapis lazuli vase of fresh, white marguerites on a marble-top entrance table hid against the wall to our left, and two imposing closet doors greeted us ahead. Still carrying bags, we walked right to another hall where we met the *petit salon*, which opened into the *grand salon*. Opposite them, across a narrow hall, were the kitchen and, behind it, the dining room, which I have been told is atypical of Parisian architecture—usually the *salles à manger*, or dining rooms, line the front façade of the flats. At the end of the hall was a staircase leading to the bedrooms. We could have taken the elevator to the bedroom floors, but Uncle Roul couldn't be certain that Grandma'Maud wasn't occupying *l'étage noble*.

We ascended the back stairs for her suite of bedrooms, and in one of the sitting rooms, two women lazed as the sun burst through the upper-story, open windows. The one sitting on the divan wore a blue dress with a gray smock over it. Her head titled backwards on a round pillow she had propped up, positioning her face directly in the sunlight of the window behind her. The other woman reclined in an armchair, one foot on an ottoman and an arm bent on the chair arm, more attentive than the other woman to the words broadcasting from the radio on the low table in the middle of the room. She wore a black duster and gray apron, and a drink I knew must be hers awaited her casual sip. Both women I estimated to be in their late twenties. The woman on the divan was thin, of medium height, and had light brown hair, although it looked flaxen as she bathed her head in the sunlight. The woman in the armchair, thin despite a big-boned frame, and also of medium height with dark brown hair, I knew to be Borbála, Grandma'Maud's maid.

Borbála, the first to notice us, started in silence, and within seconds, the other woman's head jerked at the movement into the room. They both stood, Borbála setting her drink down beforehand.

"Monsieur Semperrin," she said, bowing her head. "And you brought the grandchildren of—"

He put his finger over his mouth and advanced toward the doors leading to Grandma'Maud's chamber. Borbála smiled at the thought of the surprise, and the other woman inched over to see the sight of our grandmother's reaction; I had not known our arrival to be a surprise.

Uncle Roul leaned in the door frame between the sitting room and the bedroom after a nudge to approach our grandmother. Past her bed, Grandma'Maud sat in an armchair angled toward the balcony doors, knitting a mauve blanket at a moderate speed. The doors to the balcony ajar, a gentle breeze cut the stagnant air of an early Parisian evening. The breeze, along with a glow of light, slipped past the narrow opening of curtains covering the balcony doors of the dim bedroom. We had stepped only as far as the bed when Grandma'Maud noticed us. Her needles, knitting, and mouth dropped.

I don't know what she mouthed, but no words came out. Having seen her months ago at our parents' funeral and realizing only now how much we felt the absence of her, my sister and I rushed to her before she could stand. Her arms opened just in time for our loving and longing embrace. Thank Goodness she had dropped the needles. Her arms and the mid-length sleeves of her black dress and her love wrapped around us and held us through our sobs and hers.

"Why did no one tell me of your visit?" she asked between sobs. "Someone could have told me you were coming today!"

We said nothing and simply maintained our hug.

Finally, we loosened our hold, and Grandma'Maud's hands rose, one on each of our cheeks.

"I am so happy to see you. I have been waiting for your visit as I knew you have been in France for some time now," she said.

Madeleine-Grace leaned her cheek into our grandmother's hand and started crying again.

"What is it, my dear?" our grandmother asked, tilting her head in a bewildering empathy.

"You look like Maman," Madeleine-Grace said through her tears. It was true and untrue. A look at Grandma'Maud showed she looked nothing like our mother as our grandmother's face sagged and looked fuller and more aged than our mother's, but a closer study revealed the same almond eye shape, the same perfect curve at the bottom of the nose, the same thin lips and roundness of the mouth when she spoke.

A true compliment to Grandma'Maud, the acknowledgement as well as a ping of pain brought on more tears, not only from my grandmother but from me, too. "My dear, dear ones," she said over and over. "My dear, dear ones."

I don't know how much time passed crying in her embrace, and after our tears lessened, how much more time passed. Unless a breeze passed through the open doors, I felt warm in her embrace thanks to the heat. The mauve knitting remained in her lap, pronounced against the black I remember her wearing.

She looked past us for a moment and then pulled us to her chest. With her chin on my shoulder, she said, "I see you."

Uncle Roul, at whom I gathered she was looking, said, "I should hope so. It was father's sight that failed, not yours."

"No," she said. "I see you, Roul. You can hide nothing. Paris talks. So do Fécamp and Etretat-au-Delà."

Pulling gently from Grandma'Maud's embrace, I turned and saw Uncle Roul's face turn from sentimental calmness to disgust. He turned and walked into the sitting room where the two women stood next to each other.

"You could not have told me you were bringing Ellande and Madeleine-Grace to Paris?" she asked.

"We thought a surprise would be nice," Uncle Roul said from the other room.

"You thought so, huh? Or you were too lazy to inform me? Or you never thought to inform me?" she asked.

"Crazy," Uncle Roul said to the two women. "See what I mean?"

"*I* see what you mean because the sun is shining on you as if you were on a cloud three meters away from it. How many times have I told those two to shut the curtains? They don't heed me."

The two women exchanged glances, and the one I didn't know looked at Uncle Roul. He stepped back into the bedroom, leaving them in the sitting room, aglow.

Lowering his voice, he said, "The curtains are drawn open still. What difference does that make?"

"What difference? Ask Juliette and Adèle what difference that makes," Grandma'Maud rejoined.

"What do I care what Ju—what Adèle thinks of open curtains? She cares if the hems of my boxers don't align when they're folded, if my wife doesn't place a chocolate on my pillow case before I lay my head on it."

"As if their concerns are frivolous," Grandma'Maud said to us, although the comment was meant for Uncle Roul. "Aside from the direct order coming from their employer—"

"Ah, yes," Uncle Roul said, "all must bow to you—."

"—and you would be fine if your hired help overtly disobeyed your orders when you are paying them?"

"I would—I would simply—." Uncle Roul stammered, unsure of the point he wished to make.

"Aside from the order coming from their employer, which should be enough to see the small request through," Grandma'Maud continued, "Juliette and Adèle would object to the constantly and unnecessarily open curtains warping the wood of the divan and the tables and dying the carpets. Very damaging at times, that sun. Why is it that Juliette and Adèle know of this and my other children do not?"

Uncle Roul turned for a glimpse of the two women, both of whom heard every word despite my uncle's lowered voice. When Uncle Roul turned, Grandma'Maud ogled them.

"An early *apéritif*, Borbála?" my grandmother noted.

"I will make a snack for the children," she responded quickly, lifting her drink from the table. "Would you like one before dinner, yourself, Madame?"

"A snack for the children will suffice," our grandmother said to Borbála. Then to us, she asked, "Would you like a drink, too? You've had a long journey?"

We both nodded no for some reason.

"Bring them a *cidre*," our grandmother ordered with a smile. "We must accommodate more mouths for dinner now. You will see to it?"

"I shall see to it," Borbála responded, hurrying out of the sitting room without her drink. As soon as she arrived at the door to the hall, she stopped and turned to us. "So happy to have you back, Monsieur, Mademoiselle," and to Uncle Roul, "Monsieur." Then she left for the kitchen.

"Bertille," Grandma'Maud said with a raised voice. "I wish to accompany the children on a walk before dinner."

The other woman strutted past Uncle Roul into the bedroom to Grandma'Maud. We stepped back from her as the woman took the knitting and set it on the foot of the bed. Then she helped our grandmother from the chair and steadied her once she was fully on her feet. Our grandmother held the woman's arm for several seconds until she felt balanced enough to let go.

"I will stay behind and rest my eyes," Uncle Roul said.

"You will accompany us," Grandma'Maud said to Uncle Roul. When she said this, she first looked him in the eye and then shifted her gaze to the other woman.

When Uncle Roul saw this, he said, "I don't need to take walks through Paris with a crazy woman." He walked out of the bedroom, through the sitting room, and into the hall.

"There's plenty else he doesn't need but doesn't think twice about doing," she said, looking first at us with a smirk and then at the woman.

The woman, assured of Grandma'Maud's steadiness and full awareness, stepped over to us and extended her hand. "I am Bertille Timbert, caretaker of your grandmother. I have been her caretaker for several months now."

We greeted her cordially, our hands meeting hers.

"Your grandmother speaks often of you and of your—." Another unfinished sentence. "If we have time together, maybe you can tell me of America. I would like to visit someday."

"Perhaps you will meet a good gentleman whom you will marry, and he will take you there," Grandma'Maud said.

Our grandmother led us to the door and into the sitting room where she sighed, pulling closed the curtains after taking several steps out of her way. "Some learn better than others," she noted. We walked down the hall to the elevator, descending to street level and stepping outside.

Once on the sidewalk, Grandma'Maud said, "I told myself that you would like a stroll. I had no idea you were coming today, but I remembered that I wanted to take you for this walk—as we did with your parents the last time we were all here in Paris. Oh, Juliette and Julien." She looked up at the sky, blue with thin, white clouds but not easy to see through the foliage of the overhanging trees lining the block.

We walked with her at a moderate pace in the shade to the end of the tree-lined block and turned left. On this corner, with no trees overhead and the expansive apartment buildings at an end, we felt the directness of the sun and strange consolation of the blue and white sky. This residential enclave was quiet, but occasional car accelerations and screeches cast a din as infrequent shouts and peals of locals' laughter punctuated the air.

"We will not walk for long," she said. "You must be hungry if not tired."

While I walked at her side, I noticed Madeleine-Grace nestle herself in Grandma'Maud's arm. My sister, despite a firmness developing in her character, reverted to the little girl she was with my mother. I knew that she sought the comfort of our mother and found something different in Grandma'Maud's hold, but what might be the closest she could come to the resemblance of our mother. The reality of the difference did not deter my sister from the search for something similar, for the comfort of our mother's touch.

"It is not Etretat-au-Delà," our grandmother said as we rounded the next corner, again turning left, "but Paris is beautiful, is it not? Did you not miss it?"

"Yes," I said, but I did not say that I missed it with my parents.

My answer brought us to a stop, and Grandma'Maud angled us to face the Seine a few blocks north of us. From this spot, we could catch only a glimpse of it. We stood in that spot for several minutes, taking in quiet Paris. The debris of celebrations over last night's World Cup match for third place did not reach this neighborhood, nor did civil unrest in the aftermath of the bombing in Algiers of which our Uncle Gilbert had warned us.

"We will travel farther tomorrow, my dears," she said, resuming our stroll.

We walked around the entire block and ascended the steps of her flat. At the top, Grandma'Maud inhaled the fresh air and said that it was good to get out. Once upstairs in her flat, we found Uncle Roul sitting with Bertille on the divan of our grandmother's sitting room, my uncle with a drink. She rose upon our entrance to help my grandmother to her room.

"Borbála left your drinks on the table on the balcony," Bertille said, pulling open the balcony curtains and pushing open the doors.

Madeleine-Grace and I stepped out for our drinks and took sips as we glanced at the small park across the street below. This balcony extended not from the front façade of the building but the side, overlooking another side street and, across the way, a corner park with manicured lawn, potted hydrangeas, and short benches in both the open of the small space and under the shade of trees. It was currently unoccupied, but I knew in the morning, residents stepped out to read their newspaper there.

When I glanced into the bedroom, I noticed on the far side of Grandma'Maud's bed a pile of fabrics, a small burlap bag, and a pair of shears like those Madame Maillart had been using at the *mercerie* shop.

The sight reminded me of the gifts, so I alerted Madeleine-Grace of our neglected task. We dashed for the gifts and returned to the bedroom to present them to our grandmother who received them joyfully. She unfolded the blouses and held them up in the light coming in from the balcony, smiling and commenting on Aunt Adèle's skill; Bertille concurred. She held the bourbon to her heart mockingly, as if such a thing were as near and dear to her as we were, making us laugh. When she rifled through the selection of fabrics, smiling at the variety, Bertille rolled her eyes.

"More fabrics," Bertille said. "You are obsessive."

"They are beautiful fabrics," Grandma'Maud said, lowering them to us to feel.

"You must tell your daughter not to feed your obsessions," Bertille said. "I will ask Roul to relay this message for next time."

"Yes, you wish to relay that to Roul."

Bertille tugged at the strings of her smock with a grunt and stepped into the sitting room, saying nothing to my dozing uncle. Within moments, Borbála burst in.

"Madame!" she shouted. "I saw from the window you have more unexpected guests!"

"Who is calling on me?" Grandma'Maud asked.

We heard the closing of a door down the hall and steps and rustling and voices—one all too familiar.

"Surprise!" she said, stepping into the sitting room with a small entourage behind her. It was Aunt Melisende with Uncle Ferdinand and his great-nephews, Jules and Marguerin, inches behind her holding bags.

"Melisende!" shouted Grandma'Maud, rushing to her for an embrace.

"This is simply wonderful," Uncle Roul said, reaching for his drink and pulling a cigarette from his top pocket. He rose, crossed through the bedroom, and stepped onto the terrace for a smoke.

One of the many sitting rooms on this floor was prepared for Madeleine-Grace and me as our bedroom. These rooms had, in fact, originally been bedrooms for the Semperrin family when they moved here. I do not remember the full story of how they came into this place, nor was I ever told the full story about the Paris and Etretat-au-Delà properties. What I know is this, and it may not be entirely correct: my grandfather, Grand-père Jacques, was the grandson of yet another Jacques Semperrin, after whom he was named. This Jacques Semperrin grew up in Etretat-au-Delà in the family house of his ancestors, in the same section of the town in which lives Monsieur Vauquelin; however, more ambitious entrepreneurially than his family of fishermen and oar makers and occasional priests, monks, and nuns, he took off for Paris with some like-minded friends, Thomas Martin and Onfroi Giffard. Thomas, a carpenter, had skill with his hands, with building, and with renovations. Onfroi possessed the power of efficient management and a shrewd business sense. My great-great-grandfather Jacques exuded a charm unparalleled by anyone in France, they say, and therefore fostered a prodigious rapport with anyone he encountered. (I have to wonder if my Uncle Roul did not inherit a little of this.) They left for Paris with an idea, a goal, and did not arrive there before first exploring the countryside from Pays de Caux to L'Ile de France. After acquiring the financial support of benefactors who saw promise in this entrepreneurial trio of young friends—the pitch always left to Jacques and said never to have been refused—they converted the remains of a defunct farmhouse into an inn in the countryside outside Paris. A small staff and one of Jacques's sisters helped run the inn while a few local farmers and one of Jacques's brothers tended the farm, growing primarily wheat, juniper, and several herbs. Using abandoned equipment for a distillery already on the premises, they processed and bottled small batches of gin that they served in cocktails and sold to guests of the inn. The kitchen was run with the simple but confident knowledge of one of Thomas's sisters, Albertine, as she provided a small but stolid menu featuring the traditional Cauchois dishes that she knew. Through word of mouth in Paris and eventually through advertisements, the inn became a posh get-away for the Parisian gentry. A weekend en pleine aire, a few nights in bucolic France where the country smelled not of barnyard dross but of fresh herbs and homey meals, evenings under starlit skies, sipping cordials with friends old and acquaintances new on an extensive veranda overlooking simple fields. For some, such a get-away seemed distasteful, a step down, an occasion to intermingle with peasants at a locale much too close, and for these persons, the seaside resorts along La Manche and the train rides to destinations well beyond Paris like Biarritz and Nice, and the pampering at the spas of the mineral springs of Vichy appealed more. The word of mouth coupled with the promotions, however, did wonders, as did the exclusivity of booking no more than a Friday through Sunday stay, a condition of staying at the inn. Booked year-round, the inn established a reliable revenue and an esteemed reputation, enabling Thomas,

Onfroi, and Jacques to renovate several other farms, as well as an abandoned mill, and reopen them as inns with small, expert staffs.

The name of the first inn—and all the rest—is to me a fun, family story. The friends first named the inn "L'Auberge Revelins" after the Cauchois word for the drizzle that ends a rain, the weather conditions of the day they set out together for Paris. Now, my great-great-grandfather Jacques sought to perfect the gin being distilled at the first inn, and sampled several. They took a gamble on the recipe, hoping it would turn out how they wanted without knowing much about proportions of grain alcohol and juniper and herbs. All three insistent on a dry gin, they dangerously infused the second batch with an overload of dried cloves and fresh bay leaves. Apparently, the extra cloves and bays made it dry to perfection, and they found that they had concocted a palate-pleaser. However, Jacques wanted to concoct the perfect cocktail with it, so he experimented every evening for a week. All I know is that he included in this cocktail the gin, homemade *cidre* from Pays de Caux, and cinnamon schnapps, but wasn't content with the product. He passed the drink to Albertine, who smiled and stepped into the kitchen with the bottles. She is said to have added a secret ingredient that brought all three men to their feet with mirth as they clinked glasses. She refused to reveal her secret ingredient, and, playfully adamant about this, was therefore charged as the only person allowed to make that cocktail. Jacques insisted on calling the cocktail the Albertine after her, the woman he married soon thereafter, my great-great-grandmother. When the inn opened, the Albertine cocktail became a feature of the destination, and soon, patrons referred to it as "l'auberge de l'Albertine," or "the inn of the Albertine." And the three men renamed the inn "L'Auberge de l'Albertine." All the others were so named, and the group of inns became known as the Albertine network of inns.

The venture, a huge success, stole the attention of future businessmen, and some made bids for the company as the three friends aged. My great-great-grandfather passed the company to his son, Romain Semperrin, who ran it with Thomas's son Bertin and Onfroi's son Henri. Bertin passed away young, leaving the Albertine Inns to be expanded and run by Romain and Henri alone. When an offer came in to buy their inns by a major name in hoteling, Romain and Henri sold the Albertine network of inns for a fortune. Romain and Henri purchased mansions in Paris and raised their families there, providing not only nourishment, stability, and Normand traditions for their children, but also an education. Romain Semperrin's son, Jacques, my grandfather, studied accounting and established a lucrative career in the field himself. At the time my grandfather Jacques was a young man, his father Romain longed to return to the alabaster cliffs his father had driven him so many times on visits to family and wished to establish a base for his family to appreciate their Normand heritage. To this end, he followed the lead of good friend Lord Lalauze, the father of Lady Victorine, and built the château in Etretat-au-Delà. My great-grandfather Romain brought his family there every summer, and one summer on a visit, my grandfather Jacques met Madeleine-Maud, a friend from Etretat-au-Delà visiting a then young Lady Victorine, and they married after a courtship. Romain retired there. My grandfather Jacques brought his family there every summer, too. His family included my aunts and uncles, all of whom were raised primarily in Paris. Sometime after the Second World War, the mansion in Paris partially burned down. My grandparents purchased the newly renovated Paris flat in which I found myself at this moment. Thomas Martin's descendants, still close friends, took on renovations, including of this building, modernizing them with elevators, among other wonders, while my grandfather had hired them to restore simultaneously the mansion in order to keep the place in the family.

Here's where things get cloudy. Once my grandfather had passed, somehow my Uncle Romain came into the deed to the Paris mansion and not only stopped the restoration but *sold* the mansion. He nor his wife worked; however, it came to light that my Uncle Roul and Aunt Mirabelle and my Aunt Laure and Uncle Gilbert, none of whom worked except for Uncle Gilbert, were all in on the sale. Something I didn't learn until months after this summer is that the selling of the Paris mansion had been done behind my grandmother's back. Although their financial security had been ensured by Grand-père Jacques, they felt the need to acquire security through money for easy spending. I learned from Grand-mère Armance that neither my mother and father nor Aunt Adèle had been let in on this as they certainly would have opted to honor their parents' wishes, and, of course, their inclusion would have reduced the others' shares. As my parents never spoke of this, I did not know their views about it, nor their feelings toward the others over it.

So Grandma'Maud owned this Paris flat from top to bottom and the Etretat-au-Delà summer house, from which she seemed to have been banned. Aunt Adèle, Aunt Laure, Uncle Gilbert and their kids, and Uncle Romain, Aunt Pé, and Astride lived with Grandma' Maud in Paris from September to May and then left for the cliffs in summer, at which time Borbála stepped in as head and only maid; now she remains year-round. Bertille, I learned, appeared on the scene several months before the funeral, a hired, live-in caretaker of Grandma'Maud. To my knowledge, she spent every day except Wednesdays there, taking occasional Saturdays off, too, to stay with her family in Paris. According to Uncle Roul, she was a trained nurse, so my grandmother was under efficient care. I had heard mention of a caretaker but only met her today. Although Uncle Roul and Aunt Mirabelle resided in Rouen, they stayed at the flat in Paris often.

Aunt Melisende, she said she could not bear to part with Madeleine-Grace and me last week, and knowing of our imminent trip to Paris, revised her agenda to include another visit to Paris. Uncle Ferdinand, just as delighted to visit, enlisted once again the service of his great-nephews, Jules and Marguerin, to drive them.

"How much did they pay you to spend an entire car ride with them and a week here in Paris with my lovely mother?" Uncle Roul asked the boys.

We had enjoyed a light dinner of fried, fresh sardines, *tomates provençales*, and *gratin dauphinois* in the dining room and were enjoying a Bénédictine in the *grand salon*. Grandma'Maud and Aunt Melisende sat side by side knitting on the divan, Uncle Ferdinand dozing in an armchair, and his great-nephews on a piano bench leaning their elbows against the closed instrument keys. Uncle Roul leaned his good shoulder against one of the few panels of an ornately molded wall amid wooden shelves lined with books and knickknacks and closed cabinet doors; this wall was opposite the windows. Bertille sat on a side chair, reading from a book under lamp light, while Borbála cleaned up in the kitchen. Madeleine-Grace and I shared a settee near the piano. My sister was knitting. I sat as idly as my uncles and the boys.

"They paid us nothing," Jules said, stupefied.

"Should they have offered, we would have refused payment," added the more affable Marguerin.

"And why is that?" asked Grandma'Maud. I sensed she knew the answer they were going to give and wanted to hear it out loud.

"We are happy to help them," said Marguerin, smiling through a sip of his cordial.

"One doesn't charge family for such favors," said Jules.

Jules's seriousness made Uncle Roul laugh but brought a different sort of smile, a heart-warmed one, to the face of Aunt Melisende and Uncle Ferdinand.

"I see you, Roul," said Grandma'Maud, resting her knitting on her lap and squinting her eyes at her son.

"You see me. You have said this."

"I see you always. I see you through words I have heard from as far as Dieppe, not to mention Fécamp. Why have I heard that some prefer not to include the Semperrins in social events?"

Uncle Roul was about to take a sip of his drink and stopped. He tilted his head in wonderment. "What is this you've heard? It's ridiculous."

"Some find your company embarrassing and prefer not to have you at events. This is untrue?"

"Who has told you this?" He bounced off the wall and stood upright. "This is indeed untrue."

Uncle Ferdinand shifted in his chair, and when Uncle Roul shot him a glance, he shrugged and turned up his hands.

"So your drunkenness and your attentiveness to—certain guests— are not a reality? So your brother's anger and your sister's laments and your wives'—where do I begin with the wives? Are you saying this is all untrue?"

Uncle Roul reclaimed his spot on the wall, choosing to shake off the accusation. "Pshhh."

"I need not worry over your disparaging the good name your father and I, and his father before him, have worked—without much difficulty—to establish? Are you saying you make every effort to elevate the reputation of the Semperrin name?"

"I have done nothing to abase our name." Anger got the better of him as he stepped from the wall once more. "I have fought honorably for our country! I have—."

"You have, indeed. And what are you doing now to honor your father's good name—the name you have given to his grandchildren?" Grandma'Maud resumed her knitting after delivering these words.

"I have done nothing to tarnish our good name. You are crazy!"

"You, Romain, and Laure, I have heard, have—"

"And what of Juliette and Adèle? They are exempt?" he snapped.

"My Juliette!" Grandma'Maud lowered her knitting. After a pause, her eyes clenched, and tears erupted out.

"What of Adèle?" persisted Uncle Roul.

"My Juliette! My Léon!" said Grandma'Maud through continued tears.

"And what of Adèle?" shouted Uncle Roul, as if to make a point, or at least to shift attention off himself.

Grandma'Maud wept and did not answer, and as she wiped the tears from her eyes, Aunt Melisende said, "Adèle awaits your return in Etretat-au-Delà when she would have preferred to be here, but she *must* remain in Etretat-au-Delà, mustn't she? You know that, Roul. Who can be trusted if not her? What is it you would have your mother say? You would have her include Adèle with the brood of you? No, my dear Roul. Neither Juliette nor Adèle—their names should never be uttered in the same sentence as the rest of yours."

I think my uncle wanted to throw his glass at the wall when he turned his back on us, but he somehow refrained and stomped out of the room. Bertille rose and set down her book, looking fretful and unsure what to do. After hesitation, she took two steps in pursuit of Uncle Roul before Grandma'Maud stopped her.

"I require your assistance, Bertille," she said, her voice still crackly after the bout of tears.

Bertille glanced in the direction of Uncle Roul and then abandoned the impulse to follow after him. We rose as she helped my grandmother to her feet, and we all retired for the evening.

"Do you think Grandma'Maud is crazy?" Madeleine-Grace asked me as she dipped a *biscuit à la cuillère* into her *café au lait* at the kitchen table. Paris exposed us to a different variety of sweets, and Borbála had brought these in from a local bakery yesterday morning.

"No," I responded, glancing about the kitchen for Borbála whom I found leaning her elbow on the counter as she paged through a magazine. We were speaking softly enough that she did not hear us.

"What about the fabric?" my sister asked. She was referring to the strips of fabric we saw when Aunt Melisende escorted us into Grandma'Maud's bedroom last night for bedtime prayers. When we arrived, Grandma'Maud, lying in her bed under the covers, had a square of cotton fabric featuring the pattern of tiny pink roses with emerald green stems unfolded across her torso. She was using the shears to cut the fabric into one-inch strands slowly, relying on only the back portion of the scissor blades and never making a full snip. Aunt Melisende called her name several times before she snapped out of a hypnotic focus on cutting these strips of fabric, a pile of which I saw beside her. When Grandma'Maud realized we were in the room and awaiting prayers, her eyes refocused on us, looked about the room as if it were unfamiliar, and gazed back at her fabric. Then she set down the shears on the bedside, set the fabric, cut and uncut, on top of them, and pulled her rosary out to hold during prayers. We prayed and kissed good-night, but the sight of her cutting the fabric and searching the room for some familiarity stayed with me, and now I saw that it had stayed with my sister, too.

"I think she must be making something," I responded, unsure about the fabric. I realized I was not accounting for the vacancy in her eyes, but I did not know what else to offer my sister.

"I think she goes someplace because no one she loves is here," Madeleine-Grace said. "And now that we're here, she has to readjust to our realness."

"Where does she go?" I asked.

"Some place imaginary as I used to do when I was little. Or some place in her thoughts as I do now."

"If you're right, that means we should visit again, for longer," I said, aware that Uncle Roul planned to return with us to Etretat-au-Delà tomorrow morning—or whenever he awoke. I understood Madeleine-Grace's point because I, too, enjoyed spending time in my imaginary world of detective stories and *paquebot* adventures, but it had not occurred to me that someone so old might do the same.

While Bertille helped Grandma'Maud with her toilette that morning, Aunt Melisende made sure we did the same. She scolded Borbála for allowing us to breakfast in the kitchen when we should have been seated at the dining room table, but Borbála responded with a flippant turn of a page. Uncle Ferdinand and his great-nephews had their coffee at the table in the dining room while Uncle Roul remained in bed. Jules and Marguerin teased Borbála about being famous now, on account of Zsuzsi Kormoczy winning the French Championship in May. She lamented not having anything Hungarian to cheer with except a walnut liqueur she had brought to Paris with her after her last visit home to Veszprém. She said Grandma'Maud had joined her in the celebration and enjoyed the liqueur, but Bertille had spit hers out.

Grandma'Maud and Aunt Melisende had thought through the planning of a pleasant day. As Aunt Adèle tended to do, Grandma'Maud managed to find moments hidden to Madeleine-Grace and me to accomplish prodigious feats, in this case, the arrangement of an excursion to Notre Dame de Paris on L'Ile de la Cité. While the men had been enjoying their coffee in the *salle à manger*, Aunt Melisende, apparently unable to rely on Borbála for such a thing, prepared and packed a light lunch for us all. By nine o'clock, Marguerin was escorting us to the car that Jules had pulled to the front. Once en route, Grandma'Maud revealed the plan for the morning and afternoon.

"Do you remember last summer when you told me of your visit to the Art Institute of Chicago with your parents?" Grandma'Maud asked. "Do you remember your excitement for that visit?"

I remembered both the visit to the Art Institute and sharing the story about it with Grandma'Maud in the *salle-en-arrière* of the summer house. Her memory amazed me sometimes, especially of the seeming minutia of life. The events of February and March, in some ways, had formed a wall separating the me of the present from so much of what had happened prior to it. Memories of the summer before this one arrived with the thud of having been hurled there over the wall. Grandma'Maud, however, reflected on them more easily and more quickly than I could, and with keen awareness of detail.

"And what was the name of the painting you saw for the first time and enjoyed so much?"

"*A Sunday Afternoon on the Ile de la Grande Jatte*," I said.

"By Georges Seurat," Madeleine-Grace said, her face brightening with her smile. I wondered if the smile reflected less the knowledge of the painter and more so the memory of our parents leading us to the painting, staring closely at it, trying to count the abrupt dashes of color, all with our father and mother's hands on our shoulders.

"Good!" she said, looking at her sister with satisfaction. "And do you remember what I told you?"

Madeleine-Grace spoke up without missing a beat. "You said that on a clear day, one could see L'Ile de la Grande Jatte from the towers of Notre Dame!"

"It is a sunny day," Grandma'Maud noted. "Would you like to go with Marguerin and Jules to the top of the cathedral? It is too much for me, but the boys will take you."

"Yes," we both said in unison. The idea of standing atop a tower of Notre Dame thrilled me, and I longed to arrive on L'Ile de la Cité.

My parents, too, had been excited about taking us to the Art Institute of Chicago, especially after my father's friend, Marcel Royce, and a knowledgeable docent educated us about Seurat's painting. We saw the painting in the spring of 1957 shortly before leaving for France for the summer, and Madeleine-Grace and I were glad we had seen it when we did. Sometime this year, the Art Institute had lent the painting to the Museum of Modern Art in New York, and in April, a fire broke out there. The painting, we learned, had survived. The docent had told us of many studies that Seurat had done, so those would have been available to enjoy had the painting endured a grimmer outcome, but they would not have been the same, despite his use of the fade-repellent pigment in his earlier studies.

I had asked my mother one day after school if she or Papa had ever visited L'Ile de la Grande Jatte, which Seurat had captured so novelly through *divisionisme*, along with Sisley and Van Gogh and Monet. She was organizing the groceries she had brought home on the kitchen table, setting aside a few things she needed for dinner that night. She said that neither she nor my father had been to L'Ile de la Grande Jatte, but she added that it had earned a reputation as a nearby retreat for Parisians, similar to the Albertine Inn of my great-great-grandfather. I always thought this was neat and wondered if Jacques or Albertine or their son had considered building an inn there; if they had, it could have been in the background of Seurat's masterpiece.

The ride to L'Ile de la Cité provided time for plenty of conversation, including time to catch up with Grandma'Maud about finishing the school year in America, the trip over the Atlantic, and my Grand-mère and Grand-père Avery's short visit with Grandma'Maud in Paris after having left us in Etretat-au-Delà. "Such good people," Grandma'Maud repeated. I directed our conversation to the fire at the museum in New York and reminded her that several summers ago, while visiting Grandma'Maud in Paris, we had seen what my mother insisted on calling *Le Poète* at the Musée Rodin, located near my grandmother's flat. Madeleine-Grace did not remember this and insisted she hadn't come, but I knew she had because she asked my father to put her on Dante's lap, the image of which brought us all to laughter. Grandma'Maud asked what we should like to do the rest of summer while in France, and Madeleine-Grace responded with her wish to see a lace-making workshop near Calais, and to visit Rouen in order to see a statue of Saint Maclou, the namesake of our Galimard friend. I, however, offered no suggestions, because I honestly had no inclination or desire to go anywhere without my parents. In some ways, this whole summer felt as if I were simply along for one long ride without them, and while I entertained the fancies of everyone to distract myself and to find some amusement in these ways of passing time, I longed to hop off the ride. Even the prospect of standing atop Notre Dame de Paris piqued my interest only with a hollow excitement, with a thrill I already knew would be quickly snuffed out and somehow empty. I supposed this is what missing someone so beloved means.

Once parked, we walked the quai along the Seine, crossed the Pont Saint-Michel, and proceeded east until we found ourselves standing before Notre Dame de Paris, the heights of her masonry grandiose, her windows ethereal and sparkling, her ornamentation awe-inducing. Many people passed us, heading into the darkness of the open doors, some remaining outside snapping photos, crossing themselves in prayer, and one elderly couple falling to their knees.

"You see her, Ellande? We are in her shadow, but hers is a shadow of protection. Notre Dame stands vigilant over '*Le Berceau de Paris*,' does she not?" Grandma'Maud asked. We nodded. She was referring to the nickname of this island in the Seine, L'Ile de la Cité, as "the Cradle of Paris."

"A good mother stands guard over the cradle of her child, of her children," she said.

"Marguerin and Jules will take you to the top," Aunt Melisende said, "while Ferdinand, your grandmother, and I light a candle inside and pray. We will meet you out here."

Marguerin passed the pique-nique basket of lunch to Uncle Ferdinand.

"Take your time, my dears, and enjoy the view!" said Grandma'Maud as we stepped ahead of them into the church. Her smile big, she kept her arm extended as Madeleine-Grace stepped away.

Arriving into the nave, the boys genuflected as did Madeleine-Grace and I. Jules waited with us while Marguerin sought assistance. While we awaited his return, we took in the open interior, dim despite the glow of light through the many-colored windows and from the glass and flames of votives. Marguerin returned with a guide, a man probably in his fifties, who led us to two young couples nearby and escorted us up the long and winding staircase to the top of the tower. I saw that the solid stone around us became feeble wood in our ascent, and I was amazed at the humility behind the strength of such an edifice, of such an institution.

When we emerged on the top, the gray of stone returned, along with the dusty-blue crisp of sky, cloud-laden today, the brilliance of sunlight caught in their folds. We walked to the stone rail, and Madeleine-Grace inched up on her tiptoes to see as far as she could see. Jules stepped away from the railing cautiously and lifted Madeleine-Grace onto his shoulders for the highest view. I looked at her, well over my head, to see her squinting into the distance for a glimpse of the Ile. From my spot, as I peered over rooftops and past steeples, over entire neighborhoods and beyond borders of *arrondissements*, I saw what I thought might be the Ile but could not be sure. I certainly saw the course of the Seine winding, the quai alongside with pedestrians and automobiles, benches and trees, stands and peddlers, the density of green treetops sure to be Le Bois de Boulogne, but what I thought might be the Ile I could not be sure.

"Do you see it, Jules," Madeleine-Grace asked.

"I'm not sure," he said. I felt more at ease knowing he could not tell, either.

Maguerin asked the guide, who pointed in the direction we were all looking at the very spot we must see, but the clouds, white and bright and low, were thick. He said on a clearer day, we would be able to see it.

Leaning my arms on the top of the stone rail, still appreciative to be here, I saw in an opening between clouds, a speck I was sure to be L'Ile de la Grande Jatte, and a shutter pressed in my eye like a camera. Standing high on a tower under slow-passing clouds, bathed in the ardor of quick-acting sunlight, I saw past the expansive city to its extremity; I saw, and yet again, I felt—the stillness.

Jules set down Madeleine-Grace, and we roamed the top of the tower a little longer, exploring other views as well as the stonework and the gargoyles. The guide brought us all down, and Marguerin asked if we wanted to stop to pray. We both assented and took a seat within a pew to pray, the four of us. Both boys, one on either side of us, closed their eyes tightly and rested their foreheads on clasped hands. I felt protected by them and saw they believed in a strength beyond their own. Seeing the seriousness of their prayer, in that moment, I realized also that they took seriously their charge of us. Arguably more pious than they was my sister, eyes delicately closed but with an expression of woe imprinted on her visage as she spoke to God with all her heart.

We told the others we were not sure that we actually saw L'Ile de la Grande Jatte when we rejoined them outside the cathedral. Grandma'Maud said that we will visit another time and be *sure* to see it. After a stroll, we found two benches near the *chevet* of the cathedral, a side chapel, in the Square l'Archevêché. Among the celadon lindens and the past-bloom cherry blossoms and the foresty spruces, we ate our simple lunch of butter and radish tartines, hard-boiled eggs with aioli and caperberries, and slices of *tarte aux pommes*. And it was delicious. The Blessed Mother and Child smiled down on us from the Virgin Fountain several meters away. The number of times Madeleine-Grace looked at Them between bites of lunch compelled me to think she might as well have invited Them to our lunch. Aunt Melisende poured into little glasses iced tea, one for us each, from bottles she procured from the basket. Our light lunch complete, we exited Ile de la Cité via the Pont au Double, strolled past the booksellers and artists along the Quai de Montebello, and returned to the car for the drive to Grandma'Maud's flat. I remembered too late to search the Seine for Le Pont des Arts to compare the likeness of Signac's painting in our summer house bedroom to the real bridge. The river out of view, I reclined into the seat of the car, oddly refreshed by the climb and lunch under the lindens.

"Do you think your uncle has awakened?" Uncle Ferdinand asked us with a chuckle.

"Unless Bertille roused him, he is still sleeping," Grandma'Maud said.

"Bertille is no Gourgandine," said Aunt Melisende.

"I wouldn't be so sure," said Grandma'Maud.

Marguerin and Jules started laughing at this exchange, and I knew why—at least in part. There was no way that anyone French could name a child "Gourgandine," and the boys were curious about the backstory.

"Who is this?" asked Marguerin.

Aunt Melisende started laughing as she looked out the window, but Grandma'Maud, her eyes rolling, shook her head.

"Before Bertille," explained Grandma'Maud, "my children had found another nurse. She was attentive enough—when she was attending me—but most of the time, her head was elsewhere. Sometimes I would ring and ring, call and call, and it was hours before she came. After only two weeks of employment, one day, I called several times from my bed and was met with no help. It was about eight o'clock in the morning on a Thursday. Borbála was out for the day, and Romain and Pé, Laure and Gilbert, and Adèle had gone shopping after dropping off the children at school. Roul and Mirabelle, of course, were in Rouen. In my nightgown, I walked through the sitting room to the hall where the door had been closed. I tried to open it, but it was locked. I tried several times, turning it and shaking it, but it would not open. It was locked from the other side, I was sure. That *gourgandine* locked me in! Unsure what to do, I returned to my bed, hoping I would hear someone soon and could call for help. If I had thought more clearly, I would have immediately shouted for help from the balcony. About an hour later, I stepped onto the balcony. When I stepped out, I saw Laure and Gilbert on the park bench and started shouting for them to help me—that I had been locked in. Romain, Pé, and Adèle had evidently already come home and heard me screaming, rushing to my room as I rushed from the room to the locked door. Only when I went to the door again and turned the knob, I found that it was unlocked. The key was resting in the lock on the other side of the door, which was odd enough. The key was kept in a table drawer. Romain and Pé, of course, had arrived at the door at that very second and saw me open it, along with Adèle, and soon thereafter, Laure and Gilbert ran up. I explained that I had been locked in, and Romain and Pé said that I was crazy, that I very well had opened the door without the slightest trouble. I swore to them that I had been locked in earlier when I had called for the nurse, and they persisted that I must be crazy. Well, the nurse strolled in, asking what the problem was, and we explained the whole story. She said she did not understand, for she had been sitting on the divan in the sitting room the entire morning and only stepped out twice, once for a *café* in the kitchen, and just now for the powder room. I said that she had not been in the room when I was calling for her, locked in—or I would have had no need to get out of bed at all. Romain and Laure, they said I was crazy, and Pé burst into tears and stomped off, screaming, 'Crazy! Crazy!'"

"And then I arrived," said Aunt Melisende, with a haughty chuckle.

"I retold the story to Melisende and Adèle, and they could not figure out how or why the door had come to be locked, or how I could have passed the nurse without noticing. Of course, I knew that the nurse could not have been there without *noticing me*."

"So I took over from here," said Aunt Melisende. "Despite Adèle's protestations, the next day, I convinced Adèle to distract 'Gourgandine' while I snooped about in her bedroom. Adèle called her in while I snooped, and lo and behold, I found her agenda book. On the agenda for that Thursday, from 7:30 in the morning until 9:30 in the morning was a lovely rendez-vous with one Etienne La Fèvre, a young man who had 'called' on her. I shared the information heartily with Adèle, who questioned Borbála first, inquiring if she knew of this. Borbála admitted that Gourgandine had told her of her date but had said no one noticed she had been gone. So in front of everyone, I presented the agenda book to Gourgandine and revealed her indiscretion. She admitted to locking Madeleine-Maud in the room 'to keep her safe' in the event she awoke while she, the *gourgandine*, entertained her gentleman caller in the *grand salon*. You see, she had known the Semperrin grandchildren were at school and the Semperrin children were shopping that morning. She had forgotten Borbála had the day off and expected her to cover, but even when she knew Borbála was not around to tend to Madeleine-Maud in her stead, she went ahead with her plan."

"You are a detective," I said to Aunt Melisende.

"When I have to be," she replied casually.

"And this woman was perfectly content to let all believe I had gone crazy. She was let go then and there. If Adèle and Melisende had not believed me and thought something amiss, I never would have been exonerated. Worst of all was that Romain, Pé, Laure, and Gilbert all believed I was crazy."

Uncle Ferdinand shook his head from side to side, having heard the story already, but the two boys were incredulous, their mouths agape as they exchanged looks of shock. I think Marguerin had wanted to say more but was trying simultaneously to avoid a cyclist darting in front of our automobile.

"No, sister dearest. Worst of all is that they believed 'Gourgandine' over their own mother without question," said Aunt Melisende.

That was the worst of all, but the best of all, for me, was that from then on, this woman whose birth name I had never learned, became forever known to us as "Gourgandine," the French word for "trollop," "hussy," or "whore."

Leisurely conversation in Grandma'Maud's sitting room preceded a drowsy *mésienne*, for we were tired from the walking and the climbing and the readjusting to taking on large numbers of people. Uncle Roul had swaggered in, washed and dressed and fresh-smelling, about fifteen minutes prior to our retiring for a nap, and he was the one to rouse us from, what was for me, a deep sleep.

We enjoyed *apéro* in the *petit salon* together, the curtains open to the hushed sunlight that flitted through the leaves of the tall lindens out front. I asked if Grandma'Maud could make Albertines. She told me of a tradition that my grandfather sometimes made the cocktail for her or the children but remained as in the dark as his grandfather about the elusive ingredient known only to his Grand-mère Albertine. For fun, every time he made it, he splashed a different ingredient in, hoping it might be that secret one, although he would never know. Recalling the mirth it brought to her children and her to see her husband pick a random bottle and add a splash, even on hazard of marring the cocktail, Grandma'Maud carried on the practice. She was overjoyed when I requested it. This time, she oscillated between a bottle of the Basque liqueur *patxaran* and the *liqueur lavande* that a friend had brought her from a trip to Provence. Deciding on the *patxaran*, she splashed the digestive over the poured drinks. It made for an initial bitter burst that ended smoothly and sweetly with the refreshing cider.

Madeleine-Grace asked if she could play the piano as she had wanted to try to recall a song, and I suspected she had meant the new *tourdion* Maman had found. Grandma'Maud allowed her to do so after dinner so that she could entertain us all, which was not Madeleine-Grace's intention. We dined after a heartfelt grace from Uncle Ferdinand, who was surprised to hear his great-nephew Marguerin chime in with a special prayer request of our Lord's blessing over all of France, having been inspired to supplicate the Lord for this cause while standing on the tower of Notre Dame, overlooking the hundreds and thousands of citizens far and wide. "May France never forget her Protectress," Marguerin said, to my sister's joy especially. Uncle Roul and Grandma'Maud, affable in their interactions with each other this evening, laughed over past reminiscences involving young Roul, Alphonse, and Chardine, and even over her children's attempt to bar her from leaving for America last March. After dinner, as Borbála cleared the table, we enjoyed a cordial in the *grand salon* at nightfall.

Eager to try her hand at remembering, Madeleine-Grace raced to the piano and double-checked that her left-hand chords sounded correct. I sat beside her. She then attempted to play the melody with her right hand, which I, too, had tried to commit to memory. We could both hear the music in our heads and tried diligently to replicate it. Months ago, we never would have thought we would have to rely on our own memory of the song from having watched our mother, yet here we were trying pertinaciously to replay the song that, in our own way, was sure to honor our mother at the children's ball. Bertille was accompanying Grandma'Maud into the *grand salon* when we heard her speak.

"This tune—it is the *tourdion* from your piano in America," she declared. At least we knew our replication of it was close enough to be recognizable, but there was no way my mother could have played it for Grandma'Maud. Our mother had come across the music in February.

"Yes," Madeleine-Grace said, unceasing in her playing of the chords and attempting variations that might be more exact.

"Rise, children," she said. "I must confess, I know the tune."

We rose from the piano bench and stepped aside. Grandma'Maud opened an ornately carved wooden door of the built-in cabinet and shelving. She withdrew the topmost selection from a pile of sheet music and adjusted it on the stand. I recognized it immediately, as did my sister. It was Maman's *tourdion*—the very copy. Grandma'Maud sat at the piano, and we leaned over her shoulder for a better look at the music. The pencil annotations of my mother, light as they were, jumped off the page.

"While I was at your home in America, the house to myself one day, I saw the music opened on the piano. I thought this must have been the last piece my Juliette had played, and I touched the keys, the keys of the notes written on the score. I was touching one of the last things my Juliette had touched in the same order in which she had touched them. And I played the tune and knew straight away why my daughter had chosen such a song; it was beautiful." She played four measures of the melody with her right hand. "I confess, I packed the music with my things to play over and over on my own—for Juliette."

She wiped away a few tears and then touched the music at the margin, running her hand down the coarse paper.

"I did not think you would miss it," she said apologetically.

"We are grateful you have it," I said.

"But we need to borrow it," Madeleine-Grace added with urgency. "We are dancing to it for the children's ball!"

"Ah, you have chosen the *tourdion*?"

"We have chosen it, but we have yet to bring them the music," Madeleine-Grace said.

"Now we can, if you'll allow us," I said.

"Of course! It is a beautiful song and will be a beautiful dance, I'm sure," Grandma'Maud said. "Now let's listen."

Madeleine-Grace and I stepped back and let Grandma'Maud play the beautiful tune in triple time. Madeleine-Grace smiled widely at me, for it sounded just as Maman had played it at home. And now we had the music for it! Although we felt moved to dance, we both refrained, subsiding instead to the easy swaying of the others in the room.

When our grandmother had finished playing, as she wiped away more tears, Madeleine-Grace said, "Grandma'Maud, can't you come with us to Etretat-au-Delà?"

She looked over her shoulder at the rest of us and directed her comment to Uncle Roul when she sputtered, "I'm no longer permitted in my Etretat-au-Delà house when Romain and Roul and Laure are there, is that not correct?"

"You are crazy enough when you're alone," Uncle Roul said. "We don't need your craziness when we are all together, trying to relax."

"Again with the 'crazy,'" she said. "I think you're all crazy to say you are 'trying' to relax. You don't know how to do anything *but* relax."

"Listen to the playing," Jules said. "You could have such music with you all summer." Perhaps he did not know the summer house had no piano.

"Aunt Melisende sings for us, and we all sing along!" my sister reminded Uncle Roul.

"You could have double the music," Marguerin suggested.

"I could do without the music, including Aunt Melisende's screeching," Uncle Roul said playfully.

"I'm afraid I must say this, Roul," said Uncle Ferdinand, posturing from his armchair with philosophical aplomb. "You should want to spend every moment with your mother. Look at the little ones. There's no guarantee, Roul, that your mother will have a tomorrow for you to spend with her."

I think he knew Uncle Ferdinand had a point but refused to concede. "I don't need a sermon," he said.

Aunt Melisende laughed. "You have fallen quite behind on your Masses, nephew mine. Seems to me you certainly could use a sermon."

Uncle Roul threw in the towel, shaking his head, and let Aunt Melisende enjoy the last word. He meandered off as Grandma'Maud finished one more piece, a Chopin *berceuse*. The rest of us discussed our departure tomorrow and then engaged in casual conversation, Grandma'Maud and Aunt Melisende knitting and Uncle Ferdinand and the boys reading. Grandma'Maud asked if we wanted to play cards, but we refused the offer, preferring instead to listen to conversations and the telling of stories. Grandma'Maud's matter-of-fact recounting of a memory, Aunt Melisende's ebullient and jovial narration of a screwy incident, and Marguerin's reflective tone over any topic captivated both Madeleine-Grace and me more than *brelan* or *coinchée* or spades or gin-rummy and was all we needed for an evening's entertainment.

"Has Romain repaired the wall in the terraced bedroom?" Grandma'Maud asked. She was referring to the bedroom Aunt Laure and Uncle Gilbert occupied at the summer house.

"Laure had blockaded herself in there on my last visit. I could not see," Aunt Melisende responded.

"It hasn't been repaired yet," Madeleine-Grace noted.

Grandma'Maud shook her head with dismay. "*Après moi*," she said, French for "after me."

"*Après eux*, God only knows what will be," responded Aunt Melisende. "*Après eux*" meant "after them," and I did not understand what this expression implied.

Apparently, Uncle Ferdinand was reading something about Italy because he mentioned something about upcoming elections there. Madeleine-Grace piped up about Aunt Adèle's *piccagge aggétto in to brodo.* "Aunt Adèle said her trip to Italy was the best time of her life. She learned so much and enjoyed the convent in Liguria."

"She said she loved the smell of the hazelnut trees in Nola and the lemon trees in Sorrento. She said everything in Italy was beautiful, from the North to the South," I added.

Grandma'Maud, her eyes on her needles and jonquil-yellow yarn, said, "Adèle loved that trip so much not because Italy was so beautiful and the convent was so peaceful, but because she was with Juliette alone—and not the others." She looked up where Uncle Roul had been standing and then back at her work. "That had been the first and only time in their lives they had been together away from the others."

Aunt Melisende woke us the next morning to see us off. Even Uncle Roul woke earlier than he would have wanted. Before bedtime prayers last night, he made a promise to his mother to bring us back to Paris soon for another visit. The only one more thrilled about this promise than my grandmother, oddly, was the caretaker, who fluttered her eyelashes at the declaration. Grandma'Maud, from her bed, mocked her by squinting her eyes and smooshing her lips together, all toward Uncle Roul.

Borbála prepared us a *café au lait* and a *croissant*, which we enjoyed in the kitchen, to which Borbála was met again with Aunt Melisende's admonition. We then walked with Aunt Melisende and Uncle Ferdinand to the boys' room to bid adieux and then to Grandma'Maud's room. She was awake in bed with the covers pulled to her neck, her head propped on several pillows. The fabric, a few strands cut, rested on her lap, and the shears lay at her side next to the small pile of squares of fabrics. The inch where the curtains did not meet let in a little light in the otherwise dark room, but, as we stood at her bedside, we could see her eyes were open and fixed on something in the corner of the room, a thin column of light, yet on nothing at all.

"Madeleine-Maud," Aunt Melisende called. "Madeleine-Maud, the children are leaving."

Grandma'Maud did not budge. She did not blink.

"She gets like this," Bertille said, caressing her arm. My grandmother blinked but did not respond to the gentle touch.

Uncle Roul rolled his eyes and left the room. Aunt Melisende tried another time to shake her sister from the daze, and once she realized it would not break any time soon, she encouraged us to kiss our grandmother before leaving. We both reached with our necks over the side of the bed and kissed her on the cheek. Our kisses were not magical enough to break the spell, for she stared on, her limbs reclined but stiff, her fists tight. I wanted to wait until she actually awoke, just to be sure she was okay, but Bertille insisted she would come out of it. Uncle Roul nudged us to depart.

The ride, bright and warm and—green—the closer we drove toward the alabaster coast, lasted shorter than the drive to Paris; of course, we did not meet a nearly overturned truck with crates and hay and wandering chickens blocking the road. We did stop, however, for no more than three minutes at a farm stand selling seeds when I remembered we had neglected to purchase for Aunt Adèle her mint seeds. Uncle Roul reluctantly supplied the funds.

We pulled up shortly after one o'clock in the afternoon, and Aunt Adèle greeted us with a smile. Aside from stories of our excursion and news of Grandma'Maud, her priority was washing our travel clothes. Our priority, however, was bestowing the mint seeds, presenting the sheet music to the *tourdion*, and revealing that Aunt Melisende and Uncle Ferdinand had met us in Paris.

Uncle Roul went upstairs shortly after our arrival to bathe and sleep, and Aunt Adèle headed to the kitchen to make us a snack. Through the *salle-en-arrière* window, I saw Wischard and Laure wave from the bench in the flower island. Wischard's wave, frenetic and fast, implied an urgency to his summons, so my sister and I hurried outside.

"Come on," he said, pulling my arm toward the cliffs, and we ran there, leaving little Laure behind as she yawned and reclined on the bench.

Once at the cliffs, we plopped down, and I surveyed the sea for sails—nothing. Wischard's panting after the run, followed by the animation in his voice, claimed my attention.

"Your bedroom had more traffic than Gare Saint-Lazare!" he said. "Alphonse, Roul, Chardine, Astride—everyone got in trouble in there except Laure and me."

"In our bedroom?" I asked. That was hardly a thoroughfare of the house and certainly not the most exciting room to be in.

Wischard explained, "First, Aunt Mirabelle wanted to know why Roul wasn't with us for *apéro*, and Alphonse, thinking his brother was sleeping still, tried to get Roul in trouble by saying that he was kissing Bette Tranchaud in the bedroom and didn't want their mother to know. It was a joke, of course, but Aunt Mirabelle and Aunt Adèle leapt from their seats on the veranda and bounded up the stairs to the bedroom, which was empty. Aunt Adèle couldn't bear to leave the bed unmade and started making it. But Aunt Mirabelle heard a noise coming from your bedroom, and there she found Roul kissing Henriette Loiselier. He thought he was in a place no one would look since you two were gone."

"Why does he always kiss girls?" Madeleine-Grace asked.

"I asked him that," Wischard said. "He said, 'it feels good and will make girls want to be in bed with me.' He said I was too young to know this, but I think I'll try one day and see."

Referring to the boys and girls being in bed together, I shared, "I've heard of that. I'm pretty sure that's what's called sex." When Jimmy Mertens one day at recess said that he saw Mrs. Sizel having sex with Mr. Monroe, I pretended like I knew what he was talking about and laughed. We all did. Mary Beth Narble said he was fibbing, but Jimmy said we'd all see he wasn't when Mrs. Sizel is pregnant tomorrow. When I went home, I had recounted the words to my father and asked him what they meant. My father turned red, took a sip of the cocktail my mother had prepared him, and said he would tell me another day.

"What's sex?" Madeleine-Grace asked.

"I don't know, but it's how we were born, I think," I said.

Wischard, impatient with this unnecessary tangent, continued, "Anyway, Aunt Mirabelle made Aunt Adèle talk to Roul and punish him, so he had to do the weeding in the flower garden in front of the house. He asked if he could weed Jeuffine des Gervais's rose garden, too, and Aunt Mirabelle threw a bottle of *hydromel* across the room. It didn't break. Roul also has to go to Confession, but he says he doesn't want to. Alphonse has to go with him for lying to his mother. Poor Alphonse. I don't understand why his mother got so upset over his joke about Bette when it was just a joke."

"But what about Chardine and—Astride?" Madeleine-Grace wanted to know.

"They had gone into your room to snoop through your travel trunks, and I caught them in there!"

Now I had heard it all concerning Astride and asked, "Why were they snooping?"

"They wanted to find proof that you two were naughty," Wischard said, "so they were looking for jewelry that you could have stolen from passengers on the *paquebot* or swear words written on your magazines, but I told them you were good and not thieves or swearers. But when I left, they stayed in there to play *la balle autambourin*, and while they were playing, they must have bumped into the dresser because the vase fell and shattered."

My sister and I looked at each other, her mouth agape, my eyes bulging. Could my sister have the same memories of that vase, of my father's filling it for my mother, of my mother's smile when she breathed in the fragrance of freshly picked jonquils and mint? And now it was shattered? To Wischard, this was another detail in an intensifying story, but to me, this was a blow to my bones, to my heart, really. My attention must have shattered at the image of the vase falling because Wischard had to corral me back to his story.

"Over here, Ellande," he said. Without realizing it, my gaze had turned to the horizon. Wischard's continuation of story slowly reeled me in. He said, "They left it there and ran away. Aunt Adèle went in to tidy up, to clean the soap dish, and to replenish the towels, and found the broken vase. Don't tell Chardine and Astride, but I told Aunt Adèle I had seen them in there, so she knew it must have been them. When she yelled at them, first they said it was Roul, but Aunt Mirabelle said it hadn't been broken when she had walked in there. Then they admitted to it, and Chardine said she was going to tell her mother what they had done when Astride said to leave the mess and not say anything. Aunt Adèle accused Astride of wanting to leave it so that you two would be accused of breaking it when you returned, assuming, of course, that no one would go in there before the two of you returned. But Aunt Pé heard Aunt Adèle say this to Astride and yelled at Aunt Adèle for insinuating that her daughter would try to frame her cousins. Aunt Adèle told Aunt Pé she needed to punish her daughter, but Aunt Pé said that it was an accident and refused to punish her. She also said Aunt Adèle wasn't allowed to punish her, either."

This ending to the story sickened me, but every time I thought of the vase smashing to the floor, I thought of my father and mother. I saw them on their hands and knees, sweeping the shards into a dustpan. I saw tears in their eyes and a struggle to smile despite the pain. I knew it was Aunt Adèle who had swept the shards into a dustpan, and I wondered if she, like my fancy, wept the while she swept.

I don't know if Wischard was finished with all his updates, but I rose, as did Madeleine-Grace. Wischard must have understood our goal because he didn't skip a beat in hopping to his feet and racing with us to the house. We passed the kitchen and passed Aunt Adèle stepping out to invite us for a snack, rounded the staircase, taking two stairs at a time, and burst into our bedroom, the bedroom of my parents, the bedroom of my mother as a little girl, kept nearly the same as it had been all those years ago. Where there had been a white Limoges vase fell a slant of light through the window with nothing to illuminate.

It was hard enough seeing the vase empty every night before I fell asleep and every morning as I awoke, but it had brought some small comfort in triggering pleasant memories of my father and mother. Now, there was no vase even to stir such warming thoughts, an absence that made everything about this spring and summer seem more real. And the vase, it hadn't simply disappeared; it had been shattered, left for someone else to find, left for someone else to clean up, left for someone else to lament.

CHAPITRE 6

The paddles brushing the orange glow of the water's black blue surface before each dip and tug hypnotized me, lulled my mind into a haven before the boat arrived in harbor, before my feet touched land. The skimming and gentle swoosh of sun-streaked water mollified my eagerness to visit the island in a way that the slowly arriving morning, with its bird calls and shimmering first specks of sun and lacey breezes, couldn't. It wouldn't be long before we arrived on L'Ile d'Aobefein. Monsieur Vauquelin rowed while Aunt Adèle, Madeleine-Grace, and I imbibed the fading in of morning, alone at sea between the alabaster cliffs and the tiny cornflowers of the island known now mostly for its *marais salants*, salt marshes.

It amazed me, sitting in the boat as the first traces of sun glowed, how much we had already done this morning. Aunt Adèle had awoken us for the anticipated journey to the salt marshes; groggy as I was, I stepped from my bed easily—Madeleine-Grace, not as readily. We washed and dressed in the dark, met Aunt Adèle in the foyer, and walked into town. Aunt Adèle and I carried baskets while Madeleine-Grace carried a lantern, and my sister held my aunt's free hand. I spent the walk taking in the darkness, noting a difference between the shape night's blackness gives to a place compared to that of morning's. At night, the shapes seemed more formless and ominous, content to remain unidentifiable; in the morning, the shapes were ready to transform, ready to reveal themselves, ready to let light expose them.

When we arrived at Monsieur Vauquelin's place, he greeted us through the open window off the sidewalk, hurried through his house, and opened the door, ushering us in to the smell of fresh coffee, which I hadn't missed until now. Madeleine-Grace and I waited in the parlor with a seated, aged man I learned was Monsieur Vauquelin's Great-

Uncle Bertin. He sat in a gray chair, his arms resting on the chair's upholstered arms, his finger rubbing the groove of a nick in the wood at the end of the armrest. On the painted wall behind him, a crack rose from behind the chair to the ceiling. We had little time to meet before Alban brought out *cafés* for Aunt Adèle and us in *demitasses-sur-soustasses*. We sipped quickly as I heard movement and pots and pans from the kitchen. Monsieur Vauquelin told me his grandmother and sister were doing this and that in there. The old man in the chair and Monsieur Vauquelin smiled as they sipped, their eyes fixed on Madeleine-Grace and me, happy to see us, happy to have us in their home, happy to treat us to coffee and a day of new adventures.

Uncle Bertin rose as we departed, and he stood in the window along the sidewalk to watch our stroll toward the boat. A short while later, we arrived at Monsieur Vauquelin's small boat, tied to a bollard among a few others along a rocky parcel of shore well beneath the cliffs. With only the light of the lantern, Monsieur Vauquelin untied the ropes and saw us onto the boat. Before setting sail, he said, "You must call me Alban today, or we will not make it to the isle." The command fell on us like a terrifying superstition, albeit a self-instituted one, and we assented. A light shade of blue wanted to replace the dark sky as we drifted away from Etretat-au-Delà. Once a ways out, Madeleine-Grace and I preoccupied ourselves more with the majesty of the alabaster walls behind us than with where we were headed. Then, with the isle a short ways before us, the sun unrolled fire-orange carpets on the water for us, and I started to see the blues of atmosphere, sky, and water.

As we neared the southwest tip of the isle, I saw a man, decked in quintessential fisherman garb, walking along a dock of some sort. Still difficult to make out as orange begot blue, the dock seemed to connect several rows of poles that jutted outward from the shore, and the man's boat, tied to a pole on the dock, bobbed loosely near him. "Wandrille La Pouquette," Alban said to Aunt Adèle. "He maintains the *bouchots*."

"What are *bouchots*?" I asked as our boat crept to the man's dock.

"They are the poles you see with the nets. He catches mussels with them."

The man, perhaps in his fifties with a fat face and white and gray stubble, extended a hand to help us out of the boat. He bent at the waist to Aunt Adèle and Madeleine-Grace, and patted me on the head, saying, "You will have a delicious dinner tonight, will you not? The *moules* will be good!"

I smiled, unaware that Monsieur Vauquelin had seen to dinner on the isle. He explained that with high tide coming to an end, the *bouchots* would reveal a beautiful assortment of mussels, *moules*, to fill us, and Monsieur La Pouquette's son would be arriving soon to help him collect them from the nets and bring them to the mainland to sell.

From the dock, waving good-bye to Monsieur La Pouquette, we struggled to find our footing moving uphill over slabs of stone amid clumps of mud and vegetation. Madeleine-Grace and I followed Monsieur Vauquelin while Aunt Adèle took the tail. Dawn had arrived with us, and, although the terrain here was rugged, we could see more easily. To our left, wild sea vegetation grew amid puddles of sea water and mud, and to our right, the sea sparkled in the cradle of morning. Monsieur Vauquelin had apologized for his motorless boat, but I was grateful for the absence of the loud sounds one would emit. The voyage could have been shortened, but in the tranquil glides of the paddle, I did not mind.

A short distance from Monsieur La Pouquette's little dock and *bouchots*, a stone pathway formed, and not far beyond that, the path split, one headed to our left—the north part of L'Ile d'Aobefein—and the other to our right—the isle's south. Ahead, I could see the terrain changed, less untamed. I saw the silhouette of a structure in the distance to our left and asked what I saw.

"We have two choices," Monsieur Vauquelin stated, stopping at the fork in the path. "To the north lie the ruins of L'Ermitage Saint Ouen, fields of cornflower, and a grove of orange trees. I will show you them. To our south lie the salt marshes. We must go there first."

My excitement over seeing the salt marshes eclipsed my interest in the ruins, the walls of which I saw in silhouette. We were heading to the salt marshes at last, and Monsieur Vauquelin's invitation to help him gather the salt never escaped me. We started walking the stone pathway to the south of the isle, a path more defined and careful than our prior walk.

"What else is on the isle?" Madeleine-Grace asked, her head turning every which way.

As he led us to the marshes, Monsieur Vauquelin explained that the part of the isle from which we walked belonged to low-lying terrain, often submerged at high tide or after storms, so it remained uninhabited by humans, belonging instead to sea grass and bulrushes and samphire, to kingfishers and egrets and cranes, and, of course, to Monsieur La Pouquette's mussels. The middle part of the isle, more elevated and flat, contained the salt marshes and oyster beds to the south and the fields, groves, and ruins to the north. He noted that along the northwest shore of the island, we could spot the occasional dilapidated shack of the women who salted the cod the fishermen brought in from the open sea, all abandoned now. The easternmost portion of the isle served as home to several locals, mostly living in small farm houses, the keeper of the ancient locks on the northeast tip, and a village on the southeast so small that except for tiny Eglise Saint Martin, a few market stands, and a well, it contained only seven residences. I asked if it had a school, and Monsieur Vauquelin said it lacked even that. Madeleine-Grace asked where the priest lived, and Monsieur explained that one was assigned from the diocese to visit for Mass once a week, if that.

The area of L'Ile d'Aobefein, one of the smallest habitable isles off the coast of France, enabled us to arrive at the marshes in little time. We found ourselves following Monsieur Vauquelin onto a thick embankment, slightly elevated over a multitude of tiny, square pools of water; the embankment bordered these shallow pools to the north. Each set of pools belonged to a *saunier*; however, Alban informed us that several had been abandoned. In the distance, I saw the figure of a woman walking the thin walls separating the pools. In a slow approach to her, Alban pointed to the marsh directly to our right, noting that it had been abandoned as a salt marsh and usurped by clam scavengers who made periodic appearances on the isle to comb the mud for clams, or *palourdes*; others remained abandoned, unmaintained as well as unclaimed by newcomers.

From the wide, elevated embankment, we at last stepped down to another embankment that enclosed a collection of these square pools, and the woman turned to face us. Holding a long tool that reached into the pool of shallow water, she stiffened at our arrival so that her carriage became erect. She greeted us with a cordial smile and carefully walked over in thin canvas shoes to our sturdier ground.

"Adèle," she said, applying the customary greeting of kisses on the cheek, then did the same to us. "Ellande and Madeleine-Grace?" she said.

We nodded although the long-handled tool she was holding whose bottom had dragged the earth beneath the water surface intrigued us more than meeting her.

"Ellande, Madeleine-Grace, this is my sister, Aürnas-Marie," Monsieur Vauquelin said. "She and I are the primary salt harvesters here. This is our *marais*!"

He opened his arms, and with the crinkles along his eyes pronounced in the sun and accentuated with his bright smile, he stepped from our stop on the *tremet* along the thin clay bridges and, standing at the intersection of two, made a cheerful three-hundred-sixty degree turn. I looked at Aunt Adèle and saw her smiling just as widely, her eyes sparkling not only from the sun.

Aürnas-Marie continued with her "raking" of the pools after catching up with Aunt Adèle. In the meantime, Monsieur Vauquelin assembled us on the elevated embankment, the *talus alentours*, that surrounded the pools. I didn't understand everything he explained, but I came to learn that this *marais* comprised the third along this coast. The second, which we had passed, had fallen defunct through disuse and prey to *palourde* scavenging. Beyond Monsieur Vauquelin's, seven more well-designed *marais* lay, although not all of them functioning.

This *marais* was supplied with ocean water funneled through a small channel, an *étier*, that carried water to a large basin, a *vasière*, local to each *marais*. Clay and dirt embankments, the *tallus*, surrounded these and smaller containers of water. The water filtered through from the *vasière* to other smaller ponds before arriving in the tiny pools before us, the *oeillets*. These were the shallow, square pools that had caught my eye. Each set of *oeillets* was surrounded by lower embankments called *tremets*, some of which crossed through the grid work of *oeillets*, which were also connected by surrounding clay bridges. Small ledges of earth, *ladures*, jutted into each *oeillet* as a spot to pile the "raked" salt. Those piles were loaded into the wheelbarrow, the *brouette*, to be transported to bigger *mulons* along the embankment. So many of these terms I didn't know the words for in English. I wouldn't remember all the words nor the system. My mind raced only to using the tool as Aürnas-Marie was.

From here, Alban walked us to a shanty on the *tremet* a few steps from the clay path. "*Le cabane de saunier*," he said, noting his humble cabin as a place to store tools, collect and store the salt, and even sleep. This cabin looked like a rickety, wooden closet. He opened the door to reveal the lone room built atop the earth itself without a floor. A few blankets and pillows covered one part of it, and I imagined this to be the spot he and his sister rested. Shelves contained pails and ropes and empty bags for salt. In the corner, another *brouette* rested, piled with a few ropes and burlap bags. A wooden table with two wooden stools occupied a stark spot in the cabin; lines of light sifting through two long cracks in the wooden wall struck the tabletop. Against the wall, along with shovels and trowels and hoes and *rateaux à coquillages* and *griffes à palourdes*, clam rakes and claws, rested long, strange tools like the one Aürnas-Marie used, and another one with a different contraption at its bottom. The first Monsieur Vauquelin called a *las*, the second a *lousse*. He asked me to grab the *las*. The handle was so long and straight that I did not quite know how to wield it, and he laughed as it bobbled with my walk. He led my sister before him along the thin, clay bridge to the *oeillet* his sister was working.

"Watch Aürnas-Marie to observe the technique, and then you will help me do it," Alban said, positioning me in front of him. "The salt has settled on the bottom of these ponds, so we need to extract it to these piles—" he motioned toward the *ladure* of this *oeillet* on which was started a heap of wet salt— "so that they can begin to dry. Later, we will transport salt from each *oeillet* to the bigger one on the *tremet*—" and he motioned toward the *mulon*. Thus, salt was collected from the square pool of water, the *oeillet*, left to dry in a pile, the *ladure*, and then brought to a larger pile of salt, the *mulon*, located on the embankment: this was my understanding of the terms and the process.

I watched Aürnas-Marie dip the *las* into murky water and drag the salt toward her to the wall of the *oeillet*. She lifted it into the box at the bottom of the *las* and dumped it on the pile of salt nearby. Then she repeated the exercise, reaching far into the pool for each pull.

"When I loosen the salt from the bottom of the floor, it lifts the sediment and clay from the pool bed," Aürnas-Marie explained. "I swirl it in the water so that some of the sediment can fall away. I can't avoid all of it, but that's okay. Too much of it, though, can distort the taste of the salt. We will sift through it later once it dries, and the minerals we can't avoid add nutritional value to the salt."

"And color—this salt is called *sel gris*," Alban added. "It's a good everyday salt, coarse and flavorful."

"What do you do with all the salt?" Madeleine-Grace asked.

"Much of it goes to fishermen who use it—from the ships to the markets. Salt has been preserving food from rotting for centuries," Alban replied.

"Some of it we bag and sell at markets. There is a market here on the isle once a month, but we have more success at the weekly ones in Etretat-au-Delà, Fécamp, Dieppe, and other towns throughout Pays de Caux," Aürnas-Marie explained. "We try our hand in Le Havre and every so often Paris."

"We sell bags of *sel gris* and bags of *fleur de sel*, but we also sell salt flavored with herbs and flowers. Your aunt helps us with those, and they have been quite successful," Alban noted, smiling at Aunt Adèle.

I watched Aürnas-Marie pull the flat, rectangular board at the bottom of the *las* toward her, loading more to the wall and then onto the pile. She pushed the top of the salt pile down with the *las* and then added the newer salt to the top. She walked to the corner of the *oeillet* where salt had caked during her recent tugs through the water and pushed the thick clumps into the water and toward the *ladure*. She did this along the wall and then began again dipping the *las* into the pool's center to drag more of the newly freed salt to the pile.

"Let's try," Alban said, a bounce in his step as he turned to the *oeillet* behind us. Could he have been more excited than I? "Let's walk to the other side. This one is all yours, Ellande."

I followed Alban over the clay *oeillet* walls bordering each pool to the far wall of the adjacent pool. I was careful not to slip, watching my footing while trying to balance with the long-handled *las*. Madeleine-Grace stayed beside, circumspect for me as she said, "Careful," every time I looked to the sky to make sure the *las* was up and "Watch out" every time I checked behind me to make sure the handle wasn't dragging or going to hit anyone; it was at least two meters long.

Once in place, I asked Alban, "How do I hold it?"

He took it from me and modeled a respectable grip. He held it toward the end of the handle with two hands about a foot apart, and then gave it a bounce to advance his hands, pulling the *las* in, then again until the end of the handle was well behind him. He handed it back to me.

I held it the way he did but certainly wasn't as strong let alone as dexterous as Alban. I held it too far at the end to control it well, so I advanced my hands for a better grip. The wooden board on the end plunged into the water, and I pulled it back out, trying to bounce into a lower grip. I finally did and felt a little more in control of it.

"Now you'll want to dip it in the water and gently stir up the salt," Alban said. Across the *oeillet*, Aunt Adèle watched us while Aürnas-Marie finished on her *oeillet*. Alban stepped behind me and held the end of the *las* protruding.

I dipped the *las* in the water and swooshed it around as Alban said, "Smooth movements along the bottom of the *oeillet*. Just push and pull a few times." I followed his instructions, awkwardly wielding the *las*, thankful for Alban's guidance behind me.

After a few pushes and pulls through the water, Alban said, "Good! Now you can start harvesting the salt, Ellande. Drag the *las* through the water without touching the bottom, and pull the salt toward this *ladure* by your foot. Push the water and pull the salt."

I dipped the *las* in again and tried with all my concentration not to touch the bottom of the pool, but the *las* board, so difficult for me to balance, nicked the muddy pool bed twice. Still, I drew in a decent load of salt, although mine looked muddier than Aürnas-Marie's.

"Hold it here against the wall a moment," Alban said, "and then pull it onto the *ladure*. We'll start the pile here."

I again followed Alban's instruction, straining the salt a few seconds against the wall and lifting it to land. I did, however, lose quite a bit of salt.

"That's okay," he said. "Now repeat."

So on I continued, dipping, dragging, draining, and lifting the salt into the pile as Alban stood nearby guiding me occasionally with words but more so through the certainty of his presence. A pause to readjust and to see what I brought in also showed the figures of others on their own *marais* down the succession of plots. A woman rolled a *brouette* from her *cabane*. A man dragged his *las* over an *oeillet*. Even a child packed salt in her hands from a pile formed on the clay ledge before carrying handfuls of it to a *mulon*. Some shadows, some more defined in the thickening morning, but all those I saw were lone figures. And the solitary quality of working the salt marshes struck me—the lone sun, the lone vast sky, the lone man and woman and child working with routine movements from dawn until—whenever Alban told me to stop. Lone forces but not lonely in their work, for they all worked together.

Alban and Aunt Adèle helped Madeleine-Grace drag in some *sel gris*, but, a bit smaller than I, she had difficulty and did not seem to enjoy it. When Aürnas-Marie taught her how to load small pails of salt from the ledges and carry them to the *mulons*, she occupied herself doing that with the women, leaving the salt harvesting to Alban and me. By ten o'clock, I was sweating and took off my shirt with Aunt Adèle's permission, extracting a promise from Alban to make me re-clothe within the hour to avoid sunburn. I saw how Alban's skin came to be so bronzed.

At noon, we stopped when another woman arrived from the east of the island. She carried a basket and stopped only at our *marais*. Alban, Aürnas-Marie, and Aunt Adèle greeted her in front of the *cabane*. She greeted Madeleine-Grace, and then Alban waved me over. I had my shirt on now and approached the woman who bore a striking resemblance to Aürnas-Marie.

"Our sister, Ajurnée-Marie," Alban said. "She has brought lunch from the farm house!"

She walked into the *cabane* and set the basket on the table, pulling forth its contents as we surrounded. In under a minute, she had set out plates, utensils, and cloth napkins, glasses and bottles of iced tea, and two vegetable pies. She filled each glass for us while shooing away Aunt Adèle who was distraught over not being allowed to help.

"A light lunch for the hard workers," Ajurnée-Marie said heartily. "We will have a nice dinner at the farm later, too."

"You have been working hard, too," Aürnas-Marie said to her, and I wondered what she did at the farm besides prepare our lunch. So much more to the world of the *marais* awaited.

The sisters insisted that Aunt Adèle occupy one of the two stools, Alban the other, while the rest of us sat on the ground, the plate of food in our lap and the drink at our side. Madeleine-Grace and I ate voraciously after the work under the hot sun. Alban had given us water earlier, but the iced tea proved more refreshing than the shade of the *cabane*.

In their every movement—dispersing napkins, cutting the pies, pouring the drinks—Alban's sisters hustled, unlike Aunt Adèle, who distributed drinks and folded the napkins gracefully and unhurriedly. His sisters' actions, brisk but careful, had grown accustomed to working efficiently. I couldn't tell who among the three siblings was oldest or youngest but came to learn later that the two females were twins almost two years younger than Alban. The skin of Alban's sisters did not have the wrinkles that his did by his eyes; their skin was lighter with a few freckles on their face and arms, and their hair was lighter, too, with fiery orange highlights.

We ate serenely, mostly in silence, enjoying the feeling of growing full, the nourishment, and the deliciousness of every bite. Once we had emptied our plates, Alban asked Aürnas-Marie, "Did you fix the rug in Uncle Bertin's room? I forgot to check." Then to Aunt Adèle he explained, "He spilled on the rug, and we washed it. But when we put it down, the corner curled up, and we are afraid he will trip on it."

"When would I have fixed it, Alban? You know as well as I that I stayed on the island," Aürnas-Marie replied.

"It must get fixed soon," Ajurnée-Marie said, the concern in her voice evident.

"I will do it. I will do it," Aürnas-Marie said, shaking crumbs off her napkin directly onto the earth.

"Sure, you will," Alban said with a smirk. "*Après moi.*" He laughed after saying this, as did his sisters and Aunt Adèle.

"What does this mean, '*après moi*?'" I asked. "Grandma'Maud said it when we visited in Paris."

"It comes from the expression, *'après moi le déluge*,'" Aunt Adèle said, French for "after me the flood." "It implies that some people don't care about the havoc they wreak or making sure things are corrected or done well by the time they're dead and buried, not even for the people who come after them—their children, their grandchildren—as long as they can enjoy their life the way they want in their own time. Only *after* them will come the destruction—the flood—but they don't care as long as there's no flood during their own time."

"It's a very selfish outlook," Alban commented. "I was only joking when I said that to my sister. Why was your grandmother saying it? She was referring to your Uncle Roul? Uncle Romain? No! Your Aunt Laure!"

"Alban!" Aunt Adèle said while Ajurnée-Marie shushed him and Aürnas-Marie slapped his arm with her napkin.

"What?" he continued playfully. "They will not lift a finger to do anything. If Adèle does not do something, it won't get done. As long as they don't suffer the flood, what do they care?"

Aunt Adèle and Alban's sisters continued to upbraid him for speaking this way, but I glossed over the remainder of their conversation because I thought of my parents in that moment. For them, an "*après moi*" was already taking place. They no longer had the option to correct wrongs, to fix things, to ensure a safe environment for anyone who might outlive them. Madeleine-Grace and I were their "*après*," their after. However, I couldn't conceive of a circumstance in my life for which they hadn't insulated us, hadn't provided for our security, save their absence itself.

"*Après moi le déluge*," I thought. There was no deluge, thanks to my parents, for Madeleine-Grace and me to fear. Aunt Adèle and even Alban, it seemed to me, were continuing my parents' work.

After lunch, Ajurnée-Marie cleared the table and returned the plates and glasses to the basket. She said she expected us later at the farm and then headed there to continue her work. Alban had me step outside the *cabane* for a good look at the *marais* in order to see all that I had accomplished—amongst all of us harvesting, we had made quite a few small piles of salt. He said I had worked well, that I should be proud of how much I accomplished. Then, he left Aunt Adèle and Aürnas-Marie to continue harvesting while he led Madeleine-Grace and me on a small tour of the island.

Steps from Alban's *marais*, I saw a woman in a long, gray dress with two young daughters dredging the mud near the sea in front of the abandoned *marais* next to us. They used hand rakes to tear through the wet earth now that the tide had receded, and any shells that got caught in the rake's claw—mostly clams, *palourdes*—were dumped into a wooden bucket with metal wiring around its many openings. The *palourdes* they pulled from the rake were caked with mud. Alban saw us staring.

"Scavenging for clams," he said. "They will pass the buckets through water, freeing the *palourdes* of mud, and then wash them down so that they can be sold. Right now, Wandrille and his son are likely collecting *moules* from the *bouchots.*"

When we stepped onto the elevated embankment, I tried to catch a glimpse of Wandrille but could not see him. The bulrushes on the wild part of the island grew high. As we walked westward, we arrived again at the fork in the road. This time, we took the other branch, heading to the north part of the isle. The bulrushes here must have been cut at some point, for they weren't as tall or thick. The stone path led us through bushes and occasional cornflowers, but it was not long before we came upon a beautiful, gently swaying field of cornflowers, the *âobefeins* of the isle.

Beyond the fields of blue cornflower, I saw two amazing things: the orange trees lined neatly in their arbor, and the ruins of the hermitage to which they belonged. The fruit on the trees, each a miniature sun, punctuated the lush green of the trees, the beige of the ruins, the blue of the sky. A sweet scent, soothing like tea, both comforted and invigorated me. The cornflowers, I realized, surrounded the hermitage, and from this point on the path, I could see the orange trees through the tilting tips of the blue flowers, and the ethereal vision took my breath away. I stopped on the stone path as Alban and Madeleine-Grace walked ahead unaware of my halt to catch my breath. The stones under my feet became ancient and mystical like the trees and the hermitage and what once had dwelled here and what once had knelt in prayer here. And with this vision of beauty past and present before me, concealed in the field of blue cornflowers despite the openness of the sky surrounding me, I gulped. My eyes watered. I put my hand to my throat for a moment, unsure how to address this acute burning, this pure splendor that was bringing me to tears, this utter pain that my mother and father would never be here to enjoy with me. And I started to cry as beauty and grief wrapped around my sternum like climbing vines.

Never in my life had I experienced anything like that—the suddenness, the unexpected arrival of it, the emotions that pulled my soul to the surface of my body for one moment with a pain and beauty that made it feel unending. Only later could I say I am glad I felt it here, on L'Ile d'Aobefein.

Alban's voice ahead hit me, startling me eerily to reality. Stooped over the cornflowers, I wiped my tears from my eyes, caught my breath with my hands on my knees, and walked to the others. They had just arrived at something of a clearing, although it was more like a thin path between two cornflower fields that led to the *oranger* grove and hermitage. The flowers brushed against us on both sides as we shimmied through. Before us lay the hermitage.

More cornflowers swayed outside the low stone wall circumscribing the area of land. We stepped over the wall into the arbor. Alban walked us to a tree. He stepped beyond it into the shade while Madeleine-Grace and I stared at the low-hanging fruit from outside the grove.

"Grab one," Alban said. "We need one for tonight."

Madeleine-Grace couldn't reach one from this tree, so I wrapped my hand around one plump, bright orange and pulled it. I saw lower fruit as I peered through the rows of trees and suggested Madeleine-Grace pull one from another tree. She skipped through the shade past Alban, pulled one, and inspected it. Then we gave our oranges to Alban, who praised our picks and pocketed them in his pants.

"The monks who came here to pray hundreds of years ago kept this orange tree arbor. The hermitage may not have lasted, but the grove sure did. Monsieur La Ripleure tends to it, I believe. His enchanted hand helps maintain these trees, this place."

"What is that smell?" asked Madeleine-Grace, covering my own curiosity with the question.

"Ah," Alban said, turning to the ruins and walking through the grove toward it. "Come see, and you will understand the source of such a delightful scent." The leaves of the orange trees flitted through his lifted fingers as he walked. "The trees—they smell great, too, don't they?"

Our smile of agreement matched his as he looked over his shoulder at us. Just past the last trees in the grove appeared the highest remaining wall of the hermitage. Other walls were of varied heights, the stonework looking more solid than it probably was. Toward the topmost of this highest wall remained a cruciform aperture deliberately shaped for the monks. Alban led us around the height of this wall to a lower one, which we stepped over in order to enter the hermitage itself. Then I saw the source of the pleasant, soothing fragrance.

Growing within the ruins, along the walls and well within what must have been rooms or cells belonging to the hermits, yellow chamomile released its medicinal scent.

"Chamomile grows within," Alban said. "We think the monks were growing it in their garden, and over time, wind spread it. For some reason, the majority seems to enjoy growing within these walls instead of outside them where the garden most likely was planted. I like to think it perfumes the ground with the same healing power of these monks' prayers centuries ago. It is, to me, as if the work of the monks in prayer lingers, so powerful is prayer. Do you think it is so?"

I didn't know how to answer and just nodded yes. I stepped to the perimeter of the room and, leaning over the chamomile, I touched the stone of the highest remaining wall. I felt like a hermit of bygone days. I saw myself drying the chamomile flowers on strips of muslin as Aunt Adèle did with herbs, and, before my prayers, sipping the elixir of freshly brewed healing.

Alban continued walking through what must have been a doorway, and we followed. He explained, "I don't know much about this place. Monsieur La Ripleure told me the monks of the hermitage belonged to the larger monastery on the mainland and came here in isolation for prayer. They still lived as a community but had their own cells and devoted their lives to private prayer, except for Masses in the chapel, which was probably that building." He pointed to a part of the ruins. "Monsieur La Ripleure thinks they kept the orchard and a garden, wrote in a scriptorium, had private cells, and even operated the *écluse* for fish, which he now operates. I will show you that next!"

Continuing north-east carried us to the most elevated part of the island although not by much. As we walked through more cornflower fields with occasional hawthorns and bulrushes and wildflowers interspersed, I could see the lots of farms. Each parcel of land seemed small, as did the farmhouse itself. Alban did not initially lead us through the small stretch of farmlands, though. He brought us to the north-most tip of the island, and from an embankment paralleling the sea to our left, we could see the waves, less gentle than those on the southeast border of the isle, lap against the shore. Ahead, a formation of rocks jutted into the sea, suggesting a system of walls and water basins quite unlike those of the *marais salants*. Alban was bringing us right to it.

A few steps off the embankment led us to a hut on the rocky shore. The hut was made of both wood and stone, not much larger than Alban's *cabane de saunier*. The stone wall that formed the perimeter of the formation of rocks jutting into the sea began next to the hut, extending in each direction from the tiny edifice. The wall made a sort of enclosure around a small circle of sea, akin to the *clos masure* of the Pays de Caux countryside and the border of the hermitage ruins. An old man in a dark brown *feutre* sat on the stone wall near the hut, staring tranquilly at the sea beyond the far wall. The sleeves of his dirty white shirt were rolled at the elbow, and his top few buttons were unclasped as Uncle Roul preferred. His skin, darkened from so much sun, leathered from wind, made the white of his hair from under his cap stand out saliently.

"Monsieur!" Alban called to him, tugging him from his reverie. He smiled and rose to meet us in front of the hut, sprightly though shaky in his steps. A teenage boy stepped from out of the hut at Alban's call to the old man, pulling a hand from his pants pocket. The brown-haired boy wore a *feutre*, too, an unbuttoned, light gray shirt, and salt-stained, blue pants. Two or three connected, brown beads dangled from his pants pocket.

"Alban!" the old man said. "You have brought visitors to the *écluse*!"

The old man placed an arm around Madeleine-Grace and me as if he had known us our whole lives, or his. His smile relaxed but genuine, he stooped to introduce himself.

"I am Delphin La Ripleure, '*le Vieillard de l'Ecluse*,'" he said, extending his hand to the *écluse* he had in place. "This is my youngest grandson, Franchinot, for now, '*le Jeune de l'Ecluse*' but one day, the next '*Vieillard*!'"

The boy smiled bashfully, shaking his head from side to side at the epithet. The old man referred to himself as "The Old Man of the Lock" and to his grandson as "The Youth of the Lock," soon to be "The Old Man of the Lock" one day. I now saw that this was the lock system the hermits had established to catch fish, of which Alban had spoken earlier.

"And these are my friends, Ellande and Madeleine-Grace Avery, son and daughter of Juliette Semperrin and Julien Avery."

"From America?" he asked with a special smile. They had heard of us.

"Indeed," Alban confirmed.

The old man and his grandson removed their caps to greet us. I peeked into the hut to see two wooden chairs, a wooden table like Alban's, blankets, shelves, and all sorts of tools, knives, fishing poles, and nets. The air here smelled pleasantly of the sea and of the flowers and trees, yet also of fresh fish. Just inside the doorway was a wicker basket, a *gourbeille*, with fish from a recent catch.

"You have come to show your guests my lock? Or have you come to visit an old man?" Le Vieillard asked.

"Both," Alban explained, placing a hand on our heads. "They have been my helpers in the *marais* all morning, but for our break, we explore the isle. To appreciate L'Ile d'Aobefein fully, they must visit the *écluse*."

"You are correct," Monsieur La Ripleure said. "Although I've provided a little upkeep to it, as my ancestors have before me, this lock is as old as the hermitage itself. The hermits operated it. This was how they caught fish—by trapping them in the locks—but in a way that allowed the ones they did not need to escape back into the sea."

"I don't understand how they decided which fish to return to the sea," Le Jeune said. "The fish is so delicious."

He was joking, and we smiled, but the comment prompted a question. I asked, "What kind of fish do you trap in the lock?"

"A great variety," Le Vieillard said. "We catch sole, whiting, bream, bass—"

"We catch squid sometimes, too!" the grandson interrupted. "Those are a mess in the *trill*." The *trill* was a net they used to scoop up the fish they wished to keep.

The old man chuckled. "Those don't belong in the net. But you understand, my little ones, we catch a good variety. And Franchinot takes the boat and sells them to a man in Dieppe who buys them for a few restaurants there. We don't sell much. I bring some back to the house for myself—and my family when they visit."

"They don't visit too often," the boy said.

"They don't visit too often, no. That is why I'm grateful for visits from friends old and new," he said, first looking at Alban and then us.

The boy continued, stepping barefoot toward the *gourbeille* of fish and resting a hand on the doorframe, "We will be the last keepers of the lock because the family does not want to continue. I will not have children. Who can find a wife who would want a life like this? I will be the last."

The old man smiled despite his next words. "This brings me a great sadness. Franchinot is the only one among seven grandsons and twelve granddaughters who wished to learn the ways of the lock, of the isle. And he has been faithful to this wish, despite the sacrifices he must make. This makes me very proud of him and the work he does here. Alas, he may be right. He may be the last." He placed an arm around his grandson, pulling him from off the doorframe into his embrace. The tug shook free a few more beads of a rosary from the boy's pants pocket.

I saw he must have been praying when we arrived. When the old man released the boy, the boy pushed the rosary back in his pocket.

"Maybe you can help me one day," Franchinot said to me with a hopeful grin.

I did not see a future in keeping an ancient fish lock, but I said only, "There's too much I wouldn't know. Besides, I live in America."

The boy smiled as if he knew my answer and shrugged. The old man stepped toward the stone wall and rested a hand on it.

"It is hard to see much at low tide, but the tide will rise again," Le Vieillard said. "Do you wish to dwell a while with the children, Alban? Do the weary salt harvesters need a break, or must you carry on?"

Before Alban could respond, Madeleine-Grace said, "We can stay long enough to pray the rosary with Franchinot, can't we, Alban? We know how." She looked at Franchinot with as much hope and joy in her eyes as the sea and sky were expansive and majestic, and I didn't know how anyone could turn down her request. Franchinot's initial surprise turned to joy, his own as immense as my sister's, as he looked to Alban for permission.

Alban smiled and said, "May we all join you?"

Delphin La Ripleure and Alban pulled wooden chairs from the hut and sat outside while Franchinot secured the three of us flat but unstable seats on the wall of rock. He warned us not to be deceived by how secure the stonework looked; we must be incredibly cautious. Each of us in somewhat comfortable spots about the lock, Franchinot led us in the rosary, taking no more than twenty minutes. From our spot on the wall, the wind whirred in my ear, and we enjoyed an occasional spray of ocean foam, although the sea was tame. Everything about our short stay on the wall of the ancient lock felt fresh—the air, the wind, the scents, the words off our lips, the prayers themselves. I was praying that my parents were with me right now so that they, too, could enjoy this isle, but I knew where they were was even more beautiful.

Franchinot asked Madeleine-Grace when we finished the rosary, "Why did you want to pray with me?"

"La Vierge Albâtre wanted me to do so," Madeleine-Grace responded, turning to me casually as she ran her fingers through her hair.

The Franchinot who was so delighted to pray with us was equally as sad to see us depart. Alban encouraged him to visit one day over summer, noting that he would secure Aunt Adèle's permission. The boy and his grandfather's waves as we departed for the farms seemed interminable. Franchinot even hopped onto the wall of the lock when we drifted out of sight.

We finished our tour of the enchanting isle by walking a path through the farms, of which there were very few. He pointed out Monsieur La Ripleure's and his own, reminding us that we would be heading there in the evening. South of the farms was the tiny village— a few rows of graying, stone buildings with narrow, cobblestone streets between them, adorned with potted flowers and a few benches and chairs of the proprietors. Each street, which was more a walkway, spilled into the town square of the unadorned, stone Eglise Saint Martin, the well, and an open area sometimes used as a market.

Finally, we rounded the southeastern tip of the island to head back along the southern *marais* until we reached Alban's shack off the *talus*. He sighed, smiled, and plopped down on a stool as Aunt Adèle and Aürnas-Marie stepped over.

"And soon," he said, "We will harvest the *fleur de sel*, and you will see the true beauty of L'Ile d'Aobefein."

The long and labor-laden day wore on me, I had to admit, and I longed for *mésienne*. Alban had more work to do before the harvesting of the *fleur de sel*, but he spent a few minutes with us in the *cabane*, encouraging us to remain for a nap while he continued working. Lying on the blankets spread over the ground in the *cabane*, Madeleine-Grace and I filled the moments before dozing off with a million questions for poor Alban and his sister.

"Do you ever sleep here?" I asked Alban.

"Yes. Sometimes it's easier to stay here. We have only the one boat for now, so coordinating coming and going with all of us can get tricky. Sometimes, though, I want to stay here, especially on warm, summer nights. It's nice to fall asleep on my back, amid warm breezes, under the twinkling stars."

"May I sleep overnight here?" I asked, the thought of sleeping under the open stars amid the work I had done, amid the fields and pleasant scents appealing to me.

"If your Aunt Adèle permits you, you may sleep here."

"Do you do this all year?" I asked.

"We harvest the salt only in summer, beginning as early as late April if we're lucky, but usually not until May. The other months, we are preoccupied tending to the upkeep of the *marais*, including securing the walls of the *oeillets* with clay. The bridges, too. Without the upkeep, they can dry out and fall into severe disrepair. The summer is our harvesting, and we must work fast and we must work hard so that we have enough salt to sell throughout the year."

Lying his head on the blanket with us, his body reclined mostly on the direct ground, for our bodies occupied the bulk of the blanket. I thought he, himself, appreciated a moment of reprieve from the work, but he lifted his torso now and bent his knees toward his chest. He must have decided this was long enough a break.

"What if it rains?" Madeleine-Grace asked drowsily, unaware he was preparing for continued work.

"We are dependent on the whims of weather," he said, his arms resting on his knees. "A storm can change things and necessitate restructuring of walls, maintenance of the channels and basins, even. Once, a strong storm knocked down this *cabane*, and we had to lift it up to secure it in place, damaged wood and all."

He started to rise to his feet, but Madeleine-Grace's lethargic next question plopped him right back down.

"Does all the salt we eat come from *marais*?"

"No. Some can be harvested from salt mines on earth. Those miners—"

I did not hear the entirety of his answer because after these few words, I drifted off to the realm of dreams as if carried like the scent of chamomile and cornflower and orange trees by the breeze to the *marais*.

When I awoke, Alban was walking toward us, the sun behind him overhead, the smile on his face vibrant.

"Good timing," he said about my return to this consciousness. "It's time to harvest the *fleur de sel*. Grab the *lousse*!"

I rolled over before rising to see Madeleine-Grace gone. I glanced past Alban for a glimpse of Aunt Adèle but did not notice her, either. As I rose to my feet, I reached for the long tool against the wall at which Alban was pointing. It looked similar to the *las*, but it had something of a wooden box at the bottom. I grabbed it and passed it to Alban, more preoccupied with my search for my sister and aunt.

"My sister took Adèle and Madeleine-Grace to the farmhouse. Wandrille came with his son with a good assortment of *moules* for us. They will prepare them for us tonight. We have more important work to do first."

The heat seemed stronger now even though the hour had grown late, and the isle took on a new sort of glow—the fiery orange I observed this morning now intermingled with a thick pink. A few clouds rolled by an otherwise blue sky, heavy with warmth, with eagerness, with the prospect of new joy. Late as it was, we still had a few hours before nightfall. Alban, holding the *lousse*, guided me along the clay *tremet* to the edge of an *oeillet*.

"Look at the water," he said with a surprising animation for one who had worked longer and harder than I had, and without much of a rest.

I looked, and the surface of the water in an *oeillet* shimmered in the setting sun. Sparkles of blinding light combined with the faintest of pinks on a crystalline surface of water. It reminded me of a Chicago winter when frost crept along the panes of the house windows or the windshield of the car before we started it.

"The sparkles you see, those crystals, are the *fleurs*. Those we must harvest now. I will show you."

Alban positioned himself with *lousse* in hand on the midpoint of an *oeillet* wall. He dipped the box at the end of the *lousse* into the water at the far left wall and skimmed the surface to the right wall. The crystals entered the box, clearing the water surface. He did it again, also from left to right, harvesting another segment of salt crystals along the surface of the water. After these two skims, he emptied the box onto a piece of burlap waiting on the *tremet* beside us. The salt crystals formed a small mound there, and I noticed the color—mostly white with a vaguely perceptible pink. I crouched to look more closely. They, indeed, reminded me of frosty snowflakes.

"Take some in your hand, Ellande," Alban encouraged. "They are finer than the coarse *sel gris*. They crumble differently between your fingers, do they not?"

I took some between my index finger and thumb to examine them, to see the distinct crystals and to verify their thinness and delicateness. Then I ground them together with my fingertips. They easily made a light, white powder. Granules were still obvious, but they did not compare to the coarseness of the *sel gris*, as Alban had indicated.

"Taste," he said, licking his own index finger to show me.

I took a lick, and the salt tasted stronger to me, more acute in its saline quality, and oddly sweeter. I took another taste to determine if my first evaluation was correct, which I decided it was; however, on the second lick, I detected an aftertaste of flowers. I could not tell if I tasted the flower or if I smelled them, but the flavors of the isle—the winds and fields and the waters—had crystalized in each *fleur* of salt.

"It's good, is it not?" he asked.

"It's sweet," I said. "I think." I did not want to be wrong in my report.

"Do you taste the wind?" Alban asked me and laughed, dipping the *lousse* again into the waters of the *oeillet* to skim two more segments of *fleur de sel*. He added them to the pile.

"Are you watching, Ellande. You will do the next one—and the next—and the next!"

I rose and watched him finish harvesting the *fleur de sel* from this *oeillet*. Then he handed me the *lousse*, the handle just as unwieldy as the *las*, and I walked with it to the next *oeillet*. I felt more comfortable with these tools, though, and more confident with skimming the surface. I made sure I had positioned myself at the center of the pool, and then I dipped the box in and dragged it across the water surface to the wall, watching the salt accumulate in the box, listening to the faintest crunch and crackle noise, so pleasing to the ear. Alban suggested I unload the *lousse* after two runs. I obeyed this directive to Alban's praise in multiple "well-dones" and soon a pat on the back.

For the next hour, I skimmed the *fleur de sel* from the surface of the *oeillets* as dusk settled. All the while, Alban let me be. He covered the *sel gris* with cloth to protect it overnight. He also used a small shovel to gather the newly harvested *fleur de sel* into another wheelbarrow. By the time he had finished covering the *sel gris*, I had seen to at least seven mounds of *fleur de sel* on the ledges of the *oeillets*. The wind strengthening, warm as it remained, and the smells of flowers and sea and salt pacifying me in some inexplicable way, I felt the process of skimming the salt and the soft crackling that accompanied each collection therapeutic and satisfying. Alban was right: I felt at peace here.

Dinner at the farmhouse, a traditional favorite, had never been more welcomed and could not have tasted better. Aunt Adèle and Alban's sisters had prepared mussels in white wine and cream. A stock pot awaited our entrance, and when we were ready to eat, which was minutes after our arrival, Ajurnée-Marie dropped in Wandrille's gift of mussels. Aunt Adèle added fresh parsley that she had chopped, soon followed by several dollops of *crème fraiche*. Aürnas-Marie sliced a country *boule* of bread. Alban pulled an orange from his pocket and grated its zest over the stock pot the moment before serving. Ajurnée-Marie ladled the mussels into bowls, Aürnas-Marie tossed in two slices of bread, and they placed them before each of us on the long wooden table in the kitchen. Aunt Adèle carried a large bowl of samphire salad from the counter to the table, and Madeleine-Grace was asked to bring the rest of the *boule* over. Alban grabbed a bag of *fleur de sel* from a pile in the corner of the kitchen, opened it, and sprinkled a bit of it over every dish, smiling as he did so.

"You must taste your work," he said to Madeleine-Grace and me.

Alban led us in grace, and we began enjoying the delicious meal. We set the empty mussel shells in empty plates on the table, and within minutes, I had left only a bowl of milky broth. I eagerly dipped one thick slice of bread in, pressed it to the side of the bowl, and brought the soppy piece to my mouth—pure deliciousness. Everyone did the same in silence. Those first few minutes of dining, no one spoke; we keenly enjoyed every bite, every morsel of how much fun we had had today working, every sip of how much we had learned, every salty lick of the understanding of what good people and good company means. Then, and only then, as Ajurnée-Marie stood to dish salad into our empty bowls, did we begin to converse about the happenings of the day, from the salt harvesting to the stroll around the isle.

After the meal, Ajurnée-Marie called us to the stove. She was boiling water about two centimeters in depth in a Dutch oven and had placed a deep, flat plate over it. Its rim rested on the top of the Dutch oven even though its shape didn't mirror the circular container exactly. Steam from the boiling water underneath peeped through the gaps where the plate did not align. On the plate, she placed several thin bars of dark chocolate, which slowly melted into a puddle. Reaching beside us on the countertop, she pulled from another plate a thin, orange strip.

"Candied orange peel," she said, her eyes glimmering.

"Ah, you have enlisted help with dessert," Alban said to his sister.

"Indeed!" she replied, untying a small bag of *fleur de sel* near the plate of orange peels. "I candied these days ago. Now we will dip them in chocolate and sprinkle them with a flake of *fleur de sel* as the chocolate hardens. You can help me."

She modeled the first one, dipping the orange peel into the small puddle of melted chocolate in the plate and placing it on a clean plate. We did the same with a few strips of candied orange peel until the chocolate was done. There were many more pieces of orange, but they hadn't enough chocolate to melt. As the strips dried on the plate, Ajurnée-Marie dropped a flake or two of *fleur de sel* onto the melting chocolate. They would be ready to eat in a few minutes.

Afterwards, as Alban's sisters cleared the table, I wandered with Madeleine-Grace to the next room. I wouldn't call it a parlor or a drawing room; it was simply an open room in which were piled many bags of salt, some large, some small. Piles of empty bags lined the walls, and on a wooden table sat a pile of dried cornflower petals, a giant mortar and pestle beside it. I peeked inside the mortar to see that dried, blue petals had been pulverized, ground with the salt. One of the sisters must have been bagging them in small, cloth bags that had been dyed blue. There were several more to go. Alban entered as we observed the contents of the mortar.

"This is one of the flavored salts—*sel à l'âobefein*," he said. "Taste!"

Madeleine-Grace and I pinched a little of the bluish salt from the giant mortar and released it on our tongue. The tang of the salt hit first, followed by a drying sensation from the flower petals. It reminded me of how dry gin sat on the palate.

"What do you think?" Alban asked.

"It's smooth and dry," I said.

"How about the flavor?" he inquired.

"It's peppery," Madeleine-Grace said.

"Good! You have a good palate. *Aobefein* petals have a mildly peppery flavor that complements the salt nicely, does it not?"

"Do the flavors of salts from other *marais* have different tastes?" Madeleine-Grace asked.

"Oh, yes," Alban answered. "This is a good question. Every salt tastes of the sea, earth, and wind where it is harvested. The traits of the sea, the *merroir*, and the traits of the earth, the *terroir*, affect the flavor. The wind, too, can pass the cornflowers and dust the salt with their essence, which affects the flavor. *Sel gris* is heartier and robust, and *fleur de sel* is delicate, melting pleasantly on the tongue, and every *marais* produces a unique harvest."

Luckily for Alban, we ended the questions here, and he gave us a quick tour of the farm, showcasing the wheelbarrows of salt awaiting bagging and, for some, flavoring; the gardens of herbs around the farmhouse; the rooms for storage of salt that had to be rationed throughout the year. The place was meager yet efficient and cheerful.

Alban wanted to be sure to return us to Etretat-au-Delà at a reasonable hour, and the eight o'clock hour had just passed. He knew we were tired. While I had asked to sleep in the *cabane de saunier* for the night, Alban promised I could do so another night. The chocolate on the candied orange peel had dried with the *fleur de sel* on it, and when Ajurnée-Marie called to us, we tasted one—deliciousness. Alban kissed his sisters good-bye as we enjoyed peeling a few more strips of chocolate-covered orange peel from the plate and plopping them whole in our mouth. We, too, kissed his sisters through a profusion of thank-yous. Then Alban led us to the pathway to the village. Apparently, he had arranged with Wandrille to bring his shallop to an inlet off the village square so that Aunt Adèle and we might avoid the walk back to the other side of the isle. The short walk from the farmlands to the village called to our attention a new sound, an instrument, a voice, a melody that pierced the glowing blue darkness pleasantly.

"Monsieur Noue and his son play the *chifournie*," Alban said when we looked at him with curiosity. "They sit on a bench in the square some evenings and play the songs of the sunset, of nightfall. They won't play long, but it is beautiful, is it not?"

The men's voices sounded melodious, the man's deeper and raspier than his teenage son's. The instrument, however, was new to me. It sounded like a cross between an accordion and a bagpipe. As the song grew louder and we grew nearer, so did a light in the square. I finally saw the pair of them with a lantern at their feet. The instrument in the older man's arms looked something like a guitar or a lute without the long fretboard. I couldn't make out all the words, but I knew they sang of coming dusk.

Quaunt que l's âobefeins devyinent d's éteiles,
Anoitent mes lermes, anoite el cyil.

Alban nodded as he passed, and Aunt Adèle smiled. Madeleine-Grace and I waved, inspecting the instrument and the playing of it as our pace slowed. We didn't know the song, but something about the lilt of it made me want to sing along; I wish I had known the words. I imagined that Madeleine-Grace wanted to dance to it.

"They are jersiais. They sing in '*jèrriais*' dialect, in the *patois* of Normandie, and in *français*," Alban explained as we passed. If my translation was correct, they sang, "When the cornflowers become stars, my tears turn to night, the sky turns to night." Alban added, "It is said they found that *chifournie* on this island near the ruins of the hermitage. It is an ancient instrument."

Quaunt que l'asseiraunt t'appelle, péli-pélaunt,
Anoite el cyil, anoite men quoeu.

Madeleine-Grace and I could not take our eyes off them, the sound of the instrument and the melody so enchanting like so much about this island. "When the dusk calls you, gently, the sky turns to night, my heart turns to night." The musicians both smiled at us and bowed their heads but never stopped singing their ode to the evening, to the evenings of our lives.

Once out of the square, we descended down a stone path, pushed through bulrushes and slid over gorse, and on the water before us floated Alban's boat in the ocean, tied neatly to a pole lodged between some boulders.

Alban guided us in with only the light of the moon and the stars illuminating us. He untied the boat, and Aunt Adèle handed him the oars. To think he had to row us back to Etretat-au-Delà after how much and how long he had worked since before dawn today!

"I can row for you, Alban," I said.

He smiled and patted me on the head, holding both oars with one hand for that moment. He assumed, and rightly so, that he could bring us home more quickly on his own. Not a half kilometer out, looking back at the isle we were leaving, I saw two figures, the one in the foreground running to the edge of the town square. At first, I thought they belonged to the two jersiais men, the *chifournie* players, but the music still reached us as if they had never stopped playing nor moved from their seat. I realized, as the much older man walked slowly behind the animated youth, that the figures belonged to Delphin La Ripleure and Franchinot La Ripleure. When he could run no farther, the boy stretched on his tiptoes and waved avidly. I called Madeleine-Grace's attention to them behind us, and she turned to meet their unexpected presence and cheerful adieux with a loving smile—and moments thereafter a tear. Instead of waving, she blew them a kiss.

Blue and orange—two colors one might not want to mix but when positioned side by side, in layers, one swirling with the other so as to maintain a disparateness of color, they pair stunningly: the colors of flames flickering on votive wicks, that electric spark of match before the tiny, diamond-like blaze; the colors of providing—energy, destruction, purgation, warmth, light. But now, this enchanting place, this keeper of ancient lore and hymns, this preserver of traditions and passions and honor, expanded my conception of these colors: this is the island of blue and orange—a rising sun streaking the blackish-blue ripples of sea; that spreading glow of new day illuminating the hazy blue air, water, sky; the kingfisher with the carnelian breast and topaz plumage peering atop a pole into glowing water with searching eyes; the sweet, pale-peach life of mussels latching onto iridescent marine-blue shells; the life-giving brightness of trees dotted with oranges in an arbor surrounded by the celebration of dancing cornflowers; the pink and cantaloupe hues of freshly crystallized salt flowers held in cupped hands to hail the light blue sky and to invite the breeze to carry a waft of violet. Now blue and orange are to me the colors of a sinking island, an evanescent space on this earth, the colors of protection, preserving, and peace. They are the colors of what makes beauty evoke lamentation, the colors of wide, soul-stirring smiles and salty, pain-exacting tears. They are the colors of a place one never sees again.

Whether the sun is shining a carnelian dawn or shining a fiery sunset, it is surely as powerful, equally as bright. In the sun is perpetual youth. But the blues of the sky and sea change, clear in the morning and darkening at close of day, as they undergo a maturing, an aging. I don't know how these two colors taught me this, but I learned of pride in passing trades and practices to younger generations to uphold and maintain and improve and continue. I learned of this pride because I saw it in the eyes of the old *écluse* keeper and his grandson, the only one willing to help, and in the eyes of the *moules* harvester and his son. I heard it in the verses the old *chifournie* player sang with the boy who had inherited his father's voice and skill at holding a melodious tune. This act of continuing what had been passed—and then passing on again— is how Grandma'Maud tried to spend her life, hoping her children would embrace what was being offered. And I became most keenly aware that my mother had been doing the same through Madeleine-Grace and me. An accident had cut short her role in the passing process. It was something more tragic that aborted the process for others.

Aunt Adèle asked us to enter the house with the basket and to wait for her while she said good-bye to Alban. My sister and I hugged Alban and headed in, pushing the door an inch from shut so that we could espy them. We couldn't make out what they were saying, especially on account of raised voices from family on the back veranda. I turned from the open slot of the door to see if anyone in the family had noticed our arrival, but the main hall remained empty. Madeleine-Grace nudged me to look back through the opening, and I saw Aunt Adèle and Alban in an embrace. Then he kissed her.

Madeleine-Grace and I looked at each other and smiled, our reaction capturing a bashfulness but more so a happiness for their love. There was no doubt that both of us wanted to see them married so that Aunt Adèle could be happier and Alban could become our uncle.

Standing at the end of the walk to the front door in order to see him off, Aunt Adèle glowed in the moonlight and the starlight and the faint glow from the light of the foyer through the sidelights. Then, as if coming to the awareness that all had been a dream, she turned and walked with purpose into the house, a seriousness evident from the wrinkle that formed across her forehead that outweighed the effect of her unconvincing smile. When she shut the door, the aunts popped their heads from the back veranda into the *salle-en-arrière* for a glimpse at us arriving in the foyer.

Aunt Pé and Aunt Mirabelle scurried over holding *cendrier*s, Aunt Pé's tipping with her oblivious steps so that ashes fell on the floor. Aunt Adèle lifted the basket so that she could bring its contents into the kitchen, but she did not advance a single step beyond the foyer.

"You have returned," Aunt Mirabelle said.

"It's late," said Aunt Pé. "That was too long a day for the children, wouldn't you say? Surely picking salt couldn't have amused you for this long?"

"Salt is not a berry growing on a bush," Madeleine-Grace said. "We didn't exactly 'pick—'"

"Adèle, you must make the beds," Aunt Mirabelle said. "Roul wants to retire early this evening, and we had so much on our plate today without you here."

Madeleine-Grace and I had made our bed before we left on this day of waking before the sun rose. At least Aunt Adèle would not have to give ours her attention. It occurred to me that I could ask Madeleine-Grace to help me make everyone else's bed while Aunt Adèle unloaded the basket, but Madeleine-Grace looked so tired that I did not think she could make it up the stairs. I didn't know how much I had in me, either.

"Mirabelle had to make dinner tonight," testified Aunt Pé, "and, really, she did a nice job, but, of course, that took time."

"What did you make, Mirabelle?" Aunt Adèle asked.

"*Croque-Messieurs* for all," she answered with pride. "Everyone enjoyed it."

"I'm glad," said Aunt Adèle, skirting past them with the basket into the kitchen. Our aunts followed, and we followed them.

One step into the kitchen and Aunt Adèle halted—dishes and bowls, spoons and knives, glasses and cups, the cream and overly soft butter, the ham, a bowl of eggs, two of them cracked, emptied egg shells, loaves of bread, a plate of raided *sablés*, bread baskets with crumbs, dishcloths, pans and spatulas lined every which centimeter of tabletop and counter. Aunt Adèle stepped in and pulled a chair from the table so that she could set the basket on it, but she did not notice an opened bottle of cantaloupe liqueur had been placed on it; when she pulled, the bottle fell to its side on the chair, spilling its tart liquid onto chair and floor. She quickly lifted it.

"Too sour," Aunt Mirabelle said of the liqueur.

"This one we were saving," Aunt Adèle said, devoid of enthusiasm, cheer, even anger. "It contained the boiled rinds." She set the basket on the floor in the corner, grabbed a dishcloth from the tabletop, wet it, and headed to the spill.

Aunt Laure, little Laure, and Uncle Romain stepped into the kitchen at this moment, complaining of hunger.

"A *croque-monsieur* for dinner and nothing else!" shouted Uncle Romain before realizing we were home. "Ah, good! Adèle, you must make us a snack. Mirabelle made us a sandwich for dinner."

"What is it you do with the *croque-monsieur* when you make it, Aunt Adèle? Yours has the green layer," said little Laure. "Aunt Mirabelle did not make it the same."

Staring blankly at the spill she was sopping up, she replied, "I use herbed butter on the inside."

I could not believe all this mess resulted from such a modest meal. I didn't know if I should laugh or holler.

"Look at the children," Aunt Pé said, pointing at my face. "Did you not keep them in the sun too long? They look like over-cooked *crêpes*."

"You would know," Madeleine-Grace said.

"Adèle, I will need your help tomorrow," said Aunt Laure, pulling the back of her skirt to the front. "Young Roul was finishing his punishment in the garden in the front, and Alphonse must have taunted him. I had to break up a brawl between them in the yard!"

"You hardly broke it up," said Uncle Romain, growing irritated at being ignored. "Boys roughhouse. They didn't need you acting the heroine. Adèle, now that you're home, Roul, Gilbert, and I need a snack."

"I did not tell Adèle about the brawl to tell her about the brawl," continued Aunt Laure. "I told her because, in the midst of stopping it, my skirt caught on a rose bush and ripped at the seam. See?" And she held that part of her dress in front of her without lifting it so that Adèle, on her hands and knees over the spill, could see the threads popping out where the seam split.

"Why did you jump into the rosebush?" asked Aunt Pé. "This was your fault."

"My fault? I had to end the brawl. You'd think I was their mother," said Laure.

With little energy in her voice, Aunt Adèle asked, "Was their brawl in the front lawn or in the garden?"

"In the flowers along the front veranda," responded Aunt Laure, releasing her skirt and gliding to the counter in search of a snack.

"Then young Roul has finished the weeding in a garden that he has trampled," Aunt Adèle said, rising to her feet.

"Leave that," Uncle Romain said, "and find a snack, or make us one. It's only half past ten o'clock."

"She has to do the beds first," Aunt Mirabelle said. "Roul wants to retire early tonight."

"Roul wants to eat first!" retorted Uncle Romain. "He's starving!"

"Have the children said their evening prayers?" asked Aunt Adèle.

"They don't need to say their prayers one night," said Aunt Laure. "Gilbert would like a snack, too."

"I will gather the children for evening prayers," said Aunt Adèle, running water over the dishcloth and wringing it out in the sink, her back to us all, wringing, and wringing, and wringing.

My sister and I went to bed well before everyone else, and we did not arrive upstairs before midnight.

I was grateful for a "fattened morning," as the French say. Madeleine-Grace and I didn't leave our bed until after ten o'clock in the morning, and I wondered if Aunt Adèle had been able to sleep in, too. I hoped she had done so.

Madeleine-Grace and I spent the late morning practicing our dance and reminiscing about our day on L'Ile d'Aobefein before joining Aunt Adèle in the conservatory for attention to our outfits for the children's ball. By now, it was early afternoon. She had our outfits draped over the ironing board, not to iron them but to allow them to hang so that she could work on them. I didn't know quite what she was doing, but it involved sewing something along the hem of Madeleine-Grace's dress and the cuffs of my trousers. Madeleine-Grace was crocheting her thin, circular doilies next to me on the divan, and I was winding my grandfather's watch. As we worked, we talked about the isle, Madeleine-Grace lamented not having picked a few cornflowers to bring back, and Aunt Adèle reminded us that we were to meet Lady Victorine and Lady Léontine today to register our music for the children's ball. Madeleine-

Grace had been terrified that if we turned in the original sheets Grandma'Maud had given us that we might never see them again, so she insisted I transcribe the music onto paper. I had done so the day after our return from Paris.

As we wrapped up, Aunt Laure stepped into the conservatory holding her unraveling skirt. "You promised to mend—." She stopped when she noticed that Aunt Adèle was putting away our outfits for the children's ball. "Why do you give Ellande's suit and Madeleine-Grace's ball gown so much attention and not the others? Do you think this is fair?"

Aunt Adèle turned and looked as if she had found a bloody body like the women in my detective stories, only her scream was internal.

"You and Pé and Mirabelle made a point this year of telling me you wished to do the suits and gowns yourselves, do you not recall? You would take no suggestions from me on fabric, on color, or on design. When I offered to accompany you to the *mercerie*, you told me you preferred a shop in Rouen because Marie Loiselier mentioned a certain tailor there, and you all went without me. When I offered to embroider a bodice for little Laure's gown, you told me the gown did not need my embroidery, that what you bought was good enough. Now it is not fair that I see to Juliette's children's suit and gown?"

"All that was before we knew Ellande and Madeleine-Grace were to be included in the children's ball at all," said Aunt Laure, tossing the skirt on the ironing board.

Aunt Adèle turned her back to Aunt Laure and lifted the skirt. "If you would like my help with your children's outfits for the ball, I am happy to help however you would like."

"By now it's too late," said Aunt Laure. "Wischard's and Laure's are both ready."

"I must ready Ellande, Madeleine-Grace, and myself for a walk into town. We are registering their music for the ball, and Lady Victorine and Lady Léontine wish to accompany us." Aunt Adèle set the skirt neatly on the ironing board, smoothing it with her hand after angling it so that the ripped seam lay visibly. Then she led us out of the room to make sure we had the sheet music ready.

Aunt Laure said as we passed, "Can you not mend my skirt first?"

Ladies Victorine and Léontine met us at the end of our front walkway and commented on our tan. When they learned of our visit to L'Ile d'Aobefein with Alban, they grew giddy, hoping such a *séjour* implied a growing closeness between him and Aunt Adèle. They also pointed out the flowers in front of the veranda, a patch of them horizontal, snapped, and crushed. Lady Léontine thought maybe animals had been the culprits.

Our stroll down the road to town teased out several topics of conversation and stories, much of which pertained to society personages on the coast and in Paris, but the one that lured my ear the most strongly involved Jeuffine des Gervais. Apparently, when Lady Victorine walked to our house alone to watch *la choule* and invited Jeuffine along the way, she had probed the newcomer for information on her past and had come to some conclusions about her character.

"'Where did you stay if not in Paris with your parents?' I asked her," Lady Victorine recounted. "She said she had spent several years in Oxford, England. I assumed she meant attending one of the colleges there, what with all the hoopla last year about admitting so many women in the former men's colleges—why they must allow the sexes at that age to intermingle in the educational arena is beyond me—but no, she did not mean she attended the college. She said she enjoyed being near intellectuals and such circles, although she did enjoy a good 'bumps race' or something of the sort involving young men rowers. 'With what sorts of intellectual circles were you consorting?' I asked, and I tell you, she went on a rant about 'the cowardly followers' too afraid to think differently about their bodies, about the weaklings too docile to think for themselves, about the idiots too feeble-minded to disagree with religious teachings. In her circles, they could talk freely about the wrongness of marriage and the joke that is this life and hooey and more hooey."

"She is godless," added Lady Léontine, shaking her head.

"I think she expected me to blush and swoon," continued Lady Victorine, "as if this were the first I was hearing of dissenting talk. 'No, my dear,' I wished to say. 'I have heard such talk for years from my generation to those of my grandchildren, through wars and through peacetime, and I not only am no stranger to these 'new' ideas, but I am not so simple as to buy into them.'"

"You should have said it to her," said Lady Léontine.

"I respect that she holds differing opinions but do not respect the opinions themselves. So I nod when she talks. That's all one can do with a headstrong imbecile. A single conversation with me on a ten-minute walk will not undo her several years in Oxford, entertaining 'intellectuals' and fawning over rowers. I must add, Adèle, I think she is fawning over your brother Roul, too. Watch out for that one."

Aunt Adèle parted her lips to respond, but, thinking better of it, closed her mouth. After a moment of silence, she said, "Thank-you for the warning, Lady Victorine."

"Victorine has an eye for these things, and so does your mother," said Lady Léontine, referring to Grandma'Maud. "My eye is not so good for these things, but Victorine and Madeleine-Maud, theirs is sharp."

Although the topics changed and other stories were shared, I remained preoccupied with what Lady Victorine had shared about Jeuffine des Gervais. Could she really think life is a joke and prefer such an understanding of life to what we believe—that our life is a gift from God, the object of which is to be holy, to be good, to be happy? How could anyone be happy who thinks life is a joke? They might laugh, but could they be happy? I thought a visit to her place for more *hydromel* might occasion these queries of her. If she were so forthcoming with Lady Victorine, she might not mind sharing her thoughts with me.

Our late registration took place at Monsieur and Madame Dalmont's apartments in town. This is not where the children's ball would take place, but Madame Dalmont had organized the orchestra and the conductor to meet at her place to organize the music and to begin practicing. The other registrants had already supplied their music, and an easy exception was being made for our late presentation of song and sheet music.

A personal friend of the Countess and her factotum for the children's ball, Madame Dalmont volunteered a ballroom in her apartments for ballet lessons for young children, requiring the ballroom for formal events only so often. Today, however, the ballroom to which we were escorted housed an orchestra ready to practice and a conductor eager to have all musical concerns in order for the imminent event. The conductor spoke with a violinist in the middle of the floor while other musicians set up stands and music at their chairs, some tuning, some piecing together their instrument, some paging through the sheet music.

"Ah, Jacques and Madeleine-Grace! We were expecting you," Madame Dalmont said when a butler escorted the five of us to the ballroom entrance. She sat in an upright chair inside the double doors of the grandiose room, a table at her side where sat another, businesslike woman. Madame Dalmont could not have been much older than Aunt Adèle. "The Countess is thrilled you are attending, as am I. Yours is the last of the music to register, so Edgar is eager to learn of your selection. Edgar!"

A balding man of about fifty, jaunty in his movements, abruptly darted from his conversation with a violinist to join us at the table. I recognized him from last year's children's ball. At nice restaurants in Chicago, certain waiters, when summoned to a table, grew perturbed, but when they approached the customers, an unctuous smile smeared over their sour expression as if graciously wishing to accommodate any request: this was Edgar Cuvelier's reaction to Madame Dalmont's call.

"Edgar, I present to you Jacques and Madeleine-Grace Avery, who have arrived with their music," Madame Dalmont said.

"Ah, the late-comers," he said with a bow. "I remember you from last year, and I must extend my deepest condolences."

Everyone around us, including Ladies Victorine and Léontine, bowed their head as if taking a moment of silence. Wishing to break from this moment, I lifted the sheet music in my hands, extending the pages to the conductor.

"Which have you brought us?" he asked, taking the music from me. An accidental snarl at the prospect of some tune distasteful to him certainly did not disabuse us of his disrelish for having been interrupted.

"It's neither a *gavotte* nor a *farandole*. We have selected a *tourdion*."

He smiled, as did Madame Dalmont. Now he had been smiling all along, but his smile turned real. "A *tourdion*?" he said. "This is quite refreshing. This announcement will be melodious to my musicians' ears." He scanned the music, bobbing his head at times as if he heard it. "I am not familiar with this one, nor the composer. I think I will like it, though."

"And I have some suggestions for you about the arrangement," said Madeleine-Grace, stepping from our circle and leading him away as if in confidence over some secretive matter. His curiosity piqued, I was sure, both over her assertive approach and her suggestions for the music, he bent an ear to my sister and listened avidly. As Madeleine-Grace guided him through the music, I saw his jaunty movements soften and his stiff shoulders drop.

When they finished discussing the music, the conductor departed from us with a cordial salutation and rushed past the violinist to several musicians with the sheet music. They scrutinized it, listened to his notes, glanced at us with smiles on their faces, and tried a measure or two on their instruments. A small circle had formed around him, and I could tell this music was generating excitement among the musicians.

So could Madame Dalmont tell, for she said, "I think you've secured a good selection, and I have a feeling it will be a show-stopper."

Our *tourdion* had yet to debut, but the event would be show-stopping for other reasons. The visit to L'Ile d'Aobefein marked what turned out to be the last bit of real peace I felt this summer. What became a normalcy of lazy mornings and family quarrels at the house was coming to an end, as well. The afternoon of the children's ball certainly launched the family into unrepairable damage and betrayal, but not before the tragic event of our next visit to Grandma'Maud in Paris.

What was supposed to have been a summer stay in Etretat-au-Delà until September did not last through July.

CHAPITRE 7

"She's not crazy," Aunt Adèle said, her hands clasped in the open apron on her lap as we lazed a moment on the bench in the flower island. We had tilled a small patch of earth near the shed, away from the other islands. The family had complained so much about the scantest wafts of mint that Aunt Adèle decided to transplant the patch in the island to a new spot more out of the way, but she was planning to make it bigger than the one on the island—the reason she requested more mint seeds.

I had asked her about Grandma'Maud in anticipation of our upcoming return to Paris, and she stared at the bright, white clouds, thick and slow, on the light blue sky.

"She's not crazy," Aunt Adèle said. Then she added, "She is, if anything, disappointed."

"When we left Paris last time, nothing could break her stare. Her body seemed stiff. Something was wrong," I said, my admission meant to encourage more information from my aunt. I felt as if everyone in the family knew something Madeleine-Grace and I didn't. I was feeling this way about other things, too—that we had been left out not only of important stories but of updated lifestyles and mindsets. I had to wonder if my mother and father had been left out of something, or if they had become aware of them and opted not to tell us.

"This happens to her sometimes. The doctors are not sure of the cause. It is better you were not there to see her come out of it."

"Why?" asked Madeleine-Grace.

"Sometimes, when she snaps out of it, she has a fit first. She flails her stiff arms or slams them at her side a few times. It is abrupt and frenzied, but it lasts only a few seconds. Then she readjusts to her surroundings and acts as if nothing had happened."

"Does she even know that something had happened?" I asked.

"She doesn't remember," said Aunt Adèle, looking at her hands in her lap.

"I think she goes somewhere in her mind," Madeleine-Grace said. "And that's okay."

"Sometimes," I continued, "she cuts thin ribbons of fabric without thinking, like she's a robot."

"So you have seen that, too? Yes, the doctor says she has developed a compulsion to make those strips and that it is harmless. We don't know what prompted it nor how to explain the strange form this compulsion took, but the doctor says to let her do it. He says he has seen such things in cases of senility, but Maman's is only in the early stages, although it seems to have come much too early. The possibility of senility concerns me, but the fabric does not."

We did not have a response to this. This was not something that had been kept from my mother. In January, Aunt Adèle had sent my mother a letter, and in it, she expressed her concern over what the doctor had suggested. Our mother shared this letter with us and explained to us what senility is. My father believed that such strange behavior may have been brought on by Uncle Romain's insistence on keeping her confined to the Paris flat, and my mother could not wait to spend as much of the summer as possible with her mother. Grandma'Maud always felt calm and safe with my mother and Aunt Adèle, that much I knew for sure, and the calm of my mother's presence, we expected, might alleviate her anxieties over her entrapment let alone over anility.

Uncle Romain justified the confinement of Grandma'Maud in a way that made it difficult to argue. Last October, after our summer visit in Etretat-au-Delà where we had enjoyed so much merriment with Grandma'Maud and the rest of the family, she fell one day in her sitting room in Paris. Aunt Adèle and Uncle Romain found her late afternoon on the floor, disoriented but conscious. Aunt Adèle, the last to have seen her about three hours beforehand, reported that her mother neither had appeared nor had been behaving aberrantly as she sent Aunt Adèle to buy two kilos of chestnut flour. When the doctor arrived, Aunt Adèle and Uncle Romain listened as my grandmother admitted no recollection of the fall nor of what had precipitated it.

Through days of observation and steady visits from the doctor, she remained agitated and unsteady. After several days, Uncle Romain announced that he had conferred with the doctor and decided she would require constant observation and care and should be restricted to the familiarity of the Paris flat. That was when they hired "Gourgandine." Apparently, Grandma'Maud resisted the decree, declaring stability and familiarity more likely in her *former* Paris home— had it not been sold from under her—or her summer home in Etretat-au-Delà, which Uncle Romain had the doctor discourage, a discouragement that all but Aunt Adèle upheld adamantly.

"You aren't afraid of Grandma'Maud, are you?"

"No," I said. "We just have never seen her like that. And everyone calls her crazy."

"No one should be calling her crazy, and if she *were*, I can think of a few good reasons," Aunt Adèle uttered in her mother's defense, and then looked again at the clouds. "Do you remember when you were little, and we used to sit on this bench or by the cliffs with your mother and father and point to the clouds and call them 'islands?' And we would say, 'Jacques, whose island is that one?' and you would say, 'That one is Maman's island.' And we would say, 'Madeleine-Grace, whose island is that one?' and you would say, 'That one is Papa's island.' And we kept asking until you couldn't think of anyone left to say."

"Or until there weren't any more clouds," Madeleine-Grace said.

"So you do remember?"

"I do," she said, and I agreed.

"Aunt Adèle, did Grandma'Maud and Grand-père Jacques play that game with you when you were little?"

"They played that game with all of us when we were little."

"Will you play that game when you have children with Monsieur Vauquelin?" I asked.

Aunt Adèle looked away from the clouds and back at her hands in her lap. How rare that they were not involved in some kind of work.

"Aunt Adèle, why did Monsieur Vauquelin ask that we call him Alban for the day on L'Ile d'Aobefein?" my sister asked.

She did not answer either question. She said only, "Are you happy that Monsieur Vauquelin joins us this evening for dinner?"

I was happy to know of his imminent arrival and let my aunt know, as did Madeleine-Grace. Aunt Adèle smiled and looked as happy as we were. She looked the same sort of happy as when she spoke of that spring in Liguria and Campania with my mother.

Wischard bounded down the veranda steps and over to the flower island, trampling a lily on his last step.

"You must be careful, Wischard," Aunt Adèle said, turning her energy to the poor yellow flower to which Wischard was oblivious.

"I found this map of Paris in Maman's room. I snuck in while they were sleeping, and they didn't even notice. Now we can plan our adventure!"

We had received the best news last night in that Aunt Laure had granted Wischard permission to visit Grandma'Maud with us in Paris. His company, I knew, would increase how much I enjoyed the trip by leaps and bounds, and he was already planning adventures for us.

"There will be no such adventures without Grandma'Maud or Uncle Roul," said Aunt Adèle, lifting the broken lily from the ground. "I can find a place for this lily inside; its stem is still long enough to last a few days in a vase."

Occupying Aunt Adèle's spot on the bench, Wischard began tracing paths through the streets of Paris, saying out loud the sites as his finger passed them. I pointed out L'Ile de la Grande Jatte on the western edge of the map, and placed a finger with my other hand on L'Ile de la Cité.

"This is where we were when we tried to see the isle the last time we were in Paris, but we couldn't because it wasn't a clear day," I explained. We had told Wischard about this part of our *séjour* in Paris, but I think he had to see to believe just how far the isle was from Notre Dame. Not only did many streets, sites, and neighborhoods abound, but the Seine's winding around Le Bois de Boulogne extended the distance between L'Ile de la Cité and L'Ile de la Grande Jatte.

"Did you really climb to the top of the tower?" he asked.

"Yes, and it was a spectacular view of all Paris," I said.

"But you didn't see L'Ile de la Grande Jatte."

"It wasn't clear enough," I reiterated.

"I mean you didn't see the isle at all. You've never been there. I say we see the isle for ourselves."

"You think we should go to the isle, itself, instead of trying to see it from the cathedral?"

"Why not? That will be our first adventure!" declared Wischard, pulling the map to his lap for scrutiny. Wischard had decided—and who was I to counter—our first adventure would be a jaunt to the isle of Seurat's inspiration, itself.

Monsieur Vauquelin was sitting on the divan in the *salle-en-arrière* when Madeleine-Grace and I strolled down from our *mésienne*. Wischard heard us pass his room and followed us, map still in hand. He said he had never rested, too caught up in the locales of Paris we might explore together. Aunt Adèle had finished preparing for dinner and had only to await the family's arrival for *apéritifs*, so she joined us in the *salle-en-arrière*. Madeleine-Grace picked up her knitting, continuing with her tiny doilies; she must have formed a hundred by now.

My occasional glances at her work informed me her attention to detail had not relented in spite of our tragedies. I wondered if it had not increased, perhaps in honor of our mother. I admired my sister's ability to observe and to take to something so quickly and meticulously— knitting, crocheting, sewing, dancing—always adding her own aesthetic flair. I also admired the doilies themselves and imagined them in a pile on a bar counter at an imaginary restaurant in Chicago. I, as the bartender, would lift one, place a freshly poured cocktail on it, and slide it over a polished, walnut-finished counter to the gentleman in the black suit or the lady in the white blouse with the pearl necklace.

Monsieur noted the map of Paris on Wischard's lap as our cousin tossed his head back on a couch pillow, squeezing his eyes, and rubbed them with his fists. I think he had stared too closely for too long at the tiny streets and thoroughfares.

"If you are heading for Paris soon, you are heading into the heat," Monsieur Vauquelin said. "You are fortunate to have a place on the coast for summers."

Wischard opened his eyes and said, "'Endless nights lounging on the veranda—.' That's what mother says life in summer is—what life should be."

Monsieur Vauquelin's head turned nearly sideways. He said, "Yes, put salt around that tradition."

He remained in that position, a stone face parallel to his shoulders, before straightening his head and shaking it. He scoffed and shook his head slowly side to side as he shifted his gaze to Aunt Adèle. Wischard looked at me, unsure how to interpret what I recognized as disapprobation.

To reel him back to complaisance, we told Alban of our upcoming visit to Paris and of our possible adventures.

"Decide on a steeple before leaving," he said.

"Huh?"

"If you decide on a steeple or a common point that you can see from many directions, from many spots, you can all meet there should anyone get lost, and it helps you orient yourself if you lose your way," he explained, which made sense to us. I assumed that, unless Wischard had his way, most of our treks through Paris would be by car or, if on foot with Grandma'Maud, would be within a few blocks of her flat.

"Will you ever visit us in Chicago?" I asked. "With Aunt Adèle?"

Monsieur Vauquelin laughed. "I find traveling a kilometer outside of Normandie a challenge these days. I don't know that a seven-thousand-kilometer voyage to America is on my horizon."

"If Aunt Adèle comes, you should accompany her," I said.

"Does your Aunt Adèle have plans to visit you in America?" He directed his question to our aunt, who shook her head no, her lips downturned.

"Maman said that you were going to visit us in November for Thanks-Giving," Madeleine-Grace announced, her hopes undashed by Aunt Adèle's response.

"Thanks-Giving!" Aunt Adèle exclaimed. "How I love to hear of this holiday. I do not understand why we don't have this celebration in France, why every nation doesn't insist on this celebration."

"Not every nation had the Pilgrims arrive on the Mayflower and a special meal with the Indians," Madeleine-Grace said, smiling at the preposterousness over that exact event happening elsewhere.

"Those are the historical roots of the holiday, but the idea of a day all about giving thanks—that is something special. Tell Alban about the meal. I could use the reminder."

Tantalized by the meal as visions of the dining room table covered in autumn and harvest fare and flair, I began, "We have a turkey big enough for the whole family, friends sometimes, and left-overs the next day. Papa makes the turkey. Everyone in America has turkey, I think. We have stuffing, mashed potatoes—"

"And sweet potatoes! Those are my favorite!" interject Madeleine-Grace.

"—green beans with almonds, cranberry sauce, and, for dessert, roasted chestnuts, pumpkin pie, pecan pie—."

I had to stop to think of more dishes, but Monsieur Vauquelin exploited my pause to ask what some of these dishes were. I had said "stuffing" and "cranberry" in English, unaware of the word for them in French, so I had to explain the dishes for them as best I could.

"Your mother told me of this holiday, and she told me of all the little ways she made the meal special," Aunt Adèle said.

"Like the herbs on the rolls," Madeleine-Grace said.

"I do not know of this. What are the 'herbs on the rolls?'" she asked, curious about the food but more so interested by the mention of herbs, I speculated.

"Right before Maman puts the rolls in the oven," Madeleine-Grace delighted in explaining, having sat on the kitchen chair and observed for several years now, "she brushes them with egg whites, water, and salt. Then she presses an herb on each, like a parsley leaf or a sage leaf or a braid of tarragon, and bakes them. They look beautiful when they come out of the oven—shiny and warm—with the herb imprinted on them."

Aunt Adèle reacted with such warmth and unspoken pride at the surprise of this frivolity of our mother's. What Aunt Adèle received with tearful appreciation anyone else might have perceived as trite.

"I am making rolls tonight," she said through ragged syllables, pushing through her tears. "Would you like to apply a wash of egg whites and the herbs before I bake them?"

Of course, Madeleine-Grace consented to something so pleasant to her.

"But you still have to come to America for Thanks-Giving in November so that you can see all the dishes—the whole meal!" I said. "And Monsieur Vauquelin, you have to come, too."

"It did not occur to me to—" Aunt Adèle grew teary again, just after having dabbed her eyes with a kerchief. "I suppose I could—" then, rethinking, "I would be delighted to come to your home for Thanks-Giving in November."

Monsieur Vauquelin would not assent, but I was beyond content to hear Aunt Adèle confirm her presence at our celebration in November. I began concocting ways to convince her to stay through Christmas and New Year's Eve, picturing her rolling the dough for pumpkin pies with Maman and using the tiny, pumpkin-shaped cookie cutters to make the crust border. I foresaw Monsieur Vauquelin standing with me at the bar in the living room as I taught him how to make Papa's famous cranberry walnut cocktail with the walnut syrup Maman makes just for that drink every fall. Fondly picturing them amid the backdrop of a Midwest autumn, I did not account for the many changes that I probably should have included in my visions.

Madeleine-Grace adorned the rolls before *apéritifs*, and an hour of *cidre* sipping and *saucisson* and *cornichon* munching on the veranda came and passed quickly in the form of jabs at Monsieur Vauquelin, lulls of silence, spats between family members—this evening, between Aunt Mirabelle and Uncle Romain over Uncle Romain's "forcing" Uncle Roul to drive to Paris twice—complaints about the heat, about Grandma'Maud, and about each other, and several outbursts. Dinner passed in the dining room in the same way, as if grace beforehand had fallen on deaf ears, a grace in which Aunt Adèle expressed, more ardently than usual, gratitude for the meal and the bonds of siblings. Aunt Pé scoffed at the rolls, Aunt Laure glared at them with an eerie distress as she listened to Aunt Adèle explain the story behind them, and Uncle Roul threw one at young Roul, who had broken a cigarette on the tablecloth while rolling it, the tobacco spreading around his plates and silverware. Uncle Romain commented that the rolls lacked salt and suggested Monsieur Vauquelin had been stingy with us.

The three of us helped Aunt Adèle clean up in the kitchen after dinner, and then we walked with them into town to Monsieur Vauquelin's place. Monsieur had wished not to trouble us in accompanying him, but Aunt Adèle insisted she needed air and the walk.

Once outside his place, he darted inside and opened the window on the side of the house, next to which on the exterior side Aunt Adèle, Madeleine-Grace, and I were standing. "I wish you hadn't come all this way, but since you're here, I have something for you. My sister said she would bring them home tonight, and sure enough, they are here."

A refreshing breeze coursed by, puffing a solid white tablecloth hanging on a clothesline down the road, swaying the clothesline itself. Overhead, some birds I couldn't make out came to a landing on what I ascertained must have been the small church dome; the few blocks of shops and residences between us and the square blanketed the church from our view, but I could hear the laughter of teenagers from that direction, no doubt a small gathering of friends enjoying the starlit summer evening. Laughter had accompanied our walk to Monsieur Vauquelin's, and the warmth, the breeze, the smiles made my mind feel light for a few moments.

He extended a hand through the window to Madeleine-Grace. In it was a bouquet. "For Madeleine-Grace, a bouquet of cornflowers."

Accepting them, she smiled and thanked him. "Aunt Adèle, can we make a garland of them for my hair? For the children's ball?"

"I can try, my dove, but let's enjoy them as a bouquet for now," Aunt Adèle said, dipping her nose in to smell, as did I.

"For Ellande," Monsieur Vauquelin said, passing through the window a small pouch. I could smell its contents as soon as the pouch neared me. "Chamomile! Ajurnée-Marie made sachets for you to use like tea."

"Thank-you," I said, bringing it to my nose for a soothing inhale. Madeleine-Grace did the same.

"And for Adèle," he said, handing her a small, burlap sack.

"Thank-you, Alban," she said, accepting and untying it. Then she smiled, too. "*La menthe!*"

"Did you not say you needed some seeds for the new patch of mint you're planting?" he asked.

"Yes, and Ellande brought some back from the Pays de Caux countryside," she explained. "Now I have more than enough to extend the patch around the entire shed!"

We laughed. I couldn't see how the smell my relatives found so cloying and bothersome would not reach them with the abundance of mint she must have to plant to surround the shed.

"However," she continued, pouring a few seeds into her opened palm, "I can spare a few now that I have more than enough."

I don't know if it was the moon. I don't know if it was excitement over an unexpected gift. I don't know if the scent of cornflowers, chamomile, and mint procured an intoxicating effect. Something came over Aunt Adèle in that moment, her love resting his elbows on the sill before her, the night settling on the town as the din of town square chatter faded, the bag of mint in her hand. She took the seeds in her palm and emptied them in the narrow planter hanging on the exterior window sill. Monsieur Vauquelin lifted his resting hands so that she could drop the seeds into the planter and into the crevices of the window, a dumbstruck semi-smile on his face. Then she poured more seeds into her hand and, walking along the length of his residence, dropped pinches of seeds onto the thin strip of dirt where the stone of the sidewalk met the stone of his house. A few tiny weeds were already growing there, and she swooped to pluck them—this would be a spot for mint now. On her way back to the window, she sprinkled a few more handfuls into the planters on the windows she passed. Stepping to the doorway of his house, which he had left open a few inches, she tossed more seeds along the threshold. She turned, and a handful aimed for the cobblestone street. She turned again, and another handful aimed for the sidewalk.

Then she stopped and peeked into the sack. I could tell about half the bag remained full.

"Now you have mint, too," she said, her intoxication wearing off.

"Now I will have an abundance of mint," Monsieur Vauquelin said, returning his elbows to the sill, his clasped hands extending out the window toward us, "and it will always remind me of you."

Paris in the morning felt oddly like the coast—yes, we somehow convinced Uncle Roul to wake early for the drive in, and we had arrived in Quartier Javel by ten o'clock on a warm, sunny day. This neighborhood did not impress upon one the same bustle as those closer to "the cradle" of Paris, and I wondered if I didn't associate the industrialism of this area of Paris with the farm labor I associated with the countryside outside Etretat-au-Delà. I cannot say this part of Paris on a pleasant morning felt more sluggish than other parts of Paris, for I knew hard work had begun hours before our arrival. I simply felt an easiness here, an absence of the frenzy of Le Champs-Elysées, le Quartier Palais Royal, or le Quartier Saint Germain-des-Prés.

The absence of any frenzy that Paris could provide Wischard compensated for. He had started the ride groggy and sullen but had perked up about two hours in. Since then, he had not relented: he divulged that, unlike his parents, he was unconcerned about the upheaval in Tunisia and Algeria spilling onto the streets of Paris and about the nuclear bomb testing. Instead, he spoke, to Uncle Roul's amusement, of Annick Zouzier, who had kissed him on the ear in the courtyard outside the school because he turned his head in time to avoid the unexpected kiss landing on his lips. Worst of all, Annick just moved from Paris to, of all places, Dieppe, where Wischard faced the risk of encountering her there any time they visited his father's family. He provided an endearing sketch of Brigitte Poupière, whose inquisitive and gentle personality Wischard found appealing but whose resemblance to Astride he found so repulsive that, when she tried to kiss him in the courtyard outside school, he turned his head so that she inadvertently kissed his ear; she, however, did not move to Dieppe. He described his dream wife, which really entailed a description of his dream dessert of *tarte tatin* topped with three flavors of ice cream—caramel, vanilla, and cinnamon—doused with Cointreau, lit on fire, and topped with chocolate syrup, a treat she would know how to make and serve to him every day in the courtyard outside the school during recess as well as after dinner. His dreamy vision of such bliss dissipated the instant he erupted in distress when he realized he had left the street map of Paris on his bed.

He talked all the way up the stairs of Grandma'Maud's and only zipped his lip when we entered her sitting room. Bertille stuck her head into the sitting room from the bedroom when she heard us, and she shook her head in dismay. Uncle Roul's expression, initially embossed with a smile, turned to a scrunched brow with squinty, quizzical eyes as he marched into the dim bedroom. We crept in behind him, standing a few steps beyond the bed.

Grandma'Maud, reclined with the covers up to her neck, her head and shoulders propped against the headboard, lay with shears in hand, keenly cutting strips of green fabric, a vibrant green like the gorse that creeps along the walls of the alabaster cliffs when seen from a distance. Her precise, slow cuts, like last time, used only the deep, interior part of the blades, never snapping fully shut, yet a loose pile of recently made ribbons rose beside her.

"Maman," Uncle Roul said, receiving no response. "Maman, Ellande, Madeleine-Grace, and Wischard have come to visit. They wish to see their *grand-mère.*"

The fabric wedged between the blades of the shears, she simply pushed into the green for a slow-forming ribbon, impervious to the announcement of her son. The cuts she made were remarkably straight.

"She's crazy," Uncle Roul blurted out, throwing his hands in the air. He stepped into the sitting room and slid his hands in his pants pockets, shaking his head with disapproval.

"She needs more time in the morning," Bertille said. "She will come to soon, Roul. Just give her time." Then she looked at us children. "Find Borbála and have her make some coffee. Your grandmother will be back soon."

We sidled out, all of us having experienced this Grandma'Maud and knowing it did not last, all of us eager to see the lucid Grandma'Maud and to spend the day with her caring and warm-hearted self. Borbála was stirring a batter in a bowl in the kitchen when we entered. Uncle Roul had remained behind in the sitting room, I imagined, to coax Grandma'Maud from her state with the caregiver.

"Your grandmother has taught me a few things," she said, looking up from her stirring. "*Madeleines* for this evening. But you have been traveling all morning and must long for a *café au lait.*" She read our minds. Nudging the bowl to the center of the counter with the spatula set across the rim, she turned her attention to preparing us coffee at the stove. The batter on the end of the spatula dripped onto the countertop. I wanted to place the spatula in the bowl and clean up the fallen batter, but I did not know if that would be rude; it was my Grandma'Maud's flat, but Borbála was the maid. Instead of risking rudeness, I kept my eyes on the accumulating batter on the countertop.

As Borbála asked us about our ride and how our week was at the summer house, she made the *cafés au lait*. Wischard spotted the dripping batter, walked over, and used two fingers to swipe some and lick it off his fingers.

Over coffee, which did take place at the dining room table this time among the three of us, we discussed our game plan for tomorrow. Wischard had led us there, at first, I thought, because, as someone more accustomed to visits to this flat, he had been habituated to Grandma'Maud's preference for taking meals in there, but it dawned on me as Wischard lowered his voice that he had wished to avoid Borbála's ear. His plan for tomorrow involved evading anyone's notice.

"We'll have to make a go of it starting at eight o'clock in the morning if we want to be out the door before Grandma'Maud wakes and tries to stop us. Uncle Roul will be asleep, too. I know where Grandma'Maud keeps an alarm clock she doesn't use. We'll have to use it without Aunt Adèle to wake us up," he said.

"It's not that early," Madeleine-Grace said. "I can wake up on my own before then."

"Hooray for Madeleine-Grace," Wischard said, fluttering his fingers in the air. Even his insults amused us, for we both chuckled. "I'll send word to your American newspapers: Madeleine-Grace Avery can wake up by eight o'clock without an alarm."

"What about Bertille and Borbála?" I asked.

"They'll both be up, but they won't care about us. When we're up and ready, we'll ask Borbála to make us a *café*. Bertille will be with Grandma'Maud or in her sitting room, so we won't have to worry about her. Once Borbála makes us the coffee, she'll forget about us. So we slip out after our coffee and head for L'Ile de la Grande Jatte. It shouldn't take us more than an hour to get there and an hour to get back."

"Aren't we going to spend time on the isle?" asked Madeleine-Grace.

"There used to be prostitutes on the isle," Wischard said, apropos to what I'm not sure.

"What's a prostitute?" asked Madeleine-Grace.

"A woman whom men buy for sex," he said.

"You and this 'sex' again," she said, finishing her coffee to avert participation in this topic.

"Why do men need to buy sex?" I asked Wischard. "Can't they just ask their wives?"

"Maybe it's for the men whose wives charge them too much or for the men who aren't married," Wischard speculated.

Madeleine-Grace redirected the conversation by asking, "How can we get there without the map? Remember you forgot the map on—"

"Yes, I remember I forgot the map! Let's send that to American papers, too: the cousin of Madeleine-Grace Avery forgets maps on bedroom dressers!"

"Why are we sending this only to American papers?" I inquired.

"Fine, let's announce to all of France what an idiot your cousin is," he said, throwing up his hands.

"I think anyone in France who has encountered you knows already what an idiot—"

"Anyways," I said, cutting off Madeleine-Grace before she irritated Wischard too much and turned our morning coffee into a night on the veranda of the summer house, "we don't have a map. How can we get to the isle?"

"I was studying the map the night before we left," Wischard said. "I'm pretty sure I have the route memorized. I can't remember the name of all the streets, but when I see them, I'll know."

I have no idea why we accepted this. Wischard really wasn't an idiot despite what a goof he could be, but his confidence may have convinced us he was more capable than he was.

"What if someone asks where we were?" I asked. "Can we tell them where we went?"

"No, we can't tell them. They'll get upset. We'll tell them we walked to the Quai de Javel to see the river and helped an old widow carry groceries to her apartment in, hmmm—Quartier Charonne—and we looked at pipes in a *tabac* in Quartier Saint Georges because we wanted to get Uncle Roul a gift. That should account for a few hours."

It was settled. Wischard had devised a plan and covered our bases, and we had agreed to execute the plan first thing tomorrow. The prospect of seeing the real Ile de la Grande Jatte, of being in person where Seurat had spent his afternoons, waxed in appeal to me. Would I see the very shores and animals and trees Seurat had depicted vividly in paint after countless studies? I did not, however, want to see prostitutes. Without knowing much about them or the concept of buying sex, the topic instinctively appalled me, yet Wischard could discuss such things so casually. I knew Wischard would have plenty of comments throughout our trek tomorrow, and I enthusiastically anticipated those, too.

To pass more time, Madeleine-Grace and I played the *tourdion* on the piano in *pianissimo* to avoid riling Grandma'Maud upstairs. We had wanted Wischard to hear it, and he enjoyed it. While I played to the best of my memory and ability, Madeleine-Grace taught Wischard some of the choreography. After ten minutes, Wischard threw in the towel and plopped on the chair, announcing he liked this dance less than his and Laure's *gavotte*, which, incidentally, they had not practiced yet.

Not having heard from Uncle Roul, Bertille, or Borbála in the hour since we had first stepped into Grandma'Maud's room, we decided to check on her again. Madeleine-Grace suggested bringing her a *café*, thinking the aroma might call her to this world, so we stopped in the kitchen for a cup. Uncle Roul sat on the divan of the overly sunny sitting room, buttoning up his dark blue shirt, as we walked through to the dim bedroom. I set the coffee on a side table behind us. Bertille was leaning over the other side of the bed, gathering Grandma'Maud's pile of fabric strips. Grandma'Maud, no longer cutting, had become frozen in place, staring at the corner with rigid arms, mouth, eyes.

"She usually wakes from her cutting, but this morning, she has stiffened," Bertille said, placing the fabric in a workbag.

Uncle Roul breezed in, heading straight for the balcony. He pulled open the curtains so that the room could drink the light of late morning, so that Grandma'Maud could absorb some of its life force and return to us. He opened the doors and stepped through, leaving them open. He reached in his shirt pocket, pulled out a cigarette, and lit it for a smoke on the balcony.

Bertille stepped around to our grandmother's side of the bed, leaning over her and blocking the sun from her unflinching eyes. She held Grandma'Maud by the upper arms and jostled her.

"Madame, wake up," she said, followed by another jostle. "Madame, your grandchildren are here."

She held on for a few more seconds without stirring her, my grandmother's arms unresponsive and frozen, and then she released her. No sooner than she had let go did my grandmother start blinking repeatedly, and seconds later, start flailing her still stiff arms left and right, left and right, up and down, up and down. Her eyes flashed about the room in frenetic fear as she let out a wail. Then, in a sudden, her body became limp and her arms fell into her lap. Her eyes refocused on the terrace doors, then on Bertille who leaned in to pacify her, and finally on us. We had stepped backward and stood as stiffly as our grandmother had been before coming to. We yielded to a nimbler stance only when Grandma'Maud smiled at us.

Gently pushing Bertille away, she extended her arms to us for a hug. I cautiously stepped to her with Madeleine-Grace and Wischard, falling into her embrace first. The others followed suit.

"You have come to visit your old grandmother," she said. While she had Madeleine-Grace in her arms, she revealed she had Borbála making *madeleines* for dessert tonight.

Uncle Roul finished his cigarette and stepped into the room. "Is it possible?" he said. "I did not think it possible to awaken the dead."

"How long have you been here?" she asked. Searching for her clock, she asked, "What time is it now?"

"We have been here an hour," Uncle Roul said. "It's eleven o'clock."

"Why did you not wake me sooner?" Grandma'Maud asked.

Uncle Roul shook his head in disbelief. "The medication makes you crazy," he said.

"You said I was crazy before the medication," she reminded. "I am not crazy! I see you, Roul!"

Uncle Roul looked at Bertille who glanced at him and then away. He shook his head from side to side, and Bertille leaned again into Grandma'Maud.

"Let's get you washed and dressed so that you can spend the day with your grandchildren."

Grandma'Maud smiled, but it was not at the thought of spending the day with us. It was a furtive, knowing smile directed at Bertille.

"And how will you spend the day?" Grandma'Maud said to Bertille. "While I am with my grandchildren, how will you spend the day, Gourgandine?"

Madeleine-Grace and I exchanged glances as we stepped back to make room for Bertille at Grandma'Maud's side. Bertille glanced nervously over her shoulder at Uncle Roul, and he stepped to the bed, standing behind the caregiver, leaning over her.

"'Gourgandine'? You *are* crazy," he said in a taunting way.

"I see you, Roul," Grandma'Maud said. "And I see you, too, mademoiselle. My, how pretty you look in your make-up today. Is today some special occasion?" She lifted her head off the backboard to peer more closely at Bertille. "How is it you lost so much powder from your cheeks before it is even noon?"

At first, Bertille dropped her lip at the comment, but when she heard Uncle Roul scoff, she looked over her shoulder at him and smiled. He shrugged and walked to the balcony doors, his back to us, to his mother.

"Why don't you amuse yourselves for a short while longer," Bertille said to us, "while your grandmother gets ready."

"And then you can apply more make-up," Grandma'Maud said to Bertille.

"And then you can take more pills," Bertille replied.

His back still to us, Uncle Roul added, "The pills make her see things."

"I see what's right before me. Are you saying what I see is untrue, Roul?"

He hemmed, shifting his stance in the doorway.

"Go on," Bertille said to us. "We will get ready."

We stepped out once more, but before I could think of how to spend the next half hour, I remembered the coffee I had not given to Grandma'Maud. I turned around, and walked through the sitting room, Madeleine-Grace and Wischard remaining at the door to the hall. I entered the bedroom without any warning, having been gone only fifteen seconds. Uncle Roul had returned to the bedside, and when I rushed in, he pulled his hand away; it had been resting on Bertille's *derrière*. Bertille launched a look over her shoulder at me, and I made for the side table with the coffee as if I had seen nothing. I carried it to her, the two others clearing a path for me.

"Madeleine-Grace thought you might like the *café* first thing," I said, placing the cup in her hands. "Even the aroma gives you energy!"

"You are my thoughtful children of Juliette," she said, landing on my nose a smooch likely meant for Madeleine-Grace's. "Ellande, give the *café au lait* to Roul for now. He needs the energy more than I."

"For what do I need more energy?" he asked.

"For any number of activities you enjoy, and even some you don't enjoy, like the time you are sure to spend at the washbasin removing the stains from your shirt," Grandma'Maud said before handing me the cup with a smile.

Uncle Roul pulled different parts of his shirt forward with his fingertips in search of what she meant, and then headed onto the balcony with a muffled "Crazy"—this one did not come out as loudly as the others.

We amused ourselves in the *grand salon* by paging through some of Grandma'Maud's sheet music and trying the first few measures on the piano, and after a half hour, Bertille escorted in Grandma'Maud.

Madeleine-Grace and I, quick to regale her with tales of our excursion to L'Ile d'Aobefein, found ourselves trying to relive the memory, I thought, and our palpable elation over all that we experienced there affected our grandmother, who confessed she had never visited. Then again, she added, the only isle besides L'Ile de la Cité that she visited had been L'Ile aux Cygnes in the Seine, several blocks away, and the reference to the isles of the Seine had the three of us children exchanging grinning glances. We would soon be adding one more isle of the Seine to our short list of those visited.

Grandma'Maud probed for more understanding about Wischard's inclusion in this visit with us, wondering why little Laure had not accompanied him, to which Wischard did not have an answer other than "Maman would not permit her to go. Only me." When she asked why Wischard's parents did not visit her, he said, "They have to stay behind to watch my sister." Wischard added that his mother had called him her "representative" in Paris for now.

"Ah, I see how it unfolds," Grandma'Maud said. "Your mother has sent you, so any obligation to spend time with me has been fulfilled."

While Grandma'Maud had seeped her statement in sardonicism, Wischard did not pick up on it and responded with a proud smile, considering the responsibility of representing his mother and her "obligation" an honorable act. I looked at the piano, wondering if my grandmother might play today, and Grandma'Maud looked toward the glow of the windows. The thick, mauve curtains were pulled and banded to the side, but lacey, cream ones covered the entirety of the glass.

"Melisende and Ferdinand return tomorrow evening," she announced. "They visited with Ferdinand's nephew in Asnières and will come here next."

"Seurat painted in Asnières," I said. "And Signac."

"They did," she responded with a smile. "They have immortalized our serene Seine, haven't they, and the lands around it? Asnières, it remains a bedroom town, which is why Ferdinand goes to persuade his nephew to return to Dieppe—better opportunities for work. I will be glad when they arrive here tomorrow. I could use my sister's help."

"You have Borbála's help, and Bertille's," I said, glancing at Bertille sitting inconspicuously in a side chair near the window with a box of makeup on her lap. She may have been determining how much of each item she had left as she held containers up to the sunlight.

"Bertille, she is a nurse, and Borbála a maid, but I prefer to do things for myself. I never had a maid as a child. I never raised my children with nannies or maids, either. Romain hired Borbála four years after your grandfather's death. I remember it. I remember it because Laure had demanded that I cease wearing mourning black scarcely before four full years had passed, and I declared, to her utter consternation, that I would wear mourning black four years more—at least. That same evening, Romain announced his search for a maid. I protested, preferring to do things for myself and with my family's help, as we always had, but he persisted. Two weeks later, Borbála moved in."

"And Bertille?" asked Wischard. "She came only last fall, but you do need her, right?"

Grandma'Maud shrugged with a glance in Bertille's direction. "She gives me this pill and that pill and helps me in and out of bed. That's it. Melisende learned more caring for the wounded during the war than Bertille in all her training in Paris. I prefer my sister."

Bertille's indifference to our conversation kept her attention on her makeup.

"Did the war change Aunt Melisende, too?" asked Madeleine-Grace. "Uncle Roul said war changes a person."

"It changed us all, yes," she responded. "It did change your uncle. For a year after his return, he said no more than two words a day."

"Aunt Melisende once said that he had worked as little before the war as he did after," Wischard interjected. "He doesn't work at all now."

Grandma'Maud sighed with a grin. "Melisende says this, does she? Roul has his faults, but he is a good boy, too. He loves me, you know. Léon and Juliette and Adèle, they love me easily. Roul loves me, too, but struggles to show this love even to his mother. In that way, the war has changed him the most."

"I don't think he struggles to show his love to other women," Wischard said, eliciting a turn of the head from Bertille toward our conversation, followed by a quick lift of a perfume bottle.

"He is a good boy still," Grandma' Maud said.

"Grandma'Maud, did you wear black when Uncle Léon died in the war?" Madeleine-Grace asked.

"I did. After a year in only black grieving for him, I realized it aggrieved me also to wear black for an artist, my Léon. He went to the *Ecole Militaire* in Chamonix and learned to fight in the mountains— *Chasseur Alpin*—but he was an artist in his heart. Like your mother and her music and Adèle and her knitting, all three in their own ways. And I was wearing black for an artist such as Léon. This didn't feel right."

Her gaze returned to the glowing window, and then, on a sudden, she looked at the shelves lining the wall, the ones I was wont to sit against guarding my mother's old piano music.

"Ellande, open the second door there," she ordered with tears in her eyes but unshakily. I opened the door to reveal several shelves with papers and folders of different sizes. "On the top of the bottom pile, bring that to me."

From the bottom shelf, I lifted a thin, rectangular canvas of a painting covered in a doily. I did not remove the doily and carried the frameless canvas to Grandma'Maud as Madeleine-Grace, Wischard, and I gathered around. Uncle Roul entered just then and stood over his mother's shoulder for a glimpse at what had called our attention. We stared as she removed the doily, exposing a beautiful painting of washerwomen on the shores before the Etretat-au-Delà *falaises*.

"When Léon was a boy, maybe a little older than Madeleine-Grace is now, we were sitting around the table before *mésienne*, and my mother and mother-in-law were among us. My mother recalled how several times a year the women of Etretat-au-Delà gathered the household linens and clothes and trekked to the shores for a thorough washing. Those who had money might pay a washerwoman. The others did the washing themselves, mostly at home on their own, but several times a year, they completed *La Grande Lessive*. My mother-in-law recalled it, too—the spectacle of the women before the lapping waves, the salt water and the soap working with the women's scrubs to purge the linens of impurities, the sun piercing them with warm rays, the breaks for sips of fresh water and cold coffee in the shade of the *falaises*. '*Une grande lessive*,' we called it. And afterward, *La Grande Buée*. With just this story in his imagination as he envisioned every detail his grandmothers spoke, he painted the scene."

La Grande Lessive, or "the Great Washing," and *La Grande Buée*, "the Great Steaming," were communal efforts on the part of some coastal towns in Normandie.

We looked again at the painting, its precision of strokes and proportions, the exact hues of the ocean, the walls of the cliff, the bright sun on the shores, and the shade cast by the *falaises*. No woman in the painting was exempt from working as some scrubbed linens, some carried baskets, and some lifted an ecru tablecloth to the sun. The expressions on some reflected their toil, but on the two women holding the tablecloth to the sun, he had conveyed a delight in their work through their exhausted, exhilarated gaze.

"Wearing black for someone with such beautiful colors emanating from his heart seemed wrong," Grandma'Maud said. "But I wore the black. I held his paintings with all their colors often to my heart, but I honored him with black."

When I heard a sniffle, I looked from the painting in Grandma'Maud's lap to her face, but she was not crying. It was Uncle Roul. He wiped a tear and exited the room.

We returned the painting to the shelf and conversed longer, enjoying stories about Grandma'Maud and Aunt Melisende's childhood, about the *buée* rituals and which herbs they used, and about why Grandma'Maud's *sandwiches au jambon* tasted better than anyone else's: instead of layering a few vegetables over the ham and cheese, she tops them with a finely chopped salad of mixed greens, onions, apples, mustard, and *cidraigre*, and instead of a smear of mustard on both slices of baguette, she spreads a salty, herbed butter on one. My mother made them this way in America, but Grandma'Maud's tasted better in France.

Wischard escorted Grandma'Maud into the bedroom because he was curious about her medications, and Grandma'Maud enjoyed the attention so much from her grandson that she allowed Bertille to excuse herself for a walk to the park below. I sifted through the piano music wondering if I might not stumble upon another *tourdion*. I noted a *rigaudon*, a *danse des chapieaux*, and a few *caunchounettes*, among other numbers, but no *tourdions*. All the while, the composer's name Jacot Galienne repeated in my head. When Grandma'Maud and Wischard returned from the bedroom, I asked who Galienne was, and Grandma'Maud revealed that the name, new to her, as well, had compelled her to start a search for this man whom she presumed was young, an unknown out of some *conservatoire*. She wanted to find him, call on him, and employ him to play the *tourdion* for her, himself. I found myself on board with this idea and hoped heartily that she would succeed.

Even though he would play his own oeuvre masterfully, I would favor my mother's rendition the most, piquing our souls with the joy of her playing the way Uncle Léon's painting colored our hearts with beauty.

Madeleine-Grace and I lay in bed, having been awake for an hour already, when Wischard pushed our door open cautiously, stopping it upon its first squeak. Tousle-haired and sleepy, he lacked the grogginess we had witnessed yesterday morning, likely on account of his excitement over sneaking out. He slid through the opening in the door, surprised to see us wide awake.

"I came to wake you. I used the alarm," he whispered.

"We heard it on the other side of the wall," Madeleine-Grace said, smirking.

"You could not have heard it. I kept it under the pillow next to my head to muffle the sound. Anyway, you have to get up and get ready. I think Borbála is up because I heard something downstairs. Remember: coffee and then slip out. Hurry now! Let's get ready!" His excited words in whisper were endearing, and I had to chuckle, for which he neither understood the reason nor appreciated: the volume of his whisper was somewhat high.

We washed and dressed quickly and met Wischard at the top of the back stairs. We crept down, confident we would not wake Grandma'Maud or Uncle Roul. Taking slow steps on the balls of our feet all the way down the hall, we passed the empty dining room on our right and stopped at the entrance to the kitchen. Before even looking in, I noticed the pocket door was shut to the *grand salon* across the hall, which I had never seen before, and I heard a sound from within, assuming if Borbála weren't in the kitchen, she was cleaning in there. We found Borbála in the kitchen, setting two *brioches* on a plate next to the stove. She looked surprised to see us, and actually met us at the kitchen door and escorted us to the table across the room.

"Sit. Sit, please," she ordered. "I just made *café*, and I have *brioche*."

"Why did you put out only two *brioches*, Borbála?" Madeleine-Grace asked. "There are three of us, and four if you join us."

"Sit, please," she said again, ignoring the question. She added a *brioche* to the plate and brought it over to the table as Madeleine-Grace and I took a seat.

Remaining standing, Wischard said, "Why should we eat in the kitchen?"

"Today, you will eat in the kitchen," Borbála said. "Ellande and Madeleine-Grace eat in here when they visit."

"But Grandma'Maud says we should—" I began.

"We eat in the kitchen at the summer house," Madeleine-Grace said. "It's okay."

As Borbála set the filled cups of *café* before us, Wischard whispered, "Hurry."

We ate and drank quickly as Borbála prepared another plate of *brioches* and put on more coffee. Wischard whispered that he needed to see if the coast was clear and crept behind her through the kitchen without her noticing; how he became so adept at sneaking around boggled me. He glanced left and right down the hall and then stepped out. Not a minute later, he ran back in on his tiptoes, in stockings, his shoes in his hand. Sliding into us at the table unnoticed by Borbála, he spoke in my ear almost out of breath, "Uncle Roul and Bertille are awake."

"What?" I whispered back, and my surprise alerted Madeleine-Grace to something urgent.

Wischard leaned into my ear and whispered, "They're awake, and Bertille is sitting on top of—him."

I pushed Wischard nearly to the floor in incredulous shock. Why was he joking in this way at such a time as this, when we risked being caught before our adventure had even begun?

He bounced back and slid into me, sticking his face in my ear. "I think it's sex. I think Borbála is guarding them. They're in the *grand salon*. When we pass, you'll see!"

Madeleine-Grace was curious, but we did not let on about Wischard's claim. We waved for her to join us without a word, taking note that Borbála was looking for something in a lower cabinet. Following Wischard's lead, we removed our shoes and stepped quickly out of the kitchen and into the hall. Wischard pulled Madeleine-Grace's hand so that, when they had passed the door to the *grand salon*, she was well beyond the room and could head to the entrance in the main hall. He, however, stopped at the closed door once she passed him, and nudged his head toward the room, indicating for me to peek. I pulled the pocket door open so slightly without a sound. I did not have to scan the *salon*. In the middle of the room, Uncle Roul lay on his back on the couch, completely naked, his head against a pillow, and Wischard, God love him, was not lying about where he said he had found Bertille. Her clothes were bunched around her waist so that her legs and breasts were fully exposed as she moved up and down on top of him. Uncle Roul's head angled away from the door toward the far walls, as did Bertille's, so I felt confident they couldn't notice me. I leaned in for a closer look, noting what Wischard had observed.

I felt a pair of arms on my shoulders whipping me backward into the hall. It was Wischard, trying to keep me from getting caught by staring too long. However, he could not resist peering in one more time. His hand covered his mouth, and he glanced out of the room at me with wide eyes. I then pulled him into the hall, deciding we were taking too many chances by lingering so long. I reached for the door to pull it closed, and Wischard motioned for me to stop, saying without words to leave it open. I took his advice, but he thought better of it, deciding he could do it, himself, more safely. He gingerly grasped the door and pulled it the few inches necessary to close it, every inch of its slide back in place wringing my nerves the way Aunt Adèle had wrung the spilled liqueur out of the dishcloth. Then he let go of the door, swung his body around, and slid into me for a quick exit. As I shifted momentum for the main hall, Madeleine-Grace appeared, wondering what was taking us so long, and Borbála called for us from the kitchen, wondering where we had gone. We did not acknowledge the latter and flew toward Madeleine-Grace, rounded the corner, and took refuge in the elevator she had called. The doors shut and we began the rickety descent from *l'étage noble* to the entrance of the flat, hyperventilating the whole interminable while.

"What's wrong?" Madeleine-Grace asked. "What happened?"

"You don't like it when we talk about sex, so we can't tell you," Wischard said, and I was happy he responded this way. Describing let alone explaining anything about what we had witnessed was not something I had any desire to do, not to her, not to anyone.

When we made it down the front steps of the flat into the street, we ran as fast as we could down the block, rounded the corner, and raced toward the Seine like Atalanta trying to avoid a marriage. After another block, we had to stop, panting as we rested our hands on our knees. I glanced behind us; there were no Meleagers in sight. Poor Madeleine-Grace did not fully understand our hurry and assumed it had to do more so with a quick escape from watchful eyes.

Wischard and I were facing each other as we caught our breath, and when he grinned at me, a grin locked onto my face, as well.

"Was Uncle Roul up or something?" Madeleine-Grace asked.

"I guess you could say that," Wischard responded, and we both started laughing. It hurt to laugh so hard while panting so hard. Wischard fell over onto the sidewalk, and Madeleine-Grace, fed up but understanding that something had happened beyond her, simply shrugged.

Several minutes passed before we regained the remotest traces of composure. And then we took a more leisurely stroll to the Seine, for Wischard had declared that once we arrived there, he would know how to get to L'Ile de la Grande Jatte.

We arrived on Quai de Grenelle, L'Ile aux Cygnes before us as if floating in the river. A thin, tree-lined isle, I wished to incorporate a visit there into our walk, enabling a boast of having been to this isle, too, to anyone that might care. Uncle Ferdinand had told us that he and his friends had engaged in a leaf fight on the isle one autumn, and in spite of the warmth, I found myself trying to picture it in reds and yellows and browns. For now, however, I could tell from our spot on the quai that the walkways looked shaded and the archways the trees formed felt inviting. A short walk to the west would land us at Pont de Grenelle, capable of carrying us across the Seine with a stop on the isle. Walks with Grandma'Maud had brought us only that far. Wischard, however, told us we needed to cross the Seine at Pont Mirabeau farther west. So we began the walk past Le Pont de Grenelle, taking frequent looks at the sparkling movement of the Seine water.

As we cleared L'Ile aux Cygnes and La Quai de Grenelle became La Quai de Javel, we saw Le Pont Mirabeau ahead, the bridge to Le Quartier d'Auteuil of the sixteenth *arrondissement* northwest of the Seine, sometimes called "Arrondissement de Passy." Cautious as we bypassed La Gare de Javel thanks to warnings from Grandma'Maud and my parents about the dangers of train stations in Paris, we arrived at the bridge with circumspection. Crossing the river, I took Madeleine-Grace's hand as my other arm skirted the rail in my preoccupation with looks at the river water. Halfway across, the trees of L'Ile aux Cygnes sparkled in the distance, and I could see where Pont de Grenelle met the isle. A gust of puffy wind struck us, comforting in its strength and warmth.

Exiting the bridge landed us on Quai d'Auteuil in Paris Rive Droite, now in an entirely different *arrondissement* and neighborhood. I'm not sure why, but the river's separating us from the neighborhood of familiarity and family concerned me. I felt an uneasiness in these new environs, but not because of their unfamiliarity to me; it was because the river was not a street, not a walkway, that I could easily cross to arrive in Quartier Javel. I had the well-engineered bridge at my disposal, yet the river as a boundary felt insurmountable. As we crossed Rue de Versailles and headed west down Rue Mirabeau, I took some comfort in what I saw ahead: a steeple.

I pointed to it, not knowing to which church it belonged. "That could be our steeple," I said, referring to Monsieur Vauquelin's idea about pinpointing a common, high spot to regroup if necessary. We walked toward it and found ourselves before the entrance to L'Eglise Notre-Dame d'Auteuil, easy enough to remember for its combination of Our Lady's name and our current neighborhood or *quartier*. Off-white stonework, umber-brown doors paneled with glass under a Romanesque archway, a round, inlaid clock with brass or bronze hands, a towering spire, and a statue of a smiling Blessed Mother and Child greeted us as we approached. Pockets of people were chatting while some individuals loitered, one tossing pieces of *croissants* to pigeons.

"Let's go in," said Madeleine-Grace, stepping forward.

"We don't have time," Wischard said. "We have to get through Le Bois de Boulogne, and I'm already tired."

"So am I," concurred Madeleine-Grace. "That's one reason we should stop inside."

We were all tired already. The three of us had begun this jaunt with a sprint, and the walk to the Seine, down the Seine, over the bridge, and to the church had taken an hour already. I think my nerves about being in unknown neighborhoods of Paris wore on me, too. Wischard insisted, though, that we carry on to the woods separating us from the branch of the Seine in which La Grande Jatte was scooping its water. I had forgotten about the woods, but I recalled the patch of vast trees from our view atop Notre Dame Cathedral. I supposed I could add an exploration of the famous hunting grounds of the kings to my list of sites seen.

Agreeing L'Eglise Notre-Dame d'Auteuil would be our steeple point, we made our way west down Rue d'Auteuil, but we didn't know how far to go or where to turn. Wischard said he recalled something about Rue Michel-Ange leading us to La Porte d'Auteuil, which he remembered to be the gateway to the woods, but we did not know how to find Rue Michel-Ange—nor, for that matter, how Rue Michel-Ange would lead us to Le Bois de Boulogne. Madeleine-Grace suggested that Wischard ask someone, but he maintained a steadfast walk forward down Rue d'Auteuil. I checked the name on every street we passed and saw no sign for Rue Michel-Ange. I saw posters for Cirque Medrano showcasing a pointing clown, advertisements for Christian Dior of a woman in a blouse cinched at the waist over a long skirt, but no signs for Rue Michel-Ange. At last, we arrived at an intersection past Place Jean-Lorrain, which put our minds at ease: Rue Michel-Ange. We did not know which direction to go, though, and the intersection was strange in that we had to circle a small island to head north but in so doing found other streets as options. We turned left onto Rue Michel-Ange, unsure of ourselves.

"I remember a gate into the woods called Porte d'Auteuil, but I remember another one called Porte de la Muette," Wischard said, trying hard to jog his memory of the map.

"Were they close?" I asked. "Maybe if we keep walking this way, we will hit one. If we don't hit one, we will hit the other."

"So, we should keep walking," Wischard said.

"But when we get to the woods, how will you know how to get through them to the Seine?" asked Madeleine-Grace.

"The woods have walkways and signs," Wischard responded. "That should be the easy part."

We walked down Rue Michel-Ange for a while before arriving at a main intersection. After having passed many churches, offices, and shops, I was becoming disoriented, yet I could see another distinctive church down an adjacent block. We had no idea whether to turn onto it or to continue along Rue Michel-Ange simply because Wischard had remembered seeing this street on the map. As Wischard and I duked out what to do, trying to find some means of orienting ourselves since the spire of Eglise Notre-Dame d'Auteuil was well out of view now, Madeleine-Grace stepped in.

"I just asked that lady if we are close to La Porte d'Auteuil," she said, pointing at a middle-aged woman walking down the street with a girl about my age. We hadn't realized Madeleine-Grace had left our side. "She said we should not have walked south down Rue Michel-Ange but have stayed on Rue d'Auteuil heading west. She said we must walk back and turn left on Rue d'Auteuil."

Wischard sighed, but we wasted no time in walking the many blocks back, finding Rue d'Auteuil again, and heading west on it. By now, I needed a rest, and a snack would have been nice, as well. I did not voice either need, however.

After a while, we came upon another intersection, and Wischard convinced us to turn right, rationalizing that heading north, whether we knew where we were going or not, would bring us to the woods at some point and then to the isle. Several blocks down this street had me suspecting we were walking parallel to the woods on account of the line of treetops I saw across the street not too far from us. I suggested to Wischard that we make our way over. He preferred we find La Porte d'Auteuil or La Porte de la Muette.

Maybe Madeleine-Grace's example had paved the way for him to do the same or maybe he was growing as exasperated as I, but Wischard told us he was going to ask a nearby elderly man walking a white and brown *papillon nain* several meters from us.

"Don't ask him where we are," I said. "It's not smart to let others know you're lost."

"He's an old man," Wischard said. "What can he do to us?"

"I don't know, but ask him how to get to one of the gates. Don't ask him where we are."

"If we ask him where the gates are, he's going to know we don't know where we are!" Wischard had a point, and his frustration prompted him to lose his temper with me. He made for the old man wearing a dark brown fedora, brown slacks and blazer, and white button-down shirt. He stared intently at his tiny dog as it sniffed along the curb, the leash slack in the safeness of proximity between owner and pet.

"Pardon me, sir, but could you kindly tell us if we are nearer La Porte d'Auteuil or La Porte de la Muette?"

The man looked at Wischard quizzically, perhaps wondering why a young boy was alone or wishing to traipse through the woods. Staring across the street, he pointed with his left hand to the left. "La Porte d'Auteuil is that way, off Rue d'Auteuil," he explained. Once again, we should not have turned, it seemed. "La Porte de la Muette is that way," he said, pointing to the right. "La Porte d'Auteuil? La Porte de Passy? La Porte de la Muette? Ahh—La Porte des Ternes? Which do you prefer?"

"I don't know which we prefer," Wischard said, more confused than ever. Backtracking to La Porte d'Auteuil seemed to head us in the wrong direction despite getting us into the woods, and heading to La Porte de la Muette seemed to lead to more uncharted Paris for us.

"*La Muette?*" the old man said, a goofy smirk forming on his face that worried me a little. "Do you want to attend *La Fête?*"

"What?" Wischard asked.

"*La Fête à la Muette! La Fête à Neu-Neu!* You missed it, my friend!" he started laughing. I suspected he may have been daft.

"I want to walk through Le Bois de Boulogne—" Wischard began, but the man started singing.

"*Allée de la Reine! Allée de la Reine!*" he chanted with bizarre fervor. He dropped the leash to the ground and made a *pirouette* as he sang, the goofy smirk on his face appearing again when he finished and bowed to Wischard. I felt this confirmed his daftness to me.

Wischard looked back at me with an "Oh, brother" expression on his face. I think he would have laughed had he not been so upset.

"Are you an ornithologist?" the man asked. "Do you like to watch the birds like Pierre Belon?"

"Who?"

"Do you want to play *croquet* with Gaston Aumoitte? He will take the mallet to you!"

"Who are you talking about?"

"What does a little boy want to do in Philip's playground within the walls of Henrys?"

"I'm not a—." Wischard abandoned challenging the man. "Beyond the woods is L'Ile de la Grande Jatte. My cousin and I want to go there."

The man burst into guttural laughter, bending to pick up the leash of his oblivious, sniffing dog. When he stood up, he laughed again and walked up the road, muttering something about *La Fête à Neu-Neu*. We stood in disbelief for about a minute as he hobbled off.

"He's a good-for-nothing *boulevardier*!" Wischard erupted to me.

"Let's let him walk farther ahead, and then we'll continue the same way," I suggested. "He said La Porte de la Muette is that way, so we can try to enter there."

"Can we trust what he said, though? I don't know if he was crazy," Wischard admitted. "And Madeleine-Grace is right. Once we enter the woods, I don't know if I'll be able to lead us to the Seine."

"What about the signs?" I asked.

"I don't know. I'm getting tired," he announced to my relief. I could now suggest stopping for a snack.

"There are several *boulangeries* here, and I think we could use a bite," I said, referring to Wischard and myself. I thought to include Madeleine-Grace, too, and turning to her, I began, "And Madeleine-Grace is also—" but she was not there. I spun around. I did not see her.

"Madeleine-Grace!" Wischard called, realizing she was not in our midst.

"Madeleine-Grace!" I called, running to the corner for a look down the block. I did not see her in any direction as I stood at the intersection. I surveyed the blocks across the street and, among the few pedestrians, did not see her. Wischard ran up to me, grave concern on his face.

"Do you think she crossed the street to try to find Le Bois?" he asked.

"I don't see her anywhere over there."

"Could she have gone to find someone for directions?"

"She had to have seen we were doing the same thing. Maybe she tried to find a place for food," I suggested, scouring the building fronts for indications of *boulangeries, pâtisseries, brasseries*, any such establishment.

We started running back in the direction from which we had come, stopping abruptly before every establishment's window for a quick peek through. My heart was pounding. Why had I not held her hand the whole time as I had done while walking across Mirabeau? How could I have been so distracted by that man that I neglected her? What must my parents be thinking, having counted on me to look after her now?

We ran back as far as Rue d'Auteuil without spotting her. Cars whizzed by as did occasional cyclists, and even among the several pedestrians, I could see no indication of her. I recalled she was wearing a pink dress and tried to train my eyes to look only for pink, and with the exception of some flowers hanging outside a shop, I saw no such color.

"She has to be looking for us," I said. "She must have spotted someone or something, went to it, and then planned to meet up with us again, right? She wouldn't have wandered off purposely or left us behind."

"That means she returned to where she left us," Wischard said, picking up on what I was getting at. "And we left her where we talked to that old man."

He darted up the block, which I came to learn was Boulevard de Montmorency and indeed paralleled Le Bois de Boulogne, but not as near to it as I had thought. On his heels, I jutted my head about in so many directions hoping to catch a glimpse of her. Once in the spot where we had met the old man, we looked around again, just as we had before. I even ran to the end of the block again to check that intersection. When I met Wischard in the middle of the block, we were both panting hard, sweating through our shirts, and tears forming in our eyes. My mouth was dry, and the burning in my throat didn't alleviate it. The sun was beating down on me, but not more than the metallic guilt of heavy, linked chains ripping my soul till it bled as they strangled me. How could I have let this happen?

"I don't know where else to look," Wischard said before we ever caught our breath.

I crouched to the sidewalk in silence. I saw Wischard grab a tuft of his blond hair and squeeze. I looked at the sidewalk, my shadow distorted as it mingled with Wischard's in a patch of sun.

"We'll go to L'Eglise Notre-Dame d'Auteuil," I said. "It's the steeple point. If she couldn't find us here, maybe she knows we will pass that church to get to Le Pont Mirabeau."

I think Wischard saw logic in the idea as his head nodded with approval. One time more, we headed back down this street to Rue d'Auteuil and turned left, jogging our way down. We hadn't much energy to run any faster.

I wondered if Madeleine-Grace would be able to find her way to this church even if she had thought to meet us there. I assuaged my worries by remembering that Madeleine-Grace was the first to ask for directions and would not think twice about doing so again. Then visions of her asking the wrong person flashed before me. What if she asked someone as looney as the old man, or someone who pranked her with the wrong directions? What if she asked someone anxious to prey on a lone, young girl? With so little energy, I was surprised I could accelerate, but I did. Wischard kept up.

Glances into shops, dodges around pedestrians, reckless rushes across streets filled the path to the church, and I knew we were a ways away. My eyes had not seen pink in a while, so I lifted them to the sky hopefully for a rose-colored splash of cloud. My gaze flashing to the sky, I heard her voice.

"Ellande!" she shouted.

I halted. Wischard did, as well.

"Do you hear that?" he asked.

"Then it wasn't just me," I said, looking in different directions. I couldn't tell from where the voice had come.

"Ellande!" she called again, and I determined it was coming from behind us.

Rushing back down the block, I saw Madeleine-Grace in her pink dress running down a narrow street toward us. She had no tears in her eyes, but they were as pink as her dress, colored with angst and longing. She fell into my arms and hugged me as I wrapped my arms around her. I felt my heart beating hard with her body against mine. We hadn't released from the embrace when Wischard hugged us both, burying his head between my chin and shoulder.

Exhaustion seemed to be wrestling with relief to overrule my being as I caught my breath for what I hoped would be the last time today. When we let go of each other, Madeleine-Grace was the only one without tears.

"What happened?" I asked.

"I saw a friendly baker helping a woman carry bread to her bicycle basket, so when he was done, I ran over to ask him for help. I got the idea to ask someone exactly how to get to L'Ile de la Grande Jatte. I was only a few feet away from you at the time. When I asked him for directions, he asked me to step into the *boulangerie* and said he would write them down for me. Before I entered, I saw you approach the old man with the dog and figured I would be right out, but we were farther from the isle than we thought, so the directions took a while for him to write. When I came out, you were gone."

"We looked everywhere," I said.

"We even came back to that spot, thinking you might expect to find us there," Wischard added.

"I did go back to that spot, but you weren't there."

"We must have missed each other," Wischard said.

"Then I thought to meet you at L'Eglise Notre-Dame d'Auteuil," I said, "so we were heading there."

"That's where I was headed, too," Madeleine-Grace said with a cheerfulness over the correctness of her instincts, "because it was our steeple point. I knew enough to follow this street past Rue Michel-Ange and to keep going."

"Thank God you saw us, or we might have missed each other again," I said.

"What were you doing down this way?" Wischard asked.

"Come on," Madeleine-Grace said. "I'll show you."

She ran ahead of us down the narrow street and after several meters turned down a walkway, something like an old village causeway or passageway of cobblestone, homey and warming. With laundry lines and hanging sheets, a kitten skulking along the stone wall, and the scent of the potted flowers and hanging gardens, the little lane felt less like a Paris neighborhood and more like Etretat-au-Delà's residential town lanes. A few meters down this walkway was a small stone church, its door of oaken planks partially open. Not very tall, I could see the tarnished bell in the short tower. We stopped at the church door.

"What is this place?" I asked.

"I don't know," Madeleine-Grace responded, the blue sky reflected in the joy in her eyes. "I was hurrying down Rue d'Auteuil when someone told me to walk this way. She used my name, so I stopped. I went down the tiny street in the direction I first heard the voice and saw this little church ahead of me. Come look."

She pushed open the door to reveal the small, dark interior of the church. A few candles had been lit in the vestibule, and a few more in the shallow alcoves of the transepts. The nave could not have been more than thirty meters before the altar rail. It seemed as if an adjacent building blocked light from permeating the stained-glass windows on our right, but the ones on the left glowed with good light—many yellows, blues, and pinks. In front of one, the yellow and pink light glowing around her, stood a white statue of a smiling Blessed Mother. Her arms were outstretched. White votives lined a metal stand before her, only one of which was lit. Madeleine-Grace led us to her.

"I lit that one," she said. "I had to use a candle from the statue of Saint Anne, her mother."

Wischard and I looked into the eyes of the Blessed Mother and understood why Madeleine-Grace was not crying. Her gaze was warmth, her open arms reassurance, her smile love.

"Let's say a prayer," Madeleine-Grace said. "She helped us find each other."

We all three knelt before her. While I felt I should bow my head, I could not take my eyes off her face. Fixated on her gaze, I somehow knew that Madeleine-Grace and Wischard stared into her eyes, as well. In my prayers, I asked that God look after my mother and father in Heaven, and then I said "thank-you" over and over in my head while my heart lifted to her and to God so many things for which I was grateful, from my parents to finding my sister.

When Madeleine-Grace rose, we rose, too, and headed for the door. We crossed ourselves with holy water and stepped back into the heat, still shaded in the shadow of the church.

"Isn't it funny that I found in Paris La Vierge Albâtre?" Madeleine-Grace said.

I thought this a strange remark and said, "They look entirely different. They are not the same at all."

"Yes, they are. They have the same voice." My sister's eyes sparkled like the waters of the Seine in the sun, like the waters of La Manche from the white cliffs of Etretat-au-Delà, and she skipped down the lane in perfect joy. Enjoying my own sense of calm, I followed her, Wischard at my side, to the Rue d'Auteuil. I wish I had, but in those moments, I never thought to find the name of that church, never thought to scope out a street sign for the name of that walkway or side street.

Any fear over repercussions for sneaking off, for arriving home in early evening, paled compared to the fear I had just experienced over the possibility of having lost my sister forever. Whatever might be coming our way for a punishment, from being yelled at to having to weed the summer house, did not agitate me. I held my sister's hand for the rest of the long walk back to Quartier Javel, past L'Eglise Notre-Dame d'Auteuil, over Pont Mirabeau, up Quai de Javel, entirely without a word.

"Remember the plan," Wischard said when we ascended the steps of the flat.

"Following every other part of your plan has been so helpful. Why stop now?" Madeleine-Grace said.

"Let's just broadcast on American papers that Madeleine-Grace Avery's cousin Wischard's plan had a few holes."

Madeleine-Grace rolled her eyes and shook her head. I felt saturated in sweat, and I suspected everyone inside would see it on my clothes. I could not believe how many hours had passed, much longer than Wischard's anticipated one hour there and one hour back. We were sure to find everyone in the *petit salon* having *apéritifs* without us. From the top stair outside the entrance, I glanced toward the window of the *petit salon* on *l'étage noble* but saw nothing to indicate anyone waited in the room. The strange fancy that Aunt Melisende and Uncle Ferdinand had arrived in our absence flitted through my imagination like a white butterfly.

"Remember that we were helping a widow and seeing if we could afford a pipe for Uncle Roul," he reminded us.

We entered the flat and made our way for the *petit salon*, which we found empty. After a stop in the washroom, we found the kitchen, the dining room, and the now infamous *grand salon* empty, too. For some reason, we skulked through the hall and up the back stairs, as if we were still sneaking around or trying to avoid being seen when this time we wanted to be seen and wanted to encounter anyone.

Borbála we found in the sitting room off Grandma'Maud's bedroom. She was sitting on the chair in which I was wont to see her, reading a magazine on her lap and sipping Chambord. The late day sun pierced the room through unclosed curtains. Thick, white clouds brought with them pinks and lavenders to the blue darkening sky of evening. Madeleine-Grace did not acknowledge Borbála as Wischard and I did with a silent nod and wave; instead, she walked to the curtains and pulled them shut.

"Might be too late now," she said, "but Grandma'Maud would want them closed."

"Your *grand-mère* doesn't know what she wants right now. She's frozen stiff again. Where were you all day? Your Grandma'Maud would have worried had she known you were gone without an adult," Borbála said, flipping a page in her magazine. "Can you open the curtains until it's dark. I can't see what I'm reading."

That was it. That was the extent of any interrogation we ever received for a day of defiance, a day of unexpected discoveries, a day of harrowing confusion and distress. She never followed up with more questions or concern, and neither Uncle Roul nor Bertille mentioned our absence at all.

Madeleine-Grace opened the curtains. Bertille, who had heard us talking, waved us into the bedroom. We stepped in to find Grandma'Maud as we had on our second check yesterday morning. She stared intently with few blinks at a column of light cast in the corner of the room, her arms rigid, her left hand clenched and solid, her right hand hidden under squares of fresh green fabric on the bed beside her. Cascading from her body and onto the fabric were the ribbons, the recently made green ones topping the heaps of floral and pink and purple ones reaching to the end of the bed.

Uncle Roul stepped in from the balcony, and Bertille leaned over Grandma'Maud to intercept her stare with a wave of her hand. Then she stood up and sighed.

To us she said, "Your grandmother has had a bad day. She woke up much earlier than usual, and I gave her a pill. She woke up after noontime and seemed okay, but before long, she began cutting the fabric. When we checked on her later, she had become catatonic. That's what the doctor calls her stiffness. She has not changed from this state since. She will, no doubt, come out of it as she always does, so you needn't worry, but it's taking longer than usual."

"Why don't you call to her?" Uncle Roul suggested.

"Grandma'Maud," I said. "We need to spend a pleasant *apéro* with you, and it's getting late."

"Grandma'Maud," Wischard said, "You must tell us of your visit to L'Ile aux Cygnes!"

"Why did you give her a pill?" asked Madeleine-Grace of Bertille. "Did her head hurt?"

Bertille walked mindlessly to the stand beside Grandma'Maud's bed where a glass of mineral water, her enamel pillbox and her bronze one, and several bottles of medicine lay. "I gave her a sleeping pill because she complained of pain in her hip. I thought she could sleep through it, poor thing." She lifted a white pill from a small pile of them in the tiny, bronze pill case.

"That's not a sleeping pill," Wischard said. I did not know what the pill she held did, but I, too, recalled that the sleeping pill was a different white one she kept in the enamel pillbox with the closed lid. This way, as she had explained, she could reach for it on her own and not worry about pills falling out. The bronze one had no lid, but she didn't use those pills, she had said.

Bertille started, giving the pill a double-take. She brought it to her eye and looked at me, utterly bewildered. Uncle Roul closed his eyes and hung his head.

"It's okay," Bertille said. "It's not one that will cause a problem, I swear. In fact, it is probably not even responsible for her state."

She affected an air of nonchalance and set the pill back with the others. She must have regretted lifting it in front of us, and I couldn't believe Wischard had caught that. I did not know, however, whether to trust her assessment of the effect of taking the wrong one. Seeing Uncle Roul's composure, however, assuaged me a little.

"How did you give my mother the wrong pill? You're a nurse," said Uncle Roul.

"Maybe she had something else on her mind this morning," Wischard said, glancing at Uncle Roul, and for once in his life, he was not trying to make light of something.

"Wait on the balcony, children," Uncle Roul said. "We will try to pull her out of this. It's a beautiful evening. Wait on the balcony."

We obeyed. I was nervous to be anything but obedient. The events of the day had pulled different emotions every which way, reaching for one and slamming it into another. The revelations throughout the day had struck me in unknown ways with unfamiliar hardness, crippling me mentally. I did not wish to challenge anyone, to force a quarrel, to cause even a single ripple in illusively calm waters all the while panicking inside over the prospect of Grandma'Maud's indeed not pulling through this.

I leaned on the railing of the balcony as dusk overtook the day, as the lavenders turned purple and fused with the blue evening sky. Madeleine-Grace and Wischard sat in chairs, peeking into the bedroom periodically. I saw Bertille cry into Uncle Roul's shoulder on one glance in. Later, Borbála checked on Grandma'Maud, drink in hand. A short while later, Uncle Roul joined us on the balcony for a smoke in silence, allowing Wischard and me to share his cigarette.

By now, night had fallen, and he said to us, "I will try once more to stir her. If she does not come to, we will go down and eat without her. You must be hungry."

We nodded in agreement as he stepped into the room and explained to Bertille his intention. Bertille was her old self, confident in the lack of gravity of her mistake. Light from the lamps in the adjoining sitting room illuminated the half of the bed on which Grandma'Maud reclined rigidly.

Uncle Roul sat on the bedside in the light, his back to us, and Bertille leaned over his shoulder. Wischard and I stepped into the dark bedroom, remaining at the balcony entrance to stay out of the way. Madeleine-Grace remained in a chair on the balcony, peering over the railing at the park below.

"Maman," Uncle Roul called, his mother unresponsive.

Bertille placed her hand on Uncle Roul's shoulder. He looked up at her, and then leaned more closely toward his mother, saying, "Maman, don't be crazy. This has lasted too long. Do you wish to sleep until tomorrow? If you do, you will have no right to tease me for sleeping in. You don't want to forfeit that right, do you?"

He looked up at Bertille and smiled, slipping an arm around her waist, holding it there for a few seconds, and then pulling it back to his side.

"You would not like it either if I slept in too late, would you?" he asked Bertille.

She snickered and rubbed the shoulder on which her hand rested, moving it to his hair and scratching the back of his head. I began to think they had no idea we were watching or had stepped into the room.

"Maybe more light will help," he said. "Can you turn on the lamp?"

She released from him and turned to begin her walk around the bed where the lamp sat on the other night table. She stopped when she saw us, and then continued walking. Uncle Roul remained on the bed and whispered toward the sitting room for Borbála to start dinner. She didn't hear him and stepped into the doorway. Bertille, in the meantime, passed the foot of the bed, and after her passing, I saw Grandma'Maud blink. Wischard looked at me to verify someone else had seen what he had seen. Bertille didn't notice, nor did Uncle Roul who was repeating to Borbála what he had said.

The light turned on.

Grandma'Maud blinked rapidly, and suddenly her arms rose, still rigid. I braced myself for the flailing I was sure would ensue, but I could not brace myself for what happened next. As she lifted her right hand stiffly from under the fabric, I could see it gripped the handle of the shears. Uncle Roul felt the movement of her body and turned his attention to her without a moment to consider that the slashing of her arms meant something different this time. In the very moment he turned, she swung the shears into his side as she flailed, pulled them out, and swung them back into him, wailing in terror as her eyes darted around the room.

For a moment, everyone in that room became more frozen than Grandma'Maud had ever been. Then Uncle Roul touched his left side with his right hand and held up blood. The vacant yet searching eyes of his whitened face studied his hand and then shifted to the blood spreading on his shirt. His hand pressed the wound. Borbála screamed. Madeleine-Grace rushed in from the balcony. Grandma'Maud dropped her arms at her side, the bloody shears falling from her hands onto the covers beside her. Uncle Roul slumped, slid from the bed, and fell to the floor.

Bertille gasped and rushed to his side. She yelled for Borbála to remove us. As Borbála panted, her hand on her heart, she made for us and forcefully pushed us out of the room as we could barely walk. I passed Uncle Roul on the floor, his blood staining the rug as Bertille pushed rolls of fabric into his wound. His eyes remained opened as he panted, beads of sweat descending from his hairline. Bertille implored Borbála to call for help. The last thing I remember as she pushed us into the sitting room was Grandma'Maud lying on the bed, not fully alert, completely unaware of what she had just done.

CHAPITRE 8

Our pre-dawn ride back to Etretat-au-Delà by Jules with Uncle Ferdinand and Marguerin aboard after a sleepless night could not have been more silent, to be topped only by the deafening taciturnity of our arrival at the summer house. The creakless door opened for us by a speechless Aunt Adèle only hours after the break of day, a morning yet unbroken by screams of surprise, howls of dolor, words of attempted understanding. Some of these must have occurred prior to our arrival, for Aunt Mirabelle, young Roul, Alphonse, and Chardine had already deserted, word having reached them before we had returned. Uncle Romain had driven them. The others slept.

The emotional toll of the events and the exhaustion of the long day before in Paris, from waking to being carted away into the *petit salon* for hours became too much for the three of us. We left our travel bags in the main hall, unable to carry them, barely able to lift our legs up the stairs, and reached for our bedroom. The door to young Roul, Alphonse, and Chardine's room left open, the emptiness stung us on our walk past, Wischard in tow as he opted to sleep in our bed. Lying in my pajamas in my bed on the brink of sleep, I sniffed the foul odor of our sweat. Madeleine-Grace did not consider brushing her hair, and Wischard had been so drained that he did not change into pajamas; he flung his clothes to the floor and slipped into the bed in his underwear. The last thing I remember before falling asleep was the sight of my dresser top containing certainly no flowers for Maman from Papa, and now, no vase.

We did not wake until the next morning, not one of us.

I had awakened before the other two and checked to see that they were still sleeping, Wischard's scrunched face tense, Madeleine-Grace's tranquil and delicate. The glow of the sun suggested late morning if not noontime.

Alone in the noon light, despite the others at my side, an unaccustomed heaviness pressed on me, an overwhelming feeling that I was going to lose someone close to me; it was a sensation not of trying desperately to hold on to someone but of someone desperately letting go of me, releasing me to the full weight of the heft suffocating me, to the boulder crushing my chest, my lungs, me. I didn't feel this way when I lost my parents. That was sudden. I had no warning. Whatever this was, it felt foreboding, awful, and long-lasting.

I did not stir, content to lie still awhile, yet Madeleine-Grace and Wischard woke one after the other within the next ten minutes. No one said a word. Even when we all three propped our backs on the headboard, we remained in silence.

Throughout the next few days, through conversations with family and visitors, we learned how things had unfolded and how things were expected to unfold. We had to relinquish Wischard to his parents, having learned that Aunt Laure blamed Madeleine-Grace and me for the visit to Paris, for her son's witnessing such a horror, for her brother's having to be in Paris with an unstable woman. Wischard made several attempts to reconvene with us, either to commiserate or for simple diversion, but was hauled off by his mother every time she found him in our company. Aunt Laure did not speak to us, so disgusted with us was she. Aunt Adèle shared that Uncle Roul had been brought to hospital in Paris and, thanks to Bertille and Aunt Melisende, who had learned to dress severe wounds during the war, was in less dire shape than he could have been upon arrival there. The doctors were watching him on account of punctured organs and a chipped rib and hoped to transfer him to Rouen for continued recovery after several weeks of observation. Aunt Mirabelle and the children were in Paris and would be leaving for their house in Rouen in several days, readying it for Uncle Roul's return and recovery. Uncle Romain would return to Paris after driving Uncle Roul's family to Rouen. Through Lady Victorine, who had visited Aunt Adèle for an afternoon tea, we learned that no one was to know of what had really happened in the room that night. Madeleine-Grace and I were sworn to secrecy for the sake of our grandmother, and even our Uncle Roul, whose own children did not know the full story, was expected to keep the secret. The story Aunt Melisende had concocted placed a caring Roul seeing his mother to sleep, and, falling asleep, himself, rolling over and accidentally stabbing himself with the shears they had neglected to remove from the bed. It was nothing but a terrible misfortune during the night after Grandma'Maud had fallen asleep. Apparently, no one knew we were even there, and if anyone were to refer to our presence in the Paris flat, the story would include that we had been in our rooms sleeping, woken by the commotion of the accident. Bertille agreed to keep quiet under threat of revealing her incompetence with the medication, although she swore it could have no such effect nor any damaging effect on Grandma'Maud; nevertheless, she understood the consequences to her livelihood of such a scandal, even the mere accusation. Borbála would suffer loss of employment should she utter a word remotely contradicting the story that the others had manufactured. It was Uncle Romain who threatened both women, which surprised no one, and I still did not fully understand why. Aunt Melisende had embossed onto the will of all those with access to the Paris flat that Grandma'Maud never learn of what she had done, especially since such an act was not her fault. Poor Grandma'Maud, who had no recollection of what had happened in those few horrific moments, had apparently been calling out for us, wondering why we, too, had abandoned her there, leaving with no explanation, no good-bye.

I decided to voice this concern to Aunt Adèle and make a request of returning soon to Paris, but I had made the mistake of broaching the topic within earshot of Aunt Laure. Madeleine-Grace and I were following Aunt Adèle as she dusted the dining room, and Aunt Laure had stepped in without greeting to claim a crystal fruit basket from the hutch. Basket secured, she had stepped out of the room when I spoke to Aunt Adèle.

"Aunt Adèle, I am wondering if Jules or Marguerin or Monsieur Vauquelin can drive us to Paris—" I began just as Aunt Laure stepped in, deciding on a different container for fruit.

Stopping before the hutch, she demanded, "Why do you wish to return to Paris? Have you not done enough damage there?"

"Laure!" snapped Aunt Adèle.

"Grandma'Maud does not know any of what has happened," I explained. "She wakes to a house nearly deserted. She must feel infinitely abandoned, and I would like to explain that we had to leave, that we did not abandon her, to put her mind at ease."

Finding confident footing in justifying her condescension thanks to such a concrete act of violence, Aunt Laure lifted her chin as she said, "My mother does not deserve a mind at ease, nor does she possess a mind capable of being at ease!" Aunt Laure slammed the crystal basket on the hutch after her reply.

"No thanks to a dutiful daughter like you," Madeleine-Grace said.

Aunt Laure stared at my sister and then at Aunt Adèle, who could say nothing to defend her sister. She then rummaged through the interior of the hutch.

"Wischard feels bad for her, too," I persisted. "You don't want Grandma'Maud thinking Wischard left her, do you?"

"What do I care what my mother thinks of Wischard? Since when does the opinion of a crazy woman matter to me?"

"It's mattered to you your whole life," Aunt Adèle announced. "Isn't that why you are so scornful of her? Her opinion of you does matter, only you do not wish to change your behavior to find her favor."

"That would mean you'd have to renounce the practice of locking yourself in your room," I said.

"And by the way," Madeleine-Grace added, "You're the crazy one." Aunt Laure turned from us, lifted a crystal tray from an interior shelf, and exited, leaving the fruit basket on the hutch. Aunt Adèle waved a finger of admonition at us and continued dusting the legs of the dining room table. I did not pursue my request for a trip to Paris, figuring my sister and I could find a train to Paris on our own if necessary.

Aunt Laure's resentment of Grandma'Maud should not have surprised me, but it did nonetheless. Lady Victorine and Aunt Melisende's protection of Grandma'Maud impressed me more than my aunt's reaction disturbed me, and I took some comfort in thinking either or both these ladies would explain to Grandma'Maud that Madeleine-Grace, Wischard, and I had not abandoned her. Their loyalty to a friend, to a sister, after decades and wars and family tragedies was something I admired, something I linked to the men on L'Ile d'Aobefein as they held fast to their traditions and trades, imparting them to generations after them for preservation and the security of their descendants. Perhaps I would be castigated by some for admiring a cover-up, but I did appreciate the loyalty in it, not to mention the understanding that the wielder of the shears was, in a moral sense, not the one at fault, if it were anyone's fault.

A few days later, Aunt Adèle thought immersing us in preparation for the children's ball would benefit the children, so she encouraged all of us to practice our dances, either in the house or on the cliffs, to practice our speeches, to practice walking in our suits and gowns, to partake in one last fitting, which Aunt Adèle was presumed to undertake entirely herself.

Wischard, Laure, Madeleine-Grace, and I spent several hours engaged in these activities while Astride, to my knowledge, did nothing. Even though she had been assigned a partner for the dance and could not practice much by herself, she barely practiced the other activities. Madeleine-Grace, who had amassed a mountain of doilies by now, had taken to fashioning a few of the drying cornflowers given to her by Monsieur Vauquelin into a garland for her hair. She had twisted the stems around each other and interweaving ribbons in such a way that the flowers protruded from spots along the whole circumference, the blues and greens striking and bursting with vitality. This garland would be the only color on her person to offset the off-white of her ball gown.

As my sister sat on the couch on the veranda beside me, smoothing the bends of the cornflower stems with her fingers, Aunt Adèle ascended the veranda stairs holding a piece of paper, having come from the clotheslines in the lawn. She handed it to Madeleine-Grace, and, glancing at the writing on it curiously, I realized it contained the directions to L'Ile de la Grande Jatte that the baker had written. I worried we would have to explain ourselves as Madeleine-Grace shifted her eyes to me and then at the paper.

"I found it in your pink dress when I did the wash," Aunt Adèle said. "What pretty penmanship."

With much on her mind, she walked past us into the house, never again to bring up the topic. That she lacked the curiosity to inquire about the directions or why Madeleine-Grace possessed them astonished me. But relief at not having to explain that we never made it to the isle because we got lost—and lost Madeleine-Grace along the way—reigned, and I sighed.

On a walk back to the summer house from town one late morning, when we hit the intersection of the gravel road leading to our place, I caught the sparkling shafts of sunlight prodding through the leaves of the apple trees in the orchard, straight lines appearing and disappearing as a breeze rustled the leaves. Lured by the light and its calm, I asked Aunt Adèle if Madeleine-Grace and I could play in the orchard a while. I didn't explain that I wanted to show Madeleine-Grace the spears of light, that I wanted to see up close if the light disappeared before my eyes when the foliage blocked its path through the trees to the earth, that, through the apple orchard, I wanted to relive a moment on L'Ile d'Aobefein. She consented, asking us to make our way home within the hour.

As Aunt Adèle headed up the road for the house, my sister and I drifted into the orchard. Even though the breeze tousled the leaves and a few small *bailleuls*, a variety of Normand apple, swung in place, the orchard looked sunny—honey-thick under the trees—and still. The stillness felt stagnant, as if the apples weren't growing but just suspended in time.

"The sunlight makes lines through the trees," I said to Madeleine-Grace. "Did you see them?"

She reached for a branch and tugged on it gently, shaking the leaves and making a rustling sound. Another sound then pealed through the orchard, arresting my sister's jostling of the branch. The sounds of breaking sticks and crunching dried grass made their way to us, followed by what we recognized distinctively as laughter. My sister and I, instinctively cautious, leapt to behind the thin bole of a tree in the direction of the sounds, then to another, until we saw the strange sight of a young man, maybe twenty-one or twenty-two and buck naked, scurrying through the trees away from us, laughing and holding a magenta, satin pillowcase. On his trek away, he looked over his shoulder and toward the ground. I could tell from his frivolity and laughter that his exit was carefree despite his nudity, and that his laughter interacted with someone else.

His light skin disappeared into the trees, and I stepped around the tree to see at whom he had been glancing. In the shade sprinkled with landing and lifting sunlight, at the bottom of an apple tree, rested Jeuffine des Gervais, wrapped in pale magenta sheets. Two champagne saucers on a silver tray with partially eaten apples and half a brie in its rind rested on the protruding tree roots beside her head. As she shifted to prop her head on the tree's meager trunk, she pulled up the sheets to cover herself. Then she spotted me.

"You scared Owen away," she said, relieved, I could tell, to identify the source of sound as me. "Well, I shooed him away, really. I don't know why I did. I don't really care."

Madeleine-Grace stepped from behind the tree to my side.

"Why was that man naked?" she asked.

"I'm glad it's you, though," Jeuffine said, as if my sister hadn't spoken. "You don't care the way some others would care." She propped herself up higher so that both her back and her head leaned against the tree, all the while holding the top of the magenta sheets. Then she reached for a champagne saucer.

"Damnit," she said. "I suppose I knew that we finished these hours ago."

"We're going to go," I said, uncomfortable in forcing a conversation, unsure what even to say, had I thought it necessary to prolong this moment.

"You just arrived," she said. "Were you apple picking? Maybe your Uncle Roul hopes to make his own *cidre*. Is that it?"

I wanted to tell her that Uncle Roul would not be making *cidre* any time soon, but I could not bring myself to mention the atrocity. In my silence, Madeleine-Grace asked, "Who was that man?"

"Did you think he was handsome? He was handsome, wasn't he?" Jeuffine said. "That was Owen. He's English—an 'Oxford chap' on holiday." She said "Oxford chap" in English, and I recalled she had spent however long in Oxford, England advancing liberating causes through her discussions with whomever she discussed things. "The sky last late-night, I felt, wasn't bright enough, devoid of the number of sparkles I had wished to see, so I told Owen to take me to the orchard. Outside, under the sky instead of under a roof, here in the freeness of my uncle's orchard, I felt I could see better—see ourselves better—and I made him take me here."

"Wasn't it darker in the night than under the lamps inside?" Madeleine-Grace said.

"The lamps weren't on inside, my dears."

"But he didn't bring his clothes," I said.

"That was the point, Ellande. I pulled the sheets from the bed, made him grab the tray off the bedside table, and we ran out here." She lifted the sheets to show me although I knew which sheets she had meant. After she lifted them, she let them slide down her unclad torso.

I felt a burning in my cheeks. My wits barely about me, I stepped in front of Madeleine-Grace.

"You look as if you've seen a ghost, Ellande," she said, lifting the sheets to cover more of herself. When her arms dropped to her side, it pulled the top of the sheets down to expose her cleavage.

"We're going to go," I said again, and placed a hand on my sister's shoulder to turn her around. Madeleine-Grace looked curiously at Jeuffine but wasn't as rattled as I was.

"There's nothing to be embarrassed of," Jeuffine said. "I wish you would stay awhile. Have some brie. Owen will probably get bored and come back, and you could meet him, too."

I don't know why, but I reddened more. I felt my cheeks and neck getting hotter. The combination of standing before a beautiful, near naked woman and standing before a beautiful, near naked woman while my little sister stood next to me made me uncomfortable. Jeuffine, however, carried on as casually as ever.

My second wave of blushing must have been obvious, for Jeuffine said, "Come now, Ellande. Don't be so embarrassed. This is what they've done to you. This is what society does to you. It makes you feel embarrassed about things that are natural, things you should have nothing to be ashamed of. Owen is naked. I am naked. What difference does it make? You shouldn't be embarrassed."

"I think maybe it was private, and I'm embarrassed because I shouldn't be here," I said, glancing at Madeleine-Grace with the hope that she would drag me out of there. She stared quizzically, not at Jeuffine but at the scene, unperturbed.

"Nothing about what Owen and I did—nothing about what we are—needs to be private, my dears."

"Does anything about what you did—and what you are—place any importance on being a lady?" Madeleine-Grace asked as if in conversation about the unexpected effect of accidentally slipping a stitch while knitting a doily.

What may have been a fake smile to begin with on Jeuffine's visage dropped at first to an even-lipped shock and then to a down-turned frown. "'Lady?' Who determines what a lady is, anyway? What do you know of being a lady?"

"My mother told me," Madeleine-Grace said, taking a step in front of me. "She said that I must be a lady, and that a lady acts virtuously, that a lady crosses her legs, that a lady does not stay with a boy alone until he marries her."

I was unaware my mother had had this conversation with my sister. My father had had a "being a gentleman" conversation with me one day, so these things, I assumed, must happen differently for boys and girls at certain ages.

"What is your sister's name, Ellande?" Jeuffine asked me, staring at my sister.

"My name is Madeleine-Grace, after my grandmother Madeleine-Maud," she answered for herself.

"And do you believe your mother when she tells you these—these fancies—about what a lady should be? Who is she to say?"

After she said this, she inched her back higher against the tree and lowered the sheets, revealing more of her bosom.

"Yes," Madeleine-Grace said with a smile, "I believe my mother."

"What makes me wrong and your mother correct? Do you really want to live a life so confined? Wouldn't you rather be free, allowed to be a woman the way you want to be a woman? Wouldn't you rather not be embarrassed of your body and your behavior?"

"I'm not embarrassed of my body nor of my behavior. I'm embarrassed of *your* body and *your* behavior." Madeleine-Grace delivered this with such sincerity that a trace of insult was undetectable.

The fake smile returned to Jeuffine's lips. "Who is to say your mother's idea of a lady is the correct one?"

"My mother says that we must observe what we know of La Vierge Marie, and that will guide us—boys and girls—about how to be a gentleman and a lady. Grandma'Maud told her the same thing when she was a girl." Madeleine-Grace looked at me with an unassuming smile, unaware she was going toe to toe with Jeuffine on a topic with roots that I somehow knew ran deeper for Jeuffine than the trees in this very orchard.

"And where did your mother learn this? The Bible? Your mother would believe the silliness of a two-thousand-year-old book? *You* would? That's all it is after all. An old book."

"The book may be old, but La Vierge, I know she is as beautiful as a young lady still. Her beauty has been preserved in youth. Maman says the Truths of La Vierge's life and Those of her Son will always last."

Snapping the border of the sheets up to cover a little more of herself, Jeuffine scowled, ran the fingers of the same hand through her long, dark hair, and then dropped it in her lap. She stared at me a moment, then at Madeleine-Grace, and then at the contours of her body under the smooth, magenta sheets as she repositioned her legs.

"Your mother and I would not have gotten along very well," she said. The statement dismayed me, a jab, I felt, at my mother. I don't know why I thought it so. Maybe it wasn't so much the words but the condescension with which she said them, as if she were more enlightened than my mother, that my mother had misadvised my sister, that a crazy and misguided grandmother had misinformed my mother. I didn't wish to endure more conversation and turned to leave with my sister, justified in omitting a departing salutation.

My sister began to depart with me but stopped mid-rotation.

"My mother would not have cared," Madeleine-Grace said. Then she took my hand and pulled me through the shafts of sunlight and around the trees, out of the orchard. She was skipping as I jogged to keep up. When we arrived on the gravel road, we slowed to a walk for the short distance to the house.

I was glad to be away from Jeuffine, for I really had been embarrassed. Except for the few seconds of Bertille, I had never seen a naked woman in real life before, not by spying through keyholes like Wischard, not by an accidental intrusion into a room in which someone was changing, nor had I interacted with one. If I had not been with Madeleine-Grace, I suspected I would have been flushed and laughed, especially if I were with my friends; sometimes, we joked about such things. My friend Jimmy Mertens swore he had seen a *Playboy*, but we didn't believe him. To us, such chatter was frivolous and humorous. In this situation, it was purely uncomfortable.

Somehow, Madeleine-Grace, whom I would have pegged to be more aggrieved than I, was far from rattled. Maybe as a female, she didn't think twice about such things. She didn't seem to flinch when Jeuffine said she would not have gotten along with Maman. Whereas I grew in irritation over the comment, Madeleine-Grace volleyed back a comment of her own that accurately represented our mother. I didn't know how she did it, and so quickly, but I felt both a relief and an admiration for my sister.

When we arrived home, I stepped onto the veranda where we saw Aunt Adèle stepping out of the shed, a basket of greens in one hand while her other hand rested on the boulder overgrown with marjoram. Madeleine-Grace jumped down the veranda steps to help Aunt Adèle and to press her to teach her a new stitch, but I, hoping to avoid questions about anything that had happened in the orchard, stole back into the house and up to our room. I had no agenda in mind when I walked in and scanned the room for a velleity to call my attention. Despite everything I saw, the only thing to catch my notice was the fragrance of the peony soap from the bathroom. Having come from the orchard, I decided washing my hands might pass the time as well as anything else and did so. Lying down to devise a list of activities and tasks, I decided, might fill a few moments.

Positioning myself into a recline on the bed, I stopped mid-motion like some sculpture of Rodin in *non-finito* when the Signac painting caught my eye. Settling into a slumped lean forward, one leg folded under the other one dangling over the bed side, I peered into the pastels of the painting, further dividing the dashes that made up the calm Seine waters, the Pont des Arts, the tower of Notre Dame, splitting them in twos and threes in my lost focus, dissolving them until they no longer made concrete images. In the blur of some new abstraction by which I found myself entranced, even as the sun's glow pulsed against it, as the light faded and brightened the space between the painting and me, my mind drifted as if carried by the currents of the Seine to the memory of our visit to the Art Institute of Chicago in the spring of 1957.

My father, intent on showing us a few of his favorites, grew more excited for our visit when his good friend Marcel Royce confirmed his accompanying us. Even though we knew him only in America, Madeleine-Grace and I called him "Monsieur Royce" and not "Mister Royce." We headed to the city as a family and met Monsieur Royce next to one of the verdigris lions on the Michigan Avenue staircase outside the building. An art dealer, he knew much about paintings as a genuine passion, and a native of France like my father, he knew especially about French art. The Art Institute of Chicago contains one of the best Impressionist exhibits in the world, and I don't know who was most overjoyed to enter and delight in them, my father in his desire to share something rich with us, Monsieur Royce to stand amid what enthused and riveted him, or we children to quench a curiosity heightening in anticipation.

Monsieur Royce made a point of finding a docent or trustee of the Art Institute whom I recall only as Eugène with the French pronunciation, insisting he accompany us on our exploration through the galleries. Eugène, an associate or friend, I gathered, of the Art Institute's director and curator, several times deferentially stepped aside so that the knowledgeable Monsieur Royce could regale us with background on the provenance of certain paintings and in whose keeping some of them had at one time fallen, or anecdotes about the models or stills of some of the artists' subjects. When it came to *A Sunday Afternoon on the Ile de la Grande Jatte*, however, Eugène asserted an avid recounting of Georges Seurat's practicing and preparatory studies and even lifestyle. I remembered Eugène beginning to share his insights prior to having stopped before the painting, just as it was coming into view on our approach. A fair-skinned, clean-shaven man in his fifties, the pink appeared in his cheeks when he spoke of Seurat, and his pale blue eyes glimmered like the blues in the painting's Seine. Monsieur Royce deferred more to this man's animation than to the knowledgeable man himself.

I couldn't recall who, according to Monsieur Royce, criticized Breton's *The Song of the Lark* in France nor the criminal who had tried to steal an oeuvre of Pissarro—and that's despite my predilection at that time for detective stories—but I could relate word for word some of the tidbits I learned about Seurat from Eugène. Seurat used to spend time on L'Ile de la Grande Jatte with his friend Edmond Aman-Jean during their Ecole des Beaux-Arts days; Seurat referred to his technique as *'divisionisme'* and grew dismayed to read art critic Félix Fénéon refer to it as *'pointillisme,'* as if it were nothing more than a bunch of *points*, or dots, sprinkled onto the canvas with no particular rhyme or reason behind the placement and color of each; Paul Signac had become both a disciple of Seurat, appreciative of the scientific groundwork for Seurat's approach to *divisionisme*, and a collaborator who shared advice based on his understanding of art, technique, and their circumstances. What stood out most to me was the studiousness of Seurat. Eugène told us—and I took his word for this—that Seurat became fascinated with light's effect on optics and read intently on the science of light, the way the optic nerve worked, and how the eye perceived light and color. This prompted his exploration of his new technique. I found it amazing to learn that Seurat spent a period using black *conté crayon*, pressing the blackish clay into the work surface with different pressures to effect different gradations of darkness and light, to experiment with shadows and penumbras. Then he turned to color pigments on canvas. He spent years painting sixty *croquetons*, miniature studies of the scene, as practice for *A Sunday Afternoon on the Ile de la Grande Jatte* before committing to the final version. "Seurat was disciplined, meticulous in his facture," Eugène said.

"What is facture?" I asked, reeled in by the man's explanation and not wanting to miss out on a full comprehension, but feeling terribly ashamed of having interrupted him. Although Eugène spoke to us in French, I did not know this word.

"Facture is the process of making art—the actual working on something," he explained as if my question were not a bother, "and Seurat's came only after much study."

I peered into the dashes of Seurat's masterpiece to note the arrangement of colors side by side, awestruck that each dash and pairing of color was deliberate. Madeleine-Grace found the personages in the painting stiff and liked the painting only for the inanity of the woman holding a parasol in the shade. I didn't have much of an opinion on the painting itself, for some reason, but felt a thorough appreciation for the workmanship behind it. I detected what appeared to be dots, dashes, and even, dare I say, short strokes in what formed the sails on the boats. I caught the pinks around the light-green grass as well as the complementary oranges. I observed the swaying shadows and the sparkling water and the shimmering foliage.

When we had bid adieux to this Eugène I would never see again and to Monsieur Royce and sought to regain our bearings once outside the building, my mother requested we sit on the steps for a short while after several hours on our feet. Having plopped down under one of the lions, my father asked Madeleine-Grace and me if we had learned anything. I said that I had learned how much work goes into making a painting; I was thinking of Seurat's study of optics, his period of black-and-white *conté crayons*, and his laborious facture.

My father tilted his head in such a way that his forehead touched mine, and he said with an uncharacteristic gravitas, "The most valuable thing you can do for your children is to make sure they don't stop working, make sure they value work and recognize the dignity in it. Promise me you will remember this."

I nodded up and down, my hairline rubbing his forehead. He smiled at me then, and I said, "Maman doesn't work."

"Your mother is the best worker of us all," he declared as his smile widened. "She adds artistry to everything she does. The best workers make an art of whatever they do. And if you are smart, you will learn from her how to work."

Here I was a year later, sitting on the bed alone in the summer house when my father and mother should have been beside me, staring at the Signac painting on the wall in a room that felt lighter and lighter, not on account of the ins and outs of the sun but because of the emptiness the more and more real absence became. Yet I felt the oddest consolation in knowing that Signac would not have painted that riverscape had he not committed to apprenticing himself to Seurat, had he not learned the measured discipline, despite the time and effort, apparent through his facture.

The day before the children's ball, Uncle Romain returned to the summer house, and after several outbursts at his wife and several cigarettes, he retired to his bedroom to sleep. Aunt Laure, in the meantime, implored Uncle Gilbert to walk with her to town to meet Hardouin and Marie Loiselier, who were to drive them to their favorite tailor shop in Fécamp for a few show-stopping accessories for Wischard and little Laure's outfits for the ball. The invitation had included Aunt Adèle, but Aunt Laure had her stay home to watch us. Wischard seized the opportunity of their absence to spend time with Madeleine-Grace and me.

Aunt Adèle had dedicated today to giving all our clothing for the ball a quick, light pressing. She had the ironing board out in the conservatory along with a cushioned clothesline she had set up in the room, on which she could drape our outfits one by one after pressing. They were to stay there overnight, and we were not to touch them until we needed to wear them for the ball. Aunt Pé criticized the extra step once again, auguring that we would all wrinkle ours on the journey to the Countess's, but Aunt Adèle stressed that no wrinkles to begin with meant fewer by the time we arrived.

In his parents' absence, Wischard announced a game of *muche-muche*, which we hadn't played in a while. Madeleine-Grace preferred not to play even when Wischard tried to convince Astride not to lock her in the cellar again, a plea to which Astride refused. Madeleine-Grace agreed to play one round only, and it had to be the first round. She would do the counting, herself, and she would do it from the main hall at the statue of Jesus. This sufficed for Wischard, and so she began counting. I followed Astride to a hiding place in the *salon* simply to make sure she didn't somehow taunt my sister, whose back would be turned as she counted. Once I knew Astride had hidden, I had to find my own spot with thirty seconds remaining. I heard Aunt Pé descending the stairs, and I saw Aunt Adèle scurry from the conservatory to the kitchen to check on something in the oven. I then bolted for the conservatory, passing the ironing board with Madeleine-Grace's dress on it, the last in line, while the rest of ours hung pleasantly from the makeshift clothesline. The iron rested upright on its heel off to the side, and I was careful to avoid bumping into the board as I made for the closet. I opened the door, pulled it shut, and secured a spot on the floor cross-legged in the dark recess with a perfect view through the holes of the open-weave, rattan closet. I would know if anyone were coming for me and could recede farther into the pile of blankets in the closet, although I hadn't much more room to move.

I could hear Madeleine-Grace counting excessively slowly, ensuring a generous amount of time for us to hide. We had ten slow seconds left when, through the small holes of the door, I saw the figure enter the room. I inched backwards. I had expected it to be Aunt Adèle returning to finish the ironing when I saw the shoes, the skirt—neither of them Aunt Adèle's. I jutted my head forward and watched, to my increasing astonishment, as the figure looked at the gown curiously, glanced out the conservatory door for onlookers, and made the decision to place the iron directly on the dress. The hand pressed the iron deeply into the fabric before releasing it, turning, and hurrying out without a sound.

I froze. To my utter disappointment, I did not let register with me what had happened, what was happening. At first, I thought she had seen a wrinkle that Aunt Adèle had not caught, but how out of character it would have been for her to notice such a thing or ever to help. I considered that Aunt Adèle may have sent her in to do something to the dress since she was occupied with something in the oven. As these possibilities raced through my mind, I heard Madeleine-Grace finish counting and knew she must have started the search. I heard some voices from another room, and, wondering if Madeleine-Grace had found someone, I smelled something off. Peering through the holes of the rattan weaving, I saw smoke rising from my sister's dress, and then my heart sank. The iron had been left on its hot soleplate, not its heel—directly on my sister's dress. Just then, another figure entered the room. It was Aunt Adèle, and she stopped halfway into the room when she realized what was happening.

"No!" she screamed. She ran to the ironing board and tilted back the hot iron, ripping the plug out of the socket by the cord. She grabbed a pillow from the divan and smashed it against the dress. Puffs of smoke thickened and rose to the ceiling as the scintilla of lit lace were snuffed out. She lifted the pillow, stared at the dress, and dropped the pillow.

Then she fell to her knees and wailed, a wail so loud it could have cracked a fissure through the cliffs, a wail eerily like Grandma'Maud's when she snapped out of a catatonic spell. I pushed open the closet door and stood before her as she buried her face in her hands. The children ran in, first Madeleine-Grace and Wischard, then little Laure, and then Astride; Uncle Romain shook the house as he stomped down the stairs and into the room, demanding what the noise was all about; and Aunt Pé strolled in, placing her hands on her hips as she stood not more than a step past the doorway, peering over others' heads on her tiptoes.

Aunt Adèle did not lift her face from her hands as she sobbed, and Madeleine-Grace, sensing the source of the wails, smelling the smoke, stepped to the ironing board. Her face petrified as she took in the sight of her dress, the back of it where Aunt Adèle had sewn in frills of her own lacework all the way down the back seam, destroyed, discolored brown and charcoal gray around the frayed edges of the hole that had been burned into it.

"What the hell is going on?" screamed Uncle Romain.

I heard the back veranda door close, and Aunt Laure and Uncle Gilbert entered the *salle-en-arrière*. When Uncle Romain repeated his question more loudly, they hurried into the conservatory, standing beside Aunt Pé as they tried to assess the spectacle.

"You did this," said Madeleine-Grace, turning to Astride. "You burned my dress."

"She did no such thing!" shouted Aunt Pé. "She was nowhere around!"

"We were playing *muche-muche*," little Laure said. "She was hiding."

"So she could have been in here," Madeleine-Grace said. "She couldn't lock me in the cellar this time, so she burned my dress!"

Aunt Pé took a step into the room, eyeing the burnt dress on the ironing board. "Nonsense," she said. "Although she will never admit it, Adèle grew careless for once and left the iron on the dress. It was an accident, but it was Adèle's fault."

Aunt Adèle lifted her head from her hands but said nothing. She stared at me standing before her as she breathed heavily.

"If that's it, then it was an unfortunate mistake, and I can return to my bed," declared Uncle Romain. "Now stop screaming so a man can sleep. I have just come from a long drive after having seen my brother near death. I don't need this crap."

"You are the cause of so much of it most of the time," Aunt Laure accused him. "When it benefits you to have silence, only then can we have it?"

"When did you get here? Go back out. It was more peaceful," Uncle Romain said.

"We entered through the back veranda and spent a pleasant half-hour there without your hollering to upset my wife," said Uncle Gilbert, asserting himself as some sort of defender.

"'An unfortunate mistake' you say, Romain!" said Aunt Laure. "We make light of those, but we make lighter of the deliberate mistakes you make, don't we? Those are even less of an issue than such 'unfortunate mistakes.'"

"As always, Laure, you are crazy as ever. While you're busy villainizing me, you don't see yourself turning into your mother. Look what our mother has done to Roul! And you are already crazier!"

Aunt Laure screeched at the effrontery and burst out of the room in tears. Uncle Romain stomped off to return to bed. The room went silent as Astride skulked over to her mother, who placed a supportive arm around her. Then Aunt Adèle rose shakily, devoid of strength, of the expectation of decency. She smeared her tearful hands against her apron and then slowly looked from her apron to me. She tilted her head at me, as if to ask, "Why?" Her stare into my eyes became a gaze into me, through me, and then I truly believed she was seeing nothing of this world. She stared the way Grandma'Maud stared at the corner of the dark room, only Aunt Adèle was not immobile. She turned around, looked at the burnt dress, and surveyed the faces of everyone in the room. Then she took a step, stopped, and like a ghost, a wisp of a human, walked out of the room.

I had kept my mouth shut. I had not revealed the identity of the culprit I saw all too clearly. Such a revelation would be denied and refuted, and the culprit's self-defense would be at the expense of my reputation as a truthful person, a case of my word against hers. Little Laure and Wischard quietly stepped to the ironing board for a look at the damage before leaving the room with nervous glances at Madeleine-Grace and me. Then Astride and Aunt Pé did the same, as if paying their respects at a casket out of obligation. Uncle Gilbert never took a look at the ruined dress and stepped out, unbothered by the whole thing. Only Madeleine-Grace and I remained, both of us stepping to the dress. My sister ran her hand over the hole; pieces of burnt lace and fabric snapped off. Then she lifted the dress an inch off the ironing board and inspected the damage closely. She did not cry. With her face close to the dress, her eye followed the long, vertical seam from the hole to the hem.

I realized as I stood there watching my sister that everyone had assumed I was the first to arrive after Aunt Adèle's shrieks. No one would know I had seen anything. No one knew I had been in that room—except Aunt Adèle. And it occurred to me that that look Aunt Adèle had given me may have assumed I was the culprit, remaining quiet in my guilt over some "unfortunate mistake" I had made.

"Don't worry, Ellande," Madeleine-Grace said. "We're still going to this ball." She lifted the dress from the ironing board carefully and carried it out of the room.

I could not take my sister's advice. I did worry, but my worry was not over the children's ball. It was that Aunt Adèle might be thinking that I had caused this destruction, yet I could not tell her the truth.

The day of the children's ball, we woke up starving. After Aunt Adèle had walked out of the room, we hadn't seen her. I don't know what the others did for dinner, if anything, for my sister and I spent the evening in our bedroom. Madeleine-Grace and I, the first to descend the stairs as usual, did not find our aunt in the kitchen, eager to make us a *café au lait*. She had, however, left two cups of *café* and four *sablés* waiting on the counter for us. The coffee was still warm, so we must have just missed her. I had not heard her at all. It was hardly enough to fill us after having gone without dinner, but it helped. Then we returned to our room to wash and dress, and to tend to a few other tasks.

Last night, Madeleine-Grace had brought upstairs to our room not only our clothes for the children's ball but also one of Aunt Adèle's bags of notions and other things from her *mercerie* supplies. She also had on hand the stack of round doilies of different sizes she had been making over the weeks in Etretat-au-Delà. Throughout the evening, she had sewn the doilies into the back seam of the dress.

"Are you sure you can fix it?" I had asked last night.

Her concentration strong, fixed on aligning a stunning row of doilies of varying sizes to the seam, she replied, "Be quiet and make sure you know the *tourdion*." She was sewing them one at a time through the center of each doily. The dress, the seam, and the doilies she brought inches from her face as the needle darted in, her eye steady, her fingers exerting a concentration of their own.

From my occasional glances at my sister's progress, I surmised she knew what she was doing and was doing a good job. I could not see the burn mark, the hole, nor any indication that the dress had been marred. I, on the other hand, had been working last night on something else in preparation of the children's ball: the speech. I found it funny that it was named "a speech" when it could not last longer than thirty seconds. Despite that restriction, I had an angle to make it work, one that was true to who I was.

We had crept downstairs to do evening prayers on our own while the others drank and smoked and talked on the back veranda, and then we returned upstairs, falling asleep during a conversation about the possibility of our cousins leaving us home for the ball.

The ball began at four o'clock in the afternoon at the Countess's manor outside Etretat-au-Delà. While everyone else continued, as usual, to sleep through the morning, Madeleine-Grace and I took advantage of their absence to use the conservatory. Madeleine-Grace spent an hour finishing the sewing of the doilies down the seam of the dress. She sewed a few along the hem, the sleeves, and even the collar. Who would have thought a mountain of thin pieces of cloth used to protect tabletops from teacups could be so handy and look so beautiful? When Madeleine-Grace held up the dress for me to preview, I had to have been more impressed than anyone could have been. The circular doilies became a motif throughout the dress, subtly bringing the subdued dress to life in their abundance down the back seam, from the hidden burn hole to the hem. The color of the doilies did not match the color of the dress's fabric, but they did not look bad together.

"Aunt Adèle and Grandma'Maud taught me to knit and crochet more so than Maman, and Maman taught me to sew more so than Aunt Adèle and Grandma'Maud," Madeleine-Grace said. "I hope I did it all right."

"I think all three would approve," I said.

"Now I have to try it on," Madeleine-Grace said. "And if Aunt Adèle stays hidden, I will have to do my own hair and may need your help." I knew nothing about doing hair and really hoped Aunt Adèle would appear soon, more like her old self, and help us. She did appear, but she acted unlike any Aunt Adèle I had seen before, even more oddly than her charming freeness outside Monsieur Vauquelin's window.

After Madeleine-Grace had slipped into her dress in the conservatory, she stepped before me as I sat on the divan. The dress on her looked beautiful, and I knew I smiled at the wonder of her work because I felt that smile fade when I saw movement through the window behind her. Madeleine-Grace turned to see to what my sight was adjusting. It was Aunt Adèle in her gray dress with the pale green apron over it, swooping down in front of an herb island. We rushed to the window to see better what she was doing.

She scooped up a patch of herbs with her hands and ripped them, dropping the pieces to the ground. She did the same thing on the next herb island, yanking as many as she could by the roots in each swoop and tearing them to pieces. By her last batch, her ankles were sinking into a pile of crushed, ripped herbs.

Then she moved to the flower island that enclosed our favorite bench. Her arms became scythes, swiping through the peonies but grabbing them as she slashed, yanking them from the earth. Some were uprooted while others broke, and once in her hands, she bent them in half and dropped them at her feet. She swooped again for another slash at the flowers—the phlox and lilies—taking them from their bit of soil and rupturing them.

Moving to the next island, she trampled the flowers in the grass. As she ripped through the herbs in the next spot of soil, Madeleine-Grace and I hurried through the *salle-en-arrière* and onto the veranda. From the railing, we called her name, but if she heard us, she did not acknowledge us. We knew not to persist with calls as we watched her decimate the lovage, the parsley, and the sage as she had done to the chives both blooming and unbloomed, the tarragon, and the thyme.

Once all had been unearthed from this island so that, like the others, a patch of mostly black dirt remained, she darted past the veranda to the shed. She returned holding the bags of mint seeds Monsieur Vauquelin and I had given her, and frenzied and disheveled, strands of hair falling from her bun and fingers blackened with dirt, she dunked her hands into one bag. She pulled out a handful of mint seeds and spread them on the dirt in the island and then repeated the action. Harried and frenetic, she rushed to the next ravaged island and tossed handfuls of seeds onto it. She bolted from island to island, dipping shaky hands into the burlap bags and withdrawing a multitude of mint seeds in each clutched fist before opening them to hurl at the earth. Once she had finished Monsieur Vauquelin's seeds, she did the same with mine, only less concerned with directing them into the flower and herb beds. Now she scattered them about the lawn, around the house, near the clotheslines, between the shed and the house, and certainly on the tilled patches of fresh soil she had fashioned days ago.

Madeleine-Grace and I ran back and forth along the veranda, following her erratic course from island to island, through the lawn to the cliffs, from the clotheslines to the shed. And finally, standing before the veranda with the floppy burlap sack in hand, she turned it upside down so that the last few seeds fell at her feet and threw the sack to the ground. She wiped a tear from her cheek and smudged her face with dirt and a fresh green dye of crushed stem, and then rested her hands on her knees as she breathed heavily.

We watched in silence, not twenty meters away, from the railing of the veranda. She looked up. Whether she had noticed us before or not, for the first time since her frenzied rampage began, she saw us. A breeze scudded through the veranda, and the edges of the doilies Madeleine-Grace had sewn into her neckline lifted, catching Aunt Adèle's attention. Her head tilted as her eyes looked on Madeleine-Grace with sympathy, heartache, admiration, and tragedy. A tear dissolved some of the dirt on her face in its journey down her cheek. It dropped to the ground, and I imagined that tear would be the first to activate the mint seeds at her feet, and with its salt, would ensure their permanent growth in this place.

As another tear dripped down her cheek, she wiped it away, smearing on more dirt. She turned from us toward the cliffs and stared for a minute before turning back to see us. Then she walked away, disappearing around the house.

I will never forget the image of Aunt Adèle standing with flowers in her arms, giving them one last look before crushing them, nor that of her tear-and-dirt-stained face, head tilted, as deep, watery, brown eyes stared at Madeleine-Grace. It was a picture of the fallen that refused defeat. It was a picture of the transformation that comes after war.

We did not see Aunt Adèle again that day, not to help with our outfits or Madeleine-Grace's hair, not to offer a reprise of niceties or to review our dance, not even to accompany us to the ball. We prepared as if we would be attending, unsure of our securing a ride to the ball, but Monsieur Vauquelin did show up to chauffeur us to the Countess's manor.

Aunt Laure and Uncle Gilbert had left first with Wischard and little Laure, anxious to meet and greet society men and women for as long as they could. Aunt Mirabelle had indeed returned with Alphonse and Chardine from the Rouen house, leaving young Roul to remain not with his father in hospital in Paris but in Rouen on his own. She and the children left with Uncle Romain, Aunt Pé, and Astride. Aunt Adèle knowingly had pressed even Alphonse and Chardine's outfits.

My sister and I, dressed, groomed, sprayed, and rehearsed, remained—were literally left—behind by the others. We had stayed in our bedroom with the door closed, never once checked on. Since no one had seen Madeleine-Grace's repair to the gown, they must have assumed we could not attend. Then we heard the knock at the front door. Madeleine-Grace scampered down the stairs, forgetting something important, which I claimed in her behalf, intending to surprise her with it when she realized what was missing. Amid these recent ordeals, anyone could experience absent-mindedness here and there, including my astute sister. At the entrance, we sighed to see Monsieur Vauquelin, his hat in his hands before him.

After he dusted white salt from the seat with his cap, we hopped into his car without Aunt Adèle whose absence troubled him terribly. We told him what happened involving the dress but not what happened involving the seeds. Madeleine-Grace and I shared an understanding, without ever having spoken so, that we would carry on as if that occurrence had never happened. Disturbed by the story and Aunt Adèle's disappearance, he vowed to return to the house after dropping us at the Countess's, which to me offered relief. Although he thought Madeleine-Grace's efforts to restore the dress praiseworthy, his preoccupation with Aunt Adèle prohibited a crinkly-eyed smile, and for the second half of the drive, he remained too dumbfounded and concerned to speak. We sat in silence in the backseat, ten small bags of *fleur de sel* stacked between us. The hour neared four o'clock, and the sun of late day loomed, thick as honey and full in resplendence. As the town of Etretat-au-Delà became countryside, we drove a bumpy road lined with alternating oaks and hawthorns, and the strength of the sun pierced through their greenery and between the trees into our silent car.

When I was walking home one autumn day two years ago from the River Forest Public Library after having spent an hour there after school, I was approached by my friends Jimmy and Jack. They invited me to play "settlers and Indians," although we were getting too old for such things. We hadn't played in a while, and I suppose Jimmy and Jack were both feeling nostalgic for the games of earlier childhood and bored on a fall afternoon. The game always involved separating in twenty seconds, encountering each other, asking questions about each other cautiously, and ending in peace. Sometimes he who assumed the role of settler or Indian would find ways to prolong the discussion, thereby prolonging peace, and sometimes he who assumed the role of settler or Indian quickly acted on offering peaceful relations so as to be the first to initiate such a goodness. And once peace was reached, we would share information as settler and Indian, or switch roles and start a new game.

My only deterrent to playing with them wasn't incomplete homework nor needing parents' approval, but the cold. It was only in the high thirties, and I felt it despite my coat; I did not have my gloves, scarf, or cap, because it hadn't become this cold in autumn yet. I still accepted their invitation, and we walked closer to Jimmy's house to begin in his yard. Jack's house was two houses over, and mine was a block behind theirs. We talked while we walked to Jimmy's yard, and then began the game, playing through dusk. The game ended with me, the settler, offering the Indians use of my logs to make fires; I had brought them to the high woodpile "pyramid" behind Jimmy's garage to show them the abundant store. Knowing our parents would be calling for dinner soon and with the temperature of the November evening dropping, we opted not to play another round. Jimmy went inside, Jack walked down Jimmy's drive to his house, and I decided to climb the woodpile and jump the fence into a neighbor's backyard two houses over from mine. Only when I got to the top, I accidentally slid down the far side of the pile, and three stump-like logs rolled down the pile on top of me, pinning me between the pile and the iron fence, and when I landed, my head cracked into the metal, rendering me unconscious.

Sometime before midnight, I woke up, lodged between the woodpile and the fence, to Madeleine-Grace shaking my shoulders. I remember seeing leaves falling in the darkness, and so were snowflakes. She shouted, "I found him," so loudly it pulled me to consciousness and I became aware that my hands were freezing. She kissed my cheek, and doing so must have alerted her to how cold I had become. The temperature had dropped to the twenties. She pulled off her knit cap and tried to fit it on my head, unrolling the bottom and stretching it. Most of it covered my head. She tore off her mittens and crammed my frozen fingers and hands into them, which actually hurt. She climbed back over the woodpile to get our father who had been searching for me, and he lifted the logs with Mr. Mertens and carried me home.

I learned that Madeleine-Grace knew I had been at the library and knew my route home. Assuming I had taken the same route, she ran into every yard of every property along the path in search of me. Our mother had stayed home in case I returned while our father searched, but he couldn't keep up with Madeleine-Grace's intent combing of the short stretch between the library and Jimmy's. While neighbors were warning that a boy could die if lingering too long in this cold and theorizing about running away, kidnappings, library lock-ins, and practical places a boy might have gone, Madeleine-Grace ran into the cold and searched. And she found me, and she warmed me, and she called for help.

As this memory burrowed its way to the fore of my thoughts on our ride through the oaks and the hawthorns and heavy rays of sun on our way to the children's ball, I looked at Madeleine-Grace, elegant, resilient, and delicate, the sun flickering on her eyes as it slanted between trees, and I realized it was time I defended her, who had lost her parents at the age of nine, her who had been locked in a cellar out of spite by her own cousin, her who had been sabotaged by relatives, whose dress had been burned, whose spirits and innocence had been attacked. I had spent months in a mire of pain, uncertainty, and grief, and I had not pulled my weary feet out before more muck had been dumped into the mire, onto me, by, of all people, my relatives. I would not drag myself from the mire soon, either, but I would not let it keep me from protecting my sister. Despite not having done so well before now, one look at the dress she had salvaged was enough to encourage the vow I made in that car—to stand up for my sister from this point forward.

My parents expected this of me, and I would live up to their expectation as they had raised me to do, as they had equipped me to do.

We passed through the broad iron gate of Countess Renier's manor and rode the pebble drive to her main entrance where her formally dressed staff awaited to escort us from our vehicles. Monsieur Vauquelin, too apprehensive to step into view of others for fear of embarrassing us, put the car into park and leaned over the front seat into the backseat.

"I will check on your aunt, okay?" he said. "I know you are worried, but you needn't think about anything except amusing yourself this evening—and becoming king and queen of the ball over your cousins." He smiled at last, the sun glowing in his eyes, and the wrinkles lifting his whole face to an expression of pure gladness and—love.

His next actions struck me saliently and lastingly. He reached for a bag of *fleur de sel* and opened it. He pinched a few precious flakes between his thumb and index finger and, rubbing them into powder, sprinkled them over my head and over my sister's head. His eyes welled with tears as he tied the bag and tossed it back on the pile between us.

"Why did you sprinkle salt on us?" I asked, wondering if this were some good-luck ritual with which I had been unfamiliar.

"I needed some way of preserving who you both are right now. May this little bit of salt preserve such beauty and innocence forever."

Even though a tear rolled down each cheek, he smiled widely. I suspected that his tears had to be for Aunt Adèle, that she could not be here with us, so devastated by the actions of her own family. But I did not ask him why he cried, nor why he revered the Ellande and Madeleine-Grace he saw in that moment. I thanked him, as did my sister, and then hopped out of the car, ran around, and opened the door for Madeleine-Grace. Monsieur Vauquelin drove off as a porter met us with cordiality and escorted us through the manor house door and into the main hall for check-in.

"Ah, the last of the Semperrin children," said Madame Dalmont at the check-in table, a long, blue and black feather piercing from her dark blue hat. She pointed to our names on a list, and the young woman next to her checked us off. "The children of Juliette and Julien Avery."

Her head swooped around us searchingly. An expression of panic came over her before her mouth opened and her eyes closed in understanding.

"I was looking for your guardian," she said. "Forgive me. Your aunts and uncles have already entered and must be waiting for you." She assumed wrong. "I have not seen your Aunt Adèle Semperrin, though. Has she slipped by without my noticing? Ah, so I will greet her later in the ballroom. Now, as you may recall, just a short walk down this hall will lead you to the ballroom. You can hear the chatter. The Countess will greet you and direct you to your position on the floor."

She gave us clearance to pass, smiling as she studied our outfits now that the last of us had officially arrived. A few steps beyond the table, once the ladies had returned their attention to the list of registrants and Alistair Traver had approached the table with his parents, I stopped Madeleine-Grace.

"Madeleine-Grace, you forgot something," I said, holding something I had withdrawn from a spot between my shirt and suitcoat; I was holding it behind my back now. She looked about her person, wondering what she could have forgotten, and then patted her head, careful not to mess her hair. Her mouth dropped in shock and anger when she found her head bare. Before she could distress herself over the vacant spot on her head, I pulled the garland of cornflowers from behind my back. "Thought you might want this."

She smiled, her tight shoulders dropping as she exhaled. "Thank-you, Ellande," she said, taking it from my hands with her thumbs and index fingers. She turned it in different directions, smoothed over the stems, teased a few flowers from the coils to the surface, and kissed me on the cheek. "You smooshed it a little, but I thank you, anyway. Make sure it's straight on me."

She placed it on her head and pressed it in just the right spaces. Four bobby pins she had attached to the headpiece fastened her garland to her hair. We found a mirror in the hallway, which helped her adjust it. It was the first I had seen the two of us together in our outfits, matching creams and fabrics, dressy shoes shiny, and the salt in our hair nowhere to be seen. Once the garland sat perfectly, she faced me, and I gave her the thumbs-up. I extended my arm, and we walked to the ballroom.

The two white doors with elaborate gold molding awaited ajar, and through them I could see many people mingling, passing, and some dancing, adults and children. I could hear the live orchestra playing an upbeat tune in *moderato*. I expected to see Monsieur Cuvelier upon our entrance and was eager to hear how he incorporated our thoughts into his arrangement of the *tourdion*. Steps before our entrance into the ballroom, the countess stepped into the doorway for a gaze down the hall at the last of the registrants. Alistair and his parents had passed us while we were adjusting the garland, so we were the last to arrive. She extended her arms with welcome.

"Jacques—" she began in effusive greeting, but Lady Victorine and Lady Léontine appeared from beside her, awestruck and elated at our presence. Lady Léontine rapidly fanned herself and Lady Victorine.

"It is Ellande now," said Lady Victorine with a wink to the Countess. "I told you this."

"Ellande—for it is Ellande now—and Madeleine-Grace Avery," the Countess uttered in correction. She put her hand to her mouth. "You look beautiful—ravishing!"

"Thank-you," we said.

"Beautiful!" said Lady Léontine. "And nothing like it!"

"This is your Aunt Adèle's hand, is it not?" the Countess said.

"She has outdone herself this year," said Lady Léontine.

"Thank-you," we said, unwilling to mention Madeleine-Grace's hand in the gown.

"Where is your aunt? I have seen Romain and Laure, and, how unfortunate about your Uncle Roul! What a strange accident, rolling over on—ugh!"

Lady Victorine blushed and Lady Léontine literally bit her bottom lip. I could tell they wanted to look at each other but restrained themselves so as not to tip off the Countess of anything amiss.

"And how good of your cousin Roul to spend every moment at his father's side in hospital. It was good of your Aunt Mirabelle to bring your cousins Alphonse and Chardine here, was it not, to distract them from worry? Your Uncle Roul insisted," the Countess said with sadness.

My Uncle Roul was not even conscious as far as I knew, and no one had been at his side recently besides Aunt Melisende.

"And your poor Aunt Laure is taking it the worst," the Countess added. "She tells me that poor Wischard had been there the day of the accident, and she is most distressed for him. Nothing pains a mother more than seeing her son suffer, so you must dote on your Aunt Laure until she recovers."

"I'm sure she will insist on it," said Lady Victorine, unable to thwart the Countess's gracious concern for my family.

"The tragedies of your family have been too much to bear, I am sure. Your poor grandmother must be beside herself. You must visit as often as you can. It will be good for her to be near you. You know that?"

"We have visited her twice and count on visiting again for an extended stay in Paris after the ball," I said, sure I would make that happen despite protestations from Aunt Laure. It only then occurred to me to enlist the help of Lady Victorine, from whom I did not have to keep a secret.

"This is good of you," said the Countess. "Your Aunt Adèle must be inside. I will find her later. Now, the ball! We will start shortly, so you must find your place on the floor with the other children. Your spot, I recall, is closest the orchestra. For now, you may meet your cousins and your friends or sit at one of the children's tables until we begin. Then I will invite you to your position on the floor. You remember from last year, do you not?"

We confirmed and passed through the doorway with the ladies' continued compliments bouncing through the sunny room from one to another. I was thrilled Madeleine-Grace's dress had thrived under scrutiny, although the true test would be surviving the close inspection of the judges later. Heads turned as we walked through pockets of guests gathered around the ballroom floor, as we made for the orchestra, knowing our spot was nearby. A smile, a whisper, a wave followed every head that noticed us, and we did our best to reciprocate and receive praise graciously.

Of course, some notice was followed by scowls. In a white blouse tightened at the waist with a thin black belt and long green skirt, Aunt Mirabelle followed Madeleine-Grace and me with her stare while Monsieur Traver asked how long her husband's recovery might take. Uncle Romain, in his black and white tuxedo, was talking with Lord Galimard, Colonel Corrue, and Monsieur Darré when he caught notice of our walk through the room. His evident surprise did not surprise me. Mostly the young participants of the ball occupied the glossy parquet floor, and we greeted several familiar faces as we slowly veered around clusters of friends. We exchanged greetings with the Epilliers and their children Berthilde and Jacques and waved to Madame Emeric whose ear was being bent by a boy I did not recognize. Near the wall, to my surprise, Jeuffine des Gervais was in attendance, feigning a distracted placing of her hand on the lapel of young Louis-Baptiste Edou, who, I recalled, had married Hélène Gallet last summer; he blushed and glanced at his wife who was preoccupied adjusting a bow in her niece's hair. Across the floor, I saw Wischard and little Laure talking with Augustin and Françoise Ferrand in front of Uncle Gilbert and Aunt Laure, who were chatting with Marie and Hardouin Loiselier. Uncle Gilbert wore a white tuxedo, and Aunt Laure a long, velvet dress with a low, V-shaped neckline. I could hear them trying to find a name for the dark shade of red of her dress.

"Is it scarlet?" wondered Madame Loiselier.

"It is brick red," said Aunt Laure. "It is red like a brick, is it not?"

I wished I had a brick to throw at her face. "Is this the red you're thinking of?" I would say afterwards. I felt awful for such a thought, mostly because it would hurt Wischard.

Next to that group, Maclou and Brigitte Galimard stood, practicing their dance with Michel Fautrier and Jeanne Adrieux, but when Maclou saw Madeleine-Grace, he waved us over. We headed to them, happy to be invited by someone.

When Aunt Laure spotted us, she blanched, alerting all to something having come over her. Their heads turned toward us as Aunt Laure placed a hand on Wischard's shoulders and pulled him to her person. Upon the out-of-the-blue pull, he looked perplexedly about and saw us. Poor Wischard. He had wanted to wave to us and started to lift his arm when his mother lowered her grip from his shoulders to his arms, tightening them to stop the one from rising. We, however, smiled pleasantly at Wischard and little Laure and at the Loiseliers and met Maclou's embrace. We complimented each other's outfits, and Madeleine-Grace complimented their dancing, too.

Marie Loiselier stepped into our circle to greet us more formally, exchanging kisses and complimenting our outfits. We expressed that she looked lovely in her white silk blouse, cinched at the waist over an expansive yellow and white skirt. I had seen a similar look on the model in the Christian Dior poster we had passed in Paris.

"So good that you were able to attend. We were told you wouldn't make it. And I'm so sorry about your Aunt Adèle," she said, taking us off guard. "I'm not sure which to believe, but I know it can't be good."

"What do you mean?" I asked.

"Your Aunt Laure said she had to stay home because she caught a summer flu, but when I talked to your Aunt Mirabelle, she said that she had accidentally poisoned herself by using the wrong part of an herb in her morning omelette. Poor Adèle—she must be in such pain to miss this event. She couldn't even join a relaxing excursion to the tailor shop in Fécamp yesterday, and I had so wanted her opinion. You will give her our best, won't you?"

"Of course," I said, and as I debated asking which version of the story she thought more likely, Aunt Pé pretended to bump into her, unaware she was talking to, of all people, us.

"I'm so sorry—why, Marie Loiselier!"

It was the most forced encounter I—and Madeleine-Grace and Madame Loiselier and anyone else who had witnessed it—had ever seen. As the petite Madame Loiselier rubbed the now bruised forearm that Aunt Pé had slammed into and then grabbed, Aunt Pé saw Madeleine-Grace and me.

The amount of disgust that formed on her face could not be measured. Strengthening her ire, she surveyed Madeleine-Grace's dress to see its survival, its new touches, its beauty. No one had delivered a more severe—and obvious—reaction.

Madeleine-Grace and I smiled at her. She remained silent. In that moment, Astride tripped into her mother, lacking the deliberateness of her mother's bump while sharing an uncanny gracelessness.

"Astride," she said, "You must be more careful. Astride, have you greeted Madame Loiselier?"

Astride greeted her, and then, after a glare at Madeleine-Grace, ran off.

"She is excited about the dance," Aunt Pé said.

Maclou inserted himself into the circle, and said to Madeleine-Grace, "Later tonight, when we may dance with other partners, would you like to dance with me?"

"I would be delighted to dance with you, Maclou," my sister said.

"I could tell you stories about Normand saints as we dance," he said, enthusiastic now that his invitation had been accepted well in advance. "I know them all!"

Aunt Pé stepped between Madame Loiselier and me and walked her off the floor as strange looks surfaced on the face of Madame Loiselier. "Wasn't Astride's gown a vision?" Aunt Pé said.

"If only Adèle could have done more—" Madame Loiselier said. It was the best implicature she could muster in the moment.

"You have not heard?" Aunt Pé began. "Adèle has injured herself days ago and could not attend tonight."

"Injured? How?"

This one I enjoyed. "She twisted her ankle practicing *la choule* with Ellande. We told her this was not a sport for ladies, but you know Adèle—and those nagging children—" and this was all I could hear before they stepped out of earshot. I knew I had to ask Madame Loiselier which story she thought the most vivid.

The orchestra stopped playing mid-*prélude*, and we could see the Countess on the stage behind them signaling to the conductor. The other children on the floor and we sidled to our designated spots, ours next to the orchestra. It was then that Monsieur Cuvelier, the conductor, noticed us, and his serious demeanor about the Countess's order melted to ebullient yet warm animation over our presence and, no doubt, the playing of our fun, collaborative arrangement. The abrupt cessation of music and the commanding presence of the Countess on the stage silenced the conversations and halted movement. In an instant, she gained everyone's attention.

"Good-evening, friends, and welcome to what tonight I may call 'the Fifth Annual' Children's Ball! Can it be five consecutive years already, and for some of our children, five consecutive years participating in the ball?"

The group applauded, acknowledging the duration that, I would imagine to some, had felt like the span of a year, not five. Parents looked at children who had danced in all five, several boys and girls raised their hands to indicate five years of participation, and many looked about the room to see who was in some way signaling their membership in this company.

"This evening's ceremony will follow the schedule of, well, the past four years. We will begin immediately with introductions of couples during the couples dance round. Then, while the judges are tabulating their results, we will hold the group dance where all couples will dance to one, unpracticed number. After three finalists are announced, they will come to the stage for the speeches. A winner will be announced after judges confer, and the evening will conclude with cocktails and dancing—for all!"

To laughter and expectation of an evening of merriment, the Countess lifted her arms to acknowledge warmly the privilege of all present—children and adults—to partake in the joy. Past balls have proven the event a wonderful opportunity to mingle, to meet, to drink, and to dance. I remembered Lord Galimard saying last year as we walked out of the manor house that, when reduced to its skeleton, the children's ball was really nothing more than occasion for the adults to gather over drinks and dancing. His wife corrected him by suggesting that the children, thanks to this event, learn important lessons, so its value penetrates the falseness with which he imbued it. I did think the adults looked forward more to the entertainment of later evening than the ceremony and competition prior.

"At this time, I would like to introduce our three judges." As she named each judge, he or she stood at the judges' table along the side of the dancing area and waved to the applause of all. One judge I recognized from last year's ball; the other two were new to judging but not to such events.

"Before we begin, I would like to share a word about why I continue the children's ball," the Countess said. "As the children's ball becomes a tradition now enjoying its fifth year, the event celebrates tradition in general. I wished to provide an opportunity not only to showcase the traditions of Normandie and of our French culture, but also to share them. It is through sharing them and receiving graciously what is shared with us that these good traditions, customs, and sources of comfort may continue. We can find several events that embrace our region's folk traditions, but this event seeks to embrace something different: an appreciation of decorum and the beautiful decorum of the French. It is my hope that, with your participation, I may be able to continue the fostering of our French culture through music, just as you continue the traditions of our land through your own family customs. Thank-you for helping me realize this continuance of what makes France beautiful."

Everyone applauded. I heard my mother and father's voice in her message and saw Aunt Adèle's everyday comportment in her pride. Madeleine-Grace was clapping avidly, truly enjoying the inaugural words of the evening, eager to take in the dances, the suits and gowns of others, the speeches, the variations of old melodies, the newness of the evening rooted in the practices of the past.

"And now, we will begin the couples dance round. My trusted conductor and dear friend, Edgar Cuvelier, with the help of accomplished musicians who have sacrificed precious time to practice for this evening, have collected and mastered all the music. As usual, the most common selection was the *gavotte*, which we have designated as *Gavotte A, B, C,* and *D*. Those in *Gavotte A* will do their introductory promenade, stopping before the judges' table for introduction and inspection of wardrobe; once all couples have done so and found their positions on the floor, they will dance to the *gavotte*. The procedure will repeat with those dancing to *Gavotte B, C,* and *D*. Then we will switch to the *farandole*, for which there are only two groups, *A* and *B*. They will follow the same procedure. Then we will conclude with this year's only *tourdion*, the selection of only one couple, who will follow the same procedure. During judges' deliberations, all couples will be invited for the group dance round. Very well, then. Let the dancing begin!"

After more applause, the children moved to their fixed spots along the side of the dance floor while the adults took seats around the room or stood against the walls. The most tedious part of the evening was standing in place as others walked, subjected themselves to judgment, and danced in pairs. I wished this would be the year they offered us chairs, but such a courtesy was not to be. At least the dances moved quickly enough that we didn't notice we were standing and aching the whole time.

The first round of *Gavotte A* took place, signaled by the announcement of the Countess's assistant, who stood on the stage. Each couple strolled the perimeter of the floor, stopped before the judges to introduce themselves and have their outfits evaluated, and assumed their position on the floor. Then the orchestra began playing, and the four couples danced to the delight of us all. The participants of *Gavotte B, C,* and *D* did the same. Wischard and Laure belonged to *Gavotte B* and performed exceedingly well. We cheered avidly for them after the dance. Astride and Alistair performed to *Gavotte C*, and they managed to stay entirely in unison as they bounced to the wrong beat of every measure. I did not cheer for them. Alphonse and Chardine belonged to *Gavotte D*, the least upbeat of them all but still pleasant sounding. Our cousins stood out among the other couples as having practiced the least, and as they danced, I saw the whispering increase about the room, no doubt as news of Uncle Roul's stabbing circulated. Then *Farandole A* and *B* took place, providing a change of pace and sound after four *gavottes*. Maclou and Brigitte belonged to *Farandole A*, as did the Loiselier children. I think they did an equally good dance, but I was rooting for Maclou.

"And finally," the Countess's assistant, Madame Dalmont, announced, "we have our last dance for the evening, featuring only one couple: a *tourdion!*" Everyone applauded, perhaps at the novelty of the less common dance. This, too, promised yet another change of pace for the guests, and the knowledge of only one round of it likely rendered it more appealing and anticipated. "May the couple step forward and begin your *promenade!*"

I glanced at the conductor, and he winked and smiled. I saw two men take seats with the orchestra, one with a tympanum, the other with a *chifournie*. Things were coming together, and the twinkle in Monsieur Cuvelier's eyes and the smiles brightening the faces of the musicians as they switched music revealed that a successful arrangement had been ensured, one they were excited to perform. As we took the first step of our *promenade*, I saw through the windows those pinks and lavenders in the clouds crossing a light blue sky, the sunlight rippling over them for a final stretch before its slumber. Taking our tour around the floor, eyes winked at us, mouths smiled at us, hands waved to us, heads bowed to us—so many welcomed us—amid the few glares and stony-mouthed insults.

Before the judges' table, I released Madeleine-Grace's arm, and she stepped forward. "Madeleine-Grace Avery," she said sweetly before a curtsy. When she stepped back, I stepped forward. "Ellande Avery," I said proudly of my Basque and Normand heritage, bowed, and stepped back. Until given permission to continue to our place on the floor, we stood for scrutiny, watching the judges inspect us, lean over the table, and smile, jotting down notes. When we turned to proceed to our spot for the dance, the judges gasped, and one called us back—this did not happen. We returned close to the table, and at the center judge's request, turned our back to them. They peered at the doilies Madeleine-Grace had sewn into the once destroyed seam as whispers flittered through the room. Finally, they gave us permission to move on.

As the only couple in this round, our position was the middle of the dance floor. Madeleine-Grace and I glanced at the conductor behind us who nodded with a smile. We assumed our opening *posture gauche* and froze. The whispering stopped. The guests and other children seemed stiller than we. What speed was about to cut this stillness, like the flickering of Seurat's Seine water in stiffness of short dashes.

Then the music began, first violins and cellos, in triple time. Madeleine-Grace and I took our first steps, a *pied en l'air* and a *petit saut*, in sync with the tempo and the rhythm, meticulous to the strictures of the dance. And as the base violins phased in, I was dancing in my living room in America, Madeleine-Grace at my side, my mother at the piano, my father sipping a cocktail as he kept beat with his foot. To see the smile on Madeleine-Grace's face as I heard my mother's piano playing made my heart swell with love, with pride, and with joy. And then the tympanum came in, deep and stirring, as the *chifournie* released into the air the sound of the Normandes Isles, and the song built in intensity as it crescendoed amid a melancholic layer of harmonies. Concentrating on the steps and keeping rhythm, I still saw the musicians' eyes glowing on each glimpse past their music at us, the conductor stealing glances at us over his shoulder, and the mouths of the Countess and her guests dropping in awe at the beauty of the tune or lifting in joy at the beauty of the dance. Then I heard the first clap—Lady Victorine, an instrument in her own right perhaps, began the clap to the beat—as the song continued to rise in volume and passion and tradition, and within seconds, the other guests had joined her. Madeleine-Grace's eyes were themselves dancing, and if my smile could grow any bigger, it did so to see her delight.

The song reached its close by a drastic drop in volume and number of instruments, and while maintaining triple time but slowing the tempo, the only remaining instruments of a single violin and the *chifournie* played. The clapping stopped. Our dancing stopped, and my sister and I froze. The *chifournie* alone played the last few notes, and then silence lingered.

Madeleine-Grace and I did not move until, in a sudden, the audience erupted into applause. Anyone seated stood, and I saw Uncle Romain pull Aunt Pé from her chair. When Madeleine-Grace and I relaxed, I could not help hugging her, and the audience cooed and hoorayed. Instead of returning to our assigned position, we walked to the conductor. He extended his hands to Madeleine-Grace, who received them graciously, as I loomed over the musicians on my tiptoes, shouting "thank-you" to their gleeful reception and nods of gratitude and approval to us. I knew Madeleine-Grace should be the one taking all the credit for this feat, from the musical arrangement to the choreography.

During judges' deliberations, all couples reclaimed assigned positions and began, to the surprise of all, a *courante*. I had wanted to discuss the first round with Madeleine-Grace, but we dared not talk during the dance. We would be able to talk afterwards. The judges considered this dance, too, in their deliberations, but more weight went on the *promenade*, outfit, and couples dance. Nevertheless, we played this round cautiously, maintaining correct hand and arm placement and dancing to the beat. When the music ended, we returned to our positions for more standing, more waiting.

Madame Dalmont crossed to the center of the stage with a sheet of paper. Once again, everyone hushed quickly.

"I am pleased to announce the three couples entering the final round. I must note that one couple slated for the finalist round fell out of contention for chatting during the group dance round. We will still name three finalist couples, however."

Some parents guffawed while some chuckled. I could tell the stakes were higher to some families than others. As we had made finalists only last year and still lost, our father used to say jovially, "I don't mind if you're not a winner as long as you're not a sore loser." His attitude about baseball and soccer was a bit different, but the children's ball didn't rate with the same esteem for him.

"And the first finalists are Michel and Marie-Claire Fautrier," Madame Dalmont announced to much applause. "The second finalists are Brigitte and Maclou Galimard!"

Madeleine-Grace and I cheered! Maclou glanced bashfully at Madeleine-Grace as he turned red.

"And the third finalists are Ellande and Madeleine-Grace Avery!"

The guests erupted in applause, but so did the musicians, which was gratifyingly unexpected.

"Will the three couples ascend to the stage for the final round? One member of each pair will give a speech of no more than thirty seconds. Judges will evaluate on content of speech, articulation and poise, and finishing within the time constraint. The winning couple will be allowed to give a speech with a length of their choosing. Couples, please join Countess Renier on the stage."

We followed Maclou and Brigitte to the stage and lined up. The Countess introduced the first couple, and for this one, Michel spoke. He was my age, I knew, and the hand at his side scratched his thigh throughout a monotonous reading of notes shaking in his other hand inches from his mouth. Next, Maclou and Brigitte stood front and center. Just as Brigitte began her speech, Maclou, who was grinning widely and swinging his arms nervously, hurled himself forward on a forceful swing, throwing himself off balance, nose-diving off the stage into the orchestra. He landed on the tympanum with a thunderous roar, startling the guests and eliciting a murmur of "ohhh"s and even some chuckles. A glance at Lady and Lord Galimard revealed the former disgruntled and the latter bowled over with laughter. Lady Galimard slapped her husband on the back with her fan, but he could not stop laughing. Poor Maclou lost points for poise.

Madeleine-Grace, however, rushed to the edge of the stage and reached for Maclou, who was draped over the tympanum. She and the musicians helped him to his feet, and Maclou flashed an unabashed grin at Madeleine-Grace, as if the humiliation, the stumble, the fall in front of hundreds, had been worth it.

Brigitte did, however, finish her speech in under thirty seconds.

Then Madeleine-Grace and I were called to center stage. I stepped forward and touched the outside of my suitcoat where behind that piece of fabric lay my speech in the inside pocket. The touch was a crutch of some sort, but I never intended to read from it as Michel Fautrier had. This speech was short, and I had practiced it.

"I would like to deliver my speech in the form of a toast. And this evening, I would like to raise my glass—let's imagine it's our favorite, *calvados*—to an important person in my life." The guests chuckled at my approach, at the real raising of my arm using an imaginary glass. "I would like to raise my glass to my sister, Madeleine-Grace Avery. In raising a glass to her, I am raising a glass to the patient practice of learning time-honored practices; to the keeping of traditions as an expression of honoring our parents, our ancestors, our country, our religion; and to the unwavering protection and care of close friends and close family, as our parents modeled for us, and expect of us. And to conclude, I ask that you join me in raising your glass to my sister."

No one moved at first. Then, almost in unison, Lady Victorine and Monsieur Cuvelier raised an imaginary glass. Then Countess Renier, Lady Léontine, Lord Galimard, and from his spot by the orchestra, Maclou, raised their glass. Thiessé and Célèstène Galimard and Hardouin and Marie Loiselier, along with many others, raised their glass, as did the musicians, the judges, and the many other guests. Astride glared at us in disgust while our aunts and uncles darted stunned stares at the multifarious guests honoring Madeleine-Grace for reasons they would never understand. I stepped back, positioning myself behind Madeleine-Grace, and everyone applauded her. Madeleine-Grace stood before us all, glowing in the last glints of sunlight, in her hand-stitched dress of crocheted doilies and garland of blue cornflowers from L'Ile d'Aobefein. If I did anything right in my life, I am glad I gave her that moment. She deserved so much more.

When the applause subsided, the Countess assumed center stage once again, and asked the judges if they had reached a decision. The center judge nodded yes, and walked to the stage a folded sheet of paper, handing it to the Countess. She opened it and parted her lips as if to say the names but thought better of revealing it so abruptly.

"Children of Etretat-au-Delà, Fécamp, Dieppe, and le Pays de Caux, children of Normandie, I thank you all for another year of your dedication to this cause and to this event. You have all done so well, and we are proud of you. Friends, I am pleased to announce tonight's winners of the Fifth Annual Children's Ball: Ellande and Madeleine-Grace Avery!"

Everyone applauded again, and though the ceremony hadn't officially ended—we had a final speech to give—many of the children shrugged and left their positions on the floor to find their parents. I, too, wanted to run back to my parents. We didn't even have Aunt Adèle to run to this evening. Maybe Madeleine-Grace wasn't thinking these things, for her arms wrapped around me ecstatically. To her, she had someone. I hugged her, as well.

"Do you wish to say anything?" the Countess asked us as the room quieted.

"I think everyone would like to drink and dance," I said, eliciting a few light-hearted cheers and swells of laughter.

"I think we should all like to hear a few words," the Countess suggested, her voice once again bringing about hushes.

I had nothing to say. I had hoped my words about my sister would be the final word. My sister, however, had other plans.

"I would like to speak, if I may," my sister said.

"Please," said the Countess.

Madeleine-Grace stepped next to her, front and center. The sun had vanished and the dark blue and gray of dusk hung in the sky outside the long row of windows. I did not know what to expect from my sister, but when she began to speak, I gulped.

"I don't wish to say much," Madeleine-Grace said. "I first wish to thank the Countess for hosting this event and for helping us, through this ball, to learn the music of France and to have a fun evening together."

"Here, here!" said Lord Galimard, to the cheers of those nearby.

"And I wish to thank a few others," Madeleine-Grace continued. "I wish to thank all my aunts and uncles who are present here tonight. Many of you have noticed that does not include my Aunt Adèle. To the others, I wish to say that your actions incapacitated Aunt Adèle, but maybe you forgot I could step in when my aunt is unable. Maybe you didn't forget; you just didn't know. It didn't occur to you that someone could pay attention, could be learning, could want to know more. Maybe you didn't count on the advantages I have by being nothing like you whatsoever and the joy I take in that. So the advantages I have over you—and always will have—are what allowed me to sustain your many injuries to my dress and to myself and to my Aunt Adèle whom you have ensured stayed home this evening. I feel beyond satisfied to know, thanks to my mother and Grandma'Maud, that not only am I nothing like you, I will be nothing like you. Thank-you for being the examples of how to lead a life no one would ever want to live. Thanks to you, I see clearly that it is the examples my parents and grandparents have left after them that I will follow."

At that, Madeleine-Grace bowed and receded behind the Countess. Most eyes were not on Madeleine-Grace or me but darting around the room, searching for Semperrins, fixing on Semperrins, glaring at Semperrins as whispers and murmurs abounded.

"Thank-you, Madeleine-Grace Avery," the Countess said, taken by surprise and unsure how to follow. "Let us applaud once again this year's winner, Ellande and Madeleine-Grace Avery."

The applause, much less fervent this time, was distracted and unconvincing. Most of the attention landed on any Semperrin one could find. The Countess escorted us to the dance floor where we thanked the conductor once more. The Galimards, the Loiseliers, and others approached us with congratulations amidst questions about Aunt Adèle, all of which we answered with the vagueness that revealed a truth about her situation. Lady Victorine expressed concern for us and our return to the house, but we assured her that Monsieur Vauquelin, who had driven us here, planned to drive us back. Lady Victorine promised to check on us and Aunt Adèle tomorrow, grateful Monsieur Vauquelin had inserted himself. I saw Aunt Laure approach Marie Loiselier after the latter congratulated us, but Madame Loiselier rebuffed her with a turn of the back. Raised voices from the hall proved to belong to Uncle Romain and Aunt Pé in a scuffle with Thiessé Galimard and Colonel Corrue that escalated to pushes between the men and others breaking them up. I never saw Aunt Mirabelle and think she may have darted out to avoid any interrogation. I figured she would tell anyone who asked, weeks or months later, that she had hurried out to return to Uncle Roul's side.

We followed Lady Victorine to the hall, her concern over her husband and son piqued. By the time we arrived, the scuffle was ending as Uncle Romain huffed off down the hall, shooing away a grasping Aunt Pé. Thiessé Galimard, cooling down, smoothed his suitcoat and tie. Lord Galimard and the Colonel were encouraging him to collect himself and to return to the ballroom. Uncle Gilbert entered the hall, as did Jeuffine, grabbing his arm from behind. When he turned at the touch, he was surprised to see Jeuffine. I heard her ask him if he wouldn't mind stopping by her place after the ball to help her lug up some bottles of her uncle's *hydromel*, now that Roul was away. She did not release his arm, which he stared at for at least five seconds before looking again at her face, at her anxious expectation of the answer she wanted.

"I—I would be happy—" stammered Uncle Gilbert. "I don't know," he said, dropping his arm to his side, out of her grasp.

She reached gently for his bicep and held it, awaiting the affirmation she craved. Aunt Laure stepped into the hall and met Aunt Pé, who was in tears, but when she espied her husband with Jeuffine's hand on him, she redirected her attention to him, scurrying over. I don't know if Lady Victorine predicted what was to ensue, but she neared my sister and me and eased us toward the wall. We stood between her and Lady Léontine but out of earshot of Aunt Laure and Jeuffine, who were going at it in whispers. The chatter and music and clinks of the party overpowered the raising voice of Aunt Laure and the scratchy screeches of Aunt Pé coming to her aid. Jeuffine maintained a doll-like smile as she spoke, looking more at Uncle Gilbert than at the women. When Aunt Laure ripped her hand off her husband's arm, Jeuffine's smile straightened, and when Aunt Laure yelled in her face something about what Jeuffine might do with her bottles of *hydromel*, Jeuffine shoved Aunt Laure. Aunt Laure grabbed the arms that shoved her, and Aunt Pé screeched again as she clutched both women's arm; I couldn't tell if she was trying to end the altercation or to join in. Uncle Gilbert, red-faced, did all he could not to shout at them but was clearly commanding them to cease, which they did not do.

Lady Victorine placed a hand around my shoulder and tucked us a step back from the spectacle.

"I have encountered unfortunate rivalries such as these before," Lady Victorine said to Lady Léontine, "but for the first time in my life, I don't know who I want to lose more."

"Is it too indelicate to wish that they all three beat each other to a pulp?" inquired Lady Léontine.

Not well into the dancing after the ceremony, Madeleine-Grace and I thanked the Countess once more and departed. As I stepped into the main hall, I looked back into the ballroom and saw Wischard watching me leave. I lifted my arm to wave to him, and this time, without his mother to hold his arm down, he did not lift his. We had publicly insulted his mother. I don't know that he could forgive that. I lowered my arm, turned to the hall, and escorted Madeleine-Grace to the front entrance. We sat with the porters on the entrance steps as vehicles began to line the drive under the twinkling stars on the outskirts of Etretat-au-Delà.

Monsieur Vauquelin's auto we found in a line of others along the pebbled drive of the Countess's manor after an hour of waiting, and we hopped in with renewed elation over our victory and unity. I did not see Jeuffine approach the vehicle and started when she knocked on the driver's side window.

"May I impose on you, Monsieur, the request of a ride back to the *falaises*?" she asked, resting crossed arms at the foot of the window as she crouched to his eye level.

Widened eyes and an opened mouth when he glanced at us revealed his reluctance, but his virtue won. "We have room, yes."

I don't know that she heard his response, for she noticed Uncle Gilbert step onto the drive from the front steps. Standing alone, he pulled out a cigarette and tapped a porter's shoulder for a light. "I will make other arrangements," Jeuffine said to Monsieur Vauquelin without tearing her eyes off my uncle. "Gilbert Toutrein will drive me."

As Mademoiselle des Gervais sauntered toward my uncle, Monsieur Vauquelin quickly pulled out, grateful to have us to himself. We did not wish to recount the evening's events until Monsieur Vauquelin assured us our aunt had recovered. He explained that he had spent the past few hours with her, having found her out of sorts and overly distraught. After they talked, she calmed a little.

"I have given her a good reason to feel less ill at ease," he said. "I cannot explain it all to you now, but you will know soon."

Of course, I wondered what he could have told her to pull her from such a state of distress, but with no hints on that topic, he continued to explain that she still felt worn down by all that had transpired and would do the unthinkable: she would rest. She had promised him this and had been lying down when he left to retrieve us. This, too, brought us comfort concerning her well-being. He concluded that we should know more in the morning.

We arrived at the house before the others, and with Aunt Adèle nowhere to be found, prayed in the foyer before the statue with Monsieur Vauquelin and headed straight to bed. Thanks to Aunt Adèle's expert tailoring, the suit made for easy movements; however, to be out of the suit felt good, and the warm bursts of air from the bedroom window I had opened felt good after having been constricted. I hopped into bed, waiting for Madeleine-Grace, who was brushing her hair before the bathroom mirror.

Lights out, as she lay beside me, she asked, "Do you think Maman and Papa are angry with us?"

"No," I replied confidently. "I think they were helping us."

I fell asleep for the last time on that bed—the childhood bed of my mother, the summer bed of my parents' early marriage, the bereft bed of our first summer without them. I awoke in the middle of the night to a thud or a crash and some shouting as I had other nights here, and tried to force myself back to sleep. I knew they had returned. As I drifted, I heard footsteps in the hall near our room and a door clicking shut. Unconcerned about fallout from the ball, suspecting my aunts and uncles would argue themselves to oblivion and to sleep like any other night, I fluffed the sheets, adjusted my head on the pillow, and sunk into sleep.

CHAPITRE 9

Eeriness and sickness still hover with my memory of the next morning. I woke up about the same time as Madeleine-Grace, and my first thought propelled me from the bed: to seek Monsieur Vauquelin, perhaps on the bench outside, surrounded by an upturned, trampled flowerbed. He had promised to tell us something important this morning. If the aroma of freshly brewed coffee invited me downstairs, I would know that Aunt Adèle, up already, had surely seen him in. As we headed down the stairs, I smelled no coffee, and entered the main hall to find Uncle Romain pacing in the *salle-en-arrière* and Aunt Mirabelle, who had heard us, stepping out of the kitchen. Uncle Romain stopped at the couch when he saw us, and I locked my gaze on the bench outside the window behind him. The bench was empty.

Uncle Romain did not greet us, fixing a questioning stare on us. Certainly, he blamed us for so much already that our victory last night and Madeleine-Grace's incisive words did not position us on any firmer ground with him. If we had in any way been the cause of the fray we saw him in at the Countess's, he surely would hold it against us this morning. My agenda, however, prioritized seeking Aunt Adèle and Monsieur Vauquelin, so I said good-morning to him and Aunt Mirabelle and pivoted to check the kitchen.

"She's not in there," Uncle Romain said. "Come in here a moment."

We hesitantly stepped through the *salle-en-arrière* to sit on the couch while he took a chair. Aunt Mirabelle followed us in silence, standing at the arm of Uncle Romain's chair.

"We are taking you to Paris this morning," Uncle Romain said. "You must pack immediately. Do not disturb the others. We will leave immediately. Your Aunt Adèle is no longer here."

I looked at Madeleine-Grace who looked at me, both of our eyes sharing the discomfort of the moment, of our uncle's pronouncements and disclosure.

"Go," he said. "You must pack now."

"Where is Aunt Adèle?" I asked.

He looked at Aunt Mirabelle. After a few seconds, she nodded to him, as if giving him permission to divulge something secretive, something sensitive. He reached inside his shirt pocket and pulled out a folded piece of paper.

"She left this note," he said, brandishing it before us. "She has informed us that she left last night for the convent. She will not be returning."

Madeleine-Grace and I, fully perplexed and stunned, sat without words, as if our throats and vocal cords had been suspended on Aunt Adèle's clotheslines with the sheets, smote by warm winds as they dried. My first conclusion was that I had caused this, that she suspected me of a terrible violation of her trust. Had the misunderstanding that I had accidentally knocked the hot iron onto Madeleine-Grace's dress and not admitted to it been seen as such a betrayal that she left without a parting word?

"You must go pack now," he said, rising and walking to the picture window.

"Which convent?" asked Madeleine-Grace, struggling to voice the question.

"She did not say," he said. "Probably somewhere in Liguria."

"Did she say anything before she left?" I asked.

"We did not see—." I could not tell if he was searching for the right words or scrambling for something to say, but from the way his eyes shifted and looked at the note, I considered his behavior suspicious. "We found this note here last night. That's all. She had already left by the time we found it. Read it for yourself if you'd like."

He opened it, and I walked over to him to take it, walking it back to Madeleine-Grace at the couch. I lowered it so that we could both read.

With a neat hand and in dark blue ink, the note contained only the following: "I have chosen to devote my life to God and leave this evening for the convent. Please do not try to find me. I think you will know this has been a decision put off too long already. –Adèle."

Uncle Romain walked to me and removed the note from my hand, folding it in half and replacing it in his shirt pocket. Then he returned to the window, staring at the destroyed herb and flower islands. After a minute of silence, he turned to us. "Well? There you have it. She has left, and now we must bring you to Paris for your Grand-mère and Grand-père Avery to claim you."

"What about Monsieur Vauquelin?" I asked. I was sure he had been here last night, perhaps unaware that Aunt Adèle was even gone when we returned. He and Aunt Adèle had talked during the children's ball. I couldn't fathom how she could have reached this decision so quickly and acted on it in the short time it took for him to drive to the Countess's manor to pick us up and return with us here.

"What of him?" Uncle Romain asked, a disdain evident in his tone. "Your aunt has made her decision. And so have we. You are to return to Paris at once and remain there until your American grandparents bring you back where you belong—overseas."

They refused to entertain any further questions, not that Aunt Mirabelle had been answering any. She served solely as a chaperone of sorts, watching us pack, making sure the others were sleeping, and even blocking the staircase to the attic when I tried to sneak up to delve into Aunt Adèle's things, hoping for a clue about which convent she chose, or why she chose to leave. I was prohibited from doing so. While Uncle Romain waited in the driver's seat to start the car, loaded with our trunks, Aunt Mirabelle sat next to him for the ride, expecting straightaway to visit Uncle Roul in hospital in Paris. Outside the car, I took a last look at the front façade of the summer house, deprived of the opportunity to race one more time to the alabaster cliffs, to imagine myself on the *paquebot* leaving port on its voyage to America, to peer at the horizon where the blue sky met the blue water in a heavenly kiss. We didn't stop for two minutes of *café*. None of our cousins was roused to see us off. We slid into the backseat and embarked on a sun-flooded ride whose confusion-drenched silence outdid all the others.

We were forbidden to mention to anyone, above all to Grandma'Maud, that Aunt Adèle had joined a convent. News of the permanent decision and absence would be too devastating to her mother. Instead, they planned to tell her that an inability to accept her mistake of leaving the hot iron on Madeleine-Grace's dress triggered a breakdown, that she ran away to recover in a convent somewhere for the rest of the summer. Later they would tell Grandma'Maud that Aunt Adèle decided to stay in the convent. Any deviation from this story, we were told, would bring undue pain to Grandma'Maud. The absence of Aunt Adèle still necessitated our removal.

When we arrived in Paris, Uncle Romain broke the news of Aunt Adèle's departure to Grandma'Maud, Aunt Melisende, and Uncle Ferdinand, all of whom believed the tale with reluctance. As their sobs echoed through the flat, Uncle Romain, without a mere offering of consolation, left to drive Aunt Mirabelle to the hospital before returning, himself, to Etretat-au-Delà without further stay in Paris. A reminder to them of Uncle Roul's tragedy, Madeleine-Grace and I were left by Borbála and Bertille to wait alone in the sitting room outside Grandma'Maud's bedroom, to suffer the unending sound of her sobs.

Somehow, I can't be sure, but I think we remained at the Paris flat with Grandma'Maud for two days before Grand-mère Armance arrived for us. Devastation seemed to emanate from the walls those few days, the first few of which were enshrouded in silence, even between Madeleine-Grace and me, except for the onslaughts of weeping wont to burst forth from Grandma'Maud's bedroom. She did not leave the bedroom the whole time we were there.

Scenarios of Aunt Adèle's departure circled in my head until I grew dizzy from them, only to pick up with their dizzying hours later. I imagined a tender conversation between her and Monsieur Vauquelin, and then, after he left, a snap not unlike Grandma'Maud's—or the kind to which Aunt Adèle, herself, had succumbed when she tore through the herbs and flowers—that compelled her to scribble the note and abscond for the station. I imagined her knowing all along she was leaving for the convent and lying to Monsieur Vauquelin so that he would not convince her to stay or go so far as to propose marriage. I imagined that Aunt Adèle had been truthful with Monsieur Vauquelin about her intentions to enter religious life, and when he came to retrieve us from the children's ball, he contrived to lie to us, hoping yet to change her mind, or perhaps he was too devastated to reveal what he had just learned.

In one of our few conversations, Madeleine-Grace expressed frustration over Aunt Adèle's note, certain it should have been longer, offered more explanation, and addressed, if anyone, the two of us. In fact, Madeleine-Grace and I agreed that it would have been more like Aunt Adèle to leave us a personal note, one we should find on our pillowcase or on top of the trunk. So convinced of this course of action as likely of Aunt Adèle, we rummaged through the clothing in the trunk to seek out such a personal letter in our pockets or between the folds of a shirt. We found no such letter.

Aunt Melisende and Uncle Ferdinand vowed to track down Aunt Adèle, at least to pay her a visit to request further explanation; Aunt Melisende would demand it of the Mother Superior. She did not, however, find the departure in character and planned to visit with Lady

Victorine on her way to Fécamp. Perhaps Aunt Adèle had revealed something to her. Perhaps Lady Victorine would hear of something from someone in Etretat-au-Delà—of Aunt Adèle passing through the night, onto which train she had boarded, or something of the sort. All signs had indicated to Aunt Melisende late-in-life marriage with Alban Vauquelin, but the decision to enter the convent was still not that far off base. How she left, however, was, and Aunt Melisende assigned herself the role of detective.

While sadness certainly stuck to the late July heat those last few days in Paris, two good things came of our stay there. The first was that, through time spent with Grandma'Maud, I was able to express my sorrow for having been carted back to the summer house after Uncle Roul's accident.

"You are like your mother to be concerned about that," she said affectionately to me, dipping her hand in a pile of cut fabric strips. "So like your mother that I know you would not have left me here. You are a child. You had to go where you were taken, and my sister tells me they feared for your well-being after such a trauma. The sea air would be better for you. I'm sure she was right."

In her understanding, she likened me to my mother. I know that to Grandma'Maud such a likening rose to the pinnacle of compliments. I wished, after I was sure she did not hate me or feel deserted by me, that Madeleine Grace and I could play the *tourdion* for her, but no one's spirits soared to the low altitudes of wishing even for a little cheer. The hours passed in continued grieving and vexation. Even the request by Madeleine-Grace to visit Uncle Roul in hospital was met with a negative wave of the finger and the words, "That might not be a good idea," from Aunt Melisende. We stayed in the flat morning to night.

The other good thing to happen during these few days in Paris took place only after an incident first brought more angst to the family. The day we reunited with our American grandmother but hours before she arrived at the flat, Aunt Laure and Uncle Gilbert had arrived, Wischard and little Laure with them. Their late morning arrival heralded upheaval.

I don't know much beyond sitting at the piano with Madeleine-Grace with the keys exposed, too inhibited and uninterested to play a note. While Aunt Laure and Uncle Gilbert visited with Grandma'Maud and Aunt Melisende in the bedroom, Wischard and an exceptionally groggy little Laure stepped into the *grand salon*, saw us at the piano, and exited. A short while later, we heard hollering from upstairs, followed by Grandma'Maud shouting "No!" through convulsions of sobs.

Not until observing an altercation between Aunt Melisende and Aunt Laure had we learned the cause of the tumult. Apparently, Aunt Laure announced outright to Grandma'Maud that she had been the one to stab Uncle Roul with the shears, that it had not been a self-inflicted accident, that her hand in such an act verified her insanity because she had done it on purpose whether or not she remembered doing so. Aunt Melisende, furious over the unearthing of the secret, reviled her niece in the *petit salon* in front of Wischard and little Laure. Madeleine-Grace and I observed surreptitiously at the door.

"It was unnecessary," insisted Aunt Melisende with adamancy emanating from her core.

"It was indeed necessary," Aunt Laure countered. "She can't go on thinking she's equipped with sanity. She tried to murder my brother. She should at least know about it!"

"She was catatonic. The doctors have said it! You know this! You have seen this! She did not even know Roul was beside her when she came out of her state. Your own son can verify that."

Aunt Laure looked at Wischard, and then rattled back to Aunt Melisende, "He does not know what he saw! She did it on purpose! She tried to kill Roul because she is crazy, and she might try to kill me!"

"I might try to kill you if you keep this up," said Aunt Melisende.

"Because you are as crazy as she!"

"Yes, anyone who does not see the world as Laure Toutrein is crazy, even her own mother. Is Wischard crazy? Is Ellande crazy? How about Bertille? They all saw the same thing and reported that she was not herself and did not realize Roul was at her side. Everyone is crazy because you want to find a reason—even if you have to bend the truth—to label your mother crazy and be right about it."

"I am right about it."

"You would persist with this, even at the expense of your own son's reputation?"

She looked at Wischard again. "He is a boy, and boys sometimes lie. Grandma'Maud put him up to it!"

"No, she did not say anything to us. She was not herself!" Wischard said.

"Wischard, leave at once!" Aunt Laure snapped, but he did not leave. "I know the truth!"

Aunt Melisende stepped close to Aunt Laure, and Aunt Laure stepped backward toward her husband. He was so close already that she could not retract far.

Trying to contain an anger dangerously nearing the surface, like lava splattering before erupting through the mouth of Vesuvius, Aunt Melisende said, "I know a truth, too, Laure. You did this because you want to cut your mother from your life and need, at anyone's expense, to justify it. What's more is that you told your mother what really happened out of spite, not because of some moral conviction that she must know she is insane, not because it was the right thing to do. You did it to hurt her, and that makes you the crazy one, contriving ways of attacking the mother who has been so good to you for years, throwing in her face her generosity to you at every opportunity."

"Good to me? She knows nothing of being a good mother!" screamed Aunt Laure.

Aunt Melisende slapped her across the face with a thick, open hand. Aunt Laure fell into her husband, who stumbled backward before regaining his balance with his wife in his arms.

"That's enough!" Uncle Gilbert shouted. "Get out!"

"What would you know of being a good mother? You refuse to be anything like the good ones, so what do you know?" Aunt Melisende stepped away, her arms shaking at her side. "I thought you were the crazy one to hurt your mother so cold-heartedly, just this morning and countless times before, but now I see something. That's not just crazy. It's wicked! You, my pathetic, bratty niece, are a monster!"

"That's enough!" Uncle Gilbert repeated.

She exited the room, oblivious to Madeleine-Grace and me as she passed and shaking all the way down the hall. Aunt Laure cried and pounded on Uncle Gilbert's chest, and Wischard and little Laure receded to the wall, both of them crying, as well.

This altercation did not comprise the good to which I was referring. Before they left the flat—their home—to spend the night elsewhere, Wischard found me seated on the floor in the *grand salon*, my back against the paneled wall containing the cabinets of sheet music. To my surprise, he sat beside me. Madeleine-Grace had fallen asleep in a large armchair near the divan.

"I know you are angry with us," I said to Wischard.

He didn't say anything for a while, inciting my curiosity over his visit, his nearness to me, and I suspected he might be thinking of the words to vituperate me.

"I am not angry with you anymore," he said at last. I wanted to feel relief, but my mind would not let me. I could hear him saying something more like, "but I still detest you." He had no such addendum.

In the absence of an explanation from him, I said, "I'm glad. I'd hate for you to stay angry at me forever. And now we're supposed to go back to America, and I won't see you again this summer."

"You're going back? How come?"

"Because your mother and everyone else do not want us here anymore, and without Aunt Adèle—." It was hard to believe so much of our fate depended on her, and she, too, had left.

"I'm sorry my mother won't let us play and doesn't like you and Madeleine-Grace or your par—. But I wish you could stay," Wischard said. He didn't know what to say and was fumbling for words. I suspected he wished everything were back to normal between us, as did I, but so much had changed around us.

"Wischard, why aren't you angry with me anymore?" I asked. "We didn't speak well of your parents at the children's ball. I'm sorry, though."

"I'm angry at my mother now. It's hard to be angry at you when I might be angry at her for the same reasons you and Madeleine-Grace are." He gulped, no doubt thinking on the quarrel between his mother and Aunt Melisende. "She didn't tell the truth. If only she had told Grandma'Maud that stabbing Uncle Roul was a terrible accident, but she didn't. She told Grandma'Maud that she had stabbed Uncle Roul on purpose and, because she's crazy, had forgotten or blocked it out. We saw it, though. She didn't know she was doing it. She was just swinging the shears." He started to get choked up as he spoke.

"I know, Wischard. Grandma'Maud has done nothing but love us— and our parents. She would never try to kill her own son on purpose," I said, trying to corroborate his concept of her.

"She has lost too many as it is," he said.

He could not know how much these words stung.

"Uncle Romain says he doesn't want you back at the summer house, but if you come again, don't go into Maman's room, okay?" Wischard said. It looked as if, in his silence, he had been prodding himself to bring this up.

"Why not?" I asked.

"Not even my sister has seen. She has slept more than me since the ball. Sleeps and sleeps. I'm glad she hasn't gone into Maman's room, and if you return, you mustn't either."

"Why not?" I asked again.

"Last night, she threw things everywhere. She tore the sheets and tried to tear a blanket. She broke many things, including the mirror, the lamps, vases—." He gulped. "Don't ever look through the keyhole, okay? Ellande, do you ever see your mother do these things?"

I knew that when he said "these things," he wasn't referring only to the destruction that had apparently happened last night, but also to the outbursts at the dinner table and the bolts for the cliffs. At the prompting of this question, I considered that I had never seen my mother behave anything other than composed—playful at times—but refined always. Only now did it occur to me that one reason this summer felt so different from the others wasn't solely the absence of my parents, but the absence of the role they had played in my life. Like Notre Dame towering protectively over "the cradle" of Paris, my mother and my father had been shielding us. Aunt Melisende had tried to explain this to us at the summer house. My mother shielded us from all the unpleasantness of the world— the discord within her own family, the malice with which our aunts, uncles, and cousins regarded us, the baseness of human nature—and armed us with virtue, with a work ethic, and with noble and endearing traditions. She spent her life ensuring our protection.

That explained why this summer had been so revelatory. It wasn't because I had reached a certain age when my eyes had to be opened; that would have occurred along the course of my life in its inevitable ways even if my parents had been allowed to accompany me through more of this life. My aunts and uncles made no effort to protect me, to shield me, as they made no effort to protect, to shield, their own children, including from the worst of themselves. Was it erroneous for me to believe, had my parents been here this summer, that the quarrels I never remembered before now would not have overtly erupted at many a dinner, that awareness of Uncle Roul's dalliances would not have sneaked into our purview or made our eyes bulge in disbelief at the sight of them, that encounters with naked lovers in an orchard would not have transpired to disturb us? How many occurrences of this summer would have glossed by or been reasoned away or entirely avoided had we been huddled behind our parents by their own hands?

Wischard, more mischievous than I but possessing the same potential for sustained innocence, did not have the same protection for himself, it seemed. While Uncle Gilbert may have, at times, protected his children from their mother, their mother negated any attempt at buffering them when she carelessly reacted with latent anger and malignity. I had to wonder what precipitated Aunt Laure's violence to her room last night, but my thoughts clung more so to my new realization.

"No," I said at last. "I have never seen my mother behave that way."

Wischard looked down, his lips drooping, his chin hanging. I did not give him the answer for which he must have been hoping, and while I took pride in my mother's delineation from his, I felt bad that I could not commiserate with him in the empathetic way he craved.

"Good," he said, looking up. "I don't care what my mother says about your mother. I think it's better if you don't see it."

We sat in silence for another fifteen minutes before he spoke again, asking me why I preferred to sit against the wall with the molding jutting into my back.

"Grandma'Maud's piano music is in here, and so are some of my mother's old pieces. I feel good sitting by them," I said.

"Well, do you think you might feel good sitting on the couch, too? My back hurts!" he whispered loudly, bouncing to his feet and pulling me up by the arm. We walked to the couch and moments before plopping down, Wischard thought better of it. "Maybe this isn't the best place to sit after all. Let's find a chair."

We were thinking the same thing—an unfortunate image and memory we both didn't fully understand manifesting in our mind—and we started laughing. I hadn't laughed in days. Wischard was always good for that. And more importantly to me, we had reconciled.

Our American grandmother arrived as Aunt Laure was leaving with her family, and the last and only thing she, feigning officiousness, said to them was, "We will be grateful to know you are taking those two back with you. Please make it soon."

Soon it was. Grand-mère Armance arrived alone, my grandfather having left for America two weeks ago. She arrived perplexed and tremendously concerned over the sudden change in an itinerary comprised of nothing more than a summer spent between the coastal house and the city flat. A subdued summer stay from mid-June to September was coming to an end in mid-July.

We learned that my American grandparents, after relinquishing our custody to the care of the Semperrins, had moved on to Le Havre for a visit with Aunt Melisende and Uncle Ferdinand and then to London to see cousins. Grand-père Guarin left for America to tie up loose ends, settle our parents' affairs, and arrange for our care beginning in September while Grand-mère Armance tended to similar issues here in Europe. She had only two weeks ago traveled to Calais to spend several weeks with relatives there. She was supposed to have spent another week there before heading to Paris for several weeks and finally to Normandie, meeting us at the summer house before our voyage home.

And Grand-père Guarin was to have returned to Europe by then so that Grand-mère Armance would not have to travel with us alone. But her time in Calais was intercepted by the urgency of claiming us in Paris.

Aunt Melisende explained all, swearing Grand-mère Armance to secrecy about what Wischard and I had witnessed, knowing well that Aunt Laure might play the Ezra Pound and broadcast indiscriminately; "Laure's consequences for making public her thoughts would not be the same as Pound's, unfortunately," she said, piquing Grand-mère Armance's wonderment about my aunt. Grand-mère Armance listened without word, uncharacteristically stunned.

She did ask some questions and then asked to see Grandma'Maud, who welcomed her tearfully into her bedside embrace. They talked for several hours, mostly about our parents, but also about Madeleine-Grace and me. We sat in the sitting room listening as they talked. Grand-mère Armance's presence distracted Grandma'Maud from the pain of Aunt Laure's accusation.

We said our good-byes to Aunt Melisende, Uncle Ferdinand, and Grandma'Maud the following afternoon. The image of Grandma'Maud when we parted evoked the image of Aunt Adèle standing in the pile of felled flowers, smeared and teary and exhausted, but more so, the image of the flowers themselves, cast to the ground, one moment reaching for the sun in the fullness of aromatic life, the next strangled, ripped, and thrown.

Marguerin and Jules were kind enough to drive us from Paris to Le Havre where we waited two days until Grand-père Guarin arrived. The poor man, tired from travel, required rest before making the long voyage home.

While in Le Havre, we strolled La Rue de Paris toward La Place Gambetta one afternoon in place of our *mésienne*. Grand-père Guarin, worn as he was from travel, felt sated with sleep and treasured every step on land, especially before boarding again for a similar journey. We passed a kiosk on our walk to see the newly constructed Eglise Saint Joseph, and Grand-mère Armance told us to pick a few magazines each. I thought of the American magazines I had left on the bench in the flower island, of Uncle Roul insisting on sitting for dinner instead of bringing them in, of Aunt Adèle peeling their soggy pages from the bench after the rain. I recalled my trepidation over requesting new ones, sure that the mention of the magazines would make Aunt Adèle think less of me despite the regret I felt for her having to clean up after me and for having been careless with my belongings. Anxiety about that episode had settled within me the length of the summer, keeping me from ditching the guilt as if it were a wheelbarrow of metal pellets that had been poured into me. Standing before the magazine stand in Le Havre with no Aunt Adèle to account to, as the image of her rifting the disintegrating pages and scraping the bench replayed in my mind's eye, it dawned on me why such a menial mistake had preoccupied me, how pangs of guilt managed to wound me even now: to have been so irresponsible made me feel as if I were too much like *them*.

On board the *paquebot*, we occupied the sullen journey with little more than reading, eating, thinking, and praying. Certainly, some conversations amongst ourselves and with fellow passengers punctuated the extensive boredom, but our spirits were so low that no conversation satisfied in the least. Discussions with our grandparents about our arrangements I dreaded, a future of normalcy without our parents an impossibility.

Over a week on the *paquebot*, despite hours of observing drinks being made and sipped in the Eau de Vie Room and plenty of dozing on the *chaises longues* lining the Promenade à Tribord, had us longing for disembarkment, which finally took place in early August in New York. A train from New York transported us to Chicago, and my father's best friend in the States, Marcel Royce, drove us from the city to the suburbs. At long last, we entered the familiarity of our River Forest house. Entrance into our house from our first steps stirred mourning and loss as if one were honey and the other hot tea, only not so soothing. Although I had lived in the house for two months after my parents' accident, I expected them there, longed for a glimpse of them somewhere, wanted them to be making cocktails in the kitchen and tapping their foot in the living room. We arrived during dusk, I took a shower, and I retired to my own bed in my own room alone without a bite to eat, crying myself to sleep. When I woke up late the next morning, Madeleine-Grace was asleep in my bed.

We lived from then on in the same house with my grandparents. They kept their place in the city, letting quarters to the college student son of Monsieur Royce and later an Avery cousin from London seeking new opportunities in the States. There had been much concern over raising us in the River Forest house, a place riddled with memories of our parents; those espousing these views favored distancing us from associations of our trauma. I'm glad our grandparents kept us in this house, in this neighborhood, helping us realize the path our parents had charted for us.

I finished grade school and then continued to the Catholic high school where boys from Chicago and nearby suburbs attended. My friends Jimmy and Jack came here with me. After grade school, Madeleine-Grace attended the local all-girl Catholic high school. Both high schools were Dominican, like the college our mother had attended in River Forest.

Grand-mère and Grand-père Avery have raised us well. They have not been as attentive to us as our parents, but have been present, offered sage advice time and time again, nourished us with countless delicious meals and drinks, listened to us as we conferred with them in word and in silence, shared their customs, language, life, and love without bound. In English, French, and even a little Cauchois have we verbalized our thoughts; trace indications of patois Normand have often infiltrated our interactions, especially when at a loss for English words. Our grandparents have celebrated all the American holidays with us they had come to know before our first steps on this earth, and encouraged maintaining French holidays and customs, like tacking fish on each other's back for Poisson d'Avril, serving roast veal on Ascension, resting blessed boxwood on the graves of loved ones on Palm Sunday, and ceremoniously placing the *tréfouet*, the Yule log, sprinkled with bay leaves and boxwood, in the fireplace on Christmas Eve. Thanks-Giving that first November after our return had Madeleine-Grace and me reflecting on Aunt Adèle and Monsieur Vauquelin, wishing that they could have joined us in making cranberry walnut cocktails and adhering a parsley leaf to every roll in egg wash and salt before baking. Aunt Adèle had been so excited—intent, really—on coming for Thanks-Giving that her decision to become a nun slashed at my thin wisps of understanding all the more. She must have felt she was sacrificing so much.

We were French in ancestry but followed American customs beyond those associated with holidays. After Mass on the first Sunday of every month, plus Mothers' Day and Fathers' Day, our grandparents escorted us to our parents' gravesite where we left flowers and said prayers. The days neither Madeleine-Grace nor I became emotional tended to be the days our grandparents cried the most. Every visit reminded me that not only *we* had lost our parents but *they* had lost their children. Some Sundays after our visit, Madeleine-Grace asked me to walk her to what our mother called "The Cloister Walk" of Rosary College a few blocks from our house. I sat in the grassy common before the cloister while my sister sauntered back and forth along the Cloister Walk. She imagined my mother to have made the walk on pleasant spring and autumn days while attending college. Mere acts like these brought them closer to us, or made us feel closer to them.

To the best of my ability, I lived up to my vow in Monsieur Vauquelin's car that day he drove us to the children's ball. I looked after my sister as my parents would have wanted, and did my best to protect her, not that she usually needed it. One time, when I was a junior in high school, growing suspicious of the intentions of Luke Haskins who I noticed was latching on to my sister with a keen intensity, I decided to follow them to the field alongside the library. It was a fall day with leaves of red and yellow and brown covering much of the tree-lined perimeter of the field. They were having a leaf fight with their friends, perhaps one not dissimilar to Uncle Ferdinand's as a kid on L'Ile aux Cygnes. Luke was new, so we didn't know much about him yet, further piquing my suspicions. Unaware of my presence, lo and behold, Luke walked my sister away from the fold of friends to the wall of the library and swooped in for a kiss. Poor Madeleine-Grace—she had no idea that was coming or what it meant or how to react other than to push him in the chest, away from her face. He moved in again, and Madeleine-Grace bumped her head on the hard, exterior wall, retracting from him as he planted a kiss on her lips and squeezed her waist with his arms, a hold he had on her for only a second thanks to the speedy arrival of her older brother. I decked him, levelling him in the grass. When he got to his feet with a bloody nose, shifting his eyes to scope out an escape route, I decked him again. His being a year younger than me, albeit two years older than my sister, didn't matter to me.

I walked Madeleine-Grace home. She was shaking like a single cornflower rustled by a forceful wind. We didn't talk for the first block home as I think she was trying to make some sort of sense of what had just happened. Then she said, "Thanks. I didn't even know you were there."

It made me think of God, so I chuckled. Then I said, "You don't know when you're going to need me. You can admit you're happy I'm here to protect you."

"I don't need you all the time," she said, which has always been true. In all honesty, I have needed her more than she has needed me, and she has come through without my requesting.

"I know you don't," I said. Then in jest, I said, without meaning blasphemy, "Think of me like God. You don't need me all the time, but it's nice to know I'm there."

She responded, "I will think of you like that, but that's not how I think of God. I do need God all the time, and knowing He's there is still great."

Her understandings of these things—and her teaching me something so important through them—made another conversation we had not seem so outlandish.

The August one year after our return from France and weeks before I started high school, we received word that Grandma'Maud had passed. Aunt Melisende, who had been corresponding with my grandparents and us, informed us in a letter. My grandparents here did not think a return to France a good decision and kept us in Chicago. Madeleine-Grace and I, who always prayed for her, continued to pray here. I suspected she had many answers now about her children and saw the events of her life as they really played out, an affirmation that the ways in which her children had tried to convince her she was crazy had been nothing short of malicious stratagems; her own version of things had often been the correct version, the true one.

Through these letters we learned other things about those in France, as well. Aunt Melisende often sent tidings of Marguerin and Jules, and in one letter, we clasped our hands with excitement over news that Marguerin had entered the seminary. His was not the only vocation, however, as a few years later, Maclou Galimard announced his intention to join a monastery, which, had he not married my sister, was an inevitability. He made the announcement days before the death of his grandmother, Lady Victorine, supposedly elongating her life by three joyful days despite the pain and listlessness of slow heart failure. Aunt Melisende refused contact with the Semperrins outside of our branch, so she had no news for us about them, and she did not pursue contact with Monsieur Vauquelin as much as I wished she had, for I would have liked to hear about him and his *marais*.

Madeleine-Grace and I wondered about him and, while we speculated about whether or not Uncle Roul held the wound on his side every day and if young Roul married Henriette Loiselier and such things, we cared more about what became of Franchinot La Ripleure, the future keeper of the *écluse*, the enchanted lock, and if the Countess had sent us an invitation to the following children's ball. Of course, none of our other aunts and uncles nor our cousins contacted us. Using the summer house address, I had emboldened myself to write Wischard once, a year after our return to the States, but never heard back. Worse than not knowing of any of these persons or events was not hearing from Aunt Adèle. We had to resign ourselves to the realities of her vows, her life-long seclusion, her wish to have contact with no one in the outside world, including us.

We have not visited the Etretat-au-Delà house or the Paris flat since that summer, nor have we traveled anywhere in Europe. The truth that neither Madeleine-Grace nor I wanted to go back did not feel strange to either of us. I wonder if I ever will return.

While in my junior year of high school, I experienced a decline, one that was hard to express or define because it pertained to my emotional state. Some sort of delayed grief, or a strong resurgence of it, coupled with a new-forming guilt over my summer in Etretat-au-Delà, surfaced, and my French teacher, Père Martin, had noticed a gloomy change in my presence. I had taken French in high school to continue mastering the language and to read texts to which I had never been exposed, but my teacher was grateful to reap the benefits of a near-native, heritage speaker and my understanding of French culture, at least as it had experienced Normandie. While I was glad to be of help and to continue learning so much through stories and poetry, I came to appreciate the class for the teacher who not only taught the language but perceptively guided me. A Dominican Friar, Père Martin became a confidant, and I shared with him what had happened to my parents and the events of the summer thereafter. He listened, talked to me about these things, and sometimes talked me through them.

His concern compelled him to inform my grandparents as my guardians about my bout of depression, suggesting a counselor; however, his words of insight and his allowing me to share with him, I convinced my grandparents, sufficed. The first time I opened up to him had been after school on a Friday in his classroom. The meeting had ended in tears, and he walked me home, imparting to my grandmother what had happened. When I suggested to her that I continue talking to him, she invited him to the house where he and I spoke in private in our living room after school. He was gracious to devote three visits to me, and after each one, my grandparents treated him to a true French delight: a glass of *calvados* before his departure for the Priory.

On one of his visits, I voiced a question rhetorically as it came to my mind. Particularly troubled about Aunt Laure's behavior, I said, "I am conflicted because my mother and my Aunt Adèle had had such different experiences with their parents than my Uncle Romain, Uncle Roul, and Aunt Laure. Could my Grandma'Maud have been that drastically different a mother to my mother and Aunt Adèle than she had been to the others?"

Père Martin said that in his estimation, from everything I had shared and what he knew of parenting, some children, through no fault of the parents, embrace a different lifestyle and values from those modeled by their parents. As he explained his views, he said, "Your grandmother had not been unreasonable in her expectations of her children as far as I can see or possibly know, but it sounds as if three of her children rebelled against having to work, and indeed, against any value that called them to do more and to be more. It seems to me your Aunt Laure had to present her mother as irrational, overly demanding, too exacting, and all-out insane in order to cast herself a victim, unable to meet impossible standards imposed on her. Really, her mother's standards were not so out of line as your mother and Aunt Adèle would attest. Your Aunt Laure and the others, they were upset their mother caught everything— she saw all—because that meant she saw them not working, their laziness, their self-absorption. She saw right through to your mother and father and Aunt Adèle, too, but what she saw in them was good, so they had no objections to her keen observance of them."

His insight helped me, and in thinking through that summer by juxtaposing the events to Père Martin's insight with the distance of several years, I emerged from my depression and experienced a newfound understanding of myself and the other participants of that summer. I realized something in particular had come to bother me. They made indecency so casual: casual relationships without truly committing, without stitching any kind of seam or real bond, casual lazing while enjoying the work that pummeled the few responsible, casual lying, especially to themselves about themselves. Of what must they have convinced themselves to be able to justify it and to keep it up for a lifetime?

The summer after junior year, I had my friends over for dinner. We hung out most of the time anyway, but this evening, I wanted to do something special. Grand-mère Armance and I grocery shopped the day before, and the Saturday of the gathering, I woke up early to start preparing the dinner. I pulverized dried herbs with a pestle and mixed the powder with salt from two bags—all this for the preparation of a salt-encrusted chicken. I blanched asparagus by the bunch for several thick, large *frittate*. I hard boiled eggs without turning the yolks blue, and I let succulent pieces of tuna absorb the fresh lemon for *cundiggiùn*. I had no illusions about my ineptitude with something like *piccagge aggétto in to brodo* and considered attempting it for as long as Uncle Romain considered repairing a chair rail. The chicken, the frittata, and the salad, those I could handle. Over-ambitious with my timing, I had completed some of these preparations much too early, but by dinnertime, I was serving a delectable meal, complete with appetizers, *cidre* during dinner, and *calva* afterwards. I admit that Grand-mère Armance made the platter of light *sablés* for dessert. I put forth an effort to present every dish with the abundance and artistry of which my mother, my father, and Aunt Adèle would have approved. My oldest friends Jimmy, Jack, Clark, and Stan would not have missed such an evening, but I also invited new friends I had made in high school, along with Père Martin. I wanted to relive over and over the spectacle of their faces as they were digging into the aromatic *frittata* and tasting the juicy chicken. I knew as they smiled and reached for seconds and complimented the dishes between chews that Monsieur Vauquelin was right: "You will cook a salt-encrusted chicken for all your friends in America one day," he had foretold, "and they will be your friends for life because of it." The many requests for another dinner like this through the weeks of our senior year and the unexpected visits to my house, usually around the dinner hour, verified Monsieur Vauquelin's sentiment. I wished he could have been there to help me prepare it and to see my friends' enjoyment of it. That dinner honored him as much as my family.

Now I am a senior in high school. Years have passed since that summer, and I still stick my toe in the shifting sparkles of the Seine, still dip my hand in the lapping, sun-streaked waves of La Manche. I still see an empty vase of white in that bedroom. I still smell chamomile and think of the hermitage. Still. The still continues.

Catching me in a forlorn mood one day as I left French class, Père Martin asked me if I was okay. When I told him that every now and then sadness of that summer revisits me, he listened yet again, this time about my feelings of what had gone unfulfilled.

I expressed regret over never having told Aunt Adèle that Aunt Pé had burned my sister's dress, not I, and that I had witnessed it.

Upon hearing that regrets and guilt still floated to the surface, he made a suggestion. The year before, for our final exam, we had to write many of the prayers of the rosary in French. This year, we had to translate passages from French to English from ancient French texts like "La Chanson de Roland," "Lais of Marie de France," and "Le Voyage de Saint Brendan." I had been working on St. Brendan's, connecting with lines like, "*Vait s'en Brandan vers le grant mer / U sout par Deu que dout entrer,*" meaning "St. Brendan went towards the great sea / Where he knew, by God, that he must enter or embark." Père offered me an alternative. Instead of the translation, of which he knew I was more than capable, I should write my summer in Etretat-au-Delà. He said I should write it as it unfolded in my head, and to do my best not to remove myself from the moments of reliving it. He said it was sure to call to mind many sad events and to stir many sad emotions, but seeing the story through might help me accept what had happened and move on, leaving it in the manuscript and not dragging it like a ball and chain with me. After my grandmother granted us permission, I embarked on completing this task.

This is the manuscript. I could not write it in present tense as Père Martin had suggested; I could not relive it in that way, but I did write it. This is the story of my summer in Etretat-au-Delà the summer after my parents' death, the summer that crippled me with realizations about my family, hurtfulness, and perseverance, and the summer that catapulted me to new understandings about the life I need to live and what is worth keeping with me to share with others.

In the span of three consecutive days in late June, the old man had read the letter ten times and had absorbed every word of the manuscript twice, struggling through the first read by himself, listening as he envisioned each moment through the voice of his great-nephew who recited the second read. The boy, Collot, no older than twenty, closed the manuscript, wrestling in his mind with the implications of the story, exploring the effect of it on his great-uncle who sat before him with a serious countenance.

"I don't know why, Uncle Alban," the boy said, "but it never occurred to me you had once been in love. I knew you loved passionately the salt and your work in the *marais*, but I did not know you once loved a lady."

The gravity on the old man's face melted to a crinkly-eyed smile. "I still love that lady," he said.

The boy smiled to see the reason for such a smile on his old uncle's face. A new appreciation for an old fixture in the house was developing within.

"It was your Adèle who planted all the mint around the house," he said. "That is why you love it so much. Tonight, Uncle Alban, I will give a sprig of it to Sophie. It is delicate and beautiful like her, but now I see it has roots deeper than the soil for us Vauquelin men. It will be special for us as it is special for you—and Adèle Semperrin."

The old man's smile widened as the dusky clouds of gray, pink, and lavender passed. The voices of merchants whose stands had occupied the town square for the market today chattered on as they packed up their belongings. Collot's sister must have been among them, today's representative of the family of *sauniers*.

"Collot, please hand me the letter. I wish to read it once more," the old man said. The boy handed him the letter, and Alban read:

La Fête des Pères, River Forest, IL, U.S.A.

Dear Monsieur Alban Vauquelin,

My name is Jacques Avery, whom you once knew as Ellande, a name that has perhaps faded from your memory many years ago. Your name, however, and the person to whom it was assigned, have never left me and, in fact, only gain in fondness and appreciation the longer I live. You have a big place in my heart, and some part of it hopes you will remember me as I write after an absence from each other's lives of fifty years.

Some ten years ago, walking to the house of my birth in River Forest where I reside to this day, where I have raised my children and entertained ten grandchildren, I saw in a birch tree a robin's nest, the mother on her eggs, the father perched on the low branch. The striking powder blue of the eggs and the orange breast of the roosting parents reminded me of one of the most delightful memories of my youth, indeed, of my life. During a summer of tumult and upheaval in the life of a young boy and his younger sister, you provided a respite—a true oasis of peace—in the blue cornflower fields and orange tree arbor of L'Ile d'Aobefein. How the memories of that day flooded back upon seeing those robins and their eggs, but more so, the memories of you, a good man. For years after that, I tinkered with the idea of writing you, but I convinced myself I couldn't possibly know of your whereabouts now, nor track you down. However, one of my grandsons at university announced his intention to study abroad in France and hoped to learn more of his ancestry in Normandie on his mid-semester break. I encouraged a visit to the *bocages* for their distinctive tranquility particular to Normandie alone and to the *falaises* for a blinding peace as the sun reflects off the white and blue. I refused to tell him the location of the summer house in Etretat-au-Delà, but I did send him in search of you—to spy, if you will—at the corner house of the second block off the town square. I hope you will forgive the intrusion. One day, a young man—my grandson—spoke to a young man, about his same age, whom he saw exit the house. The boy, Collot, told my grandson that he lived with his parents, grandparents, and his grandmother's brother, Uncle Alban. Your location confirmed, I undertook with joy and also apprehension the task of writing you.

When I saw the robins and the eggs, when the slow rush of memories swelled like a rising tide, I retrieved from an armoire a manuscript I had written in high school of my summer in Etretat-au-Delà. During moments not spent looking after my grandchildren, I began to translate the manuscript into French with the intention of sending it to you. Now that, thanks to my grandson, your location has been confirmed, I am sending it to you. I wish for you to know the effect your kindness had on me. Although reading the piece may stir emotions of sadness over a lost love, our cherished Adèle Semperrin, I am hoping you might witness some of the joy you might not have known you brought her, not to mention to my sister and me.

My sister and I wondered about many people after that summer. Then I did my wondering alone. Madeleine-Grace entered the convent when she finished high school. She found a convent in Pays de Caux, Normandie, not in Liguria, the place of our Aunt Adèle's great joy. Her companionship with Maclou Galimard was my sister's only hope of married life, and when he entered the monastery, she heard her calling more clearly. She confessed to me that she had been hearing it primarily through the Blessed Mother, including during our last summer in France. She, too, holds you in the highest esteem.

After Aunt Melisende passed, we stopped hearing about those in France. I never kept up with any of my cousins, nor my aunts or uncles. One day, my cousin Wischard Toutrein contacted me before a business trip to Chicago, seeking an opportunity to meet. I gladly took him in for a few days and showed him our beautiful Chicago. He was married and had at that time two young children. He had never known of a letter I had written to him, he believed, on account of his move to Paris with his father, sister, and a nanny. He was reluctant to discuss my last summer in Etretat-au-Delà, noting his cousins' returns there had lasted no more than a week at a time for the next few summers before closing the door to any more visits; his own family did not return. He had said how unfortunate it was that Aunt Adèle had left us for "what must be Heaven to her."

(Having kept up with him after this visit, I caught snippets of news from him about family. From my last summer onward, Wischard and little Laure stayed with their father at Grandma'Maud's Paris flat while Aunt Laure stayed at Uncle Gilbert's family's house in Dieppe. When Uncle Gilbert visited Dieppe, he did not take the kids, and a nanny watched over them in Paris, sometimes for months at a time. When the children visited Dieppe, their mother took off within a day of their arrival for Paris, Deauville, London. Uncle Romain and Aunt Pé lived off the family money in Paris, neither working, and Astride never married; her parents did not provide for her, and the last Wischard knew, she had moved in her fifties to a farm belonging to a relative with many children on her mother's side. I imagine her scaring the children as she disembowels their dolls. Uncle Roul and Aunt Mirabelle went in on a place in Nice with some friends and spent their years between there and Rouen. Wischard insists that Aunt Adèle's tales of Liguria had rubbed off on Uncle Roul like the garlic on the pasta, but the closest

Aunt Mirabelle could bring herself to Italy was La Côte d'Azur. Young Roul married young and attended the military academy like his Uncle Léon; his wife left him after his fourth or fifth affair. He has many children with her. Alphonse also attended military school and married a lieutenant's daughter. Their father's tenderness for his fallen brother Léon rubbed off on his sons, it would seem, as both pursued military careers. I wonder if Uncle Roul spoke at times, in his more sentimental moments, about my mother with the same endearment with which he extolled Uncle Léon. Chardine married a man as wanton as her father but with much more money; Alphonse and Chardine both live in Rouen. Little Laure suffered several breakdowns through her teenage years, and after a short-lived attempt at painting, ran away, never to be heard of by anyone in the family.)

I visited the Ligurian "Heaven" of my mother and my aunt a few years after Wischard's visit to Chicago. It had been my first trip back to Europe, and my wife and I enjoyed the month-long trip from Liguria to Sorrento. The following year, we visited Paris, but I could not bring her—or myself—to Normandie—not to Rouen, Lisieux, Etretat-au-Delà, and not even to Fécamp for Bénédictine. I don't know that I could go even now, but my grandson's descriptions have certainly tempted me. The beauty of the terrain and people call to me, but some invisible barrier not unlike one I experienced playing *la choule* that last summer prohibits me from entering a perhaps too solemn domain.

I have made a life for myself as the proprietor of several restaurants, all in Chicago, all high-end, all featuring mostly French drinks and fare. They are small and considered "exclusive," which makes me laugh as I wish to share with as many as possible the delicacies of Normandie. We boast a special selection of Northern French and Belgian beers and ciders. However, my feature cocktail is what I now call the "Vauquelin," sure to be a household name here in the States as *hydromel* gains in popularity. When my second restaurant opened in Chicago, we made a spot for a piano in honor of my mother. Determined to showcase authentic Normand playing, I began a search for Jacot Galienne, the composer of the *tourdion* so special to us, and believe it or not, tracked him down outside Rouen! I flew him in and commissioned him to write a *tourdion* for the restaurant's grand opening—and to play the older one my mother had found, of course. Until his passing, we flew him in every July to play for us. He was a Cauchois boy who, with the help of several benefactors aware of his musical potential, studied music and published several pieces. I knew my parents and especially Grandma'Maud would be proud of my search and were smiling through Jacot's every tune. Each July with Jacot was a blessing as it rekindled my use and love of Cauchois. His presence—and certainly his music—brought the joy and beauty of Pays de Caux and Normandie to our part of the world. Through his playing and sharing stories and drinks, he contributed to a passing-on of our customs, our land.

I have three restaurants so far, all named Blue A, which sounds in English like the French "*bleuet*" for cornflower, and the "A" is for "Avery," of course. We are starred and receive exceptional attention. You must know that my restaurants reach this status after years of schooling, much hard work as bartender and businessman, and decades of appreciation for craftsmanship and attention to detail, thanks to my parents, Aunt Adèle, and you. I truly appreciate the warm reception of my concoctions after *la choule* and, years later in America, my attempted replicas of Normand and Ligurian cuisine, but after having learned much more about drinks and cuisines, after having committed years to practicing and perfecting recipes and techniques, my drinks and dishes are much improved. I am grateful for the early lessons and encouragement that launched this pursuit, this joy.

My work at the restaurants and my interactions with Jacot Galienne have helped me achieve what you, Monsieur Vauquelin, were intent on teaching me many years ago: preserving the good. I pass down Cauchois to my family as much as I can. To this day, I still use "*mésienne*" instead of "*sieste*." I still elide the "r" when saying "*cidre*." My children know the difference between the standard French "*bleuet*" and the Channel Isles' dialect "*âobefein*"—not to mention the Cauchois "*âotefeis*." As Jacot regaled us with youthful reminiscences and tales of Normandie's fishermen and farmers, priests and nuns, caretakers of apple orchards and distillers of apple spirits, as he reminded us of the resilience that rebuilt a region once devastated by war and the enthusiasm that bubbles over at the mention of *la choule* and *la tèque*, my appreciation grew for my exposure to your care with salt, to Aunt Adèle's attention to detail of process, to Uncle Léon's interpretation of La Grande Lessive, to games of *p'tits chouaux*, to gulps of *béné*, to the *bocages*, to the *falaises*, and to the alabaster homages to Our Lady who relentlessly looks over us. This is worth preserving, and in the merest of ways through my family and my work, I hope I have done so.

I leave you this manuscript to read if you so desire, and by offering my sincerest gratitude for being a light to my Aunt Adèle and for being peace for Madeleine-Grace and me that most trying time of our lives.

My prayers continue for you and your family. And when I seal this package, I will go downstairs and gather my family for a toast using the cocktail formerly—and regretfully—once named "The Jeuffine," which I have renamed "The Vauquelin." And we will raise our glass to you.

With Warmth,

Ellande Avery

The boy, standing over his great-uncle's shoulder to read as he read, said, "He has named a cocktail after us, and it is on American menus. My name is not Vauquelin, but my blood is. If it is in America, in a city as big as Chicago, it will become famous! Can we follow the procedures in the manuscript and make it this evening?"

"We can make it. I recall it tasted quite good." He set the letter in his lap and sighed heavily, but it did not carry away an angst brewing within him. "But we have a task more imminent and exigent. The boy, Ellande, he has been led to a grave misunderstanding about some of the events of that summer. You must help me, Collot, to disabuse him—and to explain to him what really happened as I know it. My hand is shaky, so I will speak, and you must write for me and send this to the address you find on the package."

Collot detected the urgency in his uncle's voice and grabbed a pen and stationery from the table drawer. As Alban dictated, the boy wrote:

Le 4 Juillet, Etretat-au-Delà, France

My Dear Boy Ellande,

What had first met your unexpected letter and manuscript with astonishment turned to elation as I read word after word. To relive that summer through your eyes impressed into my soul your pain over the scars already impressed on my own; however, to see the joy with which our beloved Adèle cared for you—for us all—called love to the surface of my soul, which was a soothing ointment over the pain. I thank you for sharing your words in translation with an old man. I thank you for not forgetting an old man and for seeing him only as he was young.

My great-nephew recalls the encounter with your grandson, having found it curious more than alarming, and thought to tell me of it. We could not, however, determine who this boy could be and never suspected a relation of the Semperrins or Averys. I am glad you sent him. Your grandchildren will always be welcomed here, and my Collot has requested your permission to engage your grandson in correspondence over the internet; that is, if he can tear himself away from his girlfriend for more than ten seconds. Now *Collot* passes flowers to his love through the window as I once did. He is the grandson of my sister Aürnas-Marie whom you met on the isle. I never married. Now Aürnas-Marie's children and their children harvest the salt of the *marais* with the good help of Ajurnée-Marie's children and grandchildren.

For years, Franchinot asked of your sister. I never had news, not having a means of contact to convey any word to you. He was found dead on the island after a severe storm one day. He must have been in his forties, but every one of his days on this earth was devoted to a simple and good life. I think Franchinot pined for your sister, but I think many did, falling instantly in love. Madeleine-Grace exuded a beauty that could incite only love or envy, revealing much about her onlookers, but making life full of woe for her. How fitting that she chose to give herself to the only One worthy of such beauty. Franchinot would be pleased to know this, for he, like me, never married, leading a solitary life on L'Ile d'Aobefein.

However, I dread to tell you all these years later, that your sister and your Aunt Adèle did not share the same calling. Your aunt did not join the convent, and it troubles me after reading your manuscript that you believed she had. You have lived all these years wondering if the lady who had cared for you believed you to be the one who burned your sister's dress. I know for a fact that she did not, but you never had the chance to learn. How this must have troubled you. Although it is years too late, perhaps I can put your mind at ease about this matter. I warn you, though, that in order to do so, I must reveal something that is sure to trouble you even more.

While you and Madeleine-Grace were at the ball, I returned to your Aunt Adèle who confessed to me that she had ripped apart the gardens and dropped mint seeds on every centimeter of land. She blamed Astride for burning the dress, although she hypothesized Pé and Laure as possibilities, too. She had a difficult time determining a motive for any, for she could not believe envy or resentment to be strong enough to drive anyone to be so hurtful to a child. When I told her Madeleine-Grace had repaired the dress and looked stunning, Adèle's old self began to reclaim her, smiling at your sister's conviction not to be bested by the others. It was then that we began to talk of our future, a future together, and ensconced in the pain and the passion of the past few days, we agreed to leave for L'Ile d'Aobefein together—with you and Madeleine-Grace. We planned to stay there to make plans for a wedding, to get word to Adèle's mother, and to begin a life together. We planned to keep you with us until your American grandparents returned for you, and we planned to see you again soon in November for your Thanks-Giving. So you see, Ellande, she could not have thought more lovingly of you, never having thought you to be the culprit for an instant.

She packed a few things quietly from her bedroom in the attic and the conservatory where she then slept so that she could awake early and sneak you two out of the house. (Did you know she often slept on the divan in the conservatory, sometimes coming down from the attic late in the night after her siblings had finally retired? Romain had never hauled the mattress she had propped against the wall in the shed. If she slept upstairs, she slept on blankets on the hard floor. After much persistence on my part, she finally acquiesced to my carrying it up, but she refused to let me fix the broken shelf in the shed or the chair rail in the dining room.) I waited that night on the bench outside to help her the next morning, and my car was ready to leave. When you and your sister came home with me, she was already asleep in the conservatory, and to bed you went. When the others came home, angry, bitter, and intoxicated, they sent the children to bed and congregated in the *salle-en-arrière*, unaware their sister slept in the next room. I watched from the darkness through the window. They lingered, argued some, smoked, and I finally left, suspecting they would never step foot in the conservatory to find Adèle. I awoke the next morning not long after sunrise and drove to the house, eager to escort Adèle and you to the isle. To my surprise, Romain and Mirabelle, who never rise early, had already left with you and your sister, and Adèle was nowhere to be found. Gilbert, after a fight and unpleasant words, swore to me that Adèle had gone, left for the convent. His efforts to bar me from the house piqued my suspicions of something terribly amiss. He told me lies that, I am embarrassed to say, I temporarily entertained. I left, scouring the train station for any vestige of her. When next I saw Romain and demanded to know what really had become of Adèle, he threatened to do irreparable harm to my family if I persisted in investigating into her whereabouts. I receded, opting to conduct my search for answers cautiously. The Semperrins did not go out of their way to make any announcement, but when anyone inquired of Adèle, they stated that she had decamped. Only if someone prodded might they hint that she had entered some unknown convent. I remained convinced something terrible had happened that night. Thanks to

Madeleine-Grace's speech at the children's ball, Aunt Melisende, Lady Victorine, and others found the story suspicious, but who could know?

That September, after they had left the house, I drove by. They idiotically and carelessly had left the veranda entrance into the house unlocked, so I entered easily. The kitchen wall where once there had been a cellar door now had a poorly painted, flimsy plank of wood covering it, its perimeter nailed frivolously by someone who didn't know how to do it right. Why did Romain not hire a carpenter? Why did Romain do this, of all the tasks he neglected, and why on his own? I found a hammer in the herb shed among some garden tools and pried the wooden batten off easily. The doorknob on the cellar door had been removed or else the plywood would not have fit, so the door swung open. I descended the wooden steps and found the cellar empty of all alcohol, but some of Adèle's jars of food remained on the back shelf. The floor had been scrubbed clean. When I went to return the plywood to the wall and moved to close the cellar door, only then I saw something curious: the ledge that Adèle and Juliette had painted white one summer had a pink hue at its closest edge. I felt a tragedy had taken place here. I felt something was being concealed, wiped away, and I did not know how to uncover some terrible secret.

I am glad your manuscript informed me of a note Romain had given you from Adèle. This should confirm all to you, Ellande. You see, your Aunt Adèle could not write well. Around the time she started school, she broke her arm. She did not attend school while her arm healed, but she also never returned. She was kept home from school even though her older siblings attended intermittently. Juliette, your mother, she had a voracious appetite for learning, one that could not be quelled, so she pursued studies with her parents' blessing, even privately amid the war. Adèle, however, was content to learn everything she could from her parents. Her knowledge of reading and writing was so cursory that she was always too embarrassed to write, even a recipe, and she never lifted a book to read. The letter you mentioned, therefore, could not likely have been written by her.

All this must be difficult for you to hear, Ellande. But it is better you should know the truth now, even late, than not at all. It pains me to think this truth may pain you, even now in your old age. Do you know why I wished you to call me Alban all those years ago instead of Monsieur Vauquelin? Because I was not much older than you whenever I was with your Aunt Adèle. She drew from me the youth and love of a school boy. I expected to be your uncle one day and did not wish to wait until my marriage to your aunt to establish the familiarity of being called Uncle Alban by you; I felt you and Madeleine-Grace, as Adèle's nephew and niece, to be my family already.

I went to the Semperrin house one day late in summer the year after you had left. I saw Romain and Pé in the lawn next to the veranda trying to uproot the mint that had overgrown the land, some plants reaching higher than the veranda railing. How they despised that mint! They didn't garden. They didn't weed. They didn't know how to work at all, so they did not know what to do with the wildly growing mint. They must have given up because, years later, I snuck around the property to see it had fallen into disrepair, and the mint, the mint they hated so much, perfumed every ounce of air and grew rampantly. Their laziness and that flourishing mint were sure to keep them away. I don't know if they returned. There was good to that house, and Adèle fortified it forever from the tyranny that could tarnish the goodness of it.

Your aunt, like the mint—through the mint—lives on, too. Do you remember the day she dropped the seeds around my residence in the moonlight? That mint still grows here in beautiful abundance, and she is here. Every inhale at my window, every walk along my sidewalk, brings the thought and beauty of Adèle to my mind, to my heart, and I smile to know she is here.

So, my dear Ellande, I leave you with these sprigs of mint from the cracks between my sidewalk and my house. When you toast next, use a mint leaf to garnish your drinks, and toast to our Adèle as many years ago you did to your good sister. Despite her odious siblings' best efforts, she lingers; she grows abundantly; she and all that she stands for still thrive. Some, they leave the flood of damage after them, destruction. What came after Adèle is the flood of kindness, the flood of duty and hard work, the flood of good traditions that might have sunk. What came after Adèle flourishes, thrives in abundance, spreads in beauty. What came after Adèle—the mint, *la menthe*!

May God bless you, your sister, and your family.

With Affection,
Alban Vauquelin

CHAPITRE 10

The heat grasped the beeches and the flax and the marguerites in a stiff hold. "That stillness again," Ellande recalled, staring through the window of the car that rolled through the Normandie countryside. Over fifty years later and that sensation of moving through the stillness had not been stifled by the heat. And just like his summer in 1958, Paris was hotter than Normandie.

Ellande looked in the backseat at Pierre, his grandson, the boy of twenty-one imbibing the *bocage* of his ancestry. Pierre, eager to take in all he could on this unexpected trip, turned to his new friend, Collot, for answers, for occasions to practice his French, for moments sure to develop a friendship between the two. Next to the two boys, deeply sunk into the backseat with a not ironic lightness, sat Alban Vauquelin, Collot's great-uncle and the uncle that should have been to Ellande. Except for a few smile-infused glances at Pierre and Collot learning from each other, Monsieur Vauquelin stared out the window at the passing *clos-masures* with a seriousness often absent from country idleness. And carrying the opposite of that seriousness was Wischard, the chauffeur for the day, driving now with a wrist on the top of the steering wheel, his legs spread casually apart, and his other hand resting on the gearstick of his automatic Mercedes. When the sun radiated through the window, Ellande saw his cousin when his hair had been blond, when sunny mischief had danced in his eyes.

The suffocating grasp of the sun lessened, released, sighed, and a breeze at last stirred some hawthorns ahead. They trailed another automobile driven by a young novice belonging to the Order of the Redemptive Cross and her passenger, Soeur Adelaide, the vocational name of the former Madeleine-Grace Avery. Less than twenty-four hours beforehand, all the men had met in Paris just south of the Seine; while in Quartier Javel, they had arranged to meet Soeur Adelaide at the convent.

Two days prior to their arrival in Paris, the *café au lait* alighted next to young Pierre in a *demitasse-sur-soustasse*—two *sablés* on the tiny Sèvre saucer—carried by Ellande. This was the ritual enacted daily in the River Forest house. That morning, however, vexation accompanied the coffee and cookie. Pierre saw in the furrowed brow and sharply raised shoulders the tense consternation that stiffened his *grand-père*. Pierre's parents had moved back into the house of their youth, the house in which Ellande had raised them, in order to help take care of the aging Ellande and his wife. That meant Pierre and his siblings, too, had moved in, and while Pierre's parents, brother, and sisters slept later, he relished in waking early to enjoy mornings alongside his grandfather, especially on the limited time his summer break from university afforded him.

"You're still bothered by Monsieur Vauquelin's letter, aren't you?" Pierre asked, holding the *sablé* between two fingers mid-air, waiting for an answer before dipping it in his *café au lait*.

The boy held it longer than he had anticipated, for his grandfather lifted his chin and his eyes to his grandson, dropped his shoulders as he sighed, and announced, "I think we're going to France. I don't see another way. I can't let this go."

Pierre's hand wasn't the only thing suspended in mid-air as his mouth dropped, as his thoughts screeched to a halt as if inches from a precipice. Then he said, "We?"

"I need some answers, and I think I should not do this alone."

Pierre's stiffened face freed a smile as he asked, "When are we leaving?"

"As soon as we can book a direct flight to Paris."

Pierre, his smile beaming, dipped his *sablé* in his *café au lait* and popped the coffee-logged sweetness into his mouth. "I'll check for flights now."

"Leave that to me, Pierre," Ellande said. "May I ask you to e-mail young Collot in Etretat-au-Delà using the e-mail address Alban sent? They should know we are coming."

Within several hours of that very morning, between seven o'clock and ten o'clock, Ellande and his grandson had secured a ticket on a midnight flight to Paris, sent word to Collot of their visit, received confirmation of Alban Vauquelin's anxious expectation of them soon, and coordinated with Wischard to pick them up from the airport in Paris to bring them to his flat in Arrondissement 15 upon his insistence they not stay in a hotel. Ellande made another phone call to incorporate another important visit but could not connect with the intended recipient at the convent: his sister. Instead, he left a message with whoever answered that his sister, Soeur Adeleide, be informed of his imminent arrival. Hasty packing and many a frenzied *jusqu'à* hid agitation over the possibility of a rash decision, but Pierre's easy acquiescence and beaming smiles reduced the occasional flaring anxieties of his grandfather. Shortly before ten o'clock, Pierre's older brother Jacques was driving them to O'Hare, and shortly after midnight, the two Averys were soaring eastward to unanswered questions, to the hot doubt of another glazed summer.

Ellande interjected apologies into flight conversation for absconding with Pierre to Paris. Ellande's eldest son Julien, who went by Ian, the father of four beautiful children, named his children after his and his French wife's parents. Jacques Ellande Avery was Ian's eldest, followed by Pierre, named after Ian's wife's father. The two daughters to follow were named Odette and Yolande after their two grandmothers. To Ellande, Ian looked somewhat like his namesake, Julien Avery. Pierre, however, was a sprightly, smiling replica of Ellande's father, more so than Ian himself. Pierre's presence always brought to Ellande the comfort of paternal closeness and protection in the shape of youth. This summer, when he saw Pierre plop a ripe piece of cantaloupe into his mouth on a humid Chicago afternoon, he saw his own father do the same amid visions of bottling cantaloupe liqueur and passing the rinds to Aunt Adèle in the summer house kitchen. It always amused Ellande that, in naming Pierre after his mother's father, his name evoked Saint Peter. "Semperrin" was a time-distorted, Normand version of Saint Pierre; in that way, his name resonated through both his parents' ancestors.

The first time Ellande noticed Pierre shut his eyes for more than a blink, they had been in the air for two hours. Ellande reprimanded himself for choosing that moment, when the boy might have finally succumbed to drowsiness for a little rest, to apologize one more time.

"I should not have been so hasty in demanding that you join me. I apologize," he said with a shake of the head back and forth.

"I told you you have nothing to apologize for," the boy said as his eyes burst open with spirited gaiety. "I'm excited to go! If I weren't here with you, I'd—*je ferais le bêtas, je serais bajas, un caleû.*" These were expressions for being a good-for-nothing Grandma'Maud was wont to use in relation to Aunt Pé, Aunt Mirabelle, and some of her own dawdling children.

"With such energy, you get more accomplished in two minutes than some people do in a year. You could never *être bajas*, *ni caleuser*, Pierre. I am grateful that you don't see this trip as an imposition."

"Not at all," the boy said. He had considered moving to France, and after his semester abroad, he knew at the least that he wanted to master the language. Hanging with Collot enticed him for this reason, as did experiencing France with his grandfather. He knew, however, that his grandfather had an agenda and an uncomfortable one at that, and he did not wish to thwart any plans of his grandfather, impetuous as they may be. "Do you really think something terrible happened to your Aunt Adèle, Pépé?" the boy asked as his thoughts turned to his grandfather's impetus for traveling.

"I am kicking myself for not seeing sooner that things didn't add up, but yes, I think something terrible happened—" he ducked his head as if one of the few passengers on the scantily occupied flight might see— "to a beautiful and good person." Pierre realized the receding of his grandfather's neck and head was not meant to muffle a comment about foul play but to hide a rapidly overtaking sentiment, a rush of mourning.

Ellande sank into his seat while Pierre let him be. After a few exchanges about a days-long *paquebot* journey to the same destination that nowadays takes hours by plane, both slipped into light, easily disturbed sleep. They had skimmed a few pages of magazines purchased from the airport bookshop and borrowed a few steady moments of airline-supplied film before they disembarked in Paris a little after two o'clock in the afternoon. With no checked luggage to await, they exited easily to Wischard's warm welcome and talkative ride to the Paris flat. Wischard did most of the talking while Ellande chimed in here and there, and Pierre exerted a valiant effort to understand the Cauchois French to which the two reverted.

Wischard insisted the two travelers shower and rest a few hours at his flat before treating them to dinner at a nearby restaurant. He made a point of passing Grandma'Maud's flat as he drove to his own, not ten blocks away.

"You purchased a flat in the same *arrondissement*," Ellande said.

"I like living where I know," Wischard retorted. "Therefore, you won't see me staying in Auteuil anytime soon." Recollecting the afternoon of losing Madeleine-Grace and the angst that had embossed the memory, the two men laughed heartily.

"It is good to laugh about it now," Ellande said. Despite the passing of time, some people can be counted on—and Wischard was to Ellande one of those special persons—if for nothing else, for a good laugh, or making the kind of story that was sure to provide a good laugh later. His hair, like Ellande's, had aged, but whereas Ellande's had grayed and silvered, Wischard's had whitened.

Once in Wischard's flat, the two travelers tossed their things in their respective rooms, showered quickly, and napped. Wischard insisted on waking them at eight o'clock in the evening for dinner whether they wished to be awakened or not, for he knew they would sleep better through the night that way. The two woke easily at eight o'clock and enjoyed a warm stroll toward the Seine to Père Martin-Pêcheur des Brandes, a restaurant of Wischard's choice.

As night was falling on Paris, the small restaurant glowed in both the dim lighting emitted from sconces and chandeliers and the clementine luminosity of a slow sunset. Low candles flickered on the tabletops. With only a small banquette of five tables, four larger square tables, a cozy alcove with a round table and its own, low-hanging chandelier, and a bar long enough to cram four sturdy stools, the tiny place exuded the coziness of a post-war bistrot. The thick scents of sautéing onions and hearty stews—*carbonnade*, Ellande wondered—invited them to relax, to enjoy reprieve from impromptu travels. Two of the four larger tables were occupied, so Wischard motioned to the empty row of tables along the banquette. Then he nodded to a well-dressed man of fifty who had stepped from the kitchen to the bar where a bartender placed drinks on a round tray oblivious to the entrance of the patrons.

"Jean-Baptiste," Wischard said to Ellande. "I frequent here. This place—the meal and the ambiance—will be pleasing to you. Jean-Baptiste's father opened it in the late sixties. It is not too busy nor ever too loud. *La carte* is small. You will find it pleasing. Then again, you are the expert."

His smirk suggested the comment a dig at some perceived sort of superiority on the part of Ellande, but Ellande recognized it as playful and devoid of derisiveness. Ellande, in response, winked at Wischard as he slid across the thickly textured, densely patterned bench to his spot at table. Wischard and Pierre chuckled as Ellande swiftly pulled a menu toward his face with one hand and pulled the small candle toward his eye with the other to convey excessive scrutiny. He raised an eyebrow and bulged his eyes. Jean-Baptiste noticed and ceased helping the bartender place a fourth drink on the tray in an earnest two steps over.

"Monsieur, everything is pleasing to you, upon your close inspection?" he said, glancing at Wischard for explanation.

All three men laughed, caught in the pantomime of a restaurant connoisseur's feigned snobbery, and Wischard explained to his acquaintance the prestige of Jean-Baptiste's new patron, Ellande Avery, and his award-winning French restaurants in America. After some banter, interview, and light conversation, the men ordered drinks and a bite to eat, and settled in to an evening of Parisian comfort.

Between the arrival of drinks and meals, Pierre glanced from the phone he had recently pulled from his pants pocket and announced, "I received a message from Collot."

"Shall we tell them to expect us in Etretat-au-Delà tomorrow morning?" inquired Ellande of Wischard at whose mercy they were for transportation. Wischard had insisted they not take the train.

"Seems we are meeting them sooner than we thought," Pierre continued. "Collot says his uncle could not wait to see you and insisted his nephew drive him to Paris to welcome us. They expect to be here in an hour and would like to know where to meet us. He says they still plan to return to Etretat-au-Delà tonight but couldn't resist seeing us."

Ellande and Wischard laughed at the cheerful anticipation catapulting the Vauquelins to Paris, and Wischard suggested simply giving them the address of Père Martin-Pêcheur des Brandes for a cordial and sweet. Pierre promptly sent the message with speedy finger work and flipped his grandfather a thumbs-up when Collot immediately confirmed.

"Vauquelin," Wischard uttered with a smile. "He was a good man." Ellande could tell Wischard was leafing through the chapters of his memory for Vauquelin's visits to the summer house. "He favored you," Wischard tagged on.

"Favored me? He did like me," Ellande conceded.

"He took you to L'Ile d'Aobefein," Wischard said in observation, not in jealousy.

Ellande suspected an envy nonetheless and defended the man. "He knew you couldn't be bothered to wake up early."

Wischard chuckled again and said only, "We had different upbringings, and that was an indication of the difference. I didn't appreciate the discipline instilled in you and Madeleine-Grace until I was older, when it was harder to come by than it was for you who were raised with it."

As a pang of guilt pricked Ellande's heart for a circumstance far from Wischard's fault, he consoled his cousin. "It was summer. It's the time to enjoy many days of sleeping in, especially children."

"Perhaps you should go back, Ellande."

"To the isle? No." Ellande's rapid response sounded reactionary.

"Why not? I can't explain it," Wischard added, "but I have a strange urge to visit that place, myself, as if it summons me. I have never been there, and you can show me around."

"I imagine it is not the same. I don't want to replace the image emblazoned in my memory of that special place." The fiery oranges and rippling blues piqued his mind. He saw the sunlight tickling the crumbling, low wall of the hermitage, the rocky barrier of the ancient lock absorbing the splash of rolling waves.

"Indeed, I'm sure it has changed, what with the increased foot traffic and the retreat center." Wischard's revelation knelled as if Ellande should know.

"I'm not aware of a retreat center."

"Your sister did not share this news in her correspondence with you? I'm surprised. It is her Order that sponsored it. I don't know much other than years ago, a small retreat house was built on the island. It is run by the Sisters. They accept retreatants and pilgrims from around the world for prayerful stays. And tourism has increased. There are a few small restaurants, shops, and inns. Now everyone wants to observe the flora and fauna, birdwatch, and visit the *marais*."

Ellande wished to express contentment for all those who might now enjoy the work of the *sauniers*, yet only his displeasure at a disturbed purity—of both the marshes and the memory—manifested in a deep sigh.

Pierre also sighed but more softly. "I'd like to see the *marais*."

"I'd like you to see them as I saw them, Pierre. But they cannot be the same, I fear. And the one thing I would like you to see most is Monsieur Vauquelin harvesting the salt—especially that *fleur de sel*, fragrant and sparkling in the late afternoon sun. He no longer works the *marais*, though."

"Vauquelin was a hard worker. I didn't come to appreciate that until later. Sometimes, we don't put things together until later in our lives, but some time the week before my first child was born, I recalled something your father told me, Ellande."

"My father? When?"

"The summer before their passing. I was helping him carry boxes of the newly made cantaloupe liqueur to the cellar, and when we ascended the stairs and stopped in the kitchen, your father said to me, 'Thank-you for your help, and make sure you know the value of working hard, Wischard. The value is often to others, but even if no one sees, it is of value to yourself.' Then he added, 'You must teach your children this one day.'" As Wischard revealed this moment, Ellande recalled the similar message his father had imparted to him after their visit to the Art Institute of Chicago, the promise he demanded of Ellande to remember: "The most valuable thing you can do for your children is to make sure they don't stop working, make sure they value work and recognize the dignity in it."

"That sounds like my father," Ellande responded.

"As I awaited the birth of my first child, I thought of your father's words, but it was Monsieur Vauquelin who came to mind—not even my own father and certainly not my mother."

Jean-Baptiste stepped from the kitchen with a tray in his hands, and using dishtowels, he placed a platter from the tray onto a tabletop trivet. The bubbling cheese over three, seawater-fresh scallops on their shell and the perfume of tarragon and butter drew all heads toward the delicious gift. "My compliments to our prestigious guests. *Coquilles-Saint-Jacques*."

The blush on Ellande's face that had answered Jean-Baptiste's graciousness disappeared at the onset of his smile upon slicing his scallop with the side of his fork and lifting it toward his mouth. He enjoyed the aroma of the tarragon and shellfish as a strand of buttery *gruyère* dripped to his plate, and then he placed the succulent morsel in his mouth for a decadent and gratifying first taste of Paris. More gratifying was his observation of Pierre mimicking his action, the grin, and the nod of approval at the deliciousness.

Over dinner—a wide, shallow bowl of *carbonnade* for Ellande and the same for Pierre, a roasted chicken for Wischard—the three caught up, but the occasion forged an opportunity for Wischard to become acquainted with Pierre, a cousin he had never known. He asked many questions of the youngster, and after Pierre's answers, turned to Ellande with an affirmation of some bond of kinship: "Just like your great-grandfather, Uncle Julien," he said, or "just like Grandma'Maud," with a light laugh. But when, after a sip, Wischard had set his wine glass on the tabletop instead of the coaster that was being occupied by his cocktail glass and Pierre had bolted to the bar and back to the table with a fresh coaster for the glass, Wischard said this time, "Just like Aunt Adèle, *n'est-ce pas?*"

Wischard wanted for Ellande and Pierre to meet his own grandchildren, currently in Dieppe, and speculated that they may meet them in Etretat-au-Delà at some point, but for the moment, he filled them in on his grandchildren, including the youngest of seven, named Victorine thanks to some whim of his daughter's husband. The name, of course, evoked humorous remembrances of Lady Victorine Galimard, whom, Wischard added, he hoped his granddaughter would be nothing like.

"And why is that?" asked Ellande through his laughter.

"She was a busybody," Wischard responded.

"She was—but she was a wise lady nonetheless. She had good insights into human nature," Ellande said in her defense. "I think that's why she got along so well with Grandma'Maud."

The conversation steered cautiously clear of the import of Ellande's return to France. Ellande expected conversation with Monsieur Vauquelin would bring him to these things, and, despite whatever curiosity Wischard may have had, Ellande sensed his reticence in the presence of Pierre. Conversation remained safe and calm and Parisian-summer balmy as the last of the sunlight wiped its palm down the front window of the restaurant. Yet no one minded, perhaps used to such tensions, and in the case of young Pierre, oblivious to them. Jean-Baptiste's not infrequent pop-ins maintained levity as a question and short conversation accompanied each one.

"Will Monsieur be so kind to share his opinion on the preparation of *porc à la Normande*?" he asked of Ellande with undue formality, with the trepidation of being perceived as encroaching on some clandestine family technique. "Does one add the cream early, allowing enough time to mingle with the apples and for the meat to absorb it, or does one add it at the end, allowing only enough time for it to warm amongst the simmering ingredients shortly before serving? I have heard true Normands prefer to add it early so that the cream not taste *crue*."

"Do both," interjected Wischard, "and stop treating my cousin like a dauphin."

"I must say," said Jean-Baptiste, "it is a pleasure to see the person who accompanied Wischard on one of his most famous tales, although he failed to share what became of you and the immense celebrity you are in America as a restauranteur. We looked you up on the internet."

"I am not a celebrity in any sense," Ellande said, shushing his host. "But what is this 'most famous of Wischard's tales' to which you refer?"

"The time you, as young boys, got lost in Auteuil on your way to L'Ile de la Grande Jatte, losing your young sister, the *gendarmes* trailing you because they suspected you had sold your sister to the circus, the terrible accident Wischard caused darting into the street to save your sister when he saw her being pulled by that madman with the tiny dog along Boulevard Montmorency, and, of course, your stop at the church where La Vierge looked exactly like the one in the small town of your summer house."

"Oh, that tale," Ellande said to Wischard, lowering his head and raising his eyes. "That is one for the books."

"I like it the best of all his intrigues," commented Jean-Baptiste, "even more so than his high school escapades, his sordid university exploits, and certainly more than the business adventures."

"And what has become of Auteuil, Wischard? Surely you have been there since the time those suspicious *gendarmes* were trailing us. Has it changed much?" asked Ellande.

"We should visit," Pierre said. "Maybe while we stroll the streets of Auteuil, you could serenade us with your rendition of Paul Anka's 'Diana,' Cousin Wischard. Have you shared stories with Jean-Baptiste of your singing?"

The surprise of the reference shocked a stupefied smile onto Wischard's face. "My cousin has also been telling stories, I see." Then he began singing the Anka song.

Before Jean-Baptiste could enjoy the serenade of anything beyond the first few measures, the door opened, young Collot holding it ajar with his foot as he guided with his left hand the much older Alban Vauquelin over the threshold. Ellande, Wischard, and Pierre stood, and realizing the arrival of Ellande's guest, Jean-Baptiste stepped to the door to hold it so that Collot could use his whole self to escort his great-uncle. Once a few steps in, Alban looked up to orient himself. He took in the surroundings as his eyes adjusted to the dim lighting, to the compact space, and finally to the three men standing before him. With the dark blue night behind him through the open door and the soft glow of the sconces illuminating him, his eyes sparkled, and when his smile formed, his teeth seemed to shine joy and calm. The smile formed when he saw Ellande.

Monsieur Vauquelin's sudden release from Collot's steadying compelled the boy to maintain proximity to his uncle amid his leap to Ellande. Ellande's outstretched arms welcomed him as the salt harvester's forehead fell like a sigh on Ellande's shoulder. When he pulled his head up to draw in a good look at Ellande whom he knew only as a young boy, his smile radiated his initial joy and calm.

As Collot eased his great-uncle into a chair, Ellande and Wischard sat, as well. The two boys exchanged handshakes and stood behind the chair of their respective elder.

"Time has been good to you, Monsieur Vauquelin," Ellande said, unable to pull his fond gaze from the man's smooth, tanned face.

"Sun and salt," Alban said. "It is a good elixir."

He looked closely at Ellande and Wischard as they gazed admiringly at him.

"I see youth has left its imprint on you, as well," he said to them both. However, it had been Ellande who received the sprinkle of salt on his head as a boy.

"Thank-you, Monsieur," Ellande and Wischard said in unison.

"Alban," he corrected, "for I was to be your Uncle Alban."

Ellande, upon this comment, glanced at a small candle newly lit on the table. Wischard took the moment to summon a vigilant Jean-Baptiste to offer Alban and Collot a beverage or a dessert. They declined for the moment, and Jean-Baptiste joined his bartender behind the bar. After introducing Pierre to Alban, and Collot to Ellande and Wischard, Wischard suggested the boys become acquainted over drinks at the bar. The boys took to this idea without prodding.

"Do you like gentian root?" Collot asked Pierre, beginning the friendship in French.

"I have not had gentian root. What is it?" Pierre rejoined in French.

"It is a disgusting *apéritif*," Collot responded. "My Uncle Alban and all my aunts and uncles and parents and grandparents enjoy it, but I do not. I am determined to like it, though. You must try it with me."

"I'm game," Pierre said, this expression delivered in English.

"What is 'game?'" Collot asked as they sauntered to the bar stools.

Thinking better of remaining, Wischard excused himself and joined the boys. Ellande and Alban watched as the three settled at the bar and spoke of the auspiciousness of Pierre's encounter with Collot on his study abroad program. The two older men spoke easily about easy topics, interrupted only once by Pierre's spitting out an inappropriate pour of gentian root *apéritif* at the bar while Collot and Wischard burst out laughing. All had grown comfortable with each other in this short span, and for Ellande and Alban, broaching more serious subjects did not take long.

"My letter stirred you, Ellande."

"For most of my life, I have lived with a misconception, under an impression of something false."

"About someone deeply important to you, no less. And deeply important to me. I had to share that with you, despite the many years separating you from your childhood summers here."

"Monsieur Vauquelin, Alban, please—" Ellande experienced a trepidation in his request, a fleeting misgiving he swatted aside, despite the repercussions— "tell me what happened that night after you brought us home from the children's ball. Tell me what I don't know."

The old man leaned into the table, forging an intimacy in warm proximity. His hands retreated to his lap as his torso inched over the table top. He looked askance at the candle flame flickering.

"I don't know so much, myself, I'm afraid. I will tell you what I know—and what I think."

Stiffening in his spot, his stare still fixed on the flame, he began, and Ellande pressed a damask napkin onto his moist forehead. Alban stepped into the memory as if it had been yesterday.

"We drove off from the ball, leaving Jeuffine behind. I escorted you and Madeleine-Grace into your house after parking, and I simply waited in the uptown garden. I heard the others arrive, and I saw them enter the house. They congregated in the backroom, which I could see clearly through the picture window, and they sent the children to bed. When they ascended the steps, the adults remained, arguing in the backroom, charging into the kitchen, drifting onto the veranda, but never taking notice of Adèle sleeping in the dark of the conservatory. I remained hidden in the garden while Romain and Gilbert smoked on the veranda, and when they finished, I felt it was safe for me to return home. I stepped through the damaged earth around the house to the drive, hopped in my vehicle, and departed for the evening.

"The next morning, when I arrived at Adèle's house eager to escort her and you out, I was alarmed to find their vehicle absent, and when I approached the front door, hoping to slip in unaware, I was shouted at by Gilbert, as if on sentry duty. He stepped out and pulled the door shut behind him. He was shouting and whispering at the same time that Adèle was not here, that I must leave. Of course, I did not believe him, and my suspiciousness increased as precipitately as my alarm. I knew something was wrong and made for the door. He blocked it with his body. I bolted around the house to head in through the veranda, and Gilbert, initially stepping to chase me, averted his course, ran through the house, and locked the back door from the outside, barricading it with his person. We stood on the veranda together. I was panting, and in the early morning light, I saw ripped and trampled stems, the wilted flower petals, the smashed, torn herbs. I angled for a glimpse of Adèle through the conservatory window, asleep on the couch or standing at her sewing machine. 'You won't find her there,' Gilbert reiterated, 'or anywhere. She's gone. She left.'

"My heart climbed into my throat. I was panting, I tell you, and I rested my hands on my knees for a moment, and the only words that could hoist themselves out of my mouth were 'You're lying.' Gilbert said, 'She left this morning. Joined a convent. Didn't even say which one. She's gone, Alban.' I didn't believe him. I couldn't. He didn't know what Adèle and I had discussed the night before, the plans we had made. 'Impossible,' I said. 'You're lying.' 'She's gone,' he said, imploring me to leave.

"I made for the door and he blocked it. I tore him out of the way, and he grabbed onto my chest, pulling me to the veranda floor. We wrestled as I struggled to get free of him, to prove him wrong. I thought they were keeping her captive; maybe they had found out about our plans and forbade her to follow through with them. I knew something was amiss. I got to my feet, and Gilbert, from the floor, wrapped his arms around my leg like an octopus and pulled me down. 'You're lying!" I shouted as he pinned me to the floor, and then he punched me in the face. As I squirmed from under him, undeterred, he punched me in the face again and said, 'It's your fault she's gone!'

"This stunned me, as you can imagine. 'What could he mean?' I wondered, but I did not ask it. He said, 'Adèle knows you left the ball with Jeuffine. It destroyed her to know, but she knows. And now she's gone.' He was, as the Americans say, grasping at straws, but I was stunned nonetheless. 'That's impossible,' I said. 'Adèle knows I am faithful to her.' Gilbert insisted my actions had brought her doubts and undue consternation, that she had felt she had no reason to stay and left for the convent. I protested I had not driven Jeuffine home and the two kids could prove it, for I left the Countess's with them. I feel ridiculous now for having wasted time defending myself when I was sure he was lying. Then Gilbert said, 'Could anyone else prove it? The kids are gone, and if you don't leave this house at once, I will make sure everyone knows of your liaison with Jeuffine. You won't be able to deny it. What would that do to your—and Adèle's—impeccable reputation? Would you put her through this?'

"As shameful as I am to admit it, I thought momentarily that it could be true, that Adèle had believed some terrible lie her siblings presented about me, so I asked Gilbert when she left and to which convent. He maintained he knew nothing of these details. Against my instincts screaming at me to stay and to scour the house for her, I instead ran to my car and drove to the train station with the hope of finding her there and explaining the misunderstanding. Of course, she was not there, and in checking the train schedule, I knew trains had left for Paris and elsewhere prior to my arrival. I didn't know what to do in those moments, and I dared not risk causing any embarrassment to Adèle if Gilbert spread his desperate lies about me. I went home to think. Over the next few days, I visited the house only to be denied access. I visited the Galimards' to learn they knew nothing and were as surprised as I about Adèle's departure. The afternoon after the ball, they visited to check on the children, but no one answered, which aroused suspicion. Lady Victorine and I both contacted several convents we knew of—no record of Adèle's presence. I learned weeks later from Lady Victorine that no one had told Madame Semperrin, your Grandma'Maud, about the permanence of Adèle's absence. When Lady Victorine traveled to Paris to visit, she inquired, and Grandma'Maud was stunned to learn of this—nor did she believe it true."

"And then you visited the summer house one day when it was vacated and realized your instincts were correct," Ellande declared, referring to the passage in Alban's recent letter.

Alban scrunched his eyes and tucked his chin to his chest. His hands rose to the tabletop gently. As tears stole from his tightly shut eyes, he said, "I touched the pink blur on the white shelf. I held my hand on it. I knew it was Adèle. I knew they had scrubbed the blood out of the place, but that shelf, it was so white that the best they could do was scrub it pink. The best they could do was never a job well-done, anyway." He clenched his hands into fists. "I should have fixed the shelf. I should have fixed the light. I should have fixed the stairs. Adèle would never let me. She said Romain or Roul must do it, but they never did. They never would! They would have been content to let the house crumble around their children's children. Maybe if I had fixed these things—maybe if I had never gone home that night—."

Ellande could see the man had, no doubt, spent countless hours over a long life contemplating "what ifs" and "if onlys," and they were resurfacing now. The old man reached over the table and placed his hands over an older man's, salt-smoothed fists that had wrapped themselves in death grips around pain and questions he despised for appearing unaccompanied by clear answers.

"There is too much you don't know. You cannot fault yourself for what was done outside of your knowing," Ellande offered.

"I have spent years wondering. I even demanded an investigation, but the authorities refused to look into it. One said I had waited too long, another that there was no basis for investigation. I think Romain had gotten to them."

"Alban, from the little you do know, do you have a theory about what happened?"

When his eyes opened, his gaze fixed again on the flame and he chuckled with palpable disgust. "I have plenty of theories, but there's no use in sharing them. The one thing they have in common is that Adèle did not leave for the convent that night. She died. I don't know how, but I think she died that night, and the Semperrins had to act quickly to hide any trace of—the tragedy."

"And Grandma'Maud? She did not pursue the possibility of something devastating having happened to her Adèle?" Ellande wondered why she had never contacted them in America about this if she knew. Could she have wanted to spare them more suffering until she knew something for sure? Such would have been in keeping with his own parents' mindset. Or had Grandma'Maud contacted Grand-mère and Grand-père Avery and divulged this, a tragic secret tucked away and kept from him by his new guardians?

"I know your Grandma'Maud pursued it through confrontations with her children, through the help of the Galimards, and with the guidance of her sister Melisende and her sister's husband, but to no avail. The Galimards told me something about the firing of the nurse, the family's frenzy over a change in the will—I don't know particulars about anything—but then Madame Semperrin, your poor *grand-mère*, passed. I should have visited Paris more, should have assisted her more." His hands clenched again under Ellande's.

"I can only imagine the frenzy a change in the will caused for my Aunt Laure or my Uncle Romain." Ellande pulled his hands back and shifted his gaze to Wischard, Pierre, and Collot at the bar. He realized the recounting had exhausted Alban, and he had learned all the new information he was going to acquire this evening. "Thank-you, Alban," Ellande said. "I know this must have been difficult for you."

Alban finally leaned back. "I have thought of you often over the years, and sometimes allowed myself to imagine a life with Adèle, you, and your sister. It never occurred to me, however, that you could not know of the lie. I'm glad I was able to tell you."

"I am glad you did tell me," Ellande returned. "I am unsure how all of this evaded us. I imagine I will never know, but I think Madeleine-Grace should know, as well. I will arrange to speak with her at the convent tomorrow."

"Let me join you, Ellande."

"You are exhausted. Go home and sleep tonight. Sleep in tomorrow. I will tell Madeleine-Grace without bothering you."

"It is no bother, Ellande. You were to visit in the morning. Come to Etretat-au-Delà in the morning as you had planned, and we will accompany you to the convent. It's not an hour into the *bocage*. You can do all the talking to your sister, but I wish to be there for you, and I wish to see her again, if that is amenable to you."

"Very well," Ellande responded easily. "We will drive to Normandie tomorrow morning and bring you with us to the convent. Are you sure you don't want to stay in Paris for the night?"

"I'm sure, Ellande. Collot is young and lively and will drive us quickly to our home. And I will expect you in the morning, as I did many years ago that summer."

He was referring to the morning of the visit to L'Ile d'Aobefein, and Ellande said with a smile, "But not quite as early."

"Ellande," Alban added, the smile returning to his eyes, "you are the salt that has not lost its flavor. Old as I am, I can know such things."

"Thank-you, Alban." Ellande lowered his eyes and then shifted his gaze to the boys.

After a fond reflection on the burgeoning friendship between Pierre and Collot, they called the boys over and explained the plan for tomorrow. Their departure was gracious and demonstrative, as if they weren't about to see each other again in hours, yet the departure with Jean-Baptiste surpassed it in effusiveness.

At the flat, when Pierre retired to his bed for the evening, Wischard pressed Ellande for information, which he begrudgingly provided on account of the unpleasant scene between Alban and Wischard's father.

"You believe Monsieur Vauquelin, don't you?" asked Wischard.

"I think I have no reason to doubt him," Ellande responded.

"I think he is telling the truth, too," Wischard admitted, sinking into the cushion of the couch they shared. "My father was a good man. I know that. But I have no illusions about him, and if ever there was someone to bring out the worst in him, it was my mother."

"What are you saying, Wischard?"

"If what Monsieur Vauquelin said is true, my father must have been protecting my mother, or under strict orders to do so."

"I wasn't expecting to, but I slept like a baby," Ellande confided to Pierre as they tossed their few bags into the trunk of Wischard's car. Pierre bounced off the balls of his feet unnecessarily to shut the trunk as he flashed a white smile at his grandfather, and Ellande added, "And *you* never need much."

Wischard, although the most sleep-deprived of the three, never lost a childhood spring to his step and brought both Ellande and Pierre to laughter as he bopped into the driver's seat of the car. They drove west toward the Vauquelins', toward La Côte d'Albâtre, toward heat-soaked uncertainties in the welcome of the new day's sun. The conversation light, Ellande pointed out some of Pays de Caux's distinctions to his grandson—the *clos masures* and the salmon, flint roofs of barns. Pierre absorbed every drop, avoiding the craving shared by all three of them for *un café*.

Not ten minutes outside Etretat-au-Delà, Ellande asked Pierre if he was looking forward to spending time with Collot. Before Pierre could respond, Wischard announced, "He is a very knowledgeable boy, young Collot—well-educated especially in literature."

"He did not mention this," Pierre said.

"You do not remember when he asked me about my sister, Laure? It seems he read about her in a novel you sent his great-uncle. Young Collot read the story aloud to him and knows all the characters."

Ellande chuckled. "I did not send a novel, *per se*. I wrote about our last summer at the house."

"Did you know, Pierre, that this morning we accompany Alexandre Dumas to the coast?"

All three laughed, but Wischard ceased laughing first when Ellande asked, "What did you answer young Collot?" The inquiry into little Laure's whereabouts brought a hush to the car ride until their arrival in Etretat-au-Delà. They parked off the town square and began the stroll to Alban's.

"I'm glad this is our stop, that we're going no farther," Wischard whispered to Ellande.

"You have an aversion to the house as great as mine," Ellande responded.

"It's not quite an aversion. It's as if there's a force around it radiating that it wants me away, and I sense it. I sense it enough to fear what it's keeping me from."

Collot's arms and torso erupted through bursting shutters a few feet down the narrow lane, his smile brighter than the morning sun clambering up the white, scrubbed walls. Thin curtains fluttered out with the young man who swapped them back inside. His wave and cheery *"Boujou!"* ushered them to the door and into the house where Alban greeted them, his expectancy as eager as his great-nephew's. To the delight of the three visitors, the aroma of bitter, orange-scented coffee preceded Aürnas-Marie stepping out with a tray of *cafés* and *croissants*.

She set the tray on a table in the entry in order to welcome the guests with embraces, kisses, and introductions to her husband, several adult children, and several more grandchildren, a few of whom were Collot's siblings. She sent them quickly ascatter to ensure her brother Alban had ample time alone with the visitors, although he needed little before heading out. Aürnas-Marie's deep and rapt respect for Madeleine-Grace manifested not only in a two-minute panegyric on the kind, young girl now dedicating her life to Jesus, but also in her announcement not to keep waiting the nun who would be expecting them whole-heartedly.

As Aürnas-Marie distributed the coffees, Ellande saw Alban seated in the parlor armchair closest the entry, the one Alban's unmarried Uncle Bertin had occupied with a complaisant grin the mornings of fifty years ago. The chair had been reupholstered in a fennel-bulb green instead of the gray he remembered, yet the white nick on the wood at the end of the arm remained. The crack in the wall from behind the chair to the ceiling lingered all these years as a bump under fresh paint; in time, Ellande knew, the crack would reveal itself through the paint as it was wont to do in the past. Unadorned, white crown molding lined the room now, a pleasant addition to a simple abode. When Aürnas-Marie handed Ellande his *demitasse-sur-soustasse*, he smiled to recognize the same, white and light blue porcelain set with the now chipped, twenty-four-karat gold rim.

For all the guests, the first sip was more heavenly than the sky-and-cloud porcelain from which they indulged. However, Aürnas-Marie wasted no time in sending them off to the convent, providing Collot with a trunk of *pique-nique*-like provisions and strict instructions never to leave the side of his shaky great-uncle. She wished the blessing of good answers in their pursuit of truth and waved them out of sight.

Wischard drove the full car into the *bocage* under drifting white clouds until they pulled through the gate of the convent and parked on the gravel outside the front entrance. Despite the short ride, all the men stretched upon stepping out of the car, more so out of apprehension before the grandiose edifice, each hoping another take the first step toward the door, each wishing someone else lead the way to Madeleine-Grace who dwelled beyond those walls.

A thin, middle-aged nun in habit affirmed Ellande in the entryway of the convent that Soeur Adelaide—Madeleine-Grace—had informed her of the visit and was expecting them. The woman was soft-spoken and gentle, and the wrinkles on her cream-white forehead and jowls were supple as if life in the convent had been good to her, reassuring Ellande about the upcoming first glimpses of his sister. She escorted the party into an anteroom to await Soeur Adelaide. Despite the chairs, no one sat. No one moved from the place to which he initially stepped. No one spoke. Pierre and Collot, standing on either side of an opened window, their hands sunk in their pants pockets, pursed their lips to feign whistling and exchanged glances in silence.

Unannounced by footsteps, a petite, habited nun stepped into the doorway. She surveyed all the visages hurriedly and when her inspection arrived at Ellande's, her eyes widened, her mouth opened, and her arms lifted, extended, and preceded her to him with a firm embrace. Ellande welled with tears before losing his voice entirely, resting his chin on his sister's veiled shoulder. Her sobs, muffled from the embrace, lasted minutes before she pulled her head from his chest for a look at Ellande's face. She kissed his cheek three times, glanced around the room, kissed his cheek three times again, studied his face, and then kissed him three times more.

Although the reunited brother and sister said little, Madeleine-Grace moved to greet the others, and each encounter brought a swell of emotion like the ocean waters gushing over the walls of the ancient lock. After her embrace of Alban Vauquelin, she sighed gratitude for his kindness those many years ago and told him that his eyes still twinkled like the sun; he, in turn, revealed that she was still the most beautiful lady in any room. She said, "In this room, I should hope so!" With Collot, she traced with her fingertips the rounds under his eyes, so similar to his great-uncle's, and walked the boy to Alban to embrace them together. Before her embrace of Pierre, she gasped, and during her embrace, in intervals cried into his chest and stared at his face; every time she looked into his eyes, she smiled and said, "Papa! Papa!" on account of the boy's remarkable resemblance to her father. These exclamations brought Ellande once more to tears. Her embrace of Wischard led the room to laughter as her cousin grew increasingly irritated at the top of her wimple striking him in the face as she hugged and rehugged him. "Can't you take that damn thing off?" he joked. She blushed but smiled all the while. The greetings alone lasted a quarter of an hour.

Another nun entered with a coffee service, allowing Soeur Adelaide to serve her guests. A few armchairs surrounded a low coffee table in front of a fireplace, and the boys pulled up upright chairs from along the wall into the gaps around the table. Everyone took a seat except Madeleine-Grace, for whom the men reserved one of the armchairs. After she served coffee, she sunk into the chair.

To Ellande she said with a wink, "It's not Bénédictine, but I'm sure it will do."

Ellande studied her fondly all the while, as did Wischard. She undeniably resembled Juliette Avery, from her petite yet stout stature to her nimble swiftness despite aging. Ellande imagined his mother to be like this had she lived to this age. To Wischard, her face took on the likeness of his Grandma'Maud, after whom Madeleine-Grace was named, in a way he had never imagined: the features—the lips, the shape of the mouth, the crown of the chin, the high cheekbones, the gleam and the vitality and the kindness of the eyes, the movements of the eyebrows—mirrored Grandma'Maud's as he remembered them, but on Madeleine-Grace, they were smaller, rounder, and smoother.

"This is an important visit, Ellande tells me. Something I must know about our family, he says," she announced after a sip of *café*.

Although Alban Vauquelin sat complaisantly motionless, Ellande shifted in his chair and said, "I have learned something about Aunt Adèle."

He recounted the story as he knew it with occasional interjections from Monsieur Vauquelin and uncomfortable acknowledgements from Wischard while Madeleine-Grace, along with the two boys, listened silently. The boys wanted it to resonate with them more than it was since it affected their families, but they didn't know the personages in what landed on their ear like little more than an interesting tale. They leaned forward in their chairs, nodded at the mention of certain names or events to show the other they knew of this, and did their best to make the story sink in. Madeleine-Grace sat still, her pink hands clasped in the black of her habited lap, and moved only to tilt her head toward the window for meditative gazes at the sky, at Heaven.

Although he had not finished sharing what he knew, he paused to observe his sister contemplating these new realities about their past, and in this break, she said, "So we do not know how our Aunt Adèle died. And we do know that she never joined a convent."

"I never should have left her that night," Alban lamented again. "Nor left you."

"And you and I," Ellande stated, "slept through what must have been a terrible, terrible tragedy."

Madeleine-Grace's eyes welled with the tears at the thought of to whatever tragic fate Aunt Adèle had succumbed that evening, the idea of her enduring any kind of suffering or experiencing any pain. Then, wiping her eyes, she said, "We slept because we were tired. We had been dancing, dancing for our dear aunt. I wish she could have seen us dancing that night."

Another silence endured.

Ellande continued and to conclude his recounting, when he added that Alban had heard talk of the family riled over a change in Grandma'Maud's will, he turned to Wischard and asked, "You know nothing of this?"

"I remember very little," he admitted. "So much of these conversations happened outside of my hearing or around me but never directly to me. By that time, I wanted to wash my hands of all of it—of all of them—and was content to experience an aversion to any mention of the will, yet—." His pause called all eyes to him. "Yet I do recall—or think I recall—talk, by my mother and uncle, of stopping everything from going to—."

With such expectancy staring at him, he knew he couldn't leave this sentence incomplete, although he suddenly cared about the ramifications of speaking.

"To Madeleine-Grace," he said at last.

"Yes, to me," Madeleine-Grace said, as if his answer were not a shock.

"Did you know of this?" Ellande asked.

"No, I knew little until now, but I am putting this together in my head as best I can, and I wondered if I might not have been willed something."

"You know something more than we do, don't you?" Wischard asked, not intently, not aggressively, but resignedly to surprises at this point in his life.

"What I know has nothing to do with Aunt Adèle or changes in wills, but I have a feeling I know who has more answers," she announced, her eyes fixing on Wischard's. "And I would like for us to learn them before the sun sets tonight."

"Who? Who can tell us?" Wischard asked, perceiving that Madeleine-Grace, for some uncanny reason, was speaking mostly to him.

"And how?" Ellande added.

"I need to request permission to leave for the afternoon. I will bring you, myself, to where I hope to find answers," she said.

"Do they allow you to leave?" Pierre asked incredulously.

"For the right reasons, and they will grant me permission. Besides," she added with a grin and a tap on his knee, "I used to be the Mother Superior. Sometimes that counts for something."

"Could be a little more humble," Wischard remarked, deliberately trying to snap like a clothesline-clean sheet the tense mystery from the air, confident in whatever Madeleine-Grace had envisioned for them. He knew her determination as a girl, as Ellande and Monsieur Vauquelin did, and he heard it in the conviction of her words: she said "will find" and not "could find," and her intonation of "before the sun sets" crisped with confidence.

"Can we come?" Collot wondered, asking for himself and Pierre.

"Of course, young man," she said, adding as she rose from her seat, "Your uncle may need you."

"Where are we going?" Ellande asked, he, along with the others, rising.

"We're going to the retreat house the Sisters built years ago—"

"You mean—?" Ellande asked.

"—on L'Ile d'Aobefein."

Not far into the *bocage* beyond the convent, Soeur Adelaide's car pulled to the side of the dusty road, and unsure of the reason, Wischard eased his car to a stop behind hers. The nun driving rolled down her window and waved Wischard over, so he pulled up alongside. Rifted from speculations on what his sister could mean by "more answers," Ellande rolled down his window next to the nun's. Before his sister spoke from the passenger seat, voices of children fluttered to Ellande's ear:

"*Calimachon borgne, monte-mei tes cornes!*" a young girl of no more than seven said. It was the first half of a nursery rhyme.

"*Calimachon tortu, monte-mei ten cu!*" the other girl of the same age responded fittingly, sliding in the second half of the rhyme like a link into a clasp.

Pierre smiled and told Collot that his grandparents had taught him that one. Collot knew it, too.

As Ellande surveyed beyond the two young girls rhyming in front of their sleeping father in the shade of a farmstand's thatch, his sister leaned forward to say, "Do you remember this place, Ellande? Do you remember the chickens—and Uncle Roul—and—"

They said in unison, "the ruins!"

Ellande realized the nuns' car partially blocked the low wall of the ruins, much overgrown with tall grass and wildflowers. Uncle Roul had pulled over here on their way to Paris because the chicken truck had veered off the road when the farmstand worker's son kicked his ball in front of it. Madeleine-Grace had helped retrieve the chickens until she was requested to desist, and Ellande and Uncle Roul had leaned against the pink wall of rubble to enjoy the skyline and a few puffs of cigarette.

Madeleine-Grace's detour offered relief to his mind preoccupied with speculations about Aunt Adèle, the horrors of her experience that last night they knew her to be in the house, the actions he could have taken to change things, the stupidity he felt for not realizing he had been lied to and that Aunt Adèle would not have abandoned him. Abandoned. It had crossed his mind several times in the short car ride thus far to abandon this pursuit of answers, for not knowing might be better. Not knowing what happened to Aunt Adèle might better preserve his memory of her, thereby honoring her more gallantly. Perhaps that was fear whispering.

"Look up there, beyond the beeches," Madeleine-Grace said.

In the distance, behind a sparse wall of beeches, the rust-colored tiles of her convent's roof shimmered in sunlight. Most of the place couldn't be seen, from this angle hidden, but beyond the trees, a straight line of roof culminated with a stone cross at its end, clearly establishing the presence of a religious edifice.

"That stop was when I first saw the convent," Madeleine-Grace explained. "And it was the first time I wanted to be in one, be in one for life."

"We can't see more than a tiny bit of roof," Ellande said.

"It took just that glimpse for me to feel the pull, to want to see the special world that roof covered and what those walls enclosed, like our mother and Aunt Adèle looking into the garden of the convent in Liguria. And when at last I entered for life, the world I saw within those walls was more grandiose than I could ever imagine; in its simplicity, I found a world bigger and more majestic than even this one we see around us now."

"You truly found where you belonged."

"Where God wanted me."

Ellande inhaled deliberately through his nose the earthy and grassy air. The sky overhead a porcelain smooth, the thick clouds floated like unanchored islands in the direction of the coast as sunlight sculpted their bisque contours. Back onto the road, the travelers coursed, heading to the sea with the clouds—heading to answers they did not know they would face.

A short walkway led them to two, tall, imposing doors of faded dark brown, like black coffee diluted with too much water. Round, brass knockers hung from each, but swaths of pink cloth and strands of green vine wrapped them so that they looked like decorative wreaths, muting the knock. Two stone vessels of potted cornflowers greeted pilgrims on either side of the doorway. Madeleine-Grace requested her entourage tarry a moment; she entered the retreat house.

Moments before, a ferryboat had brought them from La Côte d'Albâtre the short way to L'Ile d'Aobefein, to the part of the isle Ellande had known to boast only a small church to Saint Martin, a square, a few shops and residences, and the *chifournie* players. The retreat house lay within meters of the new, small dock, probably so that weary travelers and aged retreatants and eager pilgrims had little distance to walk before arriving at their lodgings. Alban, himself accustomed to what was new to Ellande, appreciated this consideration. From the dock, Ellande and the others saw two towers of the retreat center dominating the skyline, rising several feet above the steeple of the nearby church; not unlike those of Notre Dame de Paris on a much smaller scale, they were made of off-white stone, and Ellande wondered about the humble woodwork that might lay behind them. *Etaillets*— terns—crouched on the topmost ledge, and while they awaited Madeleine-Grace outside the door, another two landed on the tympanum of the main entrance.

The weight of late afternoon settled on a nigh-abandoned village's center, and Ellande fancied he could smell the oranges from the arbor and the waters from the *marais*, hopeful each breeze might carry a fleck of *fleur de sel* to his tongue. His lapses into nostalgia were rattled by the chatter of tourists passing by, a spectacle that continued both to dismay and to enthrall him. On the ferryboat, he noted two pairs of birdwatchers, a family planning to walk the perimeter of the isle, and two tourist couples who had reservations at a restaurant on the *marais*. When he had overheard this, he double-checked with Alban about its veracity to learn from the old man that several of the *sauniers* had stands or little shops right on the embankment of their *marais* and one, indeed, even had a small restaurant.

The large door opened, and Madeleine-Grace waved in her entourage. She escorted them down a main hall, dim and cool, to a courtyard surrounded by the walls of the house. Several benches lined the vacant, square garden where the fragrance of wildflowers and sea breeze invigorated the visitors. Bird chirps kissed their ears, ocean laps splashed the air, and the peal of tourists' laughter beyond the walls occasionally punctuated the tranquility. Collot led his great-uncle to a bench next to potted cornflowers, and once comfortable in his seat, he wrapped his arm around the bunch of them and inhaled. Pierre looked at sun-drenched clouds rolling over the porcelain sky, a hand forming a visor. Everyone sat except Pierre and Madeleine-Grace.

"I have explained our visit to the Sisters," she shared.

"You think someone who knows something about Aunt Adèle's death is on retreat here?" Wischard asked.

"She *lives* here," Madeleine-Grace corrected. "She does not know of our presence here today."

"Who?" Ellande asked.

When Madeleine-Grace did not respond, opting instead to look to the clouds as her great-nephew had done moments before, Wischard asked, "What do you mean, 'lives here?'"

Madeleine-Grace returned her gaze to the others and began to explain. "Many years ago, when I was established but still new to the Order, our Mother Superior announced the building of the retreat center and the necessity to send some of the nuns, cloistered though we were, to L'Ile d'Aobefein to oversee the building and, from its completion thenceforward, to staff and run the house. We were used to pilgrims at the Motherhouse in Pays de Caux, used to hospitality, used to enjoyable order. We learned that this retreat center originated with the request of a generous benefactress who would fund the entire venture, coupled with a substantial donation to the Order. She had one request: to live permanently in reclusion at the retreat house on the isle. She wished to have her own apartment, to participate in prayers at her leisure, to have her meals prepared and her clothes and linens laundered regularly with the others, but otherwise, had no special favors. Our governing body agreed to this, and over the span of a year, the retreat center was built.

"Shortly after the completion of the center but before we had opened her doors, scuttle afflicted my sisters, for a visitor had come to the convent. Mother Superior, to my surprise, singled me out to inform me this visitor, the benefactress behind the new retreat house, had requested a private meeting with *me*. She had speculated that the benefactress sought spiritual counsel, but verily was unsure about the request. Why me? I met with her for the first time in the very room we sat this morning in the convent. My shock could not have been greater to see who awaited me in that anteroom, who this benefactress was. She is the same woman we come to visit today, who sits daily alone in a suite upstairs, content to enjoy the calm of a secluded, quiet life."

"But why do you think the benefactress knows something about Aunt Adèle's death?" Wischard asked as intently and sprightly as a young boy.

Madeleine-Grace sighed, for she was revealing a secret meant to be kept, tucked away in the quiet of this isle forever. "Because she is your sister. The benefactress is little Laure."

Many extended seconds passed before the bird chirps registered, before the splashes of landing ocean waves sounded again beyond the walls. The young ones budged first, simple turns of their head to observe Wischard's reaction.

"She had come into money, she told me, and donated every last *sou* to the Order with the sole request of building the retreat center for souls like her own and permission to live there forever. She asked if I kept up with the family, and I replied that I kept up only with Ellande back in the States, that I did not maintain contact with anyone else. Assuming I'd have contact with no one else, she requested that I not mention this to my brother but to leave her here, content to remain unknown to the world and occasionally wondered about. I asked her if she understood the type of life to which she was committing, but she laughed and said, 'I'm not taking vows, Madeleine-Grace.' She said if she changed her name, it would be for entirely different reasons from mine. I did not mean to pry, but I did ask her why she wished to lead such a life. Her response was most curious. She said that she had realized too late what a gift her Aunt Juliette and Aunt Adèle had been, and this decision was her homage to Aunt Adèle as mine had been to my mother. I did not consecrate my life to Jesus for my mother, but I did not correct her. She did not explain how she came into the money, but I, at the time, wondered if she had not married and been widowed, or if Grandma'Maud had left her something, though it had been years since Grandma'Maud's death. I did not ask or investigate. It was her comment about Aunt Adèle that makes me wonder today if she knows more. What did she realize too late?"

Everyone lingered, their minds suspended by such a revelation. Little Laure had been gone for so many years, wondered about indeed. Wischard rose from his place on the bench.

"You're saying that my sister is upstairs, that she's been here for decades?" Wischard asked.

"This is what I'm telling you, Wischard."

"And you never thought to tell me?"

"I *did* think to tell you, but we had never heard from you for years—didn't know how to contact you even. It was my understanding that Ellande had no contact with you or anyone from the Semperrin side. On rare visits out of the convent, I sometimes cajoled whichever Sister was driving to pass the places I thought, God forgive me, I might catch a glimpse of my former life, but both the Paris flat and the Etretat-au-Delà house appeared deserted, unkempt." As usual, as she explained, Madeleine-Grace spoke with surety about her actions, devoid of tears or a crackle in her words.

"It's okay," Ellande assured, as if she had indeed lamented her actions. He rose and placed an arm around his sister.

"I know it is," she responded.

"Then I think little Laure may be as surprised to see us today as you are to learn of her dwelling here, on L'Ile d'Aobefein, all these years," Alban said, relying on Collot's shoulder to prop himself to his feet. "Let's go to her. And, Wischard, Ellande, despite your desire for answers—about Adèle and little Laure, herself—remember that people have mysterious reasons for the things they do and may wish to leave them mysteries. We may not get the answers we seek. In fact, little Laure may not even know what we have come to hope *somebody* knows. It wouldn't be fair to expect her to give us the answers we want when we don't know for sure that she has them."

Ellande could tell Wischard was reeling from this news and placed a firm, open hand on his back. Wischard stopped before advancing, unsure how to proceed, dumb-founded by the strangeness of his sister's actions. He didn't entirely believe it to be true, and his quizzical stare at the door into the retreat house reiterated this. He had believed all these years that his sister flitted in and out of their life, unable to anchor herself as a wife, as a mother, as a denizen of their Dieppe or Paris or even Etretat-au-Delà dwellings. He had considered—and convinced himself—that she had found a way to live off rich men when her vagabond lifestyle among the struggling and diseased artists of wannabe status proved too unstable even for her. And here she had, for decades, devoted her life to solitude, possibly even to God, in her own, withdrawn way? He truly believed that Madeleine-Grace had been mistaken—but how?

From the main hall, the visitors ascended a staircase to retreatant chambers, and after passing several doors on either side of them, came to a door at the end of a hallway. Madeleine-Grace opened it, and several steps away, another door awaited, a bigger one than those of the pilgrims' and retreatants' quarters.

Wischard inhaled. The realness filling his lungs suffocated the frivolous hope in mistaken conclusions. He knew who lay beyond that partition and how close he was to an unexpected unknown. Madeleine-Grace knocked, and someone stirred within. Steps toward the door grew louder, and then the door opened without circumspection.

Gray and shaky and rested stood little Laure, without make-up, wearing a calf-length housedress like the ones her Grandma'Maud and Aunt Melisende wore, hers beige, a thin, white, wool shawl over her shoulders despite the warmth outside. Her face petrified the moment her eyes fell on the unexpected throng outside her door, congregated and still within the confined entryway.

She released the doorknob. The door slowly swung open into her suite as she stared beyond Madeleine-Grace at the combination of young strangers and never forgotten faces of family. When she saw Wischard, her hands slowly fell to her side. She stepped aside to let in the visitors.

Madeleine-Grace's confident steps did not remove the trepidation in the steps that followed hers into the room dimmed by closed curtains and shutters. After a hesitation on account of the expression of incredulity on her brother's face, little Laure scurried to the windows, tremulously drawing the curtains and slanting the shutter shafts until the room twinkled in sunlight. She opened two French windows onto a miniscule balcony so that fresh air perked up the suite. The guests found themselves in a large, well-decorated room with many built-in, stocked bookshelves, framed paintings on the walls, an easel with a canvas propped upon it, a round dining table in one corner, a wooden desk and chair in another, and several couches, chairs, and side tables in the middle of the room. Pale pinks, whites, and taupes provided an elegance in an otherwise simple, rectangular room bordered with Belle-

Epoque flourishes like crown molding and chair rails, urns of fresh pink and white flowers, and light, sun-bleached woods.

The visitors stood just inside her door, watching her until she stopped scurrying at the balcony doors. She took slow, deliberate steps toward them, understanding their expectancy of some direction, some greeting, some word.

She opened her mouth, lifted her head as her shoulders rose, and released a long sigh. Then her eyes curiously squinted with a glimmer, the hint of a smile forming on upturned lips, and she said, "I thought this day might come—" as she walked to a built-in bookshelf and pulled a leather-bound volume off, opening the front cover to retrieve a sealed envelope, which she held in the air— "before I would ever need this. You see, I had written in here the answers to some of the questions you might have come to ask. Madeleine-Grace—Soeur Adelaide—is the only one, I thought, who might care, and I didn't even know if I'd survive her. If she survived me, she had a right to know."

"A right? A right to know what?" Madeleine-Grace asked.

"What I had done to you. What I had taken from you in order to have this life I enjoy here on L'Ile d'Aobefein. Is that not why you're here with your brother and—my brother? Someone has spoken to some lawyers who have figured everything out?"

Alban, who had been standing behind the lot of them, still holding his Collot's arm after the ascent to the second floor, hobbled forward. The exertion from the long day and the exhaustion that comes from holding perfervidly onto a hope could not hide the glint in his eye and kindness on his face. He reached out his hands to Laure, and she allowed him to take them as she, a woman unused to contact, stared at his touch. Then she looked into his eyes, his smiling eyes.

"Laure," he said sweetly but pleadingly, "we would like to know if you know anything about your Aunt Adèle's death."

As if she had been holding her breath to hear what Monsieur Vauquelin might ask, she slouched, sighing again, as if what he sought could have been worse. "That night," she said, "that is in here, too." She held up the letter once more, releasing from the old man's gentle hold, and then returned the envelope to the book and the book to the shelf.

"You know something about that night?" Ellande asked.

"I know too much—not everything—but too much," she said. "In fact, when I think about it, which I have had plenty of time to do over the years, that night is the reason I'm here—the night of the children's ball. I have been running from that night for many, many years." As if this were an admission of weakness, she looked into Wischard's eyes and added, "Some of us are resigned to live a life of running, especially when it is so tranquil." She lifted her hands and fluttered her fingers, turning her head in survey of the room.

Madeleine-Grace said carefully, "Are you able to speak about it?"

"It is not a matter of ability. It is what I have to do; it is a matter of duty. I see the way you are looking at me, Wischard. I have to speak about it so that maybe you won't think ill of me, as I imagine you have been doing for many years. I would hope that you understand why I did this, Wischard. You, too, Madeleine-Grace." To Pierre and Collot she said, "Why don't we sit?"

Chairs were assembled by the boys around the couch and everyone took a seat. Laure sat in a beige armchair, and Alban sat on the pink velvet couch closest to her, leaning forward with expectancy. Next to him sat Wischard, and across from them on velvet armchairs sat Ellande and Madeleine-Grace. Pierre and Collot stood behind the couch, looking on at something of a saga they had never conceived of being privy to hours ago.

"Where do you want to start?" Alban asked. "With the children's ball?"

"No, Monsieur," she said with a chuckle. "I will go directly to what happened after we were sent to bed. Forgive me if, as I relate this, I am terse. I want to say it and never have to say it again. I wish never to visit that night again after this. I have a feeling that after I tell you, for the first time in my life, burying that night will be possible.

"So, we were sent to bed upon entering the house—no snack, certainly no evening prayers—sent right to bed, and to bed we went. I remember ungluing the dress, not with Wischard's help, and not with my mother's. It was so hot, and we had been dancing, and I remember wanting Aunt Adèle to help me out of it. That's when it occurred to me that we hadn't even seen Aunt Adèle when we had arrived. She wasn't waiting for us downstairs, eager to hear about the ball. I wanted to sneak down for some reason, just to see her, but our parents had been in such a foul mood after the ball, the whole car ride home, that I didn't dare descend. Wischard had torn his suit off and hopped in bed, and I did the same after switching into my nighty.

"As I was drifting off, I heard raised voices and loud stomping—angry walking and yelling. I turned to Wischard," Laure said, looking at her brother who, she knew, was also reliving that night with her—but his memories went only so far— "but you were asleep. Sound asleep after such an evening at the ball. I should have been, too. I still feel guilty—oddly guilty—that I didn't fall asleep, myself, like you. Why should I have felt guilty about something so out of my control? Maybe if I had tried harder at the children's ball, I would have been more tired by the time we arrived home. Maybe if I had complained to Maman of a headache or a stomach ache, she would have given me a sleeping pill like they gave to Grandma'Maud. But the fact is, I did not fall asleep. And as I sat there awake, unable to drift into sweet dreams of winning the children's ball as my dear cousins had, I heard the arguing growing louder and the footsteps more—angry. And then I heard Aunt Adèle's voice, one of the ones growing louder. Aunt Adèle raising her voice? That did not happen. I grew concerned. I suppose I grew more curious than concerned.

"Yes, curious. I whispered to Wischard, 'Something's wrong.' I said, 'Let's see what's wrong.' But you were sound asleep, as I said, so I flung the sheets off and, on my tiptoes, walked to the bedroom door and opened it. I crept to the top of the stairs and clearly made out Aunt Adèle's voice among the others. I couldn't tell you what they were arguing about, but they were in the *salle-en-arrière*. Then I heard Aunt Adèle yelp and, from the top few steps, I saw Uncle Romain dragging her by the arm into the kitchen as everyone else followed, my mother screaming at her with the same violence in her voice that Uncle Romain possessed in his grip. Once everyone was in the kitchen, the yelling escalated—everyone chipping in with insults against Aunt Adèle—Aunt Pé's voice, Uncle Romain's—even Papa's voice was raised, but he used his to project entreaties to Maman to relent. Maman was cursing at her for pitting the children against her, for trying to outdo her at every turn so that Maman looked bad. I crept down the stairs and stood outside the kitchen door.

"Uncle Romain was yelling at her to fetch him a bottle of Uncle Julien's liqueur so that he could break it, and, of course, Aunt Adèle refused. He was drunk. From my spot, I could see Uncle Romain wrestle with the latch to the cellar door, and Aunt Adèle stepped aside as it flung open. Aunt Pé screeched at Aunt Adèle to do as her husband ordered, and when Aunt Adèle refused again, my mother began another rant, declaring that Aunt Adèle brought shame on the Semperrin family, demanding that she return to Liguria and stay forever this time—because she hated not just the sight of her but the knowing she was near.

"At this, my father once again raised his voice only to demand that my mother relent, and my mother writhed to hear him stop her, as if he were taking Aunt Adèle's side. She yelled at him and then shrieked again at Aunt Adèle, this time lunging for her. I couldn't bear it anymore, so when my father interposed again, this time with his whole body to stop Maman from attacking Aunt Adèle, I ran into the kitchen, standing between Maman and Aunt Adèle. I joined Papa's entreaties, imploring my mother to stop. Papa told me to go back to bed, and, foolishly, I shouted one more time for Maman to stop. And do you know what she did? Pulling from my father, she grabbed me by the arms—" Laure crossed her arms to show her audience— "right here, like this—" and she clutched her upper arms with the opposite hands in a grip that shook in its firmness— "and with that viciousness of Uncle Romain as he dragged Aunt Adèle into the kitchen, she flung me away as if I were a pest, a fly that needed something stronger than swatting. She threw me—."

Laure interrupted herself to gulp invisible tears. Her hands around her arms still shook, and then they stopped. Laure inhaled, finally finding breath, and continued. "In her rashness, she threw me into the cellar doorway. I crashed into the doorframe, stumbled backward, and began to fall in—to fall down—when I felt a sudden push into my back, hurling me into the kitchen table and chairs. It was Aunt Adèle. She had lunged for me, sweeping me into the kitchen to keep me from falling down the stairs—" Laure exhaled lamentation, gravity, and unspoken guilt— "but she had somehow twisted herself off balance in the process. I could see, as I spun around to face who had intercepted me, the crash into the cellar doorway. I saw her bang her head on the ledge. I saw the look of terror in her eyes as she fell. And what stays with me the most is that—I saw no one budge."

The anticipation for answers did not equip her audience for the story they had just heard. No one moved. No one spoke.

"The suspension of this moment—this silence that comes not from held breath but from a paralysis—has been my entire life since that night. Aunt Adèle saved my life and died doing it. And I could never speak of it. I remember the thumping sounds in a belabored, eerily slow fall down the steps, and I can still hear the crash at the bottom into crates of bottles, and I can still recall the—the silence. I can still see the blood on the ledge where her head hit it. I was the first to move, rushing to the top of the stairs, but I could not see her in the darkness of the cellar. My father pulled me away. Aunt Pé released a witchy, horrified shriek. Uncle Romain grabbed her by the shoulders and jostled her, shaking the voice out of her. Maman was speechless. As my father was rushing me out of the kitchen, my mother finally broke her silence.

'Look what you've done,' she said to me. Then to Uncle Romain, 'You have to fix this. Fix this!'

"I wanted to check on Aunt Adèle, but in the main hall, my father spun me around as he crouched eye-level with me and said, 'Tell no one of this.' I started to cry and moved to bury my head in his shoulder and he pushed me back. I felt so startled. I knew my mother blamed me, but I wasn't expecting him to be so abrasive. 'Do you understand me, Laure?' he said. 'You will never talk about this night! Do you understand me? Not to anyone!' I nodded. Through my tears, I nodded that I understood, but I dared not hug him or turn to him for comfort. He carried me to my room, and I slipped into bed beside my brother. I wanted so much to wake him and just—I don't know—to cry to him. But he was asleep. And I knew I couldn't tell him. Oh, Wischard, how I envied your sleep. For years I envied your sleep, for I could never really enjoy a good sleep again."

"I—I did not know," Wischard stuttered. "I wish you had woken me. I never knew."

"It is better you never knew, Wischard. I'm glad I never told you. What would we have done, two kids who knew how our aunt had died?"

"But it was an accident, wasn't it? A terrible, unnecessary accident," Wischard insisted, "but an accident nonetheless. Why could our parents not have reported this?"

"Ah, this I learned the next day. Maman told me that everyone would believe Aunt Adèle's death was no accident after what Madeleine-Grace had said about them at the children's ball. She said her own mother would not believe it an accident. She told me if I spoke of the accident, she would—she would lock me in the cellar. In that cellar, with Père La Pouque and—and Aunt Adèle's ghost. She told me if I uttered a word of this, especially to Grandma'Maud, she would tell Grandma'Maud that I was the one truly to blame. 'Because, little Laure, you are the one truly to blame,' she said. 'And no one must ever know.'"

"They made me take pills to keep me asleep for the visit to Paris a few days later so that I could not mention anything to Grandma'Maud. The morning after the fall, I felt alone, without a single companion on account of my sworn silence from Wischard and the absence of Ellande and Madeleine-Grace. But it did not compare to the feeling of utter abandonment from my mother who left us with our father and lived alone in his family house in Dieppe. She left me alone to stew in the pain and confusion of what happened that night, after having led me to believe it had been my fault. For years, I was trapped in a state of shock, of abandonment, of pain. Poor Wischard, you must have thought me crazy the way I acted out, painting one night and drinking the next, reckless with my body and my pursuits and my whims, destroying every relationship I had, destroying every success I had the potential to achieve, destroying myself, really. I left and returned and left and returned, sometimes for months on end. And then I left for good—I thought—for here."

Laure turned her gaze from Wischard, about whom she was most concerned, to Monsieur Vauquelin. His numb stare finally turned into heaving sobs.

He had his answers now.

"Laure," Madeleine-Grace said, reaching for her cousin's hand, "You have been through too much for one lifetime. You know nothing that happened that night was your fault? Have you accepted that?"

"I blamed myself for many years. I even blamed you for a while. Then, I blamed my mother, and that's where my blaming ends."

"You have been through so much, my dear cousin," Madeleine-Grace continued. "For the part I played in it, I am so sorry."

"I realized years later that you saw my mother for who she was long before I did. How could I blame you, then just a child yourself, for that? Nothing that happened was any more your fault than it was mine. And if it was, well, maybe we are even."

"Even?" Ellande asked, out of an instinctive concern for his sister.

"I have not told you how I have wronged you, dear cousin," Laure said to Madeleine-Grace whose hand did not budge from hers.

"You said you had taken something that was Madeleine-Grace's, is that correct?" Ellande inquired.

"Indeed, I did," little Laure continued. "While I was in my late teens, I floated back into Papa's Paris place, to my brother's dismay, I'm sure, and coincidentally, Maman swooped into our lives for a few nights of needless harangues. It was on that visit—not to check on her children, mind you—that I overheard a curious conversation between her and Uncle Romain. It had to do with a codicil to Grandma'Maud's will. I had pieced together that shortly before her passing, having weaned herself off Uncle Romain's unnecessary medication with the help of Aunt Melisende, Grandma'Maud had secretly amended the will. It was necessary because the original will had no provision for the event that one of her children besides Uncle Léon pass before her. No one could find the codicil, and the lawyers remained tight-lipped about the whole affair. Uncle Romain and Aunt Pé, Uncle Roul and Aunt Mirabelle, and my parents, all they knew was that they were not entitled to any part of Grandma'Maud's fortune at the time of her death and had to wait—they knew not for what. The lawyers, relations of Uncle Ferdinand, tied things up nicely to keep them at bay, and even Uncle Romain's underhanded connections couldn't accelerate the dispersal of her inheritance. Can you believe they petitioned that anything in the codicil be rendered null and void on the grounds that their mother was crazy, but Aunt Melisende and Uncle Ferdinand as well as young Marguerin and Jules, one a new priest and the other a new lawyer, could attest to the contrary.

"It was only interest in the inheritance that brought Maman back into our lives that time, but my curiosity was piqued, to say the least. So, I set out to find the codicil. The most valuable thing I learned was that the Etretat-au-Delà house and the Paris flat, along with all other properties and possessions within, were, according to the original will, to be split among all her living children except Juliette. Juliette, as a resident of America and therefore less likely to benefit from the France properties the same way as the other children, was the sole recipient of the Semperrin fortune. The codicil had two amendments: the Paris flat was to go exclusively to Ellande Avery upon his twenty-fifth birthday, and the Semperrin fortune to Madeleine-Grace upon her twenty-first birthday."

"But this never came to be," Wischard said. Then to Madeleine-Grace, he added, "Did it?"

"Not to my knowledge, but I see now that it did come to be." Madeleine-Grace stood and looked around the suite that had been housing little Laure for decades. "I deduce that my inheritance is responsible for the very walls we find ourselves in, isn't it, Laure?"

"You have surmised correctly, but you can't know how." Laure smiled and stared out the window at the coming night. "I became Madeleine-Grace. She was locked away in a convent, oblivious to any news of wills and codicils. And the lawyers, they didn't know Madeleine-Grace, and they didn't know me. As Madeleine-Grace's twenty-first birthday was approaching, I knew they might be seeking her, so I sought them first. I visited the convent—and it wasn't hard snatching a habit—and in my new identity that revealed mere inches of my face, I visited the lawyers. I told them I knew of the codicil because Grandma'Maud had told me of it, and that, as my birthday approached, I wished to transfer the funds immediately from me to the Order. This announcement gave them no reason to question my identity, for what imposter would want the money only to have it immediately transferred to nuns? I knew my mother and Uncle Romain were scheming to acquire the money, and once they found out about the codicil, they would move mountains to keep it from going to Madeleine-Grace. I didn't want it for myself, you see. I wanted nothing more than to make sure my mother didn't get it. I signed this and that, and the lawyers questioned nothing. They transferred Madeleine-Grace's inheritance to the convent while I, in the meantime, negotiated with the Order's governing body to donate the money for the building of the retreat center and my personal 'upkeep.' Remember what you said at the ball? This was my way of ensuring I become nothing whatsoever like my mother. So, in a way, Soeur Adelaide, Madeleine-Grace Avery did receive her inheritance. I'm afraid, though, I gave her no choice in how she used it."

Madeleine-Grace turned to her cousin seated on the couch with the look of a defendant awaiting sentence, and she said, "I don't know that I could have come up with a better use of that fortune."

Laure sighed and stared at her hands now resting in her lap. "You are forgiving, Madeleine-Grace," she said. "But perhaps Ellande could have benefited from that money, for I'm sure he would have been the first person with whom you thought to share it. Certainly, you don't forgive me, too, Ellande."

"I don't think it's my place to forgive or not forgive you in this matter, Laure, but if it were, I would certainly forgive you. You have shouldered an immense burden all alone, and I imagine this self-imposed solitude has provided you some sort of atonement. Who am I not to forgive you?"

"Among the lot of us, Wischard was always the most accepting, and you, Ellande, the most understanding. All these years later, you still extend that warm understanding to me, even after all I have revealed, even when I know I don't deserve it." Turning to Wischard, she began shaking again and the first visible tears manifested. "But you, Wischard, resent me. You still resent me, don't you?"

Wischard's mouth, throat—the core of his being—had dried up. No tear issued from his eyes. "You carried this burden alone because you chose not to share, not even with me."

"Do you not see, Wischard, that at that time in my life, I could not share this with you? It wasn't a matter of trust. It was a matter of fear." As he remained silent, she added, "I can see I have gravely wronged you by my behavior and my choices."

"The year you spent with us before leaving for good," Wischard said at last. "It was a whole year of Etretat-au-Delà again as you slept all day and enjoyed sordid company every evening. The last I saw of you, you were frittering away every second of your life. I must admit that when you came back, I entertained a hope that I might have a mother or at least a comfortable companion again; I had lost so many, you know. But you spent not a waking moment with me, preferring your carousing and coquetry to even a single evening with me."

"That last year, Wischard, I needed a bed and a roof while the retreat house was being built. And when it was completed, I left for good. All that time, that year of waiting, I knew would be my last with you. I couldn't bear to grow closer to you only to lose you, and I couldn't imagine letting you grow close to me only to leave you again. So I avoided you. You thought I was out nights in all the wrong circles to land that man with money to secure my life forever, but I had already taken care of that. Certainly, I spent a few nights with the wrong crowds, but most of my nights, Wischard, were drifting the quais along the Seine, back and forth, crossing the *passerelles* and idling on benches— a *flâneuse* getting used to being alone, I suppose."

Now Wischard welled with tears, and when he did, everyone did.

"You sacrificed so much—" he began.

"I am no saint!" Laure yelped, lifting her hands to her face.

"—sacrificed a relationship with me to keep me from feeling abandoned again."

"You would have talked me out of this if you knew!"

"You can bet Madeleine-Grace's fortune I would have! I would have prevented this crazy scheme—"

"The women of Semperrin blood, all crazy—"

"Crazy was not to have trusted me. I resented Maman as much as you did. I would have shared your burden, your knowing."

She sighed. "I was still young then, Wischard, and even when I thought I might share with you of all good people this terrible secret, I castigated myself for even considering it. Sure, you could have split my burden by sharing in it, but I didn't want you to have *any* of it, Wischard. I wanted to keep you in your magical sleep of an Etretat-au-Delà summer."

Wischard looked away from his sister, his heavy heart visible in his quivering lip and shaking jaw and reddened eyes.

"The one who sacrificed," Laure added, "was Aunt Adèle. She sacrificed her life in every way for us. And now you know, Monsieur Vauquelin."

"What happened that night, yes, now I know. That she lived with a sacrificial love—that, I always knew."

"May I show you something, Ellande?" Madeleine-Grace asked.

"Of course," he replied, allowing her to take him by the hand and lead the way through the courtyard, down an interior hall, up a staircase, and onto the flat roof of the retreat house. They had left Wischard in his sister's suite to catch up alone and Pierre, Collot, and Alban in the courtyard. Alban pondered the past, prayerfully, amid the undying love permeating the present. The boys continued their camaraderie, solemnly for now, in the presence of Alban Vauquelin. The two families would unite after all, all these years later, through this friendship.

Resting their hands on the smooth stonework of the parapet, Ellande and Madeleine-Grace enjoyed a view of the island—the rosy rooftops of small houses and barns, the bristling of thick foliage as birds settled within or fluttered from branch to branch and from tree to tree, the expanse of sea beyond the island.

"It's beautiful," Ellande sighed.

"Long before I became Mother Superior, I was sent here to oversee the retreat house when it was first built and opened. When the timing was right, I was able to sneak up here around sundown and look to the island's terrain, to the ocean. I breathed for a few moments, breathed freely, consciously. Up here I could take a good look beyond."

"That is the *écluse*, is it not?" Ellande asked, pointing toward the sea at the rock formation of the lock.

"Indeed. It has fallen into disrepair, into un-use, really. It has become yet another ruin with no one succeeding Franchinot to care for it."

They gazed at these new ruins in the silence of a vanishing sun.

"When I came here, much younger than I am now," Madeleine-Grace began, "sometimes, I closed my eyes, and, as I breathed in the holiness of this island, I saw myself as I was the night of the children's ball, and I danced. Right here. Alone. I danced the *tourdion* we danced for our parents, for our grandparents—the dance we wished Aunt Adèle could have seen."

Ellande bowed his head, unable to enjoy the panorama, and swallowed away the lump in his throat.

"Oh, Ellande. We did not know. We could not know."

"The image of her standing before us after destroying the garden and spreading the mint seeds looms before me," her brother admitted.

"Could we have known it would be the last time we saw her, that good lady?"

"We were the only ones to witness that."

"The only ones to see her that way, for once, so defeated," Madeleine-Grace reiterated. "It was a portrait of a lady who spent her life toiling lovingly for others. She and Alban had that toil in common. When one cares so well for the earth, the earth—the salt, the herbs—treats him well. The toil did not break Alban. The toil did not break Aunt Adèle. The malice and indifference of her family did."

"Maybe she was not so broken, not so defeated in that moment, as we assume. Alban wrote something to me that suggests otherwise. He said she fortified the house with mint to keep the malefactors away, knowing their aversion to the herb."

"So she had her wits about her after all?" speculated Madeleine-Grace.

"On some level, perhaps she did." Ellande tilted his head to the sky in exasperation and confusion. "I have been living in an illusion about her, and you designed and chased a dream for all the wrong reasons. Madeleine-Grace, does knowing this make you regret becoming a nun? Does knowing Aunt Adèle never joined a convent make you feel you did this for nothing?"

"Not at all. I did not enter the convent because I was following what I thought was Aunt Adèle's example. I joined because I was called to join by God. The beauty of my experience here is something I never want to be undone nor something I regret. I told you this morning that it took just a glimpse for me to hear the call, to yearn for the special world under that roof. When at last I entered that building for life, the world I saw within those walls was of more splendor than I could ever have imagined."

Two terns glided toward the sea, gentle, calm.

"Learning that Aunt Adèle died without ever having left us for the convent does not make me think I pursued a dream foolishly, because it was not about her. And you, Ellande, have not been living in illusion. Even amid being misinformed about Aunt Adèle, you have lived a real life—a good life—and have never forgotten her. Her presence may have, in fact, been more real throughout our lives than we could ever have known."

"She has lived with us through her influence on us, the detail we give to doing things well. That has been real. That makes her real to me," Ellande asserted.

"She has been with Maman all this time."

"Enjoying distance from their siblings, just like in the serenity of Liguria."

"My heart is in Pays de Caux, yet I sometimes think this island was our little Liguria, our special place. You see, Ellande, the little farmhouses? That one is the one we dined in with Monsieur Vauquelin and his sisters. And see those shadows so pronounced against the setting sun? Those are—"

"The ruins of the hermitage."

"Yes. When I used to come up here, I inhaled deeply, hoping for a hint of chamomile and oranges and blue cornflowers on the breeze, but not because their scents are so fragrant and calming. I hoped the smell would evoke the peace of that day we spent here, the simplicity of a different time, the safety of Aunt Adèle and Monsieur Vauquelin's protection, even amid mourning."

"Did the smell of the chamomile ever make its way to you?"

"I believe that God sent it to me—the chamomile and that peace—on the sea breeze swaddling my skin and through the tune of the *chifournie* and in the memory of young Franchinot waving good-bye to us and through the silhouette of the ruins and in the taste of *fleur de sel* in the sweetness of the air. It was a good feeling, Ellande."

"Listen. Do you hear the *chifournie* now?"

"I do."

"Why is it so faint? Aren't they below, in the square?"

"They play from their farmhouse now—the next generations of Noues. Some nights, they come to town, Monsieur Noue and his son, but mostly they play from their home. One day I visited them and gave them some piano music to transcribe for the *chifournie*. They play that tune for me. Oh, Ellande, sometimes when I think back to that summer, I wish Aunt Adèle could have heard the orchestra playing as she watched us dance. She would have been so proud."

"She would have been more proud of what you did with that dress. You did not let the others' destruction deter you from making something new and beautiful. They underestimated your skill at sewing—"

"—because they lacked it themselves—"

"—but Aunt Adèle would not have been surprised and, indeed, would have been proud of your work."

"I learned from Grandma'Maud and Maman and her. It was so easy to learn when I simply spent time with them."

"They loved that," Ellande replied. "It meant so much to them for us to spend time with them, to learn from them. For as much as they enjoyed it, we were the fortunate ones. We had them in our lives to see us through our maturation and formation, to share of their good selves, and to teach us."

"The walls around our cousins crumbled without repair. Our aunts and uncles did not spurn the old traditions in order to institute new, better ones. They simply did not want to embrace them because doing so meant work, meant having to care. I don't know if they were more so lazy or—careless. Those words struggle to escape my lips; they are swears to us. And their children, they were left to drift like the clouds, without the bulwark of religion, morality, our traditions, and even an understanding of the importance of work. *Our* parents insulated us. Now look. You pass, I am sure, these values and the good ways of our family onto your children and grandchildren."

"Maybe I have not been so good at that as you may think."

"Look at Pierre," she said with a proud smile. "You have modeled the dignity in hard work. You have loved them and made them feel loved, and they know never to doubt this love, have you not?"

"I have," Ellande responded with a look toward the orange tree grove and the hermitage.

"Then you have done what Grandma'Maud and our parents and Aunt Adèle have done for us."

"Much of what I hope I am passing down comes from before me, from what I have learned from our parents and grandparents." Ellande paused. "It is still strange for me to think there will be an after me, and for me, it is near."

The song of the *chifournie* players ended. In that moment, the absence of the tune seemed to silence even the din of the sea.

Then a new song began.

"Do you hear that, Ellande? Do you know it?"

The familiar melody of the *chifournie* stunned Ellande, prickling his skin in the warmth and inciting a smile.

"Our *tourdion!*"

"This is the music I gave to them to learn." Madeleine-Grace extended a hand, proffering a dance and a chance at living once more. "What do you say?"

Ellande took her hand. They felt the suppleness and the age of each other's thinning skin. Their eyes connected as their ears caught and synchronized with the music. They bobbed their heads to the rhythm for a few measures and then, in mental alignment, simultaneously stepped into the choreography, the dance of long ago, more slowly now but with a new life, a freshness. Madeleine-Grace held her veil to her head in the gentle lifts of the wind as if it were a crown of cornflowers the blue of a faceted sapphire. They danced the *tourdion* of their youth, this time hearing the orchestra complement the crescendos of the rustling orange trees, watching the conductor's arms rise and lower as if commanding the tides around L'Ile d'Aobefein. They saw each other's tears but more keenly heard each other's laughter. In their lack of nimbleness, they held on, not only to each other as they danced through the sunset, but to an unwavering appreciation of the stories and the work and the artistry that made their traditions and their lives beautiful.

Acknowledgements

My gratitude extends to many, to those dear to me and to those unknown. Like *The December Issue*, what I had conceived as a novella expanded organically into a novel, and the characters, stories, and themes (necessarily, in this case,) developed as well. In their growth, I found myself drawing on the teachings and influences of many. I thank my French teachers from grade school lunch programs through university. Mrs. H. and Mrs. G. from junior high, Mme. Monique W., Fr. Jacques K., and Mme. Marianne S. in high school, and Sr. Jean M. at university. Mme. Hortense B. provided an opportunity to practice my French when I felt it waning. As this book imparts the message of preserving what is good about our traditions and heritages, I thank all French teachers who strive to achieve this goal through their dedication to teaching the French language and their promoting the enjoyment of French studies. And for that matter, I thank teachers of all languages.

In writing *After Me*, I encountered two new "teachers" whose enthusiasm and commitment to preserving the traditions and dialects of Normandy took the form of a generosity and kindness that amazed me. I thank Rémi P. of Magène and Denis D. of Université Rurale du Cauchois for their care and time in helping me with dialects, especially those of Pays de Caux. Their care has elevated the accuracy of this text, and that is so special to me. To see their mission in some small way advanced through the publication of this book is gratifying.

Indispensable to important and worthwhile undertakings is hard work. I thank those who, like Julien and Juliette Avery, instill the value of hard work and who, like Aunt Adèle and Alban Vauquelin, model the grace of hard work. I am thankful to the nearby university that provided me the opportunity to teach a course that highlights the intersection of art and hard work; to Pope and now Saint John Paul II, through his encyclical *Laborem Exercens*, for reminding me of the dignity inherent in labor and the humanity of toil; and to my parents for fostering the importance of both hard work and incorporating artistry into work.

I thank those who endeavor to pass on what is good, even when ridiculous trends, whims, and mindsets emerge, if not threaten, to thwart the preservation and continuance of what is good.

Finally, I could not have done this without the support of family and friends, Anna and Nellie, and the whole CW team. *Merci*!

FOR MORE ON NORMANDY AND PAYS DE CAUX:
HTTP://WWW.MAGENE.FR
HTTP://UNIVERSITERURALEDUCAUCHOIS.E-MONSITE.COM/PAGES/PARLONS-CAUCHOIS/

ALSO BY J. SHEP:
THE DECEMBER ISSUE (2023)

FOLLOW J. SHEP ON FACEBOOK.COM/JSHEPAUTHORPAGE
AND ON INSTAGRAM AT JSHEPAUTHORPAGE
BOOK GROUP QUESTIONS AND IDEAS AVAILABLE AT
WWW.CHRISTOPHERWHISPERINGS.COM
TEACHER RESOURCES AND CLASSROOM DISCUSSION PROMPTS AVAILABLE AT
WWW.CHRISTOPHERWHISPERINGS.COM